FLASH BACK

ELUDING DESTINY
BOOK EIGHT

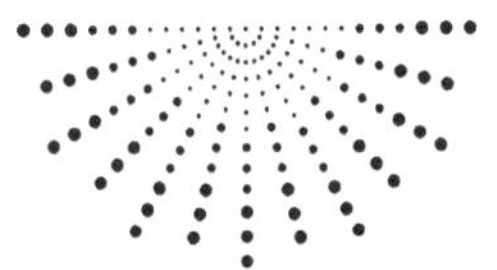

CHARLIE NOTTINGHAM

LIQUID MIND PUBLISHING

THE ELUDING DESTINEY SERIES

Eluding Destiny

The Horrors That Created Us

Aftershocks

The Precipice

Land of Light

The Quiet Army

Sacred Sins

Flash Back

The Shift

Lost to Time

Gods Among Us

The Cover Up

Blank Slate

Sign up for Charlie's newsletter and receive a free copy of the Eluding Destiny prequel, Blood Bar:

https://liquidmind.media/eluding-destiny-prequel/

CONTENT WARNING

This book contains detailed sex, mentions of drug abuse, addiction, captivity, rape, suicide, gore, violence, torture, homicide, and other adult language and situations,
It is intended only for mature audiences.
Reader discretion is advised.

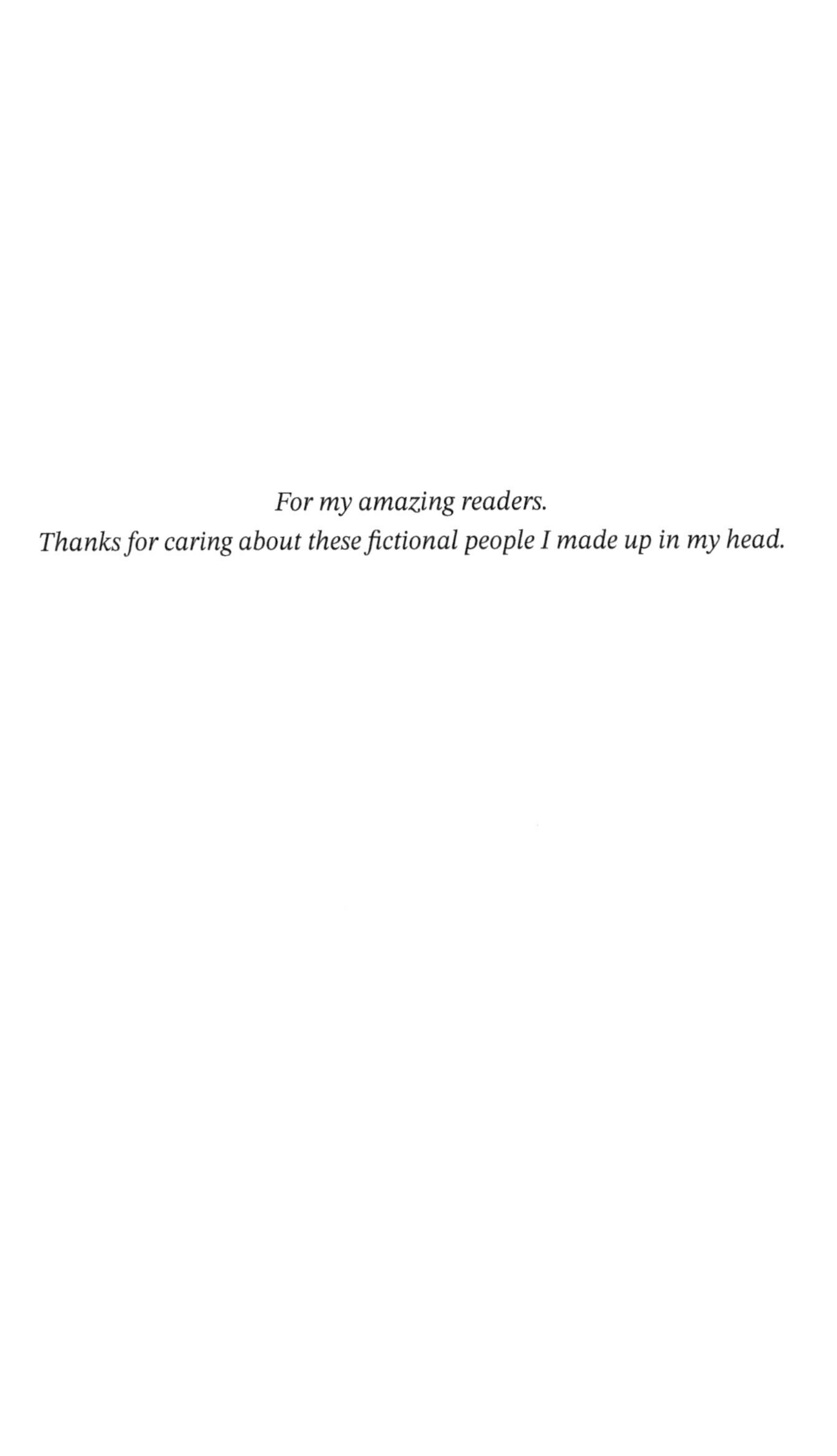

For my amazing readers.
Thanks for caring about these fictional people I made up in my head.

CHAPTER ONE

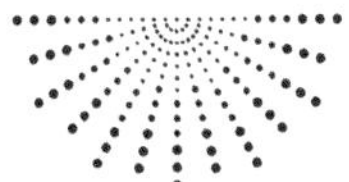

OVER THE LAST FOUR WEEKS - APRIL 30, 2022 - LAILA

At one point, nothing scared me more than becoming a mother. After losing Micah, I thought I'd be a horrible parent. But that was far from the truth. I fucked up the first three years, but I was going to make it right with the following fifteen.

My son and daughter would have good lives. They'd be as close to normal as possible for our kinds. We'd teach them to be good people. That's all that mattered to me. No matter what I had to do, I would shelter them from anything that could hurt them.

Micah had adjusted incredibly well with all things considered. But that isn't to say that every day was a breeze. There were bad ones.

About a week after we brought him home, we realized that he was deathly afraid of the dark. I usually left the wax warmer on in the bathroom at night, but the bulb burned out. I hadn't noticed, neither had Jeremy. But we certainly did when Micah erupted in erratic, uncontrollable sobs around two a.m.

I showed him that he and I always have a source of light—from our glowing eyes to our fiery or illuminated, healing palms. He relaxed a bit after that. But his panic attack still took about two hours to entirely soothe.

We also learned that Micah hated doctors. I wasn't sure if that were a result of Peterson or the hospital where we'd let them cut beneath his skin to remove the implants. Either way. His round of vaccinations the week before may have been the hardest day of my life. Had it not been for Jeremy's ever-present gentle attitude with the kids, I may have become an anti-vaxxer due to simple guilt.

Overall though, we'd gotten into the groove of having two kids. It came effortlessly. I said it before, and I'd say at a million more times over the years. We were built for parenthood. We were good at it, and we loved it.

Then again, I supposed the goddess and god of fertility were supposed to.

It'd been a good month. The first month of my life where I was able to be a wife, a mother to my daughter, and a mother to my son. It sounds so simple when phrased that way. Something most take for granted. But I treasured each and every moment. Then again, some part of me was very aware from the stockpile growing in my basement that I needed to treasure the time while I had it.

I listened to the advice the mystery CIA guys gave Adam. We got the money out of the bank like we were told to, we held our contracts in the supernatural world—we even worked a few quick cases with some allies. They went a lot quicker than they did back in the day.

Jeremy and I scheduled a meeting with the Chambers in France. Small, we told them it had to be small. No more than thirty guests with us included. I didn't trust the people working beneath the Council enough to be further outnumbered than that. They agreed. Reluctantly, anyway.

We also agreed to stay on his grandparent's vineyard for five days the following week. Chris was looking forward to it. So was Hannah. The rest of us were less than ecstatic. She and Chris were well liked by their grandparents. I think Brody held a certain place in their heart too. But the rest of us... not so much.

Regardless, we all needed the trip. Max needed the money. And in all fairness, my kids deserved a chance to at least meet their rich, stuffy grandparents.

And we'd made a deal. One we had to stick to.

The FBI and CIA went radio silent the day after those mystery-people tortured Peterson. I tried calling Tina a few times. She never called back. Jeremy called Connor only to the same end.

But still, we heeded the words they'd left in Adam's mind. I spent more time with Mom. A lot more; we saw her nearly every day. Micah loved the creek behind her house. He said he saw it before, in a dream maybe. That I wore a white dress with pretty flowers on the back.

I'm still not sure how he remembered that. Maybe from seeing memories in Lydia's mind when they were linked? Either way, it brought a smile to my lips. I'd hoped my son would be at our wedding in a little tux, but my hopes usually didn't equate to my reality. At least he was there some way or another.

As instructed, we got some damn chickens. Tink killed two. Luckily, Jeremy found them before Micah. He said we should cut them up and have them for dinner, that we'd have to get used to it if the end of the world was coming. I'd named them; there was no way I could season them and throw them in the oven. But Wyatt and Celena said they were delicious. After that though, we decided to move the coop *outside* the fenced-in section of the yard.

Jeremy threw together an eight-hundred dollar shed from the local department store on the west end of the house. We tossed up some foam insulation, bought heating lamps, and got a series of plants. Bell peppers, tomatoes, cucumbers, lettuce, spinach; the works. Micah and I worked on tending to it together, growing the leaves and fruits before trimming enough for the evening's salad and side dishes. He'd gotten a good handle on earth in that time. Milly even turned a cherry tomato green with a touch. When she did, Micah and I jumped to our feet together, clapping and cheering. She giggled and did it again. It was a life skill they'd both need, regardless of an impending apocalypse.

We invested ten thousand dollars in solar panels. Even at the time, it seemed arbitrary with Jeremy's ability to create energy. But they said it was needed and we had no reason to assume otherwise.

In our garage sat five composting toilets, ready for installation if needed. But for the time being, we enjoyed our septic system.

Thankfully, we had well water with a kick-ass filter. We bought a few cisterns and backup filtration systems to hold onto in case of a serious disaster like a collapsed well. But we didn't hook them up, just held onto them in case we'd need them.

If that wasn't enough already, I went a little doomsday prepper crazy. I pulled some strings with the underground hospital and stockpiled a large supply of broad-spectrum antibiotics. They may expire before they got used, but in an apocalypse, expired is better than nothing. Also, I got a bunch of gowns, gloves, masks, and sterile equipment. Not even for me; I could heal people. Considering the way rubbing alcohol had disappeared during the pandemic, I stocked up on that too. It was the best and least offensive cleaning product available. But I knew that if shit hit the fan, the medical field would probably be as ill-prepared as when the coronavirus hit in 2020. I wanted to be able to help.

Owning a diner made stocking up on food easy without looking odd. I loaded up on tons of canned everything. Canned beans, canned meat, canned pudding, canned nacho cheese, canned vegetables, and tons of canned fruit. Especially fruit that wouldn't survive our climate and I couldn't grow myself in the shed. I got a few quart cans of pineapple because they were Micah and Milly's latest obsessions. Pineapple on pancakes, pineapple on his PB&J, and *definitely* pineapple on his pizza. That insistence sparked a controversy deeper than the fiery political climate.

Moe's made stocking up on necessity items easier as well without clearing out shelves at the stores. Toilet paper, paper towels, hand soap, sanitizer; all the basics. I ordered a few extra boxes each time I placed the usual order.

I feel it important to bear in mind that most of the items I purchased were never intended to be used only by my massive family. I knew that if the end was coming, we'd be on the front lines. People would come to us for help. And we needed to be *able* to help.

We even cleared out a section of trees between our house and the main house. Then the guys made a project of curing the wood. We planned on saving it for lumber. We didn't know if we'd need it. But if the end was coming, we needed a safe place to keep our friends and allies who might need us. Perhaps a makeshift hospital or cabin of sorts. Our houses were large, but the end of the world is the end of the damn world. There were a lot of people out there that would need a safe place to rest their heads, and they couldn't all fit beneath my roof.

Doomsday prepping seemed so silly to me once. Now I was seriously considering digging a fallout shelter a few dozen feet underground. We decided it was too expensive. I considered it though.

It may have seemed a little excessive. But I knew it was coming and now was the time to prepare. Not panic, but prepare.

I'd been given advice once almost four years prior. Leave Jeremy, cash out my inheritance, take my baby, and start over. I didn't listen. I lost the first three years of my son's life. Not to say that I ever wanted to leave Jeremy. I wouldn't have Milly if I had. But sometimes, I still wish I'd taken that advice. Or at least been a bit more cautious than I was throughout my pregnancy. Regardless, I wouldn't make that mistake twice. Someone with more knowledge than me spoke, and I listened.

We warned people as much as we could. Others in the supernatural world, friends, and families. Leah put the word out on the dark web which apparently made it pretty far. She cited the CIA's involvement, which may not have been wise, but it got the attention it needed. We'd even started to see trending stories from major journalists—talking about odd weather changes and intense solar flares. Most weren't taking it seriously, but some did. Stores weren't clearing out, but people were establishing small stockpiles of their own.

Deep down, my core shook. But I needed to stay steadier than stone.

My kids were watching. The other survivors were watching. Leaders in our community were watching. I'd been given an army for a reason, and after seeing the warriors Jeremy and I were in our first life, I understood why.

The races in our world—Guardians, Fae, Wolves, Vampires, Demons—needed to band together. If we were divided, we couldn't fight for our world as one.

And as much as I hated Peterson, he was right.

I made a damn good figurehead.

CHAPTER TWO

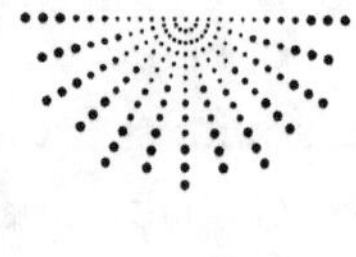

JEREMY

The familiar, homey scent of warm apples touched my nose. My ass was sore against the wooden breakfast nook bench. Soft spring air floated in from the open window behind me. It sent a pleasant chill to my skin. I listened to the kids giggling out there with Laila and Tink and wished I could go out there too.

I loved hanging out outside with them. It was my favorite thing in the world because it was their favorite thing in the world. And I wanted to enjoy it.

"You just have to focus," Hannah said.

"I am focusing," I grumbled.

"Well, not hard enough apparently. You should have been there and back by now. Chop-ch—"

"Maybe if you weren't bitching at me every two seconds." My eyes opened, meeting her blue glare. She placed either hand at her hips and huffed.

"Fine." She plopped into the chair beside the table. "But seriously, put the blindfold on. It helps."

I closed my eyes again. "I don't need a blindfold; my eyes are closed."

It wasn't that I didn't see her point. But the thing was, I didn't care about all of this right now. I just wanted to enjoy my wife and kids. I wanted to bask in the life I'd waited eons for. I finally had it all. My family, a steady income, a beautiful home.

Yeah, I needed to get used to how it felt in the whole afterlife, abyss thing. But I'd been studying. Hannah had given me something of an index with the three fundamental rules of necromancy, and I got it.

Rule number one: We can't save everyone. No matter what, there must be light in the abyss. If we saved every life that passed through, that'd throw off its balance.

Rule number two: Close the door when we leave. Metaphorically, of course, which is what we were working on at the moment. Going there, resting in the abyss for a while—getting accustomed to the peace and silence of it—and returning without bringing any light but my own back.

Rule number three: For every action, there's an equal and opposite reaction. Meaning when we put a life back into its body, death takes another of equal size in its place. That there's a balance to the abyss that can't be knocked off.

But my problem wasn't closing the door when I left. My problem seemed to be opening it. I didn't like it there. It was cold, and dark, and empty. When I had to go to save someone, I did so instantly without much thought and effort. But I didn't want to go there on my own accord. It was the personification of hanging out in a graveyard, and that wasn't my thing.

"Whatever. I'll shut up," Hannah said. "Let me know when it doesn't work and you're ready to listen."

I opened my eyes and glared. "It's not like I'm not trying, dude. But I had no choice the first time I did it. I had to bring her back."

"Should I try stabbing her?" She gestured out the window. "Probably won't get far, but maybe she'll kill me. Then you'll have to bring me back."

"Can't we just bank on it kicking in when I need it?"

"You know what you sound like?" Hannah asked. "Laila pregnant with Micah."

"That isn't fair. She didn't know—"

"And neither do we." My baby sister looked a lot more like a woman in that moment, wide, serious eyes shifting between mine. "That's why we have to do this. You have to know what you're doing. This isn't amateur hour anymore, Jeremy. The end of the world might be coming, and you need to know what you're doing to keep your people safe. You were a god once; you need to live up to what that entails."

I huffed. A god. Yeah, that may have been what people called me, but that was never how I envisioned myself.

"No, I need to know what our plan was two thousand years ago." I rubbed my temples. "We need to know whether to retreat or stand our ground. We need to know what this is going to look like. Nuclear? Natural disaster? Can we form an alliance with these people?"

"We don't even know anything's coming for sure," Hannah said. "But I know that no matter what, you need to know what you're doing with this."

I turned my gaze out the patio door. Micah's little light-up shoes glowed blue and green as Laila chased him through the yard. With each flash of those bulbs on his feet, I remembered that massive flare of white light just as blood shot like a fountain from his neck.

A knot solidified in my throat, and I shook my head. "You weren't there, Han. Something happened. It turned my hair gray." I gestured to the streaks that hung around my face. "Then some mystery CIA agents that may or may not be allies of ours from thousands of years ago tell us that we need to stock up and grow a garden and get chickens." I shook my head again. "No, it's already started. It's just a matter of time before we see it."

She fell quiet, looking out the window with me.

That image is forever imprinted in my mind. The three most important people in my world chasing one another through the early spring, wildflower-covered field off my family home's kitchen. Milly's little white dress flowing in the wind, Laila's long brown hair flying in her smiling face, Micah's bubbly baby laugh. Like something out of a 1950's movie. I could practically hear the opera singing in the background.

Still so young. Still so innocent, really. But a wonderful memory.

"When are you..." Hannah cleared her throat. "I just mean... Do you have plans?" She glanced at the basement door. "For him, I mean?"

I clenched my jaw. "Laila and I have been working up a list of things to ask him. We were hoping we'd have remembered more by now. Then we'd have more to go on."

"You haven't had any more dreams?" she asked.

"No, I've had a few. But they've been more like flashes. Seeing her walk by in some place I think is a castle. Fighting in battles and shit. We made one hell of a team on a battlefield—she healed; I held their souls in their body. We saved a lot of lives."

"And no conversations in these little flashes?"

"Not really." A good portion of them were us fucking. "Nothing worth asking Peterson."

"I think we should start asking the questions we do have though," Hannah muttered. "Kai and I can watch the kids for a few hours back at the house. Give you guys some space to... You know."

It wasn't that I was excited to torture Peterson. But I was excited to get the information we needed. I was even more excited to see what he'd look like as a corpse.

Laila and I had pushed him to the backs of our minds since we got Micah back. He'd taken so much time with our son already, we couldn't let him take any more. But Micah had adjusted well. He was doing great. And so were we.

Which was why I wasn't excited for this. We knew it was Laila he'd answer questions for. And it wasn't going to be easy for her to face that man.

"Yeah, probably a good idea. I'm going back to work when we get back from France so that'd be a good thing to cross off the list first. And the survivors want a date for the execution. So we need to get to work." I ran my fingers through my hair, letting out a deep sigh. "I'll talk to Laila when she comes in. Text me when you're free before we go."

"Pretty much whenever. I'm on spring break," Hannah said. "But we really need to work on this too, Jeremy. The biggest concern with this apocalypse is too many people dying at once. We don't know what will happen if so many souls are stuck there at the same time."

"I know, Hannah. But there's a lot on my plate right now and I'm a little overwhelmed." I ran my hand over my mouth. "I'm going to work on it, alright? But there's a lot going on. Let me get through this trip. We'll work on it around my schedule at the diner."

"Alright. We'll start working on it after the trip. But study the notes I've given you, okay? Those were Mom's rules. And they're good ones to follow."

"Yeah, I have the notecards at the house. I'll study."

"I'm serious. You need to memorize—"

"I know, Hannah. Jesus."

Her face said she didn't appreciate my tone.

I closed my eyes and rubbed my hands against them. "I'm sorry. I'm not trying to be a dick, alright? I'm just stressed out."

Hannah looked over me carefully for a moment. She continued. "Are you okay?"

A loaded question, and I knew what she was asking. If I planned on sticking a needle in my arm. But that wasn't it. I just didn't want to think about this shit. I wanted to enjoy my life. When I was happy, drugs were the last thing on my mind. And right about then, that's what I was. Happy. Life was good. I wanted to focus on that joy.

I didn't want to think about what I knew was coming.

"Yeah, I'm fine. I'm stressed, but I'm fine. I'm not relapsing in the foreseeable future if that's what you're asking. And yes, I'm still clean."

"That's not really why I asked," Hannah muttered. "This is about Mémé and Papy, isn't it?"

Yeah, I guessed it was.

I knew we had to make friends and play nice with the leaders of the supernatural community. If the world was going to end, we needed them behind us. But races aren't supposed to mix. People didn't like that I married a hybrid and that our children were massively powerful creatures. And for the most part, I didn't care.

But my grandparent's opinions were different. Not that they

mattered to me. They didn't. I could handle any shitty comments they made. But my kids weren't even three and one yet. Micah wouldn't understand why they treated him like a pariah. And he didn't deserve to. He was perfect, I didn't want them filling him with insecurities over something as arbitrary as his DNA.

"He called my marriage blasphemous. I can only keep my mouth shut for so long. And Laila's picked up a little French from me working with the kids, she's not one to bite her tongue either."

"The Chambers are going to be bending over backwards to kiss your ass. I doubt Mémé and Papy are going to be any different. You guys are a big deal in our world."

I raked my hand through my hair. "Yeah. Yeah, I hope. But if they say something shitty about my kids, I'm leaving."

"I agree. But let's hope that isn't the case."

CHAPTER THREE

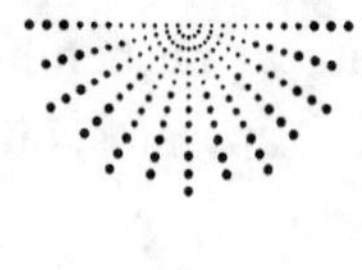

LAILA

Cool wind spilled in from the dark night. Quiet crickets chirped in the woods around the property, peacefully buzzing into my ears. I placed my hands on my hips and squinted at the suitcases on the bed.

Both kids had just fallen asleep in their rooms. And now, I was trying to figure out what the hell I'd forgotten to pack. I could feel it, I was missing something. I just couldn't tell what.

"Alright, six pairs of pants, light layers for five days, ten outfits for each of the kids, plus pajamas. I should bring toiletry items, huh?" I scratched my head. Maybe that's what I was forgetting. "Milly's skin is really sensitive. I don't want to take any risks."

Jeremy tugged off his shoes with a grin. "You do realize we can teleport back here at any given time, right?"

Of course I knew that. But I didn't want to go in the first place. If we were going to spend a week on the outskirts of Paris, I wanted to be prepared for it.

"Yes, but if I leave, I won't want to go back." I gave a smirk. "Might just leave you there to fend for yourself."

"Don't even say that." He grabbed the bottom of my shirt and toted me toward him at the edge of the bed. His hands slid from my hips up my shirt to my waist. "I really don't think I can make it a week there without you."

"Then quit trying to seduce me and help pack these bags." I looked between them and squinted. I gasped and started to the dresser. "Underwear. I almost forgot underwear."

He stood and looked at me in the mirror. "Alright, fine. I'll help. Do we have socks?"

"Laundry basket on the armchair." I glanced that way.

"What about raincoats for the kids?" Jeremy asked as he dug through the basket. "It's kinda rainy that way this time of year."

"No, but I just saw a couple at that little resale place on Main Street. I was going to grab them too, but I didn't have cash on me."

"Wouldn't be a bad idea to see if they still have them in the morning." He tucked the socks into the suitcase and tilted his head to the side. "I see a bathing suit for me, and Micah, and for Milly." He looked up with an odd smile. "Where's yours?"

"Well. If there is a pool, I am not going to be swimming."

He raised a brow. "Why not?"

That was obvious. I didn't care about my friends and family seeing my scars. Even strangers didn't bother me.

But his grandparents were different. They were important in the supernatural world. I didn't want them to look at the lashes on my back and see me as weak. I wanted them to have a healthy fear of me. And if I was standing there with my shoulders hunched in shame over marks on my skin that I couldn't change, it wouldn't send the message I was going for.

I huffed. "You know why not."

"No, I don't." He turned his head to the side a bit. "We swam at that hotel a few months before Milly was born."

I put my hands on my hips. "I brought long sleeves too, in case you didn't notice."

He made a face. "Why?"

"Because I don't want to. If you guys swim, I'll sit on the side." I looked back to the suitcase, rummaging to make sure I'd packed enough camisoles.

"Well, if you don't want to swim, then don't swim. But you have to at least bring one." He placed his hand at my hips from behind and pressed his lips to my cheek. "There's a hot tub in the basement at the guest house."

Now that... that sounded like a plan.

I couldn't remember the last time we'd had sex. The kids had a way of taking up every single moment of our time together. Any second we weren't with them, we were far too tired to fuck.

But maybe we'd have an opportunity on our little escapade to the most romantic city in the world.

"As in, private access." I smiled and turned to meet his gaze. A grin lifted his lips, his head bobbing in a gentle nod. My hands trailed up his chest and twisted around his neck. His moved to the small of my back, pulling my body against him. "So in theory. We could turn the baby monitor on, go down in the middle of the night, and relax in the hot tub."

"Or ya know." He leaned forward and touched his lips to mine. "Not relax."

A quiet laugh. I pulled away. "Well, I better grab one then."

As I meandered back to the closet, an exasperated sigh left him. "You're pretty aware of the situation with them, right?"

"Your grandparents?" I glanced at him around the closet door. He nodded, and I said, "Yeah, I think I have a good understanding. Can't really forget the man who calls you a whore on your wedding day."

"Slut, actually," he muttered. "But yeah. Yeah, I'm dreading this. Things have changed in our world since then. Everyone might be as civil as can be. We've built names for ourselves. But that doesn't mean their views have changed."

It was what it was. I didn't like the way they viewed me. It didn't bring me pleasure that his grandfather thought I was a slut. But it wasn't the first time someone called me a name, and I doubted it'd be the last.

"I'm sure it'll be fine," I said. "A few days, a couple meetings, and we'll be on our way home."

"Right," Jeremy said. "But if they say something shitty about my kids, we're leaving, Lai. I know we're trying to do what those CIA people said, but I'm drawing a line here. If they say something to our son, we're coming home. I'm not making him stay there with people who look at him as an abomination. And you either. If they say some shit about our marriage, we're leaving."

"Baby, I can handle a little bit of berating." I grabbed my swimsuit from the third drawer and turned back to the bedroom. My gaze met his as I dropped them into my suitcase. "But I agree. They say some shit about our kids and we're out."

"You shouldn't have to," he said. "And they should revere you anyway. They love the Angels so much."

"It's about the Fae blood," I said. "Don't even have that much in me but we know that's what it boils down to."

"They are your most prevalent abilities. So genetically speaking, the Fae must be a pretty strong gene in you."

"Yeah, but it could just be because they're easiest to control. Angel abilities are difficult. And we don't even know what my Guardian ability is."

"I bet it's that tree of life thing." He smiled as I sat on the bed beside him.

"Maybe." I rested my head against his shoulder. Jeremy tucked his arm around my waist and kissed my hair.

That seemed doubtful though. I had a feeling this tree of life ability tied into my soul more than my physical body. Otherwise, someone in my bloodline would have learned to use it and have granted themselves eternal life by now.

However, it wasn't like I knew much about my genealogy. But if it were so, there'd likely have been a few people walking around with the ability to live forever. Since Heylel was the only person I'd heard of with that gift, and I was the one who'd given it to him, I highly doubted that it came from DNA.

I craned up to meet Jeremy's gaze with a subject change. "I'm not looking forward to you going back to work."

He rested his head against mine. "Me neither."

"It's going to be weird doing it all without you," I muttered.

"It's not like I'm dying." He chuckled. "I'm probably only going to be there for six-hour shifts unless something comes up."

"Yeah, but seven days a week."

"It probably won't be seven days a week, you know that," he said. "There's only so much work that can be done at a place as little as ours."

"Not if we want to start stacking that saving." I thought for a moment. "We should focus on the venue downstairs. Try to get bigger crowds in. Maybe raise the prices on the liquor. Not a lot, maybe a quarter a drink, ya know?"

"That's not a bad idea," he said. "The shows bring in most of our profits anyway. Maybe we should charge an extra dollar for shows too. If we get a hundred people in, that's an extra hundred profit."

"Yeah, I hate to raise prices, but we're not gauging. A less than ten percent increase is acceptable."

"Yeah, I think it's reasonable. If we get too many complaints, we can lower it back down. But the prices have been the same since I've known you, it's about time. Adjust for inflation and everything."

After a moment, Jeremy slowly released a deep breath. "We need to talk about something."

My eyes shifted up to his. "What's that?"

His big blue eyes softened. He brushed a strand of hair behind my ear. "We have to figure out what we're doing with Peterson."

"Oh."

I knew he was right. But I liked acting like he didn't exist. He was quiet for the most part and hadn't asked for me after my repeated stab session. I knew we had to do it again; we needed a better understanding of what was really happening. But I was enjoying being a mom and pretending the last few years had been a bad dream.

"We should interrogate him at least once before I go back to work," Jeremy said. "Probably before we go to France."

I felt so gross after we'd done it last time. At least now, I knew not to expect to feel relief. He may have enjoyed hearing my screams when he hurt me, but I supposed that's one of the many things that separated the two of us. I hurt people out of necessity. He did it for shits and giggles.

After a quiet moment, I said, "Yeah. We should."

His voice was soft. "Hannah said she and Kai can watch the kids. I don't know if it's too soon, but we're free tomorrow. We should make sure we have a full day. It might take some time to recoup."

I rubbed my mouth. "Yeah. Tomorrow works."

His fingertips trailed over my open palm before he twined our fingers together. "We have that list made up, don't we?" I chewed my lip and nodded. He touched my chin, turning my gaze up to his. "Are you okay?"

"Yeah. Yeah, I just... I know he's going to say it again. That he *created* me. And he's not wrong, that's the truth. He did. Those three months inside that place and then past three years made me a different person."

"That's not—"

"Yes, it is. It is, Jeremy." My tone was sharper than I'd intended. "I'm not the same person I was."

He grew quiet, gently coasting his thumb against the back of my hand.

And the fucked-up part was that I loved the woman Peterson had created. I was stronger, and I was smarter. I learned to cope with shit because I didn't have the time to sit there and feel sorry for myself. Twenty-year-old me was pathetic. Jeremy would say that I wasn't because he loved me, but I was.

I cleared my throat. "The harsh reality is that he made me a warrior. He made me a leader. His fucked-up methods made me into a person I genuinely like. But that's the problem, I became a version of myself that I like because of the shitty lessons *he* forced me to learn. I am who I am because of him, and I hate that."

"No," he said. "Ya know what he said when we were in that cell? When you were in and out of consciousness?" I shook my head, and he said, "He said that you remembered your true self in each life. What he did, it wasn't building a version of you that didn't already exist. He just reminded you of who you really were. He didn't create you. The horrible shit he did reminded you of who you were always meant to be."

I swallowed the knot that had swelled in my throat. "Yeah. Yeah, I guess that's a better way to look at it."

He kissed my cheek and pulled my shoulders into him. I relaxed into his arms. "We should get some sleep. Big day ahead of us."

JEREMY

Charred flesh burned my lungs. Hot, humid air wafted in through a slit in the cloth of the tent. Flickering candlelight illuminated the space. I stared down at a large gash on the back of my forearm, tightly binding it in yellowing cloth.

"Nix," Véa's quiet voice said behind me.

I looked up and forced a smile. She sent a similar expression my way. The kind of smile that looked—and felt—a little pained. A white gown with buttons up the center hung over her narrow shoulders. It wasn't as provocative as the one she wore in my last memory of her. Though see-through, it covered from her shoulders to her wrists. It was beautiful though, and she was beautiful in it.

She spoke in Elvan. And every word seemed to auto-translate in my mind. "How are you?"

"Eh. I've seen better days. But I'm sure I'll see worse."

"I hope not," she murmured. She looked to the cut along my forearm. "Let me heal that for you."

I continued wrapping the cloth around my skin. "I'm all right."

"Don't be stupid." She walked into the tent and sat beside me on the makeshift cot and took my arm. As she looked over the cuts ascending it, she shook her head a bit. A *tsk, tsk, tsk* sound left her lips before her palm radiated bright light into my skin. I grimaced at the pain. "I don't know how you didn't lose limbs before I came along. Wrapping these up without washing first, that's a fast way to false hand."

I chuckled, clenching my jaw through the stinging up my arm. "Neither do I, do gràs."

Silence crept in for a long moment. She spoke again.

"What she said..." she murmured as her hand hovered over the slices along the back of my hand. "You don't think... You don't think she meant he was responsible."

"I don't know."

She dipped her head in a slow nod. She pressed her lips together and raised her hand to my other bloodied arm. "You wouldn't... You don't think that he would, do you?"

"A lot of people have wanted her dead for a long time." My jaw clenched at the pain in my bicep. "Lux though... I didn't think these politics mattered to him."

"Mm." Her eyes stayed on my skin. "I think politics are about all that matter to him. Politics and power."

She set her hand back to her lap. I turned up to meet her gaze. "Do you think he would have done that?"

Her pretty green eyes shifted between mine for a moment. She slid her gaze downward. "I've heard bits and pieces. Never details, but certain things... Fria's name has come up in some less than kind manners."

I blinked hard a few times. "From my brother?"

"Aye," she murmured. "I heard nothing of this. But he's definitely... Yes, I could see it as a possibility."

My jaw tightened, head shaking.

She was quiet for a moment. "I can speak with him when we return, if you'd like."

"No," I said. "No, I'll handle it. Thank you."

Her gaze traveled to her bare feet in the dark sand. "I am so sorry, Nix."

"Aye, thank you." I felt for the cool, Elvan ore flask on the cot. I popped off the cork and took a long gulp. I extended it to her. She took a swig, then looked down at it in her palms. For a moment, she just stared at it. She took another sip and handed it back.

"This is all so useless," she murmured. "All that bloodshed. For what?"

I took another gulp from the bottle. "Aye."

"Then why are we still here?" She met my gaze. "Why are we still fighting for him, Nix?"

"Because we have orders."

"*Orders.*" She scoffed. Her head shook, tongue running along her teeth. She gritted them tight together. "I never agreed to this. I never agreed to take *orders* from him."

"You did," I murmured. "When you married him, you did."

Her jaw clenched tighter, followed by her palms. She shook her head again. "This was meant to be a partnership. I didn't realize I was signing up to be a slave."

"You aren't a slave—"

"It's closer to slavery than freedom." Her eyes glowed when they met mine. "Don't tell me I'm wrong, Nix. We both know your brother."

I had to look away. "Aye."

She stood and walked toward the slit of the fabric that was a door. My heart sunk, probably thinking she was leaving, but she stopped there and looked out over the camps. A slow breath left her nostrils as she turned back to me over her shoulder. "Is this what you want? To fight and war? To butcher our people like we did today?"

"You know it isn't, Véa," I said. "I want this to end. But we couldn't just lie down and die either."

She shook her head once more, clenched her jaw tighter, and she stared out the opening. I stood and handed her the canteen. I looked out to the camps set up over the seemingly endless plot of sand. The moon was blue, reflecting a warm glow the color of its sun on the cool desert around us. Nearly all of the white tents appeared slightly blue by the moon's light as well. Beautiful, almost, but then a scream echoed in the distance. My eyes closed, stomach churning.

I turned away from the desert and looked at Véa.

She met my gaze. She raised the bottle back to her lips and took a long gulp, eyes still against mine. Again, she was quiet. Just looking at me. The angry glow in her eyes had softened, but something was going on behind them. She said, "They chose wrong."

"On what?"

"You," she said. "This wouldn't have happened if you were in control. The one actually fighting the battles should be the one to make the calls, not the one who sits in a room and awaits a report."

A slow breath left my nostrils as she extended the bottle back to me. Her fingers grazed mine, and our gazes met.

Judging from the comfort her touch brought, it wasn't close to the first time Nix had felt her skin.

My eyes shifted over the long damp curls that hung from her head to her ribs. I looked at her green eyes nearly glowing at the field before us. I even glanced down the front of her sheer dress, spending a second too long at her bust, then again at the dark hair of her pelvis.

I looked away and chugged what remained in the canteen. Once it was gone, I tossed it to the cot and leaned against some provisional form of a desk at the foot of it. Her eyes shifted over me, studying me.

"What is it?" I asked.

"Do you wish it would've been?" she asked. "Do you wish you would have been king?"

"No." I shook my head with a half-laugh.

Her eyes shifted from my left to right. "But does some part of you wish that you were? Not because you want the royalty, but because you could've done better than him."

"I don't know that I could."

"You'd make a better husband, at least."

My stomach flipped. I think my cheeks even grew warm.

Hers did too, but she didn't look away. "I'm sorry, I shouldn't have said that."

I cleared my throat. My mouth opened to say something before it shut just as quickly.

She took a step toward me.

As she drew closer, my heart picked up speed. But she lowered herself to the edge of the cot, reached beneath it, and lifted out another flask. She popped open the cork and took a long sip. "I should really keep my big flap shut, eh? Always say the wrong thing."

I paused, looking between her eyes and then a glance over her body. "No. You have a beautiful mind. You should always speak it."

A slight smile pulled at her lips as she handed me the flask. I took it from her and set it on the desk. When I turned back, she reached forward. I thought she was reaching for my dick at first. But her open palm covered a nasty slit at my lower abdomen.

My eyes widened when the sudden light erupted into my skin. She grinned at my shock. The wound closed shut, and she moved her palm to another cut along my rib. I grimaced for a moment. I caught her hand.

"I'm trying to help you," Véa said.

I said nothing at first, just looked at her and laced my fingers between hers.

She smiled. "What?"

I cupped her soft cheek in my hand and leaned my face to hers.

I think I expected her to pull away. Or tell me no, or say that it was wrong. But we both knew that. And we wanted it anyway.

Her hands went to my chest, warming my skin as they touched my ribs, then up to my shoulders. My fingers at her cheek slid to her sides, squeezed her tiny waist, and drew her into me. Her lips were so smooth against mine, with just the right touch of moisture. But so gentle, so sweet.

"Was that okay?" I whispered against her mouth. She opened her eyes and looked between mine, smile sliding up her cheeks. She nodded. I smiled back, pressed my lips to hers, and tugged her in closer.

Before I knew it, I was kneeling over top of her with my hand on the side of her soft, toned thigh. The rest of the world, whatever world that may have been, began to fade away. It was like everything else went black, and she was the only thing in the entire universe.

Her legs wrapping around my bare waist was the hottest tempera-ture I'd ever felt without being burned. It sent a layer of warm, anticipation-filled chills to my skin. Her lips grazing mine made my face tingle and my cock throb harder against her inner thigh. She tasted sweet, yet earthy. Almost like honey in warm tea.

Her hair against my cheek as I kissed down her neck smelled like the water of a riverbed yet held onto that sweetness I tasted on her mouth. The sound of her fast-moving breaths against my ear as my fingers grazed the wet crease between her legs forced a long sigh from my lips. My fingertips grazed the soft curls and her legs stretched farther open. I slid my fingertip along her hard, moist clit and closed my eyes in bliss at the sound of her quiet moan in my ear.

A wave of joy washed over me, and I smiled against the salty sweat dripping down her neck. Her hand at my chest drifted between her legs to my dick. My eyes closed, lips moving back to hers, taking in that sweet taste of her soft lips once more. Her moan vibrated into my mouth as she rubbed the head of my cock against her opening. A quiet breath left me and that strong, tingling sensation stretched up my body.

Her fingertips wrapped around me, slowly moving up and down. She pressed it further into the warmth of her vulva. I felt the liquid from inside her drip over my dick and pushed my body closer into hers. Not inside, but along that warm, wet crease.

That's how my entire body felt. Warm. Comfortable. This felt like making love to Laila now did. Homey, and familiar. Passionate, but not in a violent, first time, quick fuck sort of way. In a sweet, loving, *I want to be with this woman for the rest of my life* sort of way.

When her legs tightened at my hips, I slid my finger from her thigh to her opening. I spun them in a slow circular motion, wetting them against her and listening as her moan grew louder. A prideful smile heightened at my lips, and I slipped my finger inside of her. Her mouth opened against mine, and she took in a quiet gasp.

Our eyes met as I felt her muscles tighten around my fingers. Her mouth fell open, and her palm along my shaft slowed, like she'd forgotten how to move. I smiled and so did she. I started to kiss down her body, but her legs tightened at my waist. Her smile widened, and her head shook. Her hand at my shoulder slid down my bare chest. She grasped my wrist to pull me out of her.

"I want you inside of me," she whispered.

My cock throbbed against her hand, and I laughed. I lowered my lips to hers once more. I touched her neck, feeling the race of her heart beneath my fingers. I slid my hips closer to hers and pushed my dick against her clit.

Her hips arched upward until her vagina took me in. I sighed at the warmth of her muscles around me. I pushed further inside until a quiet gasp left her lips.

My knees took on my weight as I slowly pulled out and slid back in. I basked in the way her walls felt around my dick. So warm, and so *fucking* wet.

She felt different than any woman ever had. Tight, but soft. Smooth further inside but textured closer to her opening. I pushed my hips further to hers and made a grinding motion until I felt her clit against the base of my dick. A moan echoed into my mouth, and I did it again, feeling her walls tighten around me. My lips curved into a higher smile as I moved that way again and again, hearing her moan get higher in pitch with each fluid motion.

I slid my hand from her neck to her hip. The one against her chest brushed down her torso, caressing her hard nipple before grabbing her other hip. I squeezed them both and hoisted them firmly into mine. A quiet gasp left her mouth as I lifted her into the air. Her hands twisted around my neck, gently thumbing at my hair. I shifted to sit and took her body onto my lap.

She situated her dress around us while my lips glided downward. I kissed along her jaw then down her neck to her collar bone. The strap fell to her bicep, and my mouth slid to her breast.

With each brush of our fingers, each touch of our lips, each heavy breath and quiet moan, I had the urge to wrap my arms around her waist as tight as they would allow. I wanted to stay trapped in that very moment with her for all of eternity. It wasn't so much a thought, but an instinct.

My hands skimmed her hips, pushing them further down until she moaned at my ear. "Véa," I whispered.

"Mhmm?" she murmured, grinding against my pelvis. I opened my mouth to say something but snapped it shut. My head shook as my eyes closed, feeling the clench of her pelvic muscles around me.

I looped my arms around her waist, holding her tight, closing my eyes, basking in this moment. I didn't know what Nix was thinking, but I knew what he was feeling. He wasn't just aroused. This wasn't just fucking. They were making love. The kind of sex that's so beautiful, so intimate that it's almost heartbreaking.

And he felt that too. He was enjoying it. But something in his chest pinged with pain. Not guilt, true, genuine pain.

"I wished it'd have been me, too."

A quiet breath fell into my ear. Her arms tightened around my shoulders, hugging me so close that nothing could get between us. She wasn't just fucking me; she was *holding* me. And I was holding her, and that brought me so much comfort.

After a few moments, her breaths got closer together. Her moans got louder, so loud that I lifted my hand at her neck to cover her mouth. She laughed and touched her lips back to mine, grinning, struggling to stay quiet.

Just as her soft sighs grew higher in pitch behind the lips she struggled to bite together, a glowing purple light began to permeate from her body, and the euphoria flooded over me.

Then the same gray and blue, smoke-like substance started to float from my skin as well. I said, "Véa."

Her eyes opened, then grew to discs. "What's happening?"

"I don't know," I murmured, looking at her in wonder. "But don't stop."

That may not have been the first time we made love, but it was the first time our souls touched.

CHAPTER FIVE

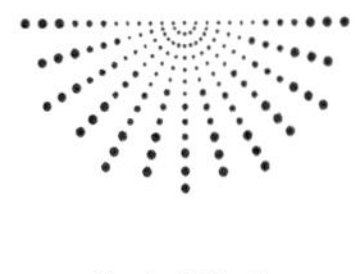

LAILA

I thought I stood within the Elder's Hall for a moment. It looked a lot like it. The dark mahogany trim, the light painted walls, the windows overlooking abundant gardens framed in glass. Even the domed ceiling. But my glance outside to the evening sky showered in bright stars and what looked like a blue planet encased with white rings reminded me that I was in a place far from what I called home. But it didn't feel much like home then either.

Smells I'd never experienced wafted into my nose and mouth. Some were familiar—yeast and bread-like—while the scent of barbecue touched the back of my throat. Not the sauce or seasoning, but meat cooked just right with only a touch of black crusted in the right places. Intoxicating, almost as much as the sweet bluish-colored liquor I sipped from a golden cup.

Music cascaded around me, sending a shiver of warm goosebumps to my skin. The melodies were a language this version of me spoke, but this me didn't understand. His voice stuck out though, as it always did. The love of my lives. But it sounded off-tune. I looked between the crowded tables to the small band playing in the corner.

An instrument—something between a ukulele and a guitar—hung around his neck. He billowed out words I didn't understand. My head tilted, as if Véa couldn't understand him either. A man beside him touched his elbow, but he laughed and shook his head, rebutting something with an uncaring smile. He lifted a glass from the table and chugged. As he set it back down, his gaze met mine.

His playful grin fell.

A hand touched my shoulder. I turned up. And I got the best, clearest image I'd seen to date of the man the world called God. Or Lux. Or whatever the fuck his name was.

He was a damn good-looking man. Strong jaw, clean-shaven, golden skin. His short blond waves fell into his brown eyes. He wore a sweet smile, the kind you'd see on a high school jock. Something between a robe and a cape hung over a thin piece of armor. Decorative, lightweight. Not the kind that would keep a sword from piercing his skin.

"Ol boaluahe." He smiled as his hand stroked my cheek. *My love.*

It occurred to me. I wasn't sure how, but I did understand this language. I just didn't understand Nix because he was drunk and belting out music.

I smiled back, though it felt strained.

A pit formed in my stomach as I looked between his warm brown eyes. I thought it was shame at first, maybe guilt. But when he leaned down and touched his lips to mine, I fought the urge to keep my teeth from trembling. Fear. Guilt and shame, but mostly fear.

As he sat at the bench beside me, I held my fake smile, but my heart raced like a deer from a coyote. His hand drifted to mine and the other slid to my knee. He continued speaking, in Enochian I believe, but all I could hear was Nix's drunken singing from the corner of the room. It sounded passionate, almost angry. And it made my heart anxiously thump harder.

Lux went on talking for what seemed like forever. He looked happy. Smiling wide, chuckling at himself. I tried to join in his laughter, but I didn't only feel guilt and fear when I looked at him. I was angry. Some part of me hated him in that moment, and it was taking everything I had to smile.

After a few minutes of his rambles that I pretended to pay attention to, I heard Nix behind me. He clanged some form of cutlery off of his glass and called out over the people. My heart thumped and the crowd fell quiet.

"Oi trian noan balit," Lux chuckled at my ear. *This will be good.*

I forced a smile and anxiously looked back to Nix. For some reason, I didn't understand, or maybe I just didn't care, what Lux was saying. But as Nix spoke, I understood it perfectly. It wasn't English, the language was much harsher. And, oddly enough, it auto-translated in my mind.

"How glad I am to feast with you all today. To share in all of this wonderful food, and drink." He paused, laughing as he lifted his glass and took another gulp. His hand sloppily rubbed against the corner of his mouth.

Someone grabbed his elbow and tried to pull him away. He ripped his hand back and turned back to the crowd. "It isn't really ours. We stole it straight from the mouths of people who did nothing but help us."

Lux stood, and the crowd began to stir. Some shouted words I didn't catch. I watched Nix stumble forward, letting out a half-laugh with furrowed brows.

"It isn't true, that's what you say? If that eases your mind, fine. Pretend then. Act like what you're celebrating isn't poisoned with innocent blood." The words left his lips like fire escaping the jaws of a dragon.

Lux started toward him, but I caught his arm. I stood and murmured something. He gave a nod. Nix went on as I continued through the crowd.

"But I was *there*." Spit angrily splattered from his lips. "I watched our soldiers die. I watched their soldiers die. I watched my mother die. They all died for nothing. For a feast and a title. A battle won in the name of light." He glanced at me coming toward him and released an ironic, drunken laugh.

"The pride we have now is far from righteous. We should be on our knees. Our hearts should hurt for what our army has done. For what we were ordered to do. Murder. Bloodshed. Death is not righteous.

And I am happy to be home, but I am ashamed to call you my people—"

I grabbed his elbow and looked firmly between his eyes. "Nix."

"Do you have something to add, do gràs? Have we not disgraced ourselves? Hmm?" His eyes held mine. "Do you believe we have the right to feast today? After what we did?"

"I believe you need some fresh air."

Laughter echoed from the crowd. My head shot toward them. I narrowed my glowing gaze at the men in tunics and robes. They swallowed hard and turned back to their drinks.

"Let's go," I murmured. He yanked his elbow away and started past me.

I followed after him, exchanging a nod with Lux.

He stomped through the stone room to a large wooden door he didn't hesitate to hold open.

"Nix," I called. He started into a snow-covered courtyard. He waved his hand at me, shook his head, and kept walking. A slow breath escaped me, watching him make it to the other side of the esplanade. He made it into a small tunnel that must have led to the rest of the world. When he did, he gripped ahold of the stone wall. Steadying himself, he leaned over to hurl.

I took off in a slow jog toward him. "Are you alright?"

"No." He coughed, lurching forward once more. More vomit spilled to the ground. I placed my hand on his back. He turned against the wall with watery eyes. He slowly collapsed against it, a few feet from the pile of vomit.

When he spoke this time, it was in Elvan. And I'd picked up a bit from the spells I'd done earlier this year, but I understood it clear as day. Every word, as if it were my native tongue. "You were right. You were right, Véa."

I lowered myself beside him and reached out for his hand, but he tugged it back. His lips curved downward, and his head shook. "Please don't do that."

"I'm sorry," I whispered.

He clenched his jaw. "We have both created our own worst nightmares. Fighting for the side we hate, killing the people we love." He paused, looking between my eyes.

I frowned. "Loving the person we can't have."

His eyes flittered from my left to my right. His voice softened. "And loving the person we can't have."

My heart ached, and I turned away.

He rolled his head against the stone wall. Slowly, he took in and blew out a deep breath. It ended in a puff of steam that clouded his face. "I just can't take this place anymore. Of course, I have to, so it doesn't matter how I feel. Not really." His nostrils flared, jaw tightening. He released a huff of a laugh. His hand rubbed against his beard. "They were helping us. And we repaid them with slaughter. A gruesome, bloody pillage."

I swallowed hard.

Nix was quiet for a moment too. He managed a smile. "At least we have each other's misery to keep us company." He bumped his shoulder against mine. I gave a quiet laugh. "Why are you so quiet?"

I glanced behind me, caught sight of a few guards in the distance, and turned back. His big, concerned eyes shifted between mine, and my stomach flipped. "I have something to—"

"There you are," a voice said behind me. My stomach clenched, and I turned with a smile. "I've been looking for you everywhere." Lux extended his hand out for mine.

I smiled, took it, and stood. "Well, I've been here."

He looked at Nix with a gentle grin. Not condescending or crude. Just kind. "Do you need help getting home, esiasch?"

"I'm not welcome inside?" Nix asked, wiping his off-white sleeve against his lip.

"Maybe not tonight."

"Shite. I didn't even get to the meat course."

Lux chuckled, extending his hand to help his brother. Nix made it to his feet and glanced at the vomit behind him. "Oops."

Again, Lux laughed. "A maid will get to it."

My jaw clenched. Tight. I wasn't sure why, that wasn't all that nasty of him to say. But for some reason, it made my heart race faster.

Nix managed a smile. "I'll see you later. Enjoy your supper."

Lux tucked an arm around my waist. "Try and get some rest, esiasch."

"Aye," Nix said. "Sleep well. And you too, do gràs."

I tried to will my lips into a smile, but faltering. Then we turned. As we started away, Lux started speaking again. Happy, bubbly. Laughing at his own jokes again. But the more he spoke, the faster my heart raced and the tighter my hands clenched. I looked over my shoulder. And my heart fell out of my chest.

Nix watched the two of us, fighting water in his eyes. His nostrils flared. He was struggling so hard to keep it inside. But he forced on a smile.

Find me later and finish what you were saying, eh? His voice spoke into my mind.

Water burned across my eyes. My chest was tight and heavy, like it was full of sand. I gave a nod.

CHAPTER SIX

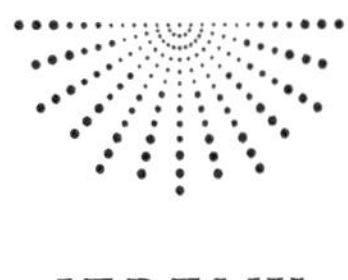

JEREMY

Laila was still asleep when I heard Milly on the baby monitor that morning. I figured she could use the extra sleep. And honestly, I was still in too much of a haze to look at her without accidentally calling her Véa.

I peeped into Micah's room. He slept soundly with Tink curled against his chest. His little arm did what it could to reach around her shoulders. She opened her eyes to look at me with Milly on my hip. She nuzzled her head against his chin.

Those two had become the best of friends lately. Any moment we were within the perimeter around the house, Tink wasn't far behind Micah. We weren't shit anymore; he was her best friend.

Chris's bed was made, and the door was open. I heard the clang of dishes and breathed in the smell of coffee. He murmured to himself as I came down the steps and sent a smile his way. "How was your run?"

That's what he did each and every morning. He woke before the sun was up, then watched it rise as he jogged through the trees. I didn't have to ask why it meant so much to him. He'd spent the last decade in captivity. There was nothing he liked more than wide-open spaces now.

"Gorgeous." Chris took a long gulp from his water and smiled back. "Have you watched the sun come up down by creek recently?"

"It's been a couple years," I said.

"You should. There's this little family of bunnies living in a little hole right off the trail. I'm surprised the wolves haven't gotten to them yet. But it's so cool, they're finally big enough to leave the nest. I've been bringing lettuce down. I hope Laila doesn't mind."

"She's got an endless supply in the shed, I don't think she cares." I put Milly in her highchair and started to the coffee pot. "There's still a trail though?"

"I took a machete to it," he said. "You guys have all this land, and you never use it."

"Kinda had a lot going on the past few years," I muttered. "Wyatt and Celena are all over the place though."

I did miss it though. Maybe I'd make a habit of taking Micah on walks down the trails I'd walked as a kid. I was headed back to work though. I didn't know how much time I'd have soon.

"Yeah, guess that's true." He walked to Milly and murmured something to her with a smile. She giggled. He chuckled and turned back to me. "Hannah said she was watching the kids today so you guys could... Ya know."

"That's the plan."

"Mind if I get in on it?" he asked. "I want to see the bastard suffer."

"As long as Laila doesn't care. I doubt he'll give you any information though. He doesn't say shit to anyone but her."

"I don't give a fuck about information. I just want to see the bastard hurt."

"I just want to see the fucker die," I muttered.

"That too." Chris sat at the bar, and I flicked on the light. "How much longer are you planning on keeping him? Holding him captive seems a little redundant."

"It's up to Lai. I hate the guy, but this is her war. It's her call."

Silence sneaked in as I got Milly a bottle and started heating her some oatmeal. Then Chris cleared his throat. "Can I torture him too then?"

"Everybody else has," I said. "I don't see why not."

"So you don't care if I cut his eyes out."

It was a good thing Milly was too young to understand what we were talking about.

"Seems justified to me. But Laila might want him to see what she's doing to him today. So ask her when she gets up. I'm sure she'll support it though."

"As long as I get to before we kill him."

"I'm sure she'll be okay with that."

I went to the pantry, grabbed the box of pancake mix, and a bag of chocolate chips. I grabbed a bowl and turned back to the counter.

"I'm excited to go to France," Chris said. "Me and Mémé were on the phone for, like, three hours last night. She's got the rooms made up for us. Oh, she wanted to know if she should stock the fridge. I figured we'd probably eat out a lot so I told her no, but I can tell her I was wrong if you want me to."

Such a strange thing we did in our family. We went from talking about torture onto the topic of family vacations seamlessly. And yet, the conversation about gore was an easier one for me to partake in.

"No, that's okay. I want every excuse to leave that we can."

"Why's that?"

Since he'd missed the last ten years, he'd missed the worst years of me. I was a shitty kid. I got into a lot of trouble. And I hadn't exactly been ecstatic to confide that in my holier than thou big brother.

I uncomfortably cleared my throat. "I'm sure you've heard about the shit I did as a teenager by now."

"I've heard you're a heroin addict." Chris's tone was as it usually was. Blatant. "But that's about it."

"Yeah, that's the short version. I don't really want to get into the long version. But I was shitty, I did a lot of shitty things. Some really cool things too. I got high as shit and broke into an animal testing facility once." I smirked. "I freed a few thousand bunnies and pigs."

"You didn't." He grinned.

"I did. Just finished paying off the fines last year." I laughed. "But yeah, shitty things too. I stole money off them a couple times. Never a lot, it didn't really hurt them. But ya know. Thievery is thievery." He nodded, waiting for me to go on. I cleared my throat. "I ODed a couple times. I got caught at school with drugs. When you died, or went missing, I guess... I don't know, man. It did a number on me. So I drowned it out."

He gave a gentle nod, but his gaze was firm. "When did you get clean?"

"Right after Annie died. I was locked in my room dope sick as shit when she did. Kind of her dying wish for me to grow the fuck up." I sipped my coffee. "So I did."

"Clean ever since?" he asked.

"No. No, I've had a few setbacks. It's not something I'm proud of. But I'm clean now. So that's what matters."

"Sure. Sure," he said. "What's your clean date?"

"August 19th, 2020."

"That's it?"

Like I'd said, it wasn't something I was ecstatic about either. But a year and a half clean was a lot harder than it sounded to someone who wasn't an addict. It made me feel pretty small when it was phrased in such a minuscule fashion. I'd busted my ass for those twenty months of sobriety.

My gaze turned to the coffee in my hand. "It's really not something I'm proud of, Chris."

He held his judgmental gaze. I licked my teeth.

"Laila and I were both in a really bad place after she got back. I fucked up when she was taken, and I didn't get my shit back together for a long time. I won't pretend that was okay because it wasn't. I should have been there for her; I should have been better. I know this. But I got my shit together after I learned my son was alive. And I've kept my shit together since unless you count Peterson injecting me that day." I paused and tightened my jaw. "So I guess my issues with Mémé and Papy boils down to the same look you're giving me right now."

His eyes widened slightly.

I never stood up to Chris when we were young. He was the smart big brother. He was the one that taught me to skateboard and play guitar. He was the one I listened to. He was the one that told me when I was being a little shit and to knock it off. But I wasn't being a little shit anymore. I was doing right by my kids and family. It wasn't fair to make me feel bad about something that was in the past that I couldn't change.

"I'm sorry," Chris murmured. "Almost two years. That's something to be proud of."

It was. And I really hoped that he meant that.

CHAPTER SEVEN

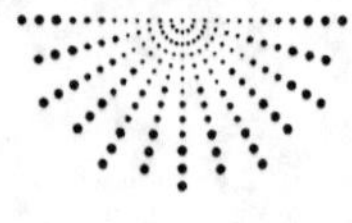

LAILA

When Jeremy woke me up, I had to do a double-take. I even sniffed his breath. He looked at me funny when I did, then gestured toward the kitchen and told me to come eat.

At breakfast, I kept looking over him. His smile was so joyous. He had his son to his left, me to his right, and our daughter just beside me. He was where he always wanted to be, even those few thousand years ago.

Lux loved Nix. He tortured us for a few thousand years. But he did let us end up here. Together, as a family, just as we'd wanted. Which, I supposed in some regard, I had to give the asshole props for. He did love his big brother.

I didn't understand though. I didn't understand why I was cheating with Jeremy in the first place. I didn't understand why I was so afraid of that man. Was he abusive? Was that why? He didn't seem to be at that party, but I guessed abusive spouses usually weren't in public.

But I knew myself. If a man were abusing me, even if I weren't as powerful in that life as I was in this one, I'd have made him pay for it. Motherfucker had to sleep sometime. I wouldn't get revenge by fucking his brother. I'd have killed him.

The anger that boiled in me when he mentioned a maid reran through my mind too. It wasn't said condescendingly and degrading toward the workers; it was just a simple statement. So why did it make me so angry?

As I put my plate in the dishwasher, Jeremy's hand caught mine.

"I'm getting water everywhere," I said.

"Sorry." He crossed his arms and leaned against the counter. "But why do you keep looking at me like that?"

"Like what?"

"Like you're not in there." He glanced at my head with a smile. "Did you remember something?"

"I did." He grinned. I chuckled, rolled my eyes, and set the plate on the bottom rack. "But unlike you, not all of my memories are about our sex life."

"Damn. So this one wasn't either?" he asked.

"No. No, but it was about you. He was there though. Lux."

"What happened?" he asked.

"I think it was some type of celebration after a war? Or a battle maybe, I'm not sure. They were speaking Enochian, I think. Maybe a splash of Latin here or there? And I understood it. Clear as day. And the same with Elvan. I think I can speak it now. I can understand it, I know that."

His brow arched. "Did you know Latin and Enochian before?"

"No. I mean, I know a little bit. A lot of the books on Angel and Guardian history were in Latin and Enochian and I had to translate them to English to read. So I guess some things stuck. But I definitely wasn't fluent. No one speaks it; there was no reason for me to learn it."

"That's true," he muttered. "But you've learned a little Elvan from those spells you were working on with Helena, right?"

"A little. But." I said, *how are you, love? The weather looks beautiful today. You don't think I'll need a coat, do you?* In Elvan.

His brows raised.

"So I guess I can speak it too."

"No shit," he murmured. "Well, that's fucking cool." He thought for a moment. "But no, I don't think you'll need a coat. Maybe a jacket though."

I tilted my head to the side. "You speak Elvan?"

"Not fluently. I understood every word of that though," he muttered. "But ya know, I can't remember actually learning it. I remember learning most languages. Not English and French, my dad spoke them interchangeably. But Spanish, I remember that. I was probably five? My dad insisted we all learn it. Latin was around the same age, for the same reason you read it. My dad said if you don't know the language, you'll never understand what the writer actually meant because you're reading one person's interpretation instead of your own." He squinted slightly, thinking for a moment.

"I learned a bit of Mandarin in middle school, Russian and German around the same time. Maybe a little younger though, when I was obsessing over the world wars. I remember learning Hindi and Italian, even Portuguese and Arabic. But I don't know where I learned Elvan."

My brow arched. I knew my man was bilingual, but damn. I didn't know he *spoke* that many. "Jesus, is there a language you don't speak?"

"I'm sure there's a lot." He laughed. "But that's weird, isn't it? That I understand a language I've never learned?"

I thought for a moment. I held my hand out in front of me and murmured a short incantation in Elvan. A honeybee appeared in my hand.

"Do you know what I just said?" I asked, cupping my hand over the bug.

"No," he said. I tossed the bee out the patio door. "Something pertaining to insects?

"Yeah. But languages evolve, right? Over time, they gradually change."

"Right."

"So maybe, you and I are speaking an older version of Elvan."

"Like the Scottish and Irish Gaelic language. One tongue that split in two and evolved from there," he muttered. "Metaphorically, anyway."

Micah appeared in front of me. My hand flew to my chest, jumping ten feet back. "Jeez oh man, kid."

He laughed and looked at Tink on the couch. "Mommy, she's bowed."

I smiled. "Is she bored or are you bored?"

He grinned, glancing back at Tink. "We'we both bowed. Can we play outside?"

"Get your shoes on, I'm right behind you." I ran my fingers over his head. "But you've got to take your vitamins first."

"Okay, I go get my shoes."

"And a jacket," Jeremy said.

Micah furrowed his brows. "I can't weach it, Daddy."

"Well, I guess I have to help you get it then." His hand brushed my shoulder as he started to the steps behind Micah. "I remembered something too. Can you grab my coffee? We can talk about it while they play."

"Damn, no wonder he hates women," I muttered.

"Nah," Jeremy said. "I've been cheated on, and it hurts. But that's no reason to treat anyone like trash. And it was arranged anyway. It's not like you married for love. You didn't even know each other."

I raised my brow. "Even if it was your brother though?"

"Even if it was my brother," he said. "I mean, yeah. It would suck. I'd be heartbroken, and I'd probably beat the shit out of him. But no, I wouldn't hate you so much for it that I expected all women in the history of forever to submit to their husbands and keep their mouths shut like they were property only to speak when spoken to. I think that's why you preferred me to him then too."

"Yeah, I guess."

I watched Micah chase after Tink in the yard and thought about the way I felt in that memory. The way I fought an eye roll when Nix was up there, and Lux leaned over and cracked a shitty joke.

"He seemed like a friendly asshole, ya know?" I said. "Like one of those guys who's super nice and friendly, then you find out he operates a dogfighting ring. Or you see him in the newspaper for having a stash of kiddy porn on his computer."

"Gross," he muttered. "I'd like to think God doesn't have a stash of kiddy porn on his computer."

I waved him off. "I didn't mean it literally."

"No, I know what you mean." He was quiet for a moment. "I don't know. If he killed my mom, I can see why I didn't give a shit about loyalty and brotherhood. And I think you and I were in love for a long while before that happened. We were close friends at least, I know that. And you already kind of hated him. You never wanted to be with him in the first place."

It still left so much up in the air. I wanted to understand *why* I'd done what I'd done. *Why* had I married him? Jeremy's last detailed memory depicted me as the Queen of the Fae, so why did I marry the king of heaven? Was it set up by our parents?

What was the whole story?

Most of all though, I needed to know why I felt the way that I did when he put his hand on my shoulder in that banquet room.

I chewed my lip. "What we just saw, that must have been a long time before the Elders. We definitely weren't married, we didn't have kids, and our bond wasn't completed."

"That's what I don't get," he muttered. "The legend says the souls were split in half by god. But that isn't true. We weren't one soul that split in half."

"No. No, we were two souls that merged. But the splitting aspect of the myth, I think that was supposed signify the curse."

"Maybe. More symbolic than I always thought but... You were scared, you said?"

"It seemed like it. When you were up there ranting, I think she thought you were going to let it slip."

"So what happened when he did find out then?" Jeremy rubbed a hand against his mouth. "Did they try to kill you?"

"I don't know. Maybe we'll find out soon."

CHAPTER EIGHT

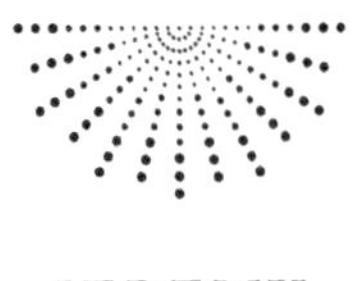

JEREMY

He looked different now.

The way that he deserved to.

A thick layer of brown framed his feminine jaw and mouth. His fair skin was whiter than a cloud. Deep purple bags rested beneath his hazel eyes. He smelled like rotten onions and the shit bucket beside him.

And I was glad. He deserved to feel how my son felt in that cell. He deserved to feel dirt on his skin and grease in his hair. He deserved to know what it felt like to be a prisoner.

"Well, good morning, Mister Peterson." Laila tossed a bottle of water to his lap. He jolted at the sudden impact on his groin. She grasped ahold of his hair and turned his face up to meet hers. "Sleep well?"

He smiled. "Verbatim, huh?"

She huffed, tongue running over her teeth. Her brow raised. "So you remember it then. What—Did I write it? Did you rehearse it like a script?"

He held his smile. "No. You left me out of the stories for the most part."

That must've been something he said to her in captivity. I was curious what the context was. But not curious enough to ask her to relive it.

"What did I cite you as then? Doctor Robert Peterson?"

"I'm mentioned scarcely. You probably didn't want to inspire me." His smile widened. "Or maybe because it was too hard to write about me."

Another huff of a laugh left her lips. She jerked his head back and slammed it to the back of the metal chair. His eyes bulged, and he gasped.

"Are you going to be a dick this whole time? Or are you going to make this easier on yourself? I can make this as painful as you decide to make it."

"Wouldn't be any fun if I was quiet. You taught me that."

She clenched her jaw. She laughed. She placed her hand over his wrist tethered to the chair. Her palms glowed red. He screamed out in pain. The burning rope fell to either side of the bar. She pulled her hands back and his screams turned to deep pants. She squatted to the ropes around his ankles.

His right hand lifted from the bar, reaching for her hair. I took a quick step forward, but Laila grasped his burned wrist and yanked him to the ground. His arms flailed to catch himself, snap sounding from his ankle. He cried out in pain. She placed either hand over his ankles and burned the ropes. He gasped in agony, crooked, clearly broken foot contorting against the cement.

I wasn't even sure why I was here. Clearly, she could handle this on her own. But maybe to make sure she didn't kill him. I knew she wanted to do that before the survivors. They deserved to see him take his last breath.

"You don't fucking touch me." She wagged her finger in his face with shining eyes. "Do it again and I'll make you watch me cut it off."

He looked up at her with panting, agonized breaths. She placed her glowing white palm over his ankle. He screamed again, backpedaling away.

I teleported beside her. I pushed my knee into his chest, relieved as the sounds of his pathetic screams turned to muffled gurgles. His hazel eyes practically begged me for breath. That made me feel pretty good, to be honest. The last time I hurt the guy, he didn't say a word. But his struggle brought me some twisted form of gratification.

I didn't enjoy watching people suffer. Not usually. But I thought back to that morning when I heard her screams as he cut through her skin. I remembered the pain surging up her whipped back as he pushed her body up and down the metal table. Then when Micah shook against Amy and Nastya's hands when they held him in place, slicing through his body like a frog in a high school lab.

And I kind of did enjoy watching him suffer.

"Thanks," Laila said.

"Any time." I stood.

I leaned against the armoire of weapons a few feet away. Laila brought herself to her feet, and Peterson looked down at his trembling, charred wrists.

"You did this to teach me," she said. "I get it. Misery builds character, right?"

"I told you from day one. Your life was cushy. And yes, it needed to be. But It needed not to be." He stared into her eyes. "I know this seems like the worst thing that could have happened but is it really? You got your happy ending. You have your husband and your son and your daughter—"

"My son?" Her eyes widened. "My son, the one who might need surgery on his knees because of what you did to him. The one who's going to be covered in scars for the rest of his life because of you."

"It had to—"

She raised her knee and thrust it into his face. He fell to the side, barely catching himself before his head hit the floor. "No, fuck you. Fuck your 'it had to happen. This had to happen, that had to happen.' Fuck that. It's bullshit. You didn't *have* to do any of this. You didn't have to do shit. You didn't have to travel back in time and torture a thousand people. You didn't have to ra—"

"It wasn't a thousand," he muttered.

"No, it was 778, right?" Laila asked.

"Seven-hundred and eighty."

I tilted my head to the side. There were three more after Micah? Had we set them free? Or were they rotting away somewhere?

"If Laila was 776, Micah was 777, who were the last three?" I asked. "Who did you take after Micah?"

"Well, you were 780." Peterson looked at me. "Short term, but still. A subject all the same."

"Then who was 778 and 779?" I asked.

"They're home now, don't worry."

Fucker.

He'd answered every one of Laila's questions, but refused to answer even one of mine. And look, I didn't like doing what I was about to. But I was good at it. Laila was too, but it tore her up inside. I'd handle this part, and she could ask the questions.

"Well, they must be important if you won't tell us." I opened the armoire and glanced at him over my shoulder. "Either you tell us what we want to know, or we torture you until you die. And I bring you back. Rinse repeat until you finally cave. And let's face it." I looked over his decrepit body and then back to his eyes. "You won't make it very long. That's why you hid. That's why you used Chris to get to us. Because you're scared."

"Of course I'm scared." Peterson's face screwed up. "I know who you are, both of you, even if you don't. But that doesn't mean I'm going to tell you anything that you are not yet meant to know because I am committed to my cause, Jeremy."

I looked over him and let out a quiet laugh. "You say that now." I grabbed a thin fishing knife from the second drawer. "Whipping hurts. It does. But there are a lot worse forms of torture."

Peterson looked at Laila and smiled. "Exactly."

"Fuck you," she said.

His smile widened. "I do like you more when you're like this. So raw. Exciting."

Jesus fuck: I just wanted to kill the bastard.

I looked at Chris at the bottom of the steps, gesturing to the chains in the wall. "We secured those, right?"

He brought himself to his feet. "They might not hold a wolf, but they can handle him."

I teleported to Peterson, grasped his shoulders, then teleported to the wall where the chains hung. As we landed, he turned toward my feet and started to vomit. I teleported to the other side just before it landed on my shoes.

Laila muttered something, eyes glowing green toward the pile of puke before it slowly slid to the drain a few feet away. Then water seeped in from a crack in the wall, rinsing it down like a hose.

"Nice," Chris said, brushing past her.

She shrugged. I took Peterson's hand and fastened the cuff around the burned skin. Chris got the other and then we each tethered a leg. As Chis clicked the one at his ankle into place, Peterson looked at him and smiled. "I told you you'd get them back eventually."

Chris grabbed ahold of his thigh and sent a bright blue current of electricity through his body. Peterson's body shook, arms contorting against the restraints.

When his body stopped shaking, he looked back up at me. "The last two want to remain nameless or I would tell you. You asked him his name, didn't you? He wouldn't tell you to because he didn't want to. I'm respecting their wishes."

"That kid you had in the last room," Laila murmured. "Why wouldn't he want us to know who he is?"

"Because it's irrelevant," Peterson said. "Knowing who they are isn't going to help you with what's coming."

"Then what will?" Laila took a few steps forward.

"Fighting as you've never fought before."

CHAPTER NINE

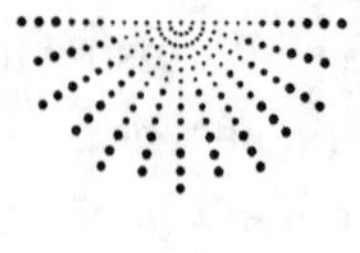

LAILA

"I've been fighting for years and I'm fucking tired." I gritted my teeth to a hard line. "You tortured me to make me strong. You tortured the others for the same reason, to be warriors. To be *my* warriors. I get that; I need to have an army to fight the war when it comes. But then you started the war. Why would you give me the tools to win only to start the war itself?"

"I didn't start the war." Peterson's face said that was an offensive thing to say. "You did. Some hundred thousand years ago."

"No, you did the sacrifice. *You* opened Pandora's box," Jeremy said. "Regardless of whatever feud we had with Lux, you're the one who started what's coming."

"It was going to happen anyway," he snapped. "No matter what course of events, they were always going to come back when they do. The cycle was always meant to break here, in this time. And yes, it could have gone differently. But if it had, you may have truly lost him. The girl too. And they wouldn't have been reborn this time because your cycle has ended. Don't you see?"

Micah and Milly. This was set up so that we didn't lose Micah and Milly; that's what it sounded like he was saying. But even that didn't make sense.

What did that mean? That we may have truly lost them?

"No. No one can understand shit when you talk in fucking riddles," Jeremy said.

Peterson released a slow, deep breath. "You'll see. A few years, and you'll see what I've seen. You'll understand. These things had to play out the way they did."

"You didn't have to take my baby." My head shook, jaw clenching tight. "You didn't have to rape me. You didn't have to torture me."

He looked at me, lips turning down. "I didn't have to rape you. But I did have to torture you. I did have to take Micah. I did, Laila."

"Why?!" Heat brightened my eyes. "Why did you have to take my son, Peterson? Why?"

His eyes stayed somber, frowning. "Because you wouldn't have let it happen. And it had to happen. Even now was sooner than I expected. I suppose there could be an issue with my calculations; this could still work if I had a number or two off. But the point remains. His sacrifice had to occur."

"But *why*?" I asked. "Why?" I looked between his eyes, practically begging for an explanation. "After everything you did to me. Everything you took from me. I deserve to know why."

He frowned. "Not because I wanted to hurt you. I never *wanted* to hurt you."

"Then why?" I said again.

Tears nearly formed in his eyes. I almost felt bad for a second. I'd never seen him anything less than business professional manner. Neat hair, shaved jaw, sparkling glasses, freshly ironed button-up and tie. But he had none of that anymore. His hair hadn't been washed in over a month. No one dared give him a razor. And we'd all be caught dead before we brushed his teeth or combed his hair.

"I've seen the other outcomes. I've seen a thousand other timelines. And this was the best one for you. This is the only one where you eventually get it all, Laila. You lost the things that meant the most to you for a time, and that was because of me, but you got it all back too. You get your happy ending."

I scoffed. "Not if the world's going to end."

"It will shift." He smiled. "It won't be the world it is now; it will be a better one. Because you saved it." He looked between us. "Because you all save it."

Jeremy's forehead wrinkled. "So let me get this straight. You're from a place in history where we saved the world. But you came back in time to make us ready to save the world."

Peterson looked at him. "One of those, 'what came first—the chicken or the egg?' sort of questions. Don't think about it for too long; it starts to hurt your head."

I paused in thought for a moment. Then my head tilted. "You said you met me once, but I wouldn't remember it. That's because it hasn't happened yet. Right?"

He turned back to me and gave a nod.

"When do we meet then?" I asked.

Peterson thought for a moment, tiptoeing around what he would and wouldn't say. "I was a young boy. You" —he glanced at Jeremy— "you two were signing books at a shop in my town."

I paused. "So in your time, I'm a celebrity."

"I suppose you could say that."

"You were obsessed with me before you met me." I turned my head to the side slightly. "I was your celebrity crush as a kid."

"It wasn't a crush." His gaze narrowed, as if that were an offensive way of phrasing his infatuation. "You are a real-life hero. The living personification of love and strength and beauty and fury all wrapped together. The great mother. I understood you, I always understood you. I studied you. I know you through and through, Laila, I have since I was a child."

I looked over him in silence, unsure of what to ask next. I had a list but standing there, it all seemed to fall from my thoughts. Processing what he just told me was hard enough.

That's where it began then. Not religion. An obsession. My very own Mark David Chapman.

Although, I supposed that was nearly the same as religion, wasn't it? Obsessing over someone that you only see glimpses of, have heard stories about, but never truly *knew*. Desperately craving that personal connection with someone... Someone you idolized. A god.

It came back to the same way I had always felt about anyone or anything being idolized.

People will do awful, unspeakable things in the name of higher beings, and that shit needed to fucking end.

"Why Amy?" Jeremy asked. "Nastya, I can see. Twisted, extremely powerful. Probably one of a handful of Witches alive with the power to conceal all that energy for so long. And the only one crazy enough to work for you. But Amy wasn't crazy. She was practically human."

"Amy was the maternal figure." Peterson turned to Jeremy. "She was the one to care for Micah when he was first born. She was kind and, frankly, easy to manipulate. I needed a healer to falsify the deaths as well. But she also believed in our cause."

There it was again. Another reference to someone else.

It had to be him. Lux. Who else would go to so much trouble to make us go through the last awful few years of our lives? It had to be the god that hated us.

But he was the one that tortured us for centuries. Why did he want us to have a happy ending? Just to take it away when the world ends?

"Our," I said. "Who's our?"

He fell silent.

Chris kicked him in the ribs. "Answer the question."

"I can't." Peterson's eyes were on me again, practically begging for mercy. "I would, but I can't, Laila."

"You can," I said. "You owe me this, Peterson."

"I owe you many things I can't give you," he said. "I wish that I could, but I am physically incapable of answering that question."

Chris made a face. "What the fuck does that mean?"

But I knew what he meant. He physically couldn't tell me.

"Him," Jeremy muttered. "Lux. That's who set this up. He sent you back here, didn't he? You couldn't have pulled this off unless you had someone all powerful behind you. It's him. That's why we still can't get in your head. Because he's in there too, isn't he?"

Peterson clenched his jaw and turned away. Jeremy grabbed ahold of his hair and ripped his head back. He stared down at him with an expression I'd never seen on his face. I never saw Jeremy as weak, not even close to it. But in that moment, his expression was more fiercely dominant than I knew he could be. His jaw was stiff, his nostrils flared, and his eyes were like daggers. And when he spoke, his voice sounded firmer than it ever had. Deep and harsh. If it weren't for the environment, it might've turned me on a little bit.

"I want to talk to him," Jeremy said.

Peterson stared at him blankly for a second. When Jeremy kept waiting, he chuckled. "What—You think that I command a god?"

"I think that if he's in there, he can hear me. And I want to fucking talk."

He released another faint laugh.

Jeremy ran his tongue along his teeth and smiled. "Alright. Well. Maybe since you're such a loyal servant, he'll come to the rescue. But if not, I'm not sorry." He looked to Chris. "Hold the chains for me, would you?"

Chris did.

Jeremy grabbed ahold of his arm and raised the thin blade to his skin. He glanced at me. "Do you want to do the honors, baby?"

Last time I had a knife on that man, Jeremy had to physically pull me off of him to get me to stop stabbing. I'd sit this one out.

"No, be my guest," I said.

He turned back to Peterson. Their gazes locked as the tip of the metal slowly sliced into his skin. His jaw clenched. Jeremy turned his head to the side a bit.

"Ya know, skinning someone alive isn't that hard. Especially when I can have you healed the moment you're about to bleed out. But do you have any idea how badly it hurts to have your skin peeled from your body?"

He gradually inched the knife upward, like slicing the flesh off a fish. Peterson's arm shook. His narrowed gaze twitched between Jeremy's. His breaths got faster together.

"They do." He glanced at me and Chris. He quickly slipped the blade up an inch or two.

Peterson gasped, then let out deep pants. But his gaze stayed steady against Jeremy.

"But it was different for them. Because unlike you, they didn't fucking deserve it." He jutted the blade further up, nearly halfway to his elbow.

Peterson screamed, rolling his head to the cement behind him.

Jeremy grabbed his face with his other hand. "I can't wait until she lets us fucking kill you because I don't like torture, but I will make this as long and painful as possible if you don't give us what we want."

"I." His gritted teeth trembled. "Physically. Can't."

Jeremy's gaze narrowed. "So you've got to hide too, huh? Started all this bullshit, put us through the worst shit imaginable for centuries and now you're too chicken shit to show your face. Just like he was. Hiding. Running."

He tightly clenched his jaw. He slammed the blade up his arm. Peterson cried out in agony as his sliver of flesh fell to the cement. My nose curled. "If you're responsible for everything that this man did, that means you wanted the cycles to end. The cycles *you* cursed us into. You wanted us to get to this point. Quit playing puppet and talk to me like a fucking man. Quit being a little bitch. I fucked your wife some thousand years ago. Time to move on and explain what the fuck you're doing."

The bloody flesh on Peterson's forearm glowed a blinding hue of gold. Jeremy pulled his hand away but held his gaze. His unblinking, empty gaze. Then the carved piece of flesh looked as it had a moment before. No longer an even slit of red muscles and tendons. Just a piece of soft white flesh.

Peterson's lips curled up in a grin. A loud, billowing laugh left his lips. He huffed. "You can't honestly believe this was all over your whore."

Most of the time, I didn't care when someone called me something like that. So why did it make my hands clench when he did? Was it because deep down, I agreed?

Or was it because he was misogynistic piece of shit?

Jeremy raised his fist and slammed it to his cheek.

His head rolled to the side, laughing again. "Tell you what. The slut leaves—"

Jeremy lifted the knife and thrust it through his thigh.

His eyes widened in pain.

"That's not how this is gonna go. You're not going to disrespect my wife."

He huffed, still smiling as he looked between Jeremy's eyes.

"We're going to talk and you're not going to call her a slut or a whore or anything else that's shitty. If this isn't about her, don't make it about her. Talk like a man instead of a little fuck boy in a locker room. Can we do that? Are we grownups here?"

He smiled, narrowing his eyes. "Fine."

"Tell her you're sorry," Jeremy said.

His brows fell far over his eyes.

"Did I stutter?"

His gaze narrowed at Jeremy. His head rolled to meet mine.

As I looked into those hazel eyes, I didn't see the man who destroyed me. I saw the man I betrayed a few thousand years ago. The one who then betrayed me. Not literally him, but his soul. It was there, right behind those eyes. It brought an instant chill to my skin and a gurgle to the pit of my stomach.

"Sorry, Véa."

"Laila," I said. "My name is Laila."

His eyes rolled. "Sorry, *Laila*." He turned back to Jeremy. "Can we talk now?"

Jeremy looked at me. "I'll be up soon, alright?"

I didn't want to be in that room any more than he wanted me there. Answers, yes, I wanted those. But Jeremy clearly had a better chance at that than I did.

I turned and started up the stairs.

CHAPTER TEN

JEREMY

His gaze slid from her back to her ass as she walked up the steps. I raised my hand and smacked him upside the head. He glared at me. "She was mine first."

Aside from my list of reasons for already hating the guy, that did it right there. He called her a whore and slut. He checked out her ass as she walked away?

That was the type of misogynistic shit that pissed me the fuck off. I never boasted about being a feminist, but this sort of thing reminded me that I was. It's not okay to denote someone because of their sexuality. But then to enjoy their sexuality a moment later? It's hypocrisy at its finest.

"Véa was your wife before Nix's. Not Laila," I said.

Chris looked between us with confusion in his eyes. "Who is this?"

"God," he answered.

"Commonly known as God," I corrected, meeting Chris's gaze. "But just one of many. There used to be a lot more before he killed them all."

"I didn't *actually* kill you." He looked back up at me. "Nothing ever dies, not really. I just, ya know. Kept you busy for a while."

That was something else Hannah had said in our training. That nothing ever dies. The day I met Heylel, he said the same thing.

But that didn't change what he'd done. Just because we lived again didn't mean that he hadn't cursed us. It didn't change that he'd slit my son's throat. It didn't change any of it.

"How long is a while, Lux?" My voice was firm. "When did this start?"

"Four thousand years or so. Maybe closer to five. Something like that."

"We wanted to lock you up for a thousand."

"And I needed you to stay busy for four."

"But maybe closer to five." I tightened my jaw.

He chuckled. "Try to look at the bright side. At least you got some really cute stories to tell. A lot of better first meetings than the real one."

"On a back road at two a.m.," I said. "That's the real one. Just because we had other past lives doesn't make this one any less real. *This* is my life. I'm not him. And she's not Véa. We are different people."

"Kind of. But not really. You actually look so much like him, it's surreal. Little pastier though." He glanced me over. "Véa had a better body too."

"So God's a douche bag." Chris narrowed his gaze. "Shocker."

"Can you just." Peterson's head rolled to Chris. Then his hand waved in a shooing motion that knocked him off his feet. "Go?"

My stomach dropped.

He had access to his abilities in here.

That meant we had this man inside of our safe space voluntarily, and he could escape at any time.

Chris brought himself back to his feet and met my gaze.

I gave a nod. If I had to, I'd teleport that fucker over a cliffside and let him fall.

Chris licked his teeth and disappeared.

Peterson—or Lux, rather—looked at the cuffs. "Do you mind?"

"Yeah, I do actually."

"I can break them," he said. "Figured I'd save you the trouble."

My tongue ran along my teeth. I reached for the keys in my pocket and undid one of the locks at his hand. "But that's it."

He rolled his eyes. "If you say so." He extended his hand. The bottle of water Laila had tossed onto his lap slung into it. He lifted it to his shackled palm, twisted off the cap, and took a gulp. His gaze shifted back to mine. "I know this guy deserves what you're doing to him, but you could give him a sandwich once in a while. I don't think he's eaten in four or five days now."

"Neither did my wife. Or my son. Or my brother." I narrowed my gaze. "He can stay hungry."

He took another sip. "Guess that's fair."

I clenched my jaw. "It wasn't even him. It was you. You told him to do all of this."

"Not all of it," he said. "But yeah. Most of it." I raised my hand and thrusted it into his face. "Ow."

"You had him take my son." I clenched my jaw tighter. "You had him torture and rape my wife. You—"

"I didn't tell him to rape your wife. But I guess I should have known that would happen. He's been obsessed with her since he was a kid. I thought that'd be a good thing for her, ya know? That he'd be kinder to her. But yeah, I probably should have been paying more attention that day." He smiled. "But let's be frank, the bitch would spread her—"

I reached forward and grasped his cheeks, squeezing my thumb and fingertips so deep that the inside of his jaw scraped against his teeth. "Don't fucking talk about her like that. And you're definitely not going to say that what he did to her makes her a slut. I don't give a shit what she did to you, you're not going fucking degrade her like that."

He blew out a slow sigh.

"But oh, I'm supposed to be okay with the torture and kidnapping." I dropped his face. "At least you didn't command he rape her, right?"

"Whether we like it or not, pain builds character," he said. "She needed to understand her abilities. She needed to master them."

"And my son?" I snapped. "Why? Why did he have to be sacrificed?"

"The more important question isn't why his sacrifice was necessary, but why I made sure you could bring him back when we did."

"I'm all ears. Explain both."

A quiet laugh left his lips. He ran his hand over the scruff of his chin. "He was a barter. His soul was both a beacon and a payment. Then you dragged him back and reneged on our deal."

"What deal?" My tone sharpened. "I don't care what life it is; I never would have offered my kid as a payment."

"No, you wouldn't. I did."

My hand clenched to a fist. "You bargained your nephew."

"Yeah, but I never planned on letting them actually have him. That's why I had him stab Véa, so that you'd remember what you are in enough time to bring him back once the sacrifice was complete," he said. "I love that kid. I'd never let anything actually happen to him."

He loved him. He *loved* him, and he let them do to him everything that they had? That's not what love looked like. I knew love, and I may not have always been great it, but I never hurt the people I love on purpose. I never knowingly tortured them to teach them a lesson.

But I supposed that's what separated him from me. I guessed that was why Véa chose me over him. If what he'd done to Micah—a small, innocent child—was how he showed his love, I didn't want to know how he showed it to a strong willed, smart ass queen.

"Then what the fuck was your plan?" I barked.

"Relax, I'm getting there."

I took in a slow, deep breath and gritted my teeth.

"The deal was that whatever souls haven't ascended at the time that they return to take their planet, they take as payment. That was the deal all twenty-five of us agreed to when we took on the souls and the responsibility of cultivating this rock. But none of us wanted to turn over any souls. The twenty-five of us made a pact. Any souls that hadn't ascended when they returned, we protect. They take none. We move them, we shelter them, we find somewhere to put them, even if it is in the abyss for a time, but we do not hand them over. And I still mean that; I won't let them take our people."

"So what does Micah have to do with it?"

A mischievous grin tugged at his lips before he pressed them together. "See, this is the part where you're going to get mad."

I felt my nostrils flare. "What did you do to my son?"

"Nothing," he said. "Well, I mean, once I did. But he's fine, his soul's been kept very safe. Your little girl too, and the others. I never wanted to actually end any of you. I just needed you distracted."

"What. Did. You. Do."

He licked his lips. "From the memories you've seen. I am the villain now? Or are you?"

"I'm pretty sure you killed my mother. So yeah, I'm gonna go with you."

He waved a dismissive hand. "Just in that life. She's fine." A half grin came to his lips. "Believe me. She's safe."

As if her being reincarnated to a new body somehow eradicated the fact that he had murdered my mother.

I gritted my teeth together. "What did you do, Lux?"

A slow breath left his nostrils. "Your son's soul is as strong as a million human souls. We made an arrangement. They come back on a designated date not too far in the distance. But if we needed more time, we sacrifice the boy. They've had their eyes on him since you and her created him. That'd buy us a few hundred years. The sacrifice worked. They felt the energy. They were just about to claim it. And then you took it back."

My jaw tightened further. "You offered my son as a consolation payment."

"Yeah, but I knew you wouldn't let that happen. But that's why I made sure you remembered what you were first." He smiled. "See? I helped you."

"I didn't need your fucking help. You never had to do this. You redirected the course of history, and for what? To protect yourself for a thousand years?"

"Mostly," he said. "Guess there was a little vengeance tied up in there. But hey, you've had some good times. It hasn't all been bad."

If we'd had five thousand years to prepare for this, not a single soul would be lost in the apocalypse. Not one. We'd had a plan in place back then. We were going to keep the people safe. And now, we had no idea what that plan was.

He hadn't just taken our lives and our children's. He took away humanity's chance at survival.

Slow, angry breaths left my flaring nostrils. "I was your brother. And you tormented me for five thousand years."

"Don't look at me like that, Nix. You took everything from me. You took my rightful place. You took my wife. You even limited my vote."

"You had more of a vote than me. I got half of a vote; you got a full one—"

"But you always agreed. The rest of you were almost always in agreement—"

"That's not my fault," I said. "And it wasn't your rightful place either. Nix was older; it was mine."

"You were a bastard—"

"Either way, I was just as entitled as you," I said. "And if I took your place, it's because you weren't doing a good job. Véa and Nix wanted peace, you wanted war."

His gaze narrowed. "Running a world isn't all rainbows and butterflies. I had to make sacrifices—"

"At the expense of lives?" I raised a brow. "What gives you that right?"

He rolled his eyes. "I can't change what I did over two-hundred thousand years ago—"

"I thought you said five."

He laughed, head tilting. "You're not stupid, you know how long humanity has existed on this world. Five thousand since you've been Nix and she's been Véa. But we're all much older than that, esiasch."

Well, that did seem obvious.

Humans had been on earth for about 300,000 years. Otherwise

meaning we had to be at least that old. But we'd lived full lives before we'd even come here.

I did the quick math though.

The Abrahamic religions started being established about 2,000 years ago. A spark of joy radiated through me at that thought. Not that I ever wanted to be adorned as a god, but it brought me some happiness to know that it took him a couple thousand years after our deaths to form his own following.

No wonder he was so pissed when people worshipped other gods. We were all long dead, and he was still busting his ass to get people to give a damn about his existence over ours.

I clenched my jaw. "It isn't just what you did then. The Abrahamic religions have ruled the world for two thousand years. As soon as the polytheistic religions moved out, yours moved in. You told trillions of people that if they don't obey you, and worship you, and beg for your forgiveness, they're going to spend their life in eternal suffering."

"What do you tell a child to keep them from going outside at night?" he asked. "'Don't go out there or the boogey man's going to get you.'"

"No, actually, I just tell them because they'll be tired if they don't go to sleep. Honesty is usually more effective than fear tactics."

"You have your ways, and I have mine."

"Your ways caused wars. Your ways caused the holocaust."

He frowned. "Well, that isn't fair. I'm the god of both sides in that argument. And that was far more about eugenics than religion, which has nothing to do with me."

I guessed I couldn't disagree with that.

"Fine. Your ways caused the Crusades. Your ways are the reason women have been treated like property since the polytheistic religions that gave them recognition disappeared. You're the reason gay people have lost their lives for centuries. You're the reason people were stoned for divorce and adultery. That's kind of a biased place to make a law, don't you think?"

"Revelation 22:18-19 I warn everyone who hears the words of the prophecy of this book: if anyone adds to them, God will add to them the plagues described in this book, and if anyone takes away from the words of the book of prophecy, God will take away his share in the tree of life.

"Proverbs 30:5-6 Every word of God proves true; he is a shield to those who take refuge in him. Do not add to his words, lest he rebuke you and you be found a liar. Deuteronomy 4:2—"

"I get the point. But that doesn't change the fact that you let more than half of the world suffer for two-thousand fucking years. And you can't tell me the stuff about women wasn't put in there by you, I know how you treated her—"

His gaze hardened. "I treated her like a queen, I treated them both like queens—"

"You treated them like property—"

"Because they were."

My head shook, nose wrinkling.

As a teenager, I remembered having a conversation with Annie about this very concept. She was born Catholic, raised in the ways of our world beneath the Council. But she viewed it a lot like I did in my early adult years.

That we did good things working for the Council, but that she wouldn't follow the religion that led it. And her reasoning was simple.

She'd said when polytheistic religions disappeared, so did a womanly higher power. That by following one god and no goddess, monotheism eroded the way women were viewed. No longer were they powerful and god-like, not by society's standards. To be like god, one would have to be a man. Women were nothing more than property and tools for reproduction. And that was why she couldn't follow the religion.

For me, that was just one of the many reasons.

I fell silent and gritted my teeth together. "You're disgusting."

His eyes rolled. "Oh, piss off. We aren't all whiney little girls like you."

"Yeah, well. Apparently, women like whiney bitches like me more than controlling assholes like you."

He gritted his teeth together.

A realization dawned on me in that moment. We were all eternal once. And evidently, he still was. I didn't expect an honest answer, but I couldn't resist asking.

"Where are you?" My head tilted. "Really, I mean. You ate from the tree of life. You've got a body out there somewhere. Where is it?"

He smiled. "When they come, when you need me, I'll be back."

"Then why are the Angels working against us?" I asked. "Why are they stockpiling weapons?"

"They're not working against you. You're fighting for the same side," he said. "They just don't know that."

I narrowed my eyes. "Well, maybe you should make it known."

He smiled. "I'll get right on that."

Something in the way he said that made it very difficult to tell where his allegiance truly was. He'd said he was fighting for the people of earth. But he had a bigger idea spinning behind those eyes. He had a plan for himself.

I hardly knew the guy. Obviously, I knew he was a prick. But I also realized in that moment that he acted on his volition. He did what was best for him; not for everyone.

It almost made me wonder. If someone were telling the story now, would they call him Thor? Or would they call him Loki, the trickster god? Had the god of tricks convinced the whole world that he was the one true god and that the rest were nothing more than fictional tales?

But I didn't know how much time I had left in this conversation. He'd said a few minutes prior that he knew when Wormwood would return. And I needed to know.

I took in a slow breath through my nostrils. "When?"

"When what?"

"When are they coming? When does it start?"

"Soon enough. Far enough. You have time, put your feet up for a while. But work on your skills with the abyss. We'll have to work together on that."

"No, give me a damn date. I need to prepare—"

"You have time," he repeated with a firm gaze. "This is your time to relax. This is your time to enjoy your life."

"Right before it comes crashing down around me." I gritted my teeth together. "I need to know how much—"

"You need to listen to the words coming out of my mouth. You. Have. Time." He looked firmly between my eyes. "I'll be back. But enjoy the time you have. Don't waste it. This reality is about to shift. When it does, nothing will be like it was. Enjoy it before it's gone. Take your children and your wife to see your favorite places. Eat your favorite foods. Attain a collection of your favorite books and instruments and anything else you want to preserve for the new world. But *enjoy it while you can.*"

"You can't just tell me that and—"

"We'll see each other again soon, esiasch."

"But you—"

His head clunked to his chest. I gritted my teeth. Peterson's head gradually lifted. "What happ—"

I punched him in the face. His head fell back to his chest.

But those words echoed through my mind.

You have time.

That's what the mystery people who'd come to interrogate Peterson had said. Obviously, it wasn't him. He was already here in Peterson's mind. But who could it have been then? And why did they say the exact same phrase?

CHAPTER ELEVEN

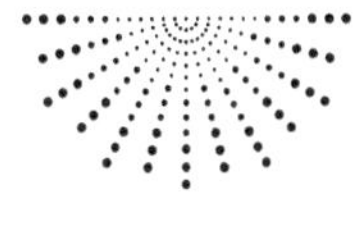

LAILA

"**S**o it was him," I murmured. My illuminated hand shined over Jeremy's swollen knuckles. "Lux caused all of this."

"Aside from that." He gestured to the scar on the side of my neck. "Yeah, he took responsibility for everything else Peterson did."

"That doesn't make Peterson any less of the enemy," Leah said. "He isn't possessed. God just channels him."

Fuck, I hated her calling him that.

He wasn't *God*. No one and everyone was God. God was a fictional concept made up by primitive people who didn't have a better way to describe those with abilities.

In some regards, a rocket scientist was a god. In others, a cardiologist was. They were more powerful than me in many ways, yet I was revered as a god once. But that didn't make them any less holy. They had abilities too. Every single person alive is a god in their own right.

The word god implies that the person it's referencing is all powerful. But no one is or can be *all* powerful. Everyone has a weakness.

"He's still the man who did it. Whether someone else told him to or not, he did it," I said. "He's going to get what he deserves. That hasn't changed."

"So wait," Chris murmured. "All of this was because God wanted to create you an army of supernatural creatures able to fight off an alien apocalypse."

"And to use your sacrifice to call them back here. We could have let them take Micah, but if we would have, that only would've bought us a few hundred years. And he'd be gone forever. I'm not sure if they would have taken you too; I'm not sure how the spell worked. But Micah was the primary bargaining tool," Jeremy said.

"Made the right decision bringing him back either way," Chris muttered. "But... But what does this mean? The world's definitely ending? For sure, without a doubt?"

Jeremy looked at the counter, slow breath leaving his nostrils. "That's what he said."

"And he wouldn't tell you when," I said.

"No. He kept saying we have time."

My face screwed up. "Isn't that what the CIA people told you too, Adam?"

Adam ran his hand over his mouth. "Yeah. But I don't think they were working with him, guys. I really don't, I trusted them."

"They could have made you trust them," Leah said. "I've done that a thousand times. It's easy."

"You don't understand, Leah," Adam said. "It wasn't like that. I'm telling you. We can trust those people."

"I believe you," Jeremy agreed. "But it doesn't matter anyway. We haven't heard from them. They did what they said they would. They pulled strings to help us get Micah back and haven't fucked with us since. I'm not concerned about them."

I thought for a moment. "If he used his powers inside of Peterson, that means he could get him out of here. He could set him free."

"We've had him for more than a month and he hasn't." Leah shook her head. "If he were going to, he would have already."

"He doesn't care about Peterson either," Jeremy said. "He's a puppet. He said something about how we could feed him a little more but didn't give a shit when I told him we don't care."

Chris ran his hand over the back of his neck. "He was working with Peterson through all of this. That's what you said."

Jeremy made a face at him. "Yeah, why?"

He fell silent, eyes against the granite countertop. "I think I've met him. There was a man. He handed me Micah on the plane. He walked us down to our cell in the second compound. He showed me around, he said 'they used to co-sleep with him, but that's probably not a good idea since you can't see' or something. I don't know." His head shook. "I don't know, guys, but I... I think I did, I think I met him."

I fell silent, running through that in my mind. I supposed it didn't make much of a difference either way. But it did tell us something.

He could teleport. But they used Chris as their transportation device. That meant he was calling the shots, but not that he was incredibly involved.

Or maybe he was just too afraid to get close to Jeremy and me on the physical level of existence.

A knot clogged my throat. "Was he around my baby?"

Chris said, "Not really. I only heard him that day. Well, I guess there was a time or two afterward, but he wasn't a part of the trinity of assholes."

At least Micah hadn't been calling him Daddy.

"This is all so fucked up," Chris said. "None of this makes any sense."

"Right now is a shitty place to pick up in the story," I muttered. "It's been a long road."

He stared at the counter for a moment. "So you guys were gods."

"I don't think we liked that word," I said. "But yeah. Yeah, apparently all the par animarum were."

"Fucking crazy." He rubbed his mouth. "And you created the Fae Realm."

"With Lucifer," Jeremy said.

"And you were, what? An Elf in your first life?"

"Apparently part Elf. Part whatever Lux is," Jeremy said. "Angel, I guess."

"And you were the queen of the fairies?" he asked me.

"According to Jeremy."

"But before you were with Jeremy, you were with him. Lux, or God, or whatever."

I said, "It looks that way."

"Crazy," Chris muttered. "Batshit fucking crazy."

"Yeah, pretty fucking weird," Leah said.

We went back to the house shortly after. Jeremy was bloodier than me, but I had a few specks on my shirt so we both grabbed showers. It was still early, barely after noon. So we planned to spend the rest of the day with the kids. Which should've been nice.

But my head was somewhere else.

Since I'd heard that odd roar when Peterson had taken us hostage, I had the notion that Lux was working with him. But suspecting it and knowing it were two far different things. It was especially strange now that I knew he was my husband once.

Considering my reaction when I'd seen that siren's naked body on Jeremy's lap, I understood how bad it hurt to find out your partner had cheated. But had it been Jenna or Celena wrapped around my husband's hips?

Yeah, I might want to kill them too.

That wasn't to say that I'd go to the lengths he had. I certainly wouldn't take it out on his children. Never, no matter how angry I was. I'd never take out my rage on an innocent child.

But I did wonder what that man thought of me.

I looked at Jeremy in the bathroom mirror, pulling my jeans up over my legs. "So did he... Did he say anything about me?"

"Not really." He brushed wet hair from his face. "Nothing worth mentioning."

"So he did then."

He tucked his hands around my waist and tugged me into his bare chest. "He said gross things that I don't agree with and don't want to repeat."

I leaned back and met his gaze. "Well now you have to tell me."

"Sexist shit. Something about you and his other wife being property. I don't know, baby. It doesn't matter."

Maybe it shouldn't have, but that actually made me feel a little better.

My jaw tightened. "It wasn't just about me then. What I did isn't what made him hate women. He's just always been a pig."

"Yeah. I think so. He viewed you as an item. *His* item. And he probably always would have if you and I didn't get together. So yeah, you cheated on the husband you never wanted to marry." He brushed hair behind my ear. "But I think that was your only way out."

I pressed my lips together and gave a nod.

"But it wasn't you, Laila. You aren't Véa. I'm not Nix. We were. But we aren't any more. That's not our life."

The trouble was, that wasn't true.

He'd planned everything. He chose when I'd get Jeremy back for good. He chose when I'd find my baby. He chose when I'd have my little girl. He'd planned all of this.

That was our true life. That was the first we'd built. Warts or not, that was our origin.

"No, it was. That was our life, Jeremy. This one," —I gestured around— "this is the life he manufactured. That life was real. It was raw. But this, all of this, has been pre-determined. These aren't even really our lives; these are the lives he sculpted for us. *That* was our real life. When we were making our own decisions. Before a plan was—"

"We do make our own decisions." He placed his hands on either side of my neck and turned my gaze up to meet his. "We chose each other. We chose our lives. He might have played some parts, but we chose how to react. We never lost our free will."

"Something poetic in that," I muttered.

He exhaled slowly. He leaned forward and kissed my forehead. "Let's go make dinner and finish packing, alright?"

CHAPTER TWELVE

JEREMY

We made mashed potatoes, asparagus, and steak for dinner that night. Steak was a big step for Micah; he was finally chewing well enough that he could handle it. Me and Chris were really excited about it. We found one of our dad's recipes, lit the grill on the back patio, and anxiously waited. They came out perfect.

Then Chris let it slip that we were eating cows. The cute, stinky animals we drove past every day. The ones that Micah got to pet a few weeks prior when we took him to the local dairy farm. All hell kinda broke loose.

Micah passionately—and loudly—proclaimed me and Chris as murderers. His brows furrowed far over his glowing blue eyes. His lower lip pouted forward. He stormed off, insisting that he would never eat with us again.

Laila was the only one of us who hadn't eaten the steak yet, so she had amnesty. She got him to eat the mashed potatoes and asparagus, but he wouldn't budge on the protein. From that point on, he'd decided. He was a vegetarian. More like pescatarian, really. He still ate eggs and fish, although probably because he didn't realize what they were. But chicken was a no-go. He wouldn't even touch pork.

Which was fine. It was his body. If he didn't want to eat meat, then more power to him. But he was judgy. Any time I ate bacon or beef in his presence from that point on, he deemed me a murderer.

He wasn't wrong, but it was rude.

We were raising a hippy. Completely of his own devices, we played no part in his humanitarian antics. He had his own opinions. A lot of them. And we prided ourselves in giving him the freedom to voice them. Even if they were annoying and judgmental.

At least his tirade gave me something to focus on aside from Lai.

She was quiet most of the night. Not with the kids, but with me. I wasn't sure if it was because of the torture or because of Lux. I tried to give her space either way. No matter which way I looked at it, it'd been a lot to take in. The kids were a good outlet for her to get it all off her mind.

I saw the point she made earlier that day. Ultimately, our lives were predetermined. Trying to see how much of them we created and how much he caused left my head spinning. I pretended that it wasn't because I could see how upset she was, but truthfully, I didn't feel much different.

The worst part? I met him, and I didn't hate him. I didn't understand it all. I didn't like him, and I thought he was a misogynistic fuckboy. I wish that I could hate him. But, although I didn't remember it all just yet, he was still my little brother. I hated what he did. I hated who he chose to be. But ultimately, even if I didn't want to, I'd always care for him.

Although, after what I'd soon see in the memories, I'd get pretty damn close to hating him.

I sat on a windowsill at least six stories high. My feet dangled in the wind below me as I took a long gulp of liquor from the flask in my hand. Cool air slid up the flowing shirt that hung on my shoulders, sending a cool shiver to the surface of my skin. The icy, wet smell of snow touched my nose. Tiny white flakes drifted from the cloudy sky to the world before me.

It looked something like a duller Seattle from the distance. High mountains stood behind the city like pillars reaching for the heavens. The buildings may have looked large from the ground, but where I saw them beside the peaks, they were as minuscule as an ant to a tree.

"You alright up there?" Véa's familiar voice called from the ground. She spoke in Elvan.

I looked down at her and smiled. From that height, all I could clearly make out were her long brown curls peeping from beneath her forest green cloak. "Alright, indeed, do gràs."

"Not too busy then?" she asked. "You could spare a moment?"

"Come on up," I called.

"Why don't you come down?" she said. "I could use the air."

I set my flask down behind me. I jumped.

Before I hit the ground, she formed a cushion of air just beneath the snowy path. I laughed and teleported to my feet with a grin.

"You could have done that from the start, you know." Véa smiled.

"Aye, but not so much fun that way." I grinned back, looking between her bright green eyes. There were red streaks through their whites. They looked swollen and puffy, even chafing on the edges. My expression softened. "What's the matter, mi lim?" *My love.*

She glanced around with her eyes, but kept her face turned on me. She forced her smile higher up her cheeks. "I'm going on a stroll; would you care to join me?"

I nodded slowly, looking between her eyes. "Of course, do gràs."

I opened my mouth to ask her something else before I heard her voice in my mind. *The walls have ears.* I glanced at the guards in armor —like she had, with my eyes, not my head—scattered around the courtyard.

"Wonderful weather, isn't it?" She gave a smile.

"It is. A bit cold for your liking though, eh?" I stood a few feet to her left, meandering the way I suppose I was expected to. My gaze shifted around the large courtyard, noting—but not looking directly at —the armored men at each exit.

"A bit." She chuckled. "Pleasant though. I didn't expect to enjoy the climate, but I do marvel at its beauty. The white against the black truly is a marvel."

"Almost as beautiful as it is in the Opshee." I continued walking, nodding cordially to the guard at a large gate before us.

"Almost." She smiled, sending the guard a nod. I followed a few feet behind. I looked over the cobblestone path leading to a snow-covered pine forest. "Just a bit too dark in the evening, don't you think?"

"Can't say I've ever minded the dark." I felt their gazes on my back as she summoned a ball of violet light to her palm.

"To each their own," Véa said.

We continued small talking until we made it a few strides into the tree line. Once we were deep enough inside, I caught her waist and looked between her eyes. "What's wrong, Véa?"

She smiled. Her head shook a bit. "Why does something have to be wrong?"

"You've been crying." I touched her cheek, grazing the sore spot beside her eye and feeling the sting against my own. "What is it? Does someone know?"

She shook her head. "No, I don't think so."

"Then what's the matter?"

She fell quiet for a long moment. She turned away and started back down the path.

"Véa," I said. "Véa, where are you going?"

"There's a bench ahead. I'd like to sit, if that's all right with you."

I teleported to her, put my hands on her hips, and then teleported to the stone bench. A smile tugged at my lips. But she was silent as she lowered herself to it. I sat beside her, careful to put a foot or two between us. "I'm sorry, was that inappropriate?"

She smiled and shook her head. "No. No, it was sweet."

I made what I could of a smile. "What's the matter then, Véa?"

Her eyes flicked between mine. She strained a smile. Then a slow, shaking sigh left her nostrils. "I'm pregnant."

My breath caught. My heart sunk. My stomach ached. It felt as though I'd just fallen from a great height, but this time, there was no cushion of wind to catch me at the bottom.

I fell quiet, still looking between her eyes. I cleared my throat and smiled. "That's wonderful. I'll be an uncle then."

She swallowed hard. "No, you'll be a father."

Silence as I stared at her, heart falling through my chest. "Are you sure?"

"Lux and I... I know my body, Nix." She pressed her lips together. "It can only be yours."

Panic started to set in. My heart raced in my chest, hands growing moist. Suddenly, my throat was so tight that even breathing felt difficult.

"He'll be gone for another quarter at least," Véa said. "I can't... By the time he returns, I won't be able to hide—"

"I know," I murmured. My hand raised to my mouth, squeezing the hair at my chin. I stood and began to pace.

"I won't tell him it's yours," she muttered. "When I tell him, I'll—"

"What do you mean when you tell him?"

"He won't know that it was you. You won't—"

I took her face in my hands. "Don't finish that thought. I won't let that happen."

She smiled as tears welled in her eyes. "Nix, we don't have another choice. He's going to know the moment he sees me. I won't be able to—"

"Then we don't let him see you," I said quickly. My head shook again. "I swore my life to protect you and I will—"

"To him," she said. "You swore to *him* that you would protect me."

"I made that oath to *you*." I looked between her eyes. "I won't go back on my word."

"You may have to." She gave a soft smile, and her hand moved to mine. She pulled it from her cheek and twined our fingers together. Her lips grazed the back of my knuckles. "But I'll be sure that you don't suffer for this."

I lowered myself to my knees, placing my hands at her hips, nearly chest to chest as I looked between her eyes. "Stop it. It won't come to that."

"It wil—"

"No." I took her face in my hands. "It will not come to that, Véa. Just give me a moment. I-I'll think of something. I will fix this."

She leaned forward and gently touched her lips to mine. I held her neck, gently grasping her face so close that it warmed my skin. My heart hammered against my chest, mostly out of fear, but I think attraction played a part too.

"No one will hurt you." I held her face with one hand and glided the other to her stomach. My forehead touched hers as I looked between her glowing green gaze. "Either of you."

"Nix—"

"No," I said. "I will find a way. I will."

Her eyes filled with tears. I twisted my arms around her waist. I tugged her body into mine, taking in the soft, sweet scent of her hair.

I stared at a dead branch jutting out of the snow a few feet in the distance. I nodded hard. "I'll find a way."

CHAPTER THIRTEEN

LAILA

At times, the dreams felt so real that I didn't even realize they were memories. Others, they felt like old movies playing behind my eyelids. The ones with Lux felt that way, at least. But they felt real when they revolved around Nix. Like the one I had tonight.

I was sleeping. I awoke to a hand over my mouth.

My hands sparked with flames in the dark room. He muttered a curse and hushed me. "It's me, it's me."

My palm ignited in violet light. Nix's blue eyes shined back at me. "What are you doing?"

"Be quiet." He hushed. "You need to pack a bag. We're leaving."

"What?" I sat forward. "What do you mean?"

"I found a way. I'll explain on the way, but we don't have much time. Get a bag." His eyes were urgent, but I noted the smile pulling at his lips. "We have to hurry. Don't worry about getting dressed, just gather what you need."

"But Venark—"

"Is waiting for us. We have to move, Véa."

And it ended.

My eyes opened to Jeremy's sleeping face curled against the pillow beside me. The sun peeked in from the edges of the curtains. I listened to the birds chirping outside the window and stared at him a moment longer.

The interesting part about those memories was the lack of completion. We both got snippets. Snippets we wouldn't be able to make sense of without one another. Like we each received pieces of the puzzle. Without our combined images, we couldn't create the full picture.

———

"Alright, I've got our bags in the living room, our passports are in my purse in there. Tink's bag is up at Leah's. I'm forgetting something though. What am I forgetting?" I looked at Jeremy in the bathroom.

He spit toothpaste to the sink and met my gaze with a smile. "The kids?"

I looked around. "I was wondering why it's so quiet. Where are the kids?"

"Hannah and Kai are playing with them out in the yard." He wiped his mouth on a hand towel. "I asked them to keep them busy while Chris and I move our stuff to the guest house."

"Oh, okay. Shit, the dishwasher. That's what I'm forgetting." I started from the bedroom.

"I wanted to talk to you, too," he said behind me. "I remembered something last night."

"So did I," I muttered. "But it was like nothing. Maybe a minute max. Probably not even that long."

"Mine was pretty lengthy. But I didn't get much out of it either. It was just you telling me you were pregnant."

I met his gaze, opened the dishwasher, and hastily put the dishes away. "That's it? No context?"

"You were married to him. Lux, I mean. You said you knew it was mine and couldn't pass it off as his. Pointed ears might've made that difficult too. And you were scared."

"Explains what I saw then," I said. "She was sleeping, and Nix woke her up in the middle of the night. He told her to pack a bag. I woke up."

He ran his tongue along his teeth, helping me unload the dishwasher. "So they're becoming chronological."

"Maybe. Maybe, I guess it looks that way." I pushed the door shut. "It's weird, isn't it? How we wouldn't be able to understand what all of this means without each other?"

He smiled. "It actually makes perfect sense if you think about it. We're bound to each other. If it weren't for each other, these memories wouldn't matter, you know?"

That was a valid point. And the reality of it gave me butterflies. We were one another's tethering point to reality in both the past and the present. There was a certain level of intimacy in that.

I smiled and looked over him for a moment. "Yeah. Yeah, I guess so."

"Sucks you haven't had any sex dreams about me though." He crossed his arms and leaned against the counter with a grin. "Just your ex-husband and sister wife."

"Ew, don't say it like that." My nose curled. "And you're the one who said it wasn't us."

"Because it isn't. But it was."

Yet, every time he referenced those dreams, he referred to Nix as I and me, not he and him. He referred to Véa as you, not her and she.

"Well, maybe my subconscious is trying to tell me the story instead of the detailed erotica version." I placed my hands at my hips with a grin. "It's not my fault that all you think about is fucking."

"I think about a lot more than fucking, thank you." He held his grin. "And at least when I am thinking about fucking, it's about you and not your sibling."

"Listen, I can't help what my soul deems as a necessary element to the story." I took a step forward and put my arms around his neck. "And I can't speak for Véa, but I can say that you're better in bed than anyone else I've been with."

His hands drifted to my hips. "Oh yeah?"

"Mhmm." I smiled.

He gripped my hips and hoisted me to the counter. "So even better than the threesome?"

"Much better than the threesome." My arms looped around his neck. "Don't get me wrong, girl knew what she was doing. But he was just alright. No skill with the hips. I don't think he even knew where my clit was. And he didn't go down on either of us which is really not—"

"Alright, thanks." His smile fell down at the edges. "Kinda killing the vibe, babe."

A quiet laugh. "I'm just saying. You're better." I leaned forward and touched my lips to his. "It's been a while though. Maybe you could remind me later."

"That's possible." He grinned and kissed me again. His hand traveled up my torso as his other hand cupped my cheek. I tightened my legs at his hips and arched a bit closer.

Then the patio door whooshed open.

"Gross, get a room," Hannah said.

As if this weren't literally our house.

"Look, Daddy!" Micah came running toward us. He looked up at Jeremy with wide eyes and an even wider smile. "You have to guess what it is."

"Hmm, I don't know. A ladybug?" He lowered himself to the ground. Micah shook his head. "A bumble bee?"

"It's a lightning bug." His palm opened, showing the slow pulse of a green firefly. "You can't see it that much 'cause it's daytime, but it was doing it. I seen it."

"That is pretty cool. But we've got to let him back outside, right? That way he can get back to his friends."

"You'we wight." He disappeared.

I laughed. Jeremy stood with a smile. "I'm going to start bringing everything over. You wanna finish getting them ready?"

"Will do."

CHAPTER FOURTEEN

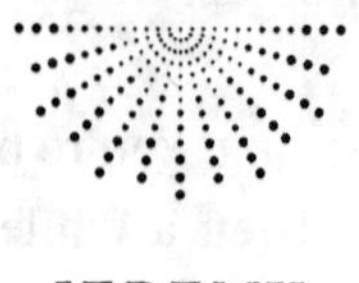

JEREMY

"So this is it," Laila muttered, lifting Milly higher against her hip.

"It's so big," Micah murmured with wide eyes.

"Too big," Kai said.

I looked up at the old mansion and blew out a deep breath. At least five copies of our house could fit inside the monstrosity, and our house wasn't small. Two rounded towers stood three stories high at each corner, and another two on the back side. I couldn't count the windows to the many rooms if my life depended on it.

Ivy grew along the stone walls coated in dainty pink flowers; Mémé's touch to make the ominous house feel a bit more pleasant. But the few flowers couldn't thaw the ice that home held.

It was beautiful, I'll admit that. But in the same way that a Catholic church is beautiful. It wasn't homey and comforting. It was fancy and uppity.

The large iron gate clicked shut behind us. Micah took a step closer to my legs. I touched his hair and looked down at him with a smile. "Do you want to knock?"

He looked to the door then back to me. His head shook.

Chris laughed. "What's wrong, bud?"

"It looks scawy," he muttered.

"It kind of does look scary," Laila murmured.

"It's not scary." Chris laughed. "Just wait until you see the back yard."

"Come here, kid." I leaned down, hooked my hands beneath his arm pits, and lifted him to my hip. His arms tightened around my neck as I started to the doorway.

"You don't like it hewe, huh?" Micah asked.

I smiled. "No, I do like it here. I just don't like all of the people here."

"Why?"

A slow exhale.

The place, I loved.

France had to be one of my favorite places in the world. The weather was beautiful, the rolling hills coated in grapes were tremendous, and the culture enthralled me. I had a thousand positive memories in this mansion.

Le reveleion de noel—a midnight dinner on Christmas Eve they hosted each year through my childhood. Meals with my dad and siblings on the terrace, Easter egg hunts Sunday mornings delivered by the bells that'd flown to Rome to be blessed by the pope. An odd tradition, but one that fascinated me far more than the Easter Bunny as a child.

I just hated my grandparents. But I did love this place.

"Ask me that in ten years, alright?"

"That's a long time. I don't think I'll wemembew," Micah muttered.

I laughed as I climbed the few steps to the door. "Ya know what my favorite thing was about coming here was when I was a kid?" He shook his head, and I gestured to the heavy, custom knocker on the dark red door.

A perfectly sculpted grapevine framed the edges. It was shaped like a shield with a bunch of grapes as a lip, clearly some type of Guardian symbolism.

"Slamming that damn knocker as loud and as many times as he could before Papy came to the door yelling." Adam laughed behind us.

I smirked and looked at Micah. "You wanna do it too?"

Micah frowned. "I don't want no one to yell."

"Well, that's boring." I smiled, grasped ahold of the knocker, and smacked it off the door a good twenty times.

"You're a child," Hannah said.

I grinned. "Old habits die hard."

Laila rolled her eyes and fought her smile.

When I didn't hear the peddle of footsteps behind the door, I looked back at Micah. "You sure you don't want to try? It's fun."

He glanced at Laila for approval. She chuckled. He smiled and gave a nod. I leaned forward, watching his little fist grasp ahold of the metal and hit it off the door once or twice. "You can do better than that." I grinned, remembering my dad smiling at me and saying something similar before it became a tradition for him to hold me up and let me beat that knocker off the door.

"Look at you teaching our son to be a troublemaker," Laila said.

I grinned over my shoulder. Then the big door creaked open.

"Oh mon Dieu," Mémé's murmured as I turned back. Her wrinkly hand lifted in front of her mouth, crystal blue eyes filling with tears. She looked over us all with a beautifully depressing gaze. Like seeing us was her dying wish.

"Bonjour, Mémé." Chris smiled, took a step forward, and lowered himself to hug her tiny frame. Her watering eyes closed, arms tightening around his neck.

She chuckled, holding him close. "Bonjour. Bonjour amour."

Micah bashfully laid his head against my chest. He raised his hand to his mouth, chewing the nail of his thumb. I gently tugged it from his lips. That'd become something of a nervous tick of his we were trying to break. Laila put her hand on my back. She smiled, and I sent one back.

Mémé pulled away and looked at Micah. "You must be Micah, mon petit."

"Bojour," Micah murmured.

"Hey, Mémé." I smiled.

"Hello, mon cher." She leaned forward, giving me what she could of a hug with Micah on my hip.

"You remember my wife." I gestured to Laila. "And this is our daughter."

"Nice to see you again, dear." She smiled at Laila and looked to Milly. "My word, the pictures don't do her justice. Or him." She looked at Micah. "Looks so much like Jeán."

"Or ya know." Chris smiled. "Us."

Adam cleared his throat behind me. I took a step closer to Laila, giving him room to brush past with Jenna and Luka. "We're back here too, you know." He grinned. "Salut, Mémé."

"Oh my." Her smile widened, looking at the blond baby in his arms. "Look at that hair!"

"Takes after his mom." He kissed Jenna's crown and smiled.

Mémé looked at her and forced a smile. "Luka, you said."

"Luka Jeán Callidy." Jenna smiled as she slid her fingers over his head.

"Not Skoulda?" she asked.

In fairness, they gave him Dad's middle name. That was more than I would have done. He didn't need the surname too.

Adam pressed his lips together. He forced a smile. "We thought about hyphenating, but we decided it'd be too long."

"Mm." Mémé pursed her lips before summoning a smile. "Let's get out of the cold then. Come in, let's have a seat while we wait on Papy."

"Guess I don't get an introduction," Kai muttered. Hannah hushed him.

"At least you got to come," Brody grumbled. "Gwen isn't welcome."

CHAPTER FIFTEEN

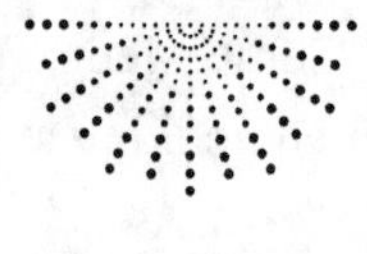

LAILA

The home felt more like a castle. Extravagant didn't come close to describing it. I'd just showered, and I still felt too dirty to sit on the antique sofa that probably cost more than my house.

The main house back home carried many of this one's characteristics, but more Americanized. The ceiling towered at least twice as high, but the intricate swirl work on them was identical. I think Melissa, Jeremy's mom, preferred the wood floors because everything my feet touched was impeccably polished white marble. It had to be old, it definitely looked original, but there were no signs of wear and tear. In fact, nothing looked worn.

All of the mahogany crown moldings reflected the light of the golden chandelier above us, and I didn't see a scratch or nick no matter how hard I squinted. The floral wallpaper could have walked straight out of 1965. But it didn't peel at the corners. No gray cast from smoke crested the tops.

I took pride in my ability to keep a clean house. But if I rubbed a white glove along any surface in that room, I'd smudge the sparkle away before a smidge of gray touched my finger. If Mémé ever came to my home, she'd probably demand Jeremy file for divorce. But in my defense, I didn't have a million maids fluttering about in cute little dresses with rags at their hips.

"So how is your shop, dear?" Smiling, Mémé handed me a glass of red wine.

"The diner, you mean?" Milly reached for the cup in my hand, and I set it on the coffee table. Jeremy grabbed a coaster and lifted my glass overtop of it. I gave an awkward *sorry* expression, and he smiled.

"Yes, your diner. I'm sorry, my English is not perfect." Mémé sat at the chair diagonal from me.

"Oh, that's alright. Yeah, we're doing pretty good right now. People got to eat, ya know?" I said.

She awkwardly smiled. "Sure."

"How are sales this year?" Jeremy asked.

"As usual, I believe. People got to drink." She shot me a friendly smile.

Chris gestured to his wine and said something in French.

Chuckling, Mémé said something back.

Everyone in the room who spoke French laughed. Kai, Jenna, and I exchanged awkward glances. Then Jeremy said, "Chris asked how long it was aged and Mémé said she doesn't care, she just drinks it."

"Oh." I let out an awkward, forced laugh.

This was weird. So, so weird. I didn't know what the hell they were saying. I knew I wasn't liked. This was *not* where I wanted to be. I couldn't wait for dinner to be over so I could take my kids up to the Eiffel Tower and look at the city.

"Papy should be done with his meeting soon. I hoped we could have an early dinner together before you go out to see the sights. That was your plan, no?" Mémé asked with a look between us.

"That is the plan," Adam said.

"Well, we have a few cars. Please, have a drink. We have plenty," Mémé said. "And I've got a few specialty cases for you to take home. That cousin of yours, she'll like them."

"Sister," Chris corrected with a smile. "She's our sister, Mémé."

"Sure." She forced another smile. She looked to Micah. "Mon petit, would you like something to eat? It looks like you could use some meat on those bones, and I know how you Americans love to eat." Micah leaned his head further into Jeremy. "We have all kinds of pastries. Éclairs, macarons, madeleines. You name it, amour."

"You'd like eclairs." Jeremy nudged his shoulder against Micah's. "They have chocolate on them."

"No thank you," he muttered.

"He's a little shy," Chris said. "Maybe we could show him the garden tomorrow while Jeremy and Laila are at that meeting. He loves being outside."

She gave a sad smile and looked him over. "I bet."

Milly fussed in my arms, reaching for my wine on the table again. "Babe, do you have her cup over there?"

"Yeah." He rummaged through the bag. He smiled at Mémé. "It's just water. Ne t'inquiète pas."

She laughed and shook her head. "I've been looking for a reason to get new furniture. Why do you think I opened a bottle of red?"

I smiled. Maybe she wasn't so bad. She had been kind at the wedding. Her gaze was still judgmental, but she was remotely likable.

It was interesting to see her though. Hannah looked a lot like her. They had the same thick black lashes and petite stature. The other siblings must've gotten their height from their grandpa's side.

I laughed, and Milly took the cup. "I thought it was because red's just better."

A grin played at her lips. She glanced at Jeremy. "I do like this girl."

"Yeah, me too." He smiled at me.

Mémé said something to Hannah in French. I heard a door shut a few rooms away followed by a billowing laugh. One that I knew pretty well. I tilted my ear that direction, wondering if I was hearing things. Then his voice carried, and I turned to Jeremy.

He tilted his head to listen closer. He looked back to his grandmother. "Mémé, who is Papy meeting with?"

"The Monarch of the Northern region here. I think you know him. Raymond or—"

"Roland." I glanced at Micah and then at Jeremy.

It wasn't that I hated Roland, or that I didn't trust him. He was relatively likable, really. But I was hesitant about anyone I didn't trust with my whole heart around my children. And this was the man who liked to snack on me once a month. My babies surely tasted a hell of a lot like I did. Then again, Roland was practically ancient. I knew he had good control over his thirst.

"Well, you speak of the devil." His voice came from the doorway. A smile edged up his warm brown cheeks, honey eyes shifting over us, then locking with mine. He adjusted his impeccable back jacket, tightening it against his toned chest. "I didn't know we were meeting again so soon, mon ange."

I pulled Milly a bit closer. "Not 'til next month."

"Who's that?" Micah asked, craning past me to meet his gaze.

"Just a friend of me and Mommy's," Jeremy said.

"Is that…" Roland began, starting into the room. He leaned down a bit to meet Micah's gaze. His eyes widened, and his lips heightened in a grin. "I suppose it has to be. So you're the little man the whole world's been in such a rut over."

Jeremy tugged Micah tighter to him. Chris stood. I met his gaze and shook my head a bit. Roland was the man who'd helped us bring our son home. He wouldn't hurt him. Not the kind of guy I'd invite over for a cookout, but the kind I was okay with standing within a few feet of him.

I looked at Roland and smiled. "Roland, this is our son Micah. And Micah, this is Roland. He's one of the many people who helped us bring you and Uncle Chris home."

Chris's shoulders relaxed. He took a sip of his wine but kept his gaze steady on the buff, well-dressed man a few inches from my son.

"What is you?" Micah asked. "I don't feel nothing."

Roland's smiling mouth fell open, eyes widening slightly. He laughed. He glanced at me and pointed at Micah. "Teaching him to insult so soon?"

"Only insulting if it's true." Jeremy smiled.

Roland laughed and met his gaze. "Can I show him?" Jeremy nodded. Roland turned back to Micah, lifted his lips, and let his canines drop from his gums.

"That's all?" Micah asked.

His eyes opened further, and he laughed again. He looked at Jeremy. "You're coaching him."

With a proud smirk, Jeremy said, "I'm not."

"Well, yes, son. That's all. But bear in mind, power is not always measured by the abilities in your hands. Power is often measured by the people you know and the power *they* hold." He glanced at me and smiled. I smiled back. He turned to Milly. "And this is the little one. Milly, I believe you said?"

"My little girl." I kissed her hair. He reached out to touch her hand, but I tugged her closer. My head shook. He could talk to my children, but no, he could not touch them.

He smiled, letting his hand drop back to his side. "Smell the Fae in this one. A lot like you, mon ange."

Jeremy licked his teeth and sent him a cordial smile. "So we've been told."

"Désolé de te faire attendre," a voice said in the doorway. I looked up.

Raphael stood in the large, cased opening. He was about the same height as his grandsons, at least an inch or two above six feet. Streaks of silver that hadn't made it to his ponytail hung around big blue eyes. His neatly trimmed salt and pepper beard framed his diamond-shaped face. He wore a finely pressed white shirt over medium-built shoulders. A pair of finely pressed black slacks hung from his hips to his shiny black shoes.

Even at his age—which I imagined was around seventy—he was an attractive man. A lot like how I imagined Jeremy would look in a few decades. But he didn't have the softness in his gaze that my husband did. He held his shoulders so high. Some may call it confidence, but I called it arrogance.

"Papy." Hannah grinned, started to her feet, and wrapped her arms around her grandpa. Chris smiled, setting his wine to the end table. Jeremy and Adam exchanged a less than joyous expression. Kai, Jenna, and I all anxiously looked between one another.

"Salut ma chère," was all I caught from what he said. He smiled and whisked her hand to him, examining the engagement ring. He pursed his lips. "Curieusement familiar."

I think that meant *this looks familiar.*

"Oui," Hannah said. "Oui, c'était à ma mère."

Yup. She said, *it was my mother's.*

He turned to Kai and raised a brow. "Couldn't afford to buy her one yourself?"

"Papy." Hannah made a wry face.

Kai cleared his throat and smiled. "Aye, I could but she wanted her mum's. Who am I to argue with tradition?"

He huffed. "You don't seem like one to pride himself in tradition."

"Nice to see you too, Papy." Jeremy stood, trying to pull the attention off of race before it reached that point. "I don't know about you, but we're starving."

He turned to Jeremy and struggled not to narrow his gaze. "Of course. Let's eat. Will you be joining us, Roland?"

Roland looked at me and Jeremy as if to ask permission. Jeremy didn't give much of a response, but I smiled. He was more my kind of people. Rich and uppity or not, he wasn't as holier than thou. Maybe he'd help with some icebreaking.

He turned back to Raphael and smiled. "I would love to. Thank you."

CHAPTER SIXTEEN

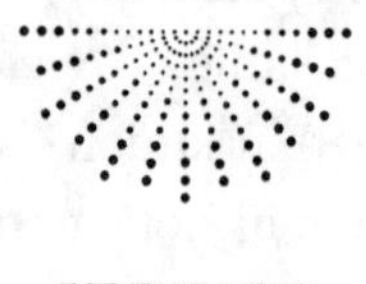

JEREMY

"*Le mariage aura donc lieu en juillet?*" *So the wedding will be in July?* Mémé asked from the end of the long table.

"Oui, c'est de toute façon l'espoir. Nous venons de choisir un gâteau la semaine dernière." *Yes, that's the hope. We just picked out a cake last week.* Hannah smiled and squeezed Kai's hand. She looked back to Mémé. "Vous serez là, non?" *You'll be there, right?*

"Nous ne le manquerions pas," *We wouldn't miss it,* Mémé said.

"They actually wanted to ask you guys something." Brody patted a napkin against his lip and gave a smile. "Would you guys be open to letting them have the wedding here?"

Bold of him. I was sure they'd decline, but maybe being put on the spot by one of their favorite grandsons, they'd at least consider it. If I were the one to ask, they'd surely say no. But that sweet, innocent smile of Hannah's had always been hard for them to refuse.

Papy's scoffed and took a sip from his wine. Mémé looked at Hannah, head tilting. "Is that right, ma chèr?"

Hannah's cheeks grew red. She smiled. "I do love it here. I remember coming to a few weddings on the terrace as a kid. It was always so beautiful. But I understand if you guys have too much going on."

90

Papy ran his tongue along his teeth, sipping from his glass once more. He murmured something I didn't catch. Mémé glared his way and smiled back at Hannah. "Give me a call one day next week. We'll talk it over."

I smiled. So did Hannah.

We all knew what that meant. Yes, but Mémé had to convince Papy not to be a dick about it first.

"So this is your brother and your sister." Roland gestured between Kai and Hannah with his fork. Laila nodded. He turned his fork to Chris. "If I didn't know better, I'd say you're your father reincarnated."

I chuckled. We got that a lot.

Chris and I were the spitting image of our dad. His shoulders were a more narrow than mine, his nose a hair longer. But we did look a lot like our dad. Which wasn't a bad thing. Whether I had strong feelings about the man or not, he wasn't bad looking.

Adam and Brody looked a tad more like Mom. We all got the vibrancy of Dad's eyes and his jet-black hair, but their faces were a bit smaller than mine and Chris's. They were a few inches shorter too. Granted, taller than most, around six feet, but they were slightly broader too. Not fat, just a little bulkier than Chris and me.

Although, our lack of exercise could've played a part in that.

Roland chuckled and glanced down the table. "So many of you. Please, I'm sure I'll forget, but introduce me. Hannah Skoulda, judging by those eyes." He smiled. "And you look a lot like Laila, so you're the other twin."

"Aye." Kai smiled. "Kai Callidy."

"And that's Adam. A year older than me, a year younger than Chris." I gestured to him beside Kai. "And that's his girlfriend, Jenna, and their son Luka."

"Also my sister," Laila said.

His brow arched as he looked between them. "Oh?"

"Laila was adopted," Jenna said. "There's no blood relation, but I'm the only one she's known since birth so brownie points for me."

Roland chuckled and smiled over her. "Human then."

She pressed her lips together and raised her head in a nod.

"And that's Brody." I gestured toward him at the edge of the table.

He smiled, moving his head up and down as he looked over us. "A beautiful family. The resemblance to Jeán within the five of you is uncanny."

"You knew our dad?" Adam asked.

"Oui." He reached for his wine and took a sip. "We were good friends for a time."

"What happened?" Adam asked.

Mémé gritted her teeth. Papy rolled his eyes. Roland glanced at them and laughed. "A tale for another time."

The dining room door quietly opened. Two maids carried out plates of food. "Merci," I said as she set the plates in front of Micah and me.

Scallops. Something Micah could eat and—thankfully—something he wouldn't recognize as an animal.

"Alors dis-moi, Jeremy." *So tell me, Jeremy.* Papy took a sip from his wine. "Comment est ton prisonnier?" *How is that prisoner of yours?*

I gave him a look. "On peut en parler quand mon fils n'écoute pas." *We can talk about that when my son isn't listening.*

"Il est quoi? Deux? Il ne sait pas ce que je dis. Votre femme non plus, mais c'est une conversation que nous pourrons avoir plus tard." *He's, what? Two? He doesn't know what I'm saying. Neither does your wife but that's a conversation we can have later.*

I didn't feel the need to comment on how Micah was listening to every word we were saying. Papy wouldn't believe how smart he was, I'd get pissed off he called my kid dumb, and a fight would start. So I went with the safer route.

"Comme ça," *As is this,* I said.

He huffed and leaned back in his seat. "Join me on the terrace this evening then."

"Or we could discuss it at the Chamber's Meeting tomorrow."

"We will." He smiled. "But I'd appreciate a quick briefing beforehand. Seems our friend has more knowledge on the subject than your own grandpére."

"Wonder why that is," I muttered as I cut Micah's food.

What's that about? Laila said into my thoughts, glancing at me over her wine.

Peterson.

What about him?

Just wants to know what we know. Probably thinks I'll tell him more than we tell everyone else. But that's not going to happen. His loyalty's with the Elders and the Council. I don't trust him enough to tell him anything we won't tell the rest of them.

We'll go over what's off-limits after we eat.

I sent her a nod.

Micah gently tapped my shoulder. "What is it, buddy?"

He pointed to his lobster bisque and curled his nose. "I don't like it."

"That's okay, you don't have to eat it. You're probably getting full, huh?" I asked.

He nodded, moving his hand over his belly.

Formal French meals were massive. We'd already made it through the L'Aperitif—a light serving of bread with cheese, some olives, and nuts. Then was L'entrée—the soups, in this meal's case. Now the fish course, which had just arrived. Next was the main course. The salad would follow, more cheese after that, and then a dessert course.

Laila didn't seem to mind. Neither did I; I loved these big meals. But Micah was little, and still adjusting to what it was like to eat more than the minimal amount of food needed to survive. He snacked a lot throughout the day because that's how we ate in our family. But it was different here. Snacking was practically unheard of in this part of the world—or at least in this household. My grandparents had large, long meals that lasted hours. I was sure he'd end up puking if he ate all of these courses back-to-back.

"I'm not a fan of soups either, mon petit," Mémé said from her end of the table. "If I wanted a drink, I'd have one."

He smiled at her. He eyed the scallops and tilted his head to the side a bit. "They smells good though."

"These are one of my favorites," Laila said on the other side of him. "But I don't cook them because I always mess them up."

He took a bite and chewed for a moment. "Can you cook these at home, Daddy?"

"I can. I think we have some in the freezer, don't we?" I asked.

"Yeah, we should cook them soon. They'll be going bad in a week or two."

"You froze scallops?" Roland asked. "A crime against humanity."

"Always better fresh," Mémé agreed.

"I like it," Micah said.

I wasn't surprised at how scarcely Papy spoke to me, Laila, and Micah during dinner. When he did, it was a quick snarky remark. Roland also acted as a good buffer—whether I liked the guy or not. But I brushed most of what Papy said off. Until the main dinner course came to the table. Magret de Canard. A meal I loved. Salt and peppered potatoes, a simple salad of greens and goat cheese, and baked duck.

Of course, I knew what Micah would say the moment that I started to cut into it. "Muwdewew."

I laughed.

"Just eat the potatoes, kid." Laila gave a playful grin.

"But it's touching." He wrinkled his nose. "Look, the juicy stuff's on them."

"Then eat the salad," I said.

Mémé glanced over his plate. "What's the matter, mon petit?"

His little head shook. "I's not a muwdewew."

"A murderer?" Roland asked, trying to stifle his laugh.

Micah nodded. Papy broke out in dramatic cackle. "Oh, you're not?"

He shook his head again.

"Well, then you belong to the wrong family, son."

True as that may have been, it wasn't an appropriate thing to say to my kid. Especially considering the way the first few years of his life had been. My son didn't like violence, and I didn't want him to view us as aggressive people. Because the truth was, we weren't. Not unless we had to be.

"Papy," I said sharply.

"What? It's the truth, your wife's ki—" He coughed. His hand flew to his chest, struggling at the crick in his throat.

"You're not having that conversation with my two-year-old," Laila said with a firm, glowing green gaze. She'd politely kept her mouth shut throughout this meal. I was glad that was what came from her lips when she broke her silence.

It wasn't rude. It wasn't impolite. But it got her point across to watch what the fuck was said around our children.

They didn't need to know what we'd done for them. Yeah, she'd killed hundreds of people to bring Micah home. But he didn't deserve that burden on his shoulders. It was hers, and mine, and we were content to carry that weight. Micah didn't need to.

Papy reached for his water. His nostrils flared, jaw tightening at the realization that Laila was the source of his cough. I glanced at her and smiled.

"What'd he say?" Micah asked.

I smiled. "Just grown-up stuff."

Papy narrowed his gaze at Laila. "You did that?"

Her brow raised, tongue sliding along her teeth. She must have said something into his mind because his jaw tightened. His gaze stayed hard against hers. He huffed and sipped his wine.

What'd you say? I whispered into Laila's thoughts.

I can do a lot more than that.

CHAPTER SEVENTEEN

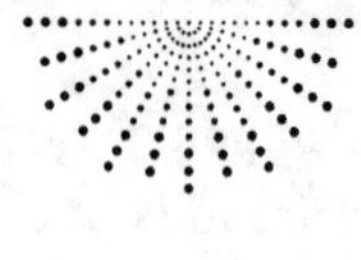

LAILA

We rushed through the créme brûlée. I don't think anyone at that table felt close to comfortable except for Roland. He seemed pretty amused at the tension.

Mémé insisted we unpack our bags and head to the city. We finished eating around four-thirty, which left us a good bit of time to tour. I was excited to see the Eiffel Tower. I'd seen it once a few months after I got my powers but only at a passing glance. Jeremy and I spent most of our time in a cheap hotel that day.

Mémé prepared to wobble down the path beside the vineyard that led to the guest house to show us around, but Chris insisted she relax. Jeremy assured her they remembered the way.

When we made it out the back door onto the rear terrace, I marveled at the beauty for a moment. The rolling hills of grapes looked like something straight out of a romance movie. Cool, whistling wind brushed against my cheeks as the soft, floral scents snuck up my nose.

Off to the right beside a large brick building, I smiled at the field of purple. It was hard to tell at the distance, but it looked like lavender. I'd have loved to run through it and breathe in that smell.

A few hundred yards ahead, I took in the quaint guest home. The cottage stood two stories high with cream-colored stucco walls framed in deep brown trim. Each window curved at the top like something from a story book.

"Well, that was the most awkward dinner of my life," Jenna muttered.

"Can't disagree with you there," I said, watching Chris chase after Micah down the path. Hannah and Kai tagged close behind them with hands cupped together, giggling like the kids in love I suppose they were at the time.

"Makes me really glad that my mom was American, ya know? Only had to see them on the holidays." Jeremy passed me Milly and pulled his jeans up his hips.

"Your grandma's nice though."

"She's not. But she tries," he said. "She's nice to the kids at least."

"Not mine," Jenna mumbled.

"They'll get used to it," Adam said. "Or they won't, and we won't visit again. I've got my trust fund either way."

"So bizarre to be disliked for being normal," Jenna said. "No offense, guys."

"None taken," I muttered.

Well, a little taken. We weren't *abnormal*. We just weren't ordinary either.

"What's all that about anyway? Aren't you guys supposed to protect the human race?" Jenna asked.

"Yeah, but not fuck them," Jeremy said. "It's because of the weakening in the gene pool. If too many of us have kids with humans, a few generations later, no one will have power."

"So wait." Jenna's head tilted to the side. "You guys only have three abilities in your bloodline. If you're not mixing with humans..."

Brody laughed. He cleared his throat. "Yeah, incest wasn't uncommon until the last century or so."

"Ew." I grimaced. "Wait. Wait, hang on. Is that why your Skoulda genes are so strong? Is that why our son looks like your clone?"

Jeremy let out an awkward laugh. "Did you notice Mémé's comment about Luka's last name?" I looked at him with a curled lip. "Yeah, her maiden name's Skoulda too."

"Oh god." Jenna looked down to Luka. "Maybe that's why he has that weird toe thing."

Gross. So, so gross. But then again, I'd left a man for my brother-in-law, so I supposed I wasn't in any position to judge. That was different though; we didn't share blood. Well, at least, I hoped we didn't. The memories hadn't shown me enough to know that for certain yet.

"They're third cousins. There aren't any birth defects at a distance like that," Jeremy said.

"It's still weird," Jenna said. "I couldn't fuck my cousin if it was to save my life."

"You don't have any cousins," I said.

"We don't know that. I could have a million cousins out there."

"Yeah, and since you don't know who your dad is, you could've already fucked a couple." Adam grinned.

Actually, I did know that. Mom and I had been writing up a family tree. She didn't know much about Dad's heritage—I'd filled what I could of that in from Moe's journal. But she'd written down Jenna's dad's name. He, like Mom and my dad, was an only child. So, no, Jenna didn't have any cousins out there.

The difficult part in writing that family tree was an obvious detail. Mary was my biological mother. Of course she was on it. But the trouble laid in her father. God.

AKA, my husband a few thousand years ago.

That thought had sent a chill down my spine. He was clearly the one that decided which soul went into which body. And he'd chosen to place me in his granddaughter.

Although I had no intentions of reenacting the life we lived in that time, it was still creepy.

Jenna shoved Adam's shoulder. He laughed and tossed an arm around her waist.

Brody laughed. "So now you know why we never let them set us up."

"But your dad was an only child, right?" I asked. "You don't have any cousins either."

"No, but Papy had a brother with, like, ten kids," Adam said.

I grinned. "With Mémé's sister?"

Jeremy laughed. "No, he didn't marry in the Skoulda bloodline. They're Guardians though. Just powerful telepaths, I think."

"No, they're psychometric too," Brody said. "Still my cousins though. I can't bring myself to do it."

"Psychometric?" Jenna asked. "What the hell is that?"

"The ability to touch an object and know its history," I said. "It's actually a really cool power."

"Pain in the ass power," Jeremy said. "Who was it? Camille that had to lock herself in her room for a year?"

"Yeah, I think," Brody said. "She's the only one I considered it with, ya know?"

"Ew, dude," Jenna said.

"Always had a thing for the crazies," Adam muttered.

"No, she has a different dad. She's not actually a Skoulda," Jeremy said to Jenna.

I raised a brow. "Oh, yeah? Did you consider it too?"

"She's three years younger than you so no." He crinkled his nose a bit. "And she was really weird."

"She was cute though," Brody said.

"Yeah, if you like quiet, greasy creeps," Adam said.

"Well, that's mean," Jenna said.

"She actually got super hot. We're friends on Facebook," Brody said.

I laughed, looking at Brody. "You do still have a girlfriend, don't you?"

"What, I can't find another woman attractive?" Brody asked. "You've got a lady boner for Roland."

My cheeks warmed. "That's not true."

It was totally true.

Roland was a beautiful man. Those muscles, his peppered gray hair, that strong jawline. And his aesthetic. Eternally in a suit, always in freshly ironed slacks, well-maintained facial hair. Throw in his mature way of speaking and any woman into men would drop her panties for him in a second. The fact that he'd drunk my blood a few times, and turned me on as he did, certainly played a part in my attraction.

But I wasn't gonna say that in front of Jeremy. I knew how inferior he made him feel. And I thought my skinny white boy was just as handsome either way.

"Really?" Jenna asked. "'Cause I kinda do."

"Honestly, not even mad," Adam muttered. "He's like a cross between Henry Cavill and Johnny Depp."

Jeremy rolled his eyes and adjusted Milly's diaper bag on his shoulder. "Why do you think Papy was meeting with him anyway? He'll be at the Chamber's Meeting. All of the Monarchs will."

"Probably to see how close he was with you guys," Brody said. "See who he's more likely to be loyal to."

I raised a shoulder. "That's what I'd do."

But I wasn't worried about that. Roland had made it abundantly clear how much he respected me and Jeremy's allegiance. I was sure he'd back us up in there.

Jeremy lowered his voice. "Listen, nobody tell anyone what we've learned from Peterson. Not Mémé, not Papy. Not even a maid. Just tell them Laila and I are the only ones who've interrogated him. You know nothing."

"Well, I don't speak French. So shouldn't be an issue for me," Jenna said.

"Yeah, I wasn't planning on it," Adam said.

A valid point. The Chambers knowing who and what we were in our first life couldn't be a good thing. They were loyal to the Elders, which operated directly beneath the Archangels that had killed us some few thousand years ago. It was best they didn't know who we'd once been.

"Mommy!" Micah called from the steps of the cottage. "Mommy, look! Thewe's fishies!"

I teleported to him with a grin, turning my gaze up to the sky. "I don't see any fishies."

"Not up thewe." He giggled.

"Isn't that where fishies normally hang out? Don't they fly in the sky?" I grinned, still looking at the blue atmosphere above.

He laughed. "That's biwds, silly."

I turned to him. "Where are the fishies then?"

"Down thewe." He pointed to the pond at the edge of the steps. "See? They not in the sky."

"Oh, that's right. Fish live in the water." I playfully tapped myself in the head.

"Even I know that," Micah said.

"'Cause you're the smartest kid in the world." I ran my fingers through his hair with a smile.

CHAPTER EIGHTEEN

JEREMY

Showing Laila, Micah, and Milly around Paris brought back a thousand memories. Dad took us there a lot. Less frequently after Mom died, but we still stopped by every few months. Even if it were just to get some real fresh bread or to grab a crepe from his favorite street vendor.

I didn't like my grandparents, but I did love that city. Everything seemed so much more natural. Most of the women didn't wear pounds of makeup like they did in America.

The street vendors sat at their tents selling produce from their gardens and small farms. Local children practically roamed free along the roads, bumping into Micah with smiles before mumbling a 'pardon' or 'je suis désolé.' People brushed past one another at a far closer distance than Laila was used to, nor comfortable with when it came to the kids.

But I loved it. And I'd missed it. It'd been years since I made a trip.

It felt like home. But it was bittersweet too. Because as we walked those busy, shuffling streets, I heard Lux's voice in my mind. And I couldn't help but wonder how long its beauty would last.

When I stared up at the Eiffel Tower, holding Milly at my hip and gazing at the lights inside, I thought about its history. It took two years to build, starting in 1887 and ending in 1889. Two years. It took two years to build one of the most beautiful pieces of architecture the world had ever seen.

It'd take two minutes for someone as powerful as Laila to destroy. It may take two seconds for a hostile alien enemy.

I was scared. I'd been scared ever since we the flash of white inside that shed turned my hair gray.

As we rode up to the second floor, I pretended not to think about it. Micah nearly had a panic attack at the sounds of the cranks pulling the elevator up the incline.

Laila leaned down and whispered something about how she'd teleport him straight to the ground if something went wrong. He gestured to the people around, asking what would happen to them. She laughed and promised to teleport them to the ground too.

Kai had never been to a human city, not even Pittsburgh that was only an hour or two from our home on a good day. His expression as he gazed out over the balcony was priceless. The city looked smaller from up there, but I don't think he'd ever seen such a vast area flooding with life from a perspective like that.

Laila was too thrilled by the allure of the view to notice my angst. But I'll never forget how beautiful she looked pointing to the boats floating along the river with our daughter on her hip and our son hugging her thigh. It felt like a dream.

As we drove back to the guest house, I stared out the window in deep thought. I started forming a mental list of the places I'd seen that I wanted them to see. I'd taken Laila to plenty of places. But most of them were private coves and silent beaches where we engulfed ourselves in each other. I hadn't taken her to many of the places I knew she wanted to see but hadn't managed to cross off of her list.

The Parthenon, which felt a little arbitrary to visit after realizing we may have been the gods those people built the structures to honor. But still, I'd seen it and she hadn't.

Taj Mahal. I loved Taj Mahal. We needed to visit it soon. Machu Picchu. She visited it with Jenna when we broke up a few years back, but I wanted to see it with her.

Stonehenge and the Galápagos Islands. The Isle of Skye, Lake Tekapo in New Zealand, and the Great Pyramids. The Great Barrier Reef, and the Grand Canyon. And Antelope Canyon, one of Earth's most magnificent works of art that often gets overlooked.

Angel Falls in Venezuela where the highest waterfall in the world was perched. I'd teleported into a small cranny along the wall behind the falls once as a teenager. I always told myself I'd take the girl I was going to marry there, but I'd almost forgotten that it existed in the past few years.

I didn't know how long any of those places would be around. But I knew I wanted to make memories with my wife, our son, and our daughter at each of them in case they weren't there much longer.

"Hey," Laila whispered, rolling her head against my shoulder.

I turned my gaze from the window to meet her green eyes. I smiled. "Hey."

"Whatcha thinking about?" She grinned back.

"All the places I want to take you." I glanced at Micah sleeping against her shoulder and willed my lips into a smile. "All the places they need to see."

"Oh, yeah?" She grinned. "Like where?"

"Like The Great Wall of China. And the Colosseum."

"Eh." Her nose curled. "Both of those places have pretty bloody histories. How about Barcelona? I love all those vibrant colors."

"We'll put it on the list." I smiled and kissed her forehead. I glanced at Milly sleeping in her car seat in the row ahead of us. "We should make sure the kids are up to date on all their vaccines. I could use a few boosters too."

Her fingers grazed Micah's forehead. "We should get a lot of pictures."

I guessed it was on her mind too.

"Yeah," I muttered. "Yeah, we should."

She nuzzled her head closer against my chest. I twisted my arm around her shoulder. I rested my chin on her head and took in the floral smell of her hair. I looked over the kids and twined my fingers between hers.

"After we get the kids in their beds, do you want to go check out that hot tub?" She grinned, looking up to meet my gaze.

I smiled and touched my lips to hers. "You're not too tired?"

"It feels like six o'clock. I won't be able to sleep for hours."

"Hours, huh?" I grinned, grazing the side of her neck.

"Can you guys keep the dirty talk in the bedroom?" Brody grumbled. "You're, like, group cuddling with your kid and talking about fucking."

Laila leaned forward and smacked his arm. "We're talking about jet lag, perv."

"Uh-huh," he muttered. "Can you make sure you leave it running for a while when you're done? That way any of your bodily fluids get evaporated by the heat."

I laughed as the car came to a slow stop. "I'll get her, you get him?"

"Works for me." Laila carefully tucked an arm beneath Micah's knees and disappeared.

I reached into my wallet and passed Brody some cash to hand to the driver. "Merci."

"Merci beaucoup monsieur. Passe une bonne nuit." *Thank you very much, sir. Have a good night.*

"Vous aussi." *You too.* I grasped ahold of Milly's car seat and reappeared in the adjoining bedroom to ours.

Laila situated the blanket up over Micah's chest, tucking his stuffed lion and lamb on the pillow beside him. I shimmied the buckle at Milly's chest, and her arms jerked forward.

Don't risk it, just let her stay in there. She'll be up in an hour or two when she pees anyway, Laila's voice said in my mind.

I clipped the buckle back into place. *Valid point.*

I left the car seat on the ground and tiptoed through the door to our bedroom. As I clicked the door shut, Laila's hands reached for the buttons on my shirt. I laughed, swiveling around and placing my hands at her hips. "Well, you're in a hurry."

"I've drunk a little more than a bottle of wine today, and it's been, like, two months." She reached to her tiptoes and pressed her lips to mine. "The kids are asleep, and we're in Paris. Opportunities like this are few and far between these days."

"Can't disagree with you there." I smiled, finding the button on her jeans. She teleported us to the bed and climbed onto my lap. I lifted her shirt over her shoulders, and she undid the buttons at my chest. I rolled over her, yanking her jeans down her legs as she unbuckled the belt at my hips.

And the door swung open.

"Hey, Papy wanted—" Chris began. "Oh, shit. Sorry." The door clunked back into place. Laila clunked her head against the pillow. I closed my eyes and plopped my head to her bare chest. Chris said, "Didn't mean to kill your mood. But Papy wants to talk to you, Jeremy. He said it won't be long."

"It can't wait, like half an hour?" I called.

"I think he wants to go to bed. And he saw your car pull up so... Yeah, probably not."

A deep sigh escaped my nose.

"Go ahead," Laila said. "I'll get Mills changed and back to bed."

I kissed her again. "Just don't fall asleep on me."

"I'm wide awake." She smiled. "I told you. I'll be up for hours."

"There he is." Papy's hands rested on the stone banister overlooking the vineyard from the top of the terrace. A fat cigar hung from his lips. His fingers wrapped around a glass of red wine. The nearly empty bottle sat beside another sparkling stemware on the barrier. "How was your trip to the city?"

"Wonderful." I smiled, ascending the stairs. "As always."

"First time that wife of yours has seen your hometown, isn't it?" He clipped the end of another cigar, passing it to me when I got close enough.

"First time she's gotten a good tour. I wouldn't really call it my hometown. More like a pleasant past time." I forced a smile as he handed me a lighter. "Micah really liked it though."

"Well, he's got a lot of us in him." He sipped his wine. "Playing any instruments yet?"

"Little bit of guitar. He hasn't had much time to practice, but we'll get there." I lit the cigar and leaned against the banister. "He really likes the sax though."

He chuckled and poured the last bit of wine into the second glass. "So did Jèan."

That he did. Dad loved music of all different kinds from all around the world. I remembered listening to jazz with him in the mornings on the way to school. He was a good musician too, but his calling had always been strings. Maybe I'd inherited that from him too.

I smiled. "Never very good at it though."

"All that smoking, how could he be?" He passed it to me.

I cleared my throat. "I'm alright, thanks."

"Suit yourself." He tilted his head back and chugged. He sipped from his other glass. He looked out over the fields and then back to me. "You've been sober then?"

Not a conversation I wanted to have, so I went the quicker route. "Oui."

He smiled. "Good for you. Really. You've built a nice little life for yourself."

His attitude was so much different than I'd anticipated it'd be. He was calm. Smirking—the closest his grumpy face could get to a smile. I knew how he felt about my marriage and family; he'd made it incredibly clear. But now, he was being... almost kind.

I cleared my throat. "So what's this about, Papy?"

He chuckled. "We both know what this is about."

Ah. Peterson.

"We don't know much."

He met my gaze, wiping wine from his lip. "What do you know?"

I raised a shoulder. "He's from the future. He knows what's coming. But he won't tell us what it looks like or what we need to fight it."

"What is it?" he asked. "What's coming?"

I let out a slow breath and chewed my lip. "They call themselves Wormwood."

"As in, the biblical Wormwood?" I nodded, and his brows furrowed. "Well, what is it?"

"We don't know. We've tried torturing it out of Peterson, but he won't budge. He says that we need to learn it in our own time."

He made a face. "How do you know they're coming then?"

"Besides the time traveler in my basement? The prophecy of a dead Witch."

I lied. I knew it was coming because of my personal conversation with the god he worshipped. But that story was far too complicated to divulge, even if he would believe it.

"Nastya La Fay," Papy said. I nodded, and he released a slow breath. "Her father. Thomas, he'll be at the meeting tomorrow."

"I assumed. Moriah's going to be there."

"The youngest of the sisters, no?" I nodded, and he said, "She helped you bring them home."

"She did. More than once."

He took a slow sip from his glass as he looked out over the field. The wind dusted ashy hair into his blue eyes. For the first time in my life, I saw something behind them I didn't realize he could feel. Fear.

"Thomas isn't pleased about the death of his daughter, Jeremy."

I huffed. "Well, I don't really give a damn."

"If I were married to your wife, neither would I. But you should know to use caution. Men like Thomas La Fay are ruthless."

Thomas La Fay was a rich old bastard with a big mouth. Just like everyone else on the Chamber. He could say some shit, he could start some shit, but I didn't care. His daughter slit her own throat, and that wasn't my problem.

"So are we," I said. "And no one's taking anyone in our family down. If Laila's name doesn't scare them off, she can terrify them pretty quick."

"Witches have ways."

"And we've got a better one."

Papy pulled in a slow drag off of the cigar. After a moment, he blew it out in a slow puff. "For your sake, I hope you don't need to." Silence crept up for a moment or two. He turned to meet my gaze. "Do you know why your son mattered so much to this man?"

"Not really. Nastya said in a letter to her sister that it had something to do with the bond Laila and I share." Not a lie. Not the whole truth, but not a lie.

He arched a brow. "That's true then."

"It is." I turned my head to the side a bit. "I was sure that news made it here by now."

"It had. But I suppose I wanted to hear it from the source." I gave an awkward nod. His head tilted. "How can you be sure?"

I raised my hand, watching the gray and blue light slide from my skin. The luminance faded and bright orange flames appeared in my palm. He clutched his chest and took a quick step backward. "I can access her abilities. Can't use them as well as she can, but" —I closed my palm to a fist— "I think that serves as proof."

"Does it affect her?" he asked. "When you do that?"

"Does it drain her, you mean?" He nodded, and I shook my head. "Not at all."

"Fascinating," he murmured.

"Yeah. Yeah, I'm very grateful for it."

He grew quiet once more. He took another hit of the cigar and looked between my eyes. "That's the only reason you know of that made your son so important?"

"To my knowledge."

"Well, you can set the record straight tomorrow then. Rumor has it that your son's sacrifice would have brought on the end of the world. But you did prevent the sacrifice, didn't you?"

"Yeah. You saw him, he's here."

He looked over me with some type of all-knowing gaze. He knew the truth already. But I don't think he wanted me to admit it aloud either. "Of course. But many leaders have pointed out signs. The Witches, especially. Astrologically speaking, it looks like a new cycle is beginning. That could mean many things. But most fear that the end of this one is the end to all things."

"The man we have tied up in the basement who came from at least fifty years in the future says otherwise."

"And what does he say then, Jeremy?"

"That we have time."

Although that was true when I said it, it wasn't so for the rest of the world.

CHAPTER NINETEEN

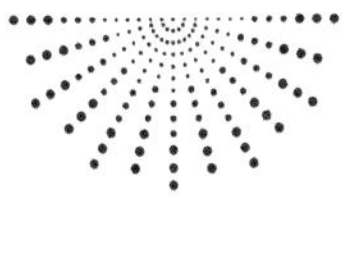

LAILA

Much to my surprise, Milly fell right back to sleep after I changed her diaper and fed her a bottle. I lay her back down. I checked the baby monitor, adjusting the angle to see both Milly in the crib and Micah on the bed.

I tiptoed back to our room and plopped onto the bed. I looked around, taking in the homey feel of the cottage. For a guest home, it was still pretty big. But a comfortable kind of big, like our house. Our rooms were on the third floor. It was more like a refurbished attic than an actual floor, but I liked it. The steeped cedar ceilings felt cozy. The green walls reminded me of the cool, sage color we covered in Micah's old nursery. The one he never got to live in.

I pushed that thought from my mind as I looked at the clock. Twelve-thirty. We weren't checking out the hot tub. Regardless, I could use a bath. I grabbed my toiletry bag, nightie, and a towel from my bag.

I'd used the bathroom downstairs earlier; I hadn't even noted the one off of our room until Jeremy mentioned it. But as I opened the door, I got one of those fuzzy feelings in my stomach. It just looked so quaint. Pretty, black and white checkered tiles lined the floors. A cute white pedestal sink stood on the right. An intricate, antique framed mirror hung on the yellow wall above it. The clawfoot tub stood a foot or two from a large window on the left that overlooked the French countryside.

After rinsing down the cobwebs, I poured some body wash into the warm water and climbed inside. My body seemed to meld into that bathtub. I always loved claw foot tubs. We'd considered putting one in our master bathroom when we built the house. We decided against it though, figuring it wouldn't be the safest option for the kids.

A few minutes after the grandfather clock rang downstairs, I saw Jeremy making his way up the cottage steps. I went on with my bath, relaxing in the water and breathing in the smell of lavender.

I heard him call my name in the room, and I softly yelled, "In here."

He pushed open the bathroom door with a smile. "So no hot tub?"

I extended my arms around the cool ceramic. "Well, this is a tub. And the water's pretty hot."

Jeremy smiled. "Think we can fit? Might be a little tight."

I fought the urge to say 'that's what she said' and kill the mood.

"That's okay." I grinned.

Jeremy laughed quietly. He kneeled beside me and touched his lips to mine. "Sorry I took so long. Papy won't shut up when he's drunk."

"It's alright. The kids are still asleep." I reached for the buttons on his shirt. "And we both know that if we wait for the mood to build up, Milly's going to wake up all of three seconds before one of us is about to come. So chop-chop."

He laughed, unbuckling his pants as I unbuttoned his shirt.

***

When we finished up in the bathroom, we kindled some flames in the small fireplace a few feet from the foot of the bed and curled up beneath the blankets. The smell of smoke touched my nose, and the crackle of the fire made me bubble with comfort. Rain drizzled quietly outside the window accompanied by an occasional flash of lightning in the distance. My head rested against his chest, counting the beats of his calm heart.

"Ya know what Micah said about the cheeses the maids left out in the kitchen?" I asked, rolling my head up to meet his gaze.

He twirled my wet hair between his fingertips and smiled. "No, what?"

"Apparently, it smells like Uncle Wyatt."

He laughed, and then silence set in for a moment. His smile fell, and his face grew a bit more serious. "Ya know, I was thinking about something on my walk back here."

"What's that?"

"Well, right now, no one knows the truth about what I am. What I did. What we did." He paused. "Micah's sacrifice wasn't the final seal. Bringing him back was the final seal."

I thought hard for a second. "His sacrifice, it'd buy us a few hundred years. That's what Lux told you."

He paused. "If everyone else knew that... In theory, they might think that completing the sacrifice would prevent what's coming."

"It very well might," I muttered.

But that wasn't an option.

Nope.

I didn't care. I would never, *ever* sacrifice my child. Not in a million years. No one would ever hurt that sweet, innocent little boy. Even if it could save the world. Or buy it a few hundred years.

"Yeah. Yeah, it could." He clenched his jaw. His head shook. "We can't let anyone find that out."

"We better talk to everyone in the morning," I said. "Make sure everyone's on the same page."

"I talked to Chris earlier. Anyone asks him what happened that day, he's telling them the truth. That bitch was in and out of his head until she killed herself. Then we got him back to the house and went back to destroy the evidence before the police got to it."

I gave a slow nod. "Good. Good. The last thing we need is to have to kill off our own people. We need alliances."

"It's not like it'd make much of a difference anyway. This is coming one way or another. Whether it be in a year or two hundred, they're coming back. And honestly, Peterson's right. It's best it happens in a time when we have someone as strong as you to fight it."

"And you." A crack of lightning brightened the room as I swept my fingertip along his jaw. "We should work on mastering each other's abilities."

"Not a bad idea. Hannah's been pretty insistent on me learning the ropes with necromancy."

"Well, when we get home, we can study together. And then we'll work on you learning my Fae abilities. They come a little easier than the Angel ones."

The door to the adjoining room creaked open. Micah's quiet little voice said, "Mommy?"

I sat up with a smile. He stood in the doorway with his stuffed lion tucked beneath his armpit. His fist rubbed against his eyes.

"Yeah, baby?" I asked.

"I... I think Milly's kind of scawed. Maybe me and hew should come in hewe with you."

I chuckled.

"Milly's scared?" Jeremy asked with a smile, sitting up to see him. "Isn't Milly sleeping?"

I smacked his chest and smiled at Micah. "Come on and lay down, baby."

Micah walked across the room and climbed up into the bed. He crawled between Jeremy and me. He laid his head against my chest facing Jeremy.

"It's okay to be scared, kiddo," he said.

Micah tucked my palm against his chest. "I's not scawed."

Jeremy smiled and pushed hair from his face. "Well, it'd be okay if you were. You're somewhere you've never been before. I'd be scared too."

"I's not."

He laughed. "Alright."

The lightning roared outside, and he jumped. "It's just a little rain. Just close your eyes, I've got you."

He reached out for Jeremy's hand. "Daddy?"

"Yeah, buddy?"

"Can you sing?"

A chuckle left his smiling lips. He took Micah's palm and sang a song we wrote together a few years prior. I couldn't remember the lyrics if I tried, but I remember how fast the melody sent me and Micah to sleep.

I'll never forget how safe the sound of his voice made me feel either. It must've done the same for Micah because his hand wrapped around the stuffed lamb released so effortlessly. But my arms tightened at his waist.

We'd do anything we had to to keep our baby safe. We'd fought for him. We'd killed for him. We'd nearly died for him.

And we'd do it again.

To halt the apocalypse or not, no one was going to lay a hand on my son.

CHAPTER TWENTY

JEREMY

"*Trois omelettes au fromage et une autre tasse de café quand vous avez un moment s'il vous plait,*" *Three cheese omelets and another cup of coffee when you have a moment please,* I said to the server as I handed him our menus.

"Bien sûr." *Of course.*

"How do you talk like that?" Micah asked.

"In French?" He nodded, and I chuckled. "Well, my mom and dad spoke French a lot. So I learned to speak both at the same time."

"Do you think I'll be able to say it that good too?" he asked.

"Si vous essayez vraiment fort."

"I don't know what that means."

I smiled. "If you try really hard."

He smiled back.

I leaned back in the iron chair and took a look over the bustling Paris street. The smell of morning bread filled my lungs. Warm sun shined against my skin, chilled by the cool spring breeze. Cars honked in the distance.

It felt so good. I was in the most beautiful city in the world with the most beautiful people in mine. My wife sat beside me; long dark hair tucked into a neat ponytail at the back of her head. Milly was in her stroller next to her, pigtails flying in the wind. And Micah sat to my right sipping his cup of orange juice with a joyous smile.

Damn. If I'd have known I'd be living this moment two years ago when I was burned out on pills, I'd have stopped in an instant. Life was finally how I wanted it to be.

"So where are we going when we leave here?" Laila asked, spooning Milly a scoop of yogurt. "I always wanted to see Notre Dame. Guess that's not an option anymore."

"It's supposed to be done for the Olympics in 2024," I said. "We can come to see it then."

"Yeah, but it won't be the original," she said. "I don't even know what art was saved and what's ruined. That's the saddest part, I think. Losing all that history."

"Yeah. Yeah, did you know it took almost two hundred years to build?"

"And a day to burn," she muttered. Ironically, the same thing I'd thought about the Eiffel Tower the day before. "But you know, all that money pledged to rebuild it kind of pisses me off. I can see spending money to save history but that much? When there are millions of people worldwide still recovering from a pandemic?"

I took a sip from my coffee. "Yeah, that's true. That money was pledged before COVID hit though."

She shook her head. "Regardless. It could be put to better use."

"No, I agree. When you rebuild something that old, it kind of removes the history. It's like creating a duplicate. You might as well just take a virtual tour."

In my eyes, as long as the history was saved, the artifacts themselves didn't matter that much. We knew exactly what every item in that building looked like. We could rebuild it. What sucked was when entire cultures got washed away. Like that Native Americans prior to the English invasion and the Irish before the Norman invasion. That was far more painful than some lost paintings of naked babies.

"I don't like these." Micah crinkled his nose at the blackberries in the cup before him.

I grabbed one and popped it into my mouth. "Who doesn't like blackberries?"

"They's souw," he said.

As I chomped, the bitter flavor exploded on my tongue. My nose curled too, but I reached for my water. "They are a little sour."

"You sure don't like a lot of fruits and vegetables for choosing to be a vegetarian, kid." Laila smiled. "You like the strawberries though, right?"

"They's good."

"How about the Luxembourg Gardens?" I turned back to Laila. "We'd have enough time to see it before the meeting."

"Ooh, yeah. That's a good idea," Laila said.

"Who awe you meeting?" Micah looked at Laila. "Am I meeting anyone else?"

"No, you're going to stay with Uncle Chris, Uncle Adam, and Aunt Jenna," Laila said.

"Well, who awe you meeting then?" He looked at her and then at me. "Is something wong?"

I smiled. "No, everything's fine, buddy."

"Pwomise?"

"I promise. Now eat those strawberries before Mommy takes them all." She smiled and tossed another slice into her mouth.

Micah said, "Hey!"

"I told ya, man. She'll eat them all if you don't get to them first."

He slid the cup closer to him, he ate another.

I visited the Luxembourg Gardens once as a child, but I didn't really remember it. That made seeing it with the three of them more thrilling.

We got amazing pictures that day. Though old and faded now, they still hang throughout our home.

Micah took one of Laila and I kissing Milly's cheeks on a bench in front of a row of pretty pink flowers. I took one of the three of them, then one with each, and she did the same. The selfies with all four of us came out pretty bad, but we kept them. We kept way more than any normal person would have wanted. But I can't say it wasn't necessary.

Then we started back to Mémé and Papy's. On the way, we stopped in their village and bought a bunch of random shit. Micah begged for a little trinket box he'd end up using well into his adulthood. Laila got a bunch of plants she couldn't find at the department store back home she planned to add to her garden. We found a handmade blanket for Milly we'd later end up throwing out because it irritated her skin.

Both kids fell asleep on the way back. When we arrived, we lay them on the couch with Chris, Adam, and Jenna. Then we walked to the mansion for the meeting we'd both been dreading for weeks.

"You double-checked with everyone this morning, right?" Laila asked quietly as we walked down the cobblestone path. "Everyone knows what to say?"

"Everyone's on the same page. As far as they all know, we prevented the sacrifice." I tucked an arm around her waist and kissed her forehead.

She took in a deep breath and gave a fast nod. "There's going to be telepaths here. Make sure you keep your guard up."

"It always is."

CHAPTER TWENTY-ONE

LAILA

Slow, calculated breaths drew into my lungs as I looked at the men and women shuffling through the grand French doors. A lot of the faces weren't only familiar, but friends.

Janis and Elijah Wilson, Guardian-Vampire hybrids known for taking in orphaned supernaturals in our community. Roland Allard, the North American Monarch. Not to mention the other six Monarchs we'd formed something of a bond with when making treaties the year prior. Audrey Cott, the leader of a nest of Vampires in a central section of the United States—another person I'd grown to call a friend. Moriah La Fay, of course. Dayo, a high priestess from Africa with a lot of pull in this community that Helena introduced us to.

There were a few others we knew. But it was still about a fifty-fifty split of allies and uncertainty.

When the meeting came to a start, Papy stood before the foot of the table and made a pleasant toast I didn't understand. But I certainly raised my glass and took a sip. I'd need a whole bottle by the time it was over.

After the toast, Papy spoke again in French. I caught a word here or there, but not enough to make sense of.

"It may help if we speak in a language that we all understand,"

Jeremy said beside me. "As far as I know, everyone here speaks English. Not everyone speaks French. If we're looking to discuss our mutual knowledge, it doesn't make much sense to use a language that's gibberish to a number of the guests."

Papy glanced at me and huffed. "I said that a lot has been going on in the world lately, and it's about time we all share what we know."

I dipped my head in a nod.

"So let's address the elephant in the room then," an older man beside Moriah said. His cold blue eyes cut deep into mine. Heavy wrinkles eroded his pale cheeks. He wore a suit two sizes too tight for his chubby frame. Twinkles from the chandelier above reflected against his shiny bald head. "What happened to this Robert Peterson?"

"A lot of suffering." I sipped my wine. "But do you really care about what happened to him? Or do you want to know what we've learned from him?"

"Both." He stared me down. "And while we're on the subject, why don't you share what you did to my daughter?"

"Your daughter?" I raised a brow. I looked at Moriah beside him. "Oh. Nastya."

"Anastasia," he said. "I believe you were the last person to see her alive."

"We both were, actually," Jeremy said.

"Well?" he asked. "What did you do?"

I let out a huff that turned to a scoff. "I burned her body after she stabbed herself in the throat."

"My daughter was many things but suicidal was not one of them," he snapped.

"I didn't think so either, but that's what happened," I said.

He leaned forward, tie bunching up in his thick neck. "And I'm supposed to take your word?"

"Would you like to see my memory of your daughter ending her life, Thomas?" Jeremy asked. "Because if you really want to see it, I'll show you. But once you see something like that, it'll replay in your mind every day until you die."

"Yes, I would. I would like to see it."

Jeremy arched a brow, shaking his head. "If you say so." The man's eyes flicked shut. The twenty or so gazes around the room studied his face, waiting for the reaction. When it came, he jumped, and his eyes flung open.

I stopped it right before the light. Don't worry, Jeremy's voice said into my mind.

He panted hard, looking at me and Jeremy with flaring nostrils. "How did the others live?"

"We healed them," Jeremy said.

"You aren't Fae," a woman a few seats down said.

"No, but my par animo is."

"That's a myth," a voice further down chimed in.

"So is your god." Jeremy's head turned to her. "But that doesn't mean he isn't real."

"I'll believe it when I see it," the woman said.

Jeremy lifted his sleeve and brought a bright orange flame to his palm. He looked at me. I extended my hand. Bright bursts of blue electricity swirled from my skin. Gasps and hushed chatter started throughout the room.

I closed my hand and looked between the well-dressed people around the table. "Not that we owe you proof. That's not why we're all here, is it? To debate mine and my husband's love life?"

"I agree, this is irrelevant," a man at the end of the table said.

"You saved them, and you let my daughter die," Thomas said. "Not very heroic of you."

Wasn't sure that what I was about to say would form me any friendships, but it needed said. I owed that man nothing. His daughter was my villain. She deserved far worse than she'd gotten.

"I never claimed to be a hero," I said. "And even if I was, Nastya deserved to die. She helped that man hold my son and almost a thousand others captive for more than a decade. I just wish someone would've gotten to her sooner because it would've saved thousands of people from years of pain that you can't even imagine. You can hate me all you want. I don't give a shit. She made her bed—"

"She was my daughter—"

"Well, you raised a shitty person." I felt my eyes glow in their sockets as I looked between his pale-blue glare. "Your daughter held my two-year-old to a table while that monster cut him open and jammed rocks into his body. Don't expect me to feel guilty for her death. I didn't kill her. She chose this. She did it, not me. So take it up with her in the next life."

His jaw clenched, and his nostrils flared. I watched his hand clench to a fist atop the white tablecloth.

A voice spoke at the end of the table near Papy.

"Let's talk about what really matters then, shall we?" the older man searched for my gaze. I recognized him. Jeremy was tagged in photos with him on Facebook from his teenage years. With Olivia at his side. Eric Ainsworth, her father. "The two of you, you're connected to the apocalypse somehow."

"It seems like it," Jeremy said.

"What do you know about it then?" he asked. "Is it true? Is the end truly coming?"

"That's what we've been told," I said. "The man responsible for all the kidnappings, the man we have in our custody. He claims to be from the future. He says it's coming. But he refers to it as the beginning of a new world. I believe he's from a time pretty distant in the future. When whatever's coming has already passed."

His face screwed up in confusion. "And what does this have to do with you?"

"He said that it was to build an army. An army I'm supposed to lead, apparently."

"You?" Eric chuckled, arching a brow.

"Yeah, me," I said. "You asked what Peterson said and that's it. What—do you want me to lie?"

He laughed still, leaning in the high back antique chair. "No. No, I'm sorry. That just seems a little silly to me."

"Oh yeah? Why's that?" My head tilted.

"You're, what? Twenty?"

I had to wonder, was it really about my age though? Or did it have something to do with the fact that I didn't have a cock dangling between my legs?

"Age has little to do with destiny and leadership, Eric," Roland said. "Joan of Arc was thirteen when she led the French Army for the first time. Alexander the Great took entire countries before he made it to his twenties. Mozart wrote his first symphony at eight."

"I'm twenty-four." I looked between Eric's eyes. "Yes, I am young. But considering my bond with my husband, whether everyone here believes that or not, our souls are probably older than everyone in this room combined. And no, I've never fought a war. Not a formal one with titles and swords and armor. But I've been fighting a war since 2019 when I was kidnapped. And a month and a half ago, I ended it. After saving over seven hundred lives, taking out at least five hundred soldiers single-handedly, and without a single casualty on our end. So yes, sir. I am young. And no, I didn't ask for an army. But I have one. And I have the power to fight a war. Whether I'm the one you would have chosen or not, these are the cards in front of us."

"Let me ask you something there, Laila. Can I call you Laila?" Thomas asked.

I crossed my arms against my chest. "That's my name. So yeah, that'd make the most sense."

A few quiet laughs sounded throughout the room.

He smiled and sipped his wine. "Tell me, Laila. Why did it take longer for your son and brother-in-law to die than my daughter? I saw it. They all stabbed themselves at the same time."

I knew what he was getting at. But I retained my poker face. I'd be damned before I admitted that Jeremy was a necromancer. That was practically a death sentence in this world, and I wanted no part in a battle for his life at this moment.

"I'm not a doctor, I couldn't tell you."

"Huh." He narrowed his eyes and leaned forward in his seat. "Because, see, I've heard rumors. Rumors about you, and you." He glanced at Jeremy. "That whole family of yours, really. I've heard stories about how close you've come to death oh-so-many times. I can't help but wonder how that is. How you've been stabbed through the heart and lived to tell the tale."

"Well, having a healer on hand can take care of things like that pretty quick."

"Sure. Sure, maybe." He looked over me. He glanced at Jeremy. "But maybe it's even broader than that."

"What are you suggesting, Thomas?" Papy said.

He tilted his head in that direction but kept his gaze on my husband. "You know what I'm suggesting, Raphael."

"Your daughter was the one practicing black magic, don't look to my kin to cast your blame."

"What are you getting at, Thomas?" Eric said. "You aren't implying that these two have ties to necromancy, are you?"

"That's exactly what I'm suggesting," Thomas said.

Jeremy laughed. "That's ridiculous."

"Is it? Is it really?" His gaze narrowed. "Because I can't see a child surviving a wound like that. Not one so weak and frail, especially."

"And what is it that you think happened then?" I asked.

"I think that the sacrifice was completed," Thomas said. "I think they all died, and you brought back your son and brother and left my daughter to die."

"I already told you, she killed—"

"Yes, but then you let her remain dead!" His piercing eyes darted between Jeremy's. "You hold the key to the other side, don't you?"

"I have no idea what you're talking about," Jeremy said.

"You're a liar." Spit flew from Thomas's curling lips.

"You will not talk to my grandson that way—"

"The grandson you call a rogue." He glared at Papy and spun back to Jeremy. "Just admit it. I know it's so; just say it."

"You don't know what you're talking about—"

Thomas chanting an incantation cut him off. Jeremy started to cough. Blood rolled from the corners of his eyes and nostrils.

I raised my hand and grasped ahold of the wind in his lungs. My eyes glowed, watching him struggle to pull in a air. The room fell silent, watching me keep that man from breath without even standing from my chair. I looked to Jeremy. "Are you okay?"

He lifted his napkin to his nose. "Yeah, I'm good."

I released my hold on Thomas. He took in a long, heaving gasp. I studied him carefully as his breaths returned. Slow, uneven pants left his nose as we stared each other down. Everyone in the room watched us, waiting for the retaliation one of us was sure to initiate.

But he disappeared.

I turned to Jeremy.

Moriah's fast, anxious voice cut through the silence.

"Where is your son, Laila?"

I shot my head around to meet her worried gaze. "I'll fucking kill him."

Jeremy took my hand, and we teleported.

CHAPTER TWENTY-TWO

JEREMY

When we landed in the living room of the guest house, Thomas stood beside the couch chanting fast. Chris held his hands around his head, letting out a banshee-like cry. Micah lay crying on the ground with blood pouring from his eyes and nostrils. Milly squealed in the bouncer, reaching for me as blood rolled from her tear ducts.

Blood started to pour from my eyes too, but I didn't even feel it. All I felt was fury burning through my body like fire to gasoline.

I teleported behind him and placed my arm around his neck in a chokehold. He gasped. I ripped him back and teleported to the field outside the window.

Honestly, I can't say what I did to him when we got there because I don't remember it. Everything went red. I heard him gasping and moaning, then beginning another incantation. I felt the ache in my fists as I cracked them into his body, hearing only his groans once more.

And I just kept going. I don't know how many times I hit him. He tried to fight, back but he was in his seventies and at least and half my size. He stood no chance. Especially when I felt my hands erupt in flames.

After a while, he stopped attempting to fight back. Only then did I start to see without the red haze of rage. His hands outstretched beside his head in surrender, begging me to stop.

I did, I stopped hitting him. I kneeled above him, staring down at the blood that covered his face. But I wasn't done. I couldn't be. I had to make a point. That's what he was trying to do. Threaten our family in front of the Chambers to make it clear that he outranked us. He wouldn't kill my kids; he thought I could bring them back. But he thought that hurting them would assert his superiority over us.

He wanted to prove a point, and so did I.

I grabbed ahold of him by his shirt and teleported above a volcano in Hawaii I visited a few years back with Laila. I watched the lava beneath us as we started plummeting toward it. I teleported a few dozen yards above him. His arms flailed out for me, eyes wide in fear as a scream left his lips.

I teleported to him again, just a few yards before he hit the molten lava. I grasped ahold of him and teleported to another spot. A cliffside, the one Laila and I jumped from when we were running from his daughter. He fell to the grass vomiting. I grasped his shirt again and teleported to the air above the water. I let go.

His arms reached into the air around him, legs kicking as he quickly fell to the icy water. I teleported to the bubbles in the waves, grasping ahold of his thrashing body. We reappeared in the sand just outside the water. Not far from the place where Laila woke up in the sand a year or so prior.

Thomas vomited again, spitting water to the sand. He struggled deep breaths into his lungs. I kneeled beside him and wrapped my hand around his throat.

"I didn't kill your piece of shit fucking daughter, but I wish I did. I wish I could turn back time and torture that cunt just like she tortured my son. Like she tortured my wife. Like she tortured almost every person in our god damned world."

He grasped for my hand at his throat as I stared between his eyes.

"I'm glad that bitch is dead. The world's a better place for it. But I swear to fucking god, you come near my children again, and I will do worse things to you than you can imagine. You think this was scary? Falling into the ocean? My hand around your throat?" I squeezed tighter, and his eyes bulged.

"This is nothing. Cast on my kid or wife or brother or sister one more fucking time, and I swear on my mother's grave that you will never see the light of day again. I don't care who you are or how much power you think you have. Try me again, Thomas. Fucking try, and I will end you."

His terrified eyes jerked between mine, still grasping at my hand on his throat.

Good. He should be scared.

I'd killed for my kid plenty of times. I'd do it again in a blink.

Finally, I released his throat. I clenched his shirt and yanked him to his feet. I teleported back to the dining hall where it'd begun only a minute or two before.

The room echoed with gasps as I threw Thomas to the ground. I wiped salty water from my face, pushing my sopping hair behind my ear. I looked between the terrified faces.

"Let me make something abundantly clear to all of you." I didn't realize my voice got as deep as it did in that moment. "Regardless of how or why this is happening, it's fucking happening. I don't know when. I don't know how. None of us do. But the world we know is coming to an end. We don't know what the Council or the Elders want, we don't know what side they're on, but they'll come to you to enforce whatever side of the war they're fighting for.

"As for me and my family, we're going to fight like hell to save this world. The people, the animals, the planet itself, every race known to Earth. That's who we're fighting for. We won't be taking blind orders from the Elders or the Angels. We're going to do what we think needs done to save the world our kinds have called home for as long as history has been recorded.

"Aside from the man in our custody pending execution, we don't want anyone to die. We don't have time to fight each other. We don't have time to give a shit about petty vendettas.

"Yes, Nastya La Fay is dead. By her own hand, but it would've been mine if I had the chance. I'll be the first to admit that. Because no person, absolutely no one, deserves to live after holding a thousand innocent people hostage. I don't care how important or powerful you are. Your title and bloodline mean nothing if you accept and assist in the kidnapping, torture, and rape of innocent fucking people. And anyone who disagrees with me is more than welcome to stand here and debate it, but I think we all have a pretty good understanding that those things should and will not be fucking tolerated."

A few people nodded, some even clapped.

"My wife and I have no enemies. But anyone who threatens my children is committing suicide. I lost my son once and I refuse to go through that again.

"You all know what my wife and I are capable of. We aren't cruel, we don't enjoy violence, but we do what we fucking have to. I could have killed Thomas just now, but I didn't because I don't want to fight the people I plan to call allies. But back me into a corner, threaten my family, and I will do what I have to. And that's not a threat, it's a fucking promise."

The room remained quiet as the guests stared over me. A grin lifted Roland's lips as he rocked back in his chair. He took a long gulp from his wine and stood. "The North American and Central French packs stand behind the Callidy Skoulda alliance. We're on your side, Jeremy. Fuck the Elders, and fuck you, Thomas. Attacking a toddler. Are you no better than that daughter who caused all of this in the first place?"

Moriah sat beside Thomas on the floor wiping his bloody cheek with a napkin. He was barely conscious enough to open his eyes.

Audrey stood and met my gaze. "You know that our kind stands behind you, love. Not only the ones back home but worldwide, to my knowledge. We may have a few straggling nomads that don't, but the masses know who their allies are. We stand with you."

"We do." Janis met my gaze with a smile. "We stand with you. We'd rather save the world than our alliance to the Council."

I gave a civil nod as Dayo, a high priestess of a large coven that spanned Africa, stood. "Every one of my Witches stands behind you and your wife. We hold no respect for" —she glanced at Thomas and crinkled her nose— "people who support the torture and murder of children. We'd be Christians if we did."

A quiet laugh left me.

Before I knew it, every leader around that room stood and pledged their allegiance to Laila and me. Although, they weren't really pledging themselves to us. They pledged themselves to their planet, to their people, and to their home.

We didn't expect them to pledge their lives to us. That's not what we wanted. We didn't expect blind obedience. We just needed to be certain we were all on the same page.

Fuck the Elders. Fuck the hierarchies of barking Angels. Fuck anything that wasn't pure intent to save the god damned planet.

We all had one common enemy. We needed to unite to fight it.

CHAPTER TWENTY-THREE

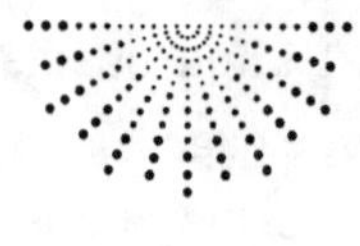

LAILA

"What the fuck was that?" Chris yelled as I clutched Micah into my arms. He sobbed uncontrollably, to the point where he could barely bring a breath into his lungs.

Milly screamed in the bouncer. I teleported her into my arms. I rocked back and forth with Micah on my left and Milly on my right. I shifted back and forth, murmuring *shh*, over their cries. But somehow, my hammering heart was louder than their weeps.

"What just happened?" Brody rushed into the living room. He gasped at the sight of blood on our faces.

"Mommy." Micah made out between gasping cries. "I-I-I's sc-c—"

"I know. I know, it's okay, baby. I'm right here; nobody's going to hurt you. It's okay." I ran my fingertips through his hair and kept rocking back and forth. "It's okay."

"What the fuck just happened, Laila?" Chris said.

I met his gaze. "Thomas La Fay."

A deep breath drew into his lungs. His nostrils flared. He tightened his jaw. "I'll kill him."

Aches started at my fists and soared up my arms. "Jeremy's got it."

"I-I-I," Micah began, struggling to finish his sentence through his sobs. "I want to-to go h-h-ho-ome."

"Okay, baby." I nodded against the top of his head. "Okay, baby, we'll go home."

He pushed his head further into my chest, still unable to stop his cries. Milly's balled fist rubbed against her watery, bloody eyes, smearing red down her cheeks.

I looked down at my crying children covered in their blood, and a terrible realization washed over me.

So long as we lived in this world, there was no safe place for my babies outside of our home. Their parents were two of the most powerful people on the planet. There would always be a target on their backs.

After I got Micah and Milly to stop crying, I took them to the bathtub to wash off the blood. Micah remained unusually quiet. Traumatized. I tried to hold a smile and tell him everything was okay, but I don't think he believed me. Not that I blamed him. I didn't believe me either.

I cleaned myself up. I wiped the blood from my cheeks, rinsed my hair, and changed my clothes. Micah curled against my chest and fell asleep on the couch as I waited for Jeremy to return. I manipulated his and Milly's minds to forget the whole ordeal, convincing him he played too hard with his uncle before falling into a much-needed nap.

When Jeremy walked in the front door, he met my gaze.

"We're going home," I stated.

He gave a gentle nod. "I'll pack the bags. I told Papy I'd meet with him in a couple of hours though. I can make a quick trip back after we get the kids settled in."

"What happened after I left?" I asked.

"I beat the fuck out of Thomas." He extended his swollen forearm for me to heal. I raised my palm from Milly's chest and covered his hand. He grimaced as the swelling went down and the small cuts molded shut. "I thought about killing him. I would have. But that'd open a can of worms we don't have the energy to deal with. So I took him back to the meeting and gave a little impromptu speech. Everyone agreed with me. Everyone pledged their groups to our cause. Thomas basically committed social suicide. But no one raised any brows about the necromancy stuff, so I guess that's good." He slid his hand over Milly's cheek from behind the couch. "Are they alright?"

"They're okay. It took them almost the whole time you were gone to stop crying. But they're alright. Micah was terrified. Milly was more confused than anything. I took the memories from them."

Another slow breath left his lips. He leaned down and kissed Micah's head. As he straightened back up, he ran a hand through his hair. "Maybe Celena and Wyatt can watch the kids when I go to meet with Papy. That way you could be there—"

"I'm not leaving my kids with anyone."

His head tilted. "Not even at the house?"

"That fucker's in the basement. If he wanted to, he could climb right out and come to the house and—" I stopped. "I'm staying with them. You can let me know what he said when you get back."

His head lifted in a nod. He touched his lips to my forehead. "Okay, baby. I'll go get cleaned up and pack the bags. You can head back now."

"No. He'll be confused if he wakes up at the house. We'll wait until they're up."

"That works." Jeremy started up the steps.

My phone buzzed on the table. Moriah.

I slid the green bar and raised it to my ear. "He's lucky Jeremy got him out of here."

She was quiet for a second. She cleared her throat. "Yes, he is."

"Did you know he was going to do that shit?" I snapped. "Did you know he was going to—"

"Of course not, Laila. You know I would've told you. I knew he was angry—"

"He has no right to be!" Micah stirred against my chest. I took in a slow breath, closed my eyes, and carefully let it out. "If he would have done something about her when she made the sacrifice that got her exiled, none of us would have suffered. None of us would have endured all the bullshit that we have for the past—"

"I know. I know, and I agree. I'm very sorry. Truly, I am."

I closed my eyes and rubbed my eyes. I wasn't angry at her, not really. This wasn't her fault, I knew that. All she'd ever done was help us. I was just... Pissed. And terrified.

Nowhere felt safe for my babies anymore. They were too young to defend themselves. I was only one person, and as much as I loved spending each waking moment with them, that wasn't possible.

My babies weren't safe anywhere in this world. My innocent, sweet children were constantly at risk. They would be until Peterson was dead. And even then, they were only safe in my home's borders.

After a quiet moment, Moriah said, "How is he? Is he alright?"

"They're fine. They're *both* fine."

"Both?" she asked.

"Yes, both. He tried to kill my daughter and my son, Moriah."

"That bastard," she murmured.

"Yeah. Yeah, I should hunt him down and slit his throat, but I'm trying not to stoop to his level."

"His days are numbered anyway, love, I wouldn't worry. He was diagnosed with cancer a little more than a month ago. Word hasn't got out yet, but I hope that eases at least some of your worries."

Good. Karma would get to him, and I wouldn't have to.

"Not really." I gritted my teeth. "But thanks for the info."

"Sure," she muttered. "Again, Laila, I just want you to know how sorry I am."

"Thanks."

The call grew quiet.

"I've got to go. I'll talk to you later."

"All right, darling. I just—"

I shuttered the phone and tossed it to the couch.

CHAPTER TWENTY-FOUR

JEREMY

"You're sure you can't stay a little while longer?" Mémé asked with a sad smile. "It would be wonderful if we could have another meal together."

"I don't think so," Laila said. "But you're welcome to visit us. We've got a few spare bedrooms if you'd like to stay for a night or two."

I agreed with Laila. Clearly, if someone had an old vendetta against us, they were going to try to use this time while we were out of our safety bubble to get their revenge in. My kids had been through enough for one day; we needed to go home. But that didn't make it suck any less.

This meant a lot to my grandma. She'd been asking us to visit since Milly was born. I'd blown her off for the most part because I was worried about how Papy would treat the kids and Lai. But he'd been remotely decent. Not exactly joyous and excited, but I could never expect that from him anyway. Cordial was more than I'd dreamed he was capable of.

Now I felt so bad to take her grandkids away. She must've been so lonely in this big house. Papy always worked a lot. This was probably the most fun she'd had since we were kids and came to visit. It wasn't often after Dad died because Annie was incredibly busy and there weren't many opportunities between all of our schedules and the time difference, but she did love to see her grandchildren. Her eyes always looked big and dopey when we'd leave, just like they did now.

Mémé struggled to hold her forced smile. "Maybe. This one's birthday is coming up, isn't it?" She touched Milly's hand.

"It is. And Micah's is in June." I smiled back.

It'd be nice if they came to the birthday parties. I'd get to show off my pride and joy—the house. I knew it wasn't exactly their taste, but that house was still my baby. Any opportunity to show it off was one I'd like to exploit the hell out of.

"You'll be having a party, won't you?" Mémé met my gaze.

Laila smiled. "I can text you the details. It's going to be in about three weeks."

She looked at Laila and smiled. "I'll be there."

"Thank you for having us again," Laila said. "I'm sorry to leave so soon, but with all things considered. Well, you know."

"Sure." She lowered herself to Micah and touched his cheek. "You behave for your mommy and daddy now, mon petit."

He smiled back. "I will."

"He always does," I said. "I'll be back in a few hours to meet with Papy. You'll be up, won't you?"

"I should be. See me first in case he tries to take all of your time."

I laughed. "Will do."

I lifted Micah to my hip and teleported to our living room.

As I put him on the couch, Micah asked, "Why'd we leave, Daddy?"

I blew out a sigh, kneeling beside him. "Ask me that in ten years, alright?"

He rolled his eyes. "You say that all the time."

I laughed and roughed up his hair. "That's because you ask a lot of questions you're too little to understand the answers to."

"I not too little." He crossed his arms against his chest. "Why'd we leave?"

I lowered myself to the couch beside him. "Remember when you asked if I liked it there? And I said I liked the place, but I didn't like all the people?" He nodded and I said, "Well, one of those people did something bad. Your mom and I were worried about you and Milly. So we wanted to bring you back here to make sure you're safe."

"Oh," he murmured. "See? I not too little."

I chuckled, looking him over. "Yeah, I guess you're smarter than I give you credit for, huh?" He nodded with a grin. "Do you want to take a walk with me to go pick up Tink?"

His head bobbed in a fast nod. A smile stretched across his lips. "I miss hew so much."

"I bet she misses you too." I laughed. Laila landed in the kitchen. "We're going to take a walk to grab Tink. Do you want to come?"

"No, I've got some laundry to start. You guys go ahead." She smiled and placed Milly in her highchair. "We'll be here. I'll start dinner."

I glanced at the clock reading twelve thirty-four. "I think it's technically lunch."

"Jesus," she muttered. "I guess it is. Well, I guess I'll whip something up to munch on and prep dinner."

"Sounds like a plan to me. You got your shoes on, kid?"

"Yep." Micah hopped to his feet. "I'm weady to get my doggy."

Laila and I laughed. I kissed her and Milly goodbye.

"He did what?" Leah's eyes glowed, jaw clenching. "He tried to kill my babies?"

"Well, *my* babies," I muttered. "But yeah. Yeah, I think he thought that if he killed them, I'd bring them back. Force me to use my powers to prove that I have them, sort of thing. Or maybe he was just trying to egg me on so I'd kill him and have problems with the Chambers. I don't know what was going through the dude's head."

"And you didn't kill him?" she asked. "You didn't slit his fucking throat?"

"He's high ranking. That would have started a war, so no. I didn't kill him. Beat the living shit out of him though." I looked to the patio where Micah sat beside Tink, telling her about his trip as if she understood him. Although, maybe she did. Those two did seem to understand one another.

"Well, you should have. I would have." Leah's head shook, teeth clamped together. "Laila didn't?"

"No, Laila dealt with the kids while I dealt with him. She's still pretty upset, I think."

"No shit, Sherlock. She just got him back and then someone tried to kill him. I'd be burning shit to the ground." A calming breath left her nostrils, and the brightness in her eyes dwindled. "Is that when you left? Just in the middle of the meeting?"

"No. No, I took him back to the meeting. The other Chambers were pretty quick to agree with me after that. Looks like we've got their support in whatever's coming."

She arched a brow. "All of them?"

"Just about. There were a few stragglers but for the most part, yeah. We may not agree on everything, but none of us want the world to end."

The door swung open. Micah toddled through the threshold, yelling, "Daddy!"

"Micah!" I smiled, returning his wide-eyed gaze.

He ran to me and raised his closed fist with a grin. "Guess what I found."

"I don't know, what did you find?"

His hand opened. In his palm rested a balled-up pill bug. "It's a woly poly."

"That is definitely a roly poly."

"I'm going to keep him, I think. Can he stay in my room?"

"If you really want to. He probably won't live for very long if you do."

"What will happen then?"

"He'll probably die."

"Like Amy?" he asked in a nonchalant tone. "I nevew see him again?"

My breath caught. Leah fell silent too. He looked up at me so innocently, like that conversation was entirely casual. I didn't know what to say at first. I knew that he knew Amy died. But I hadn't thought about the impact it made on him.

The way he said that last line, 'I never see him again,' made my heart hurt.

Yeah, I hated that bitch. I was glad she was dead. But he wasn't. He cared for her. She'd been kind to him. And I killed her.

"Daddy?" Micah asked.

I cleared my throat. "Yeah. Yeah, buddy, like Amy."

"I take him back outside then." He darted out the back door.

"That, ladies and gentlemen, is the sound of my heart shattering," Leah muttered.

CHAPTER TWENTY-FIVE

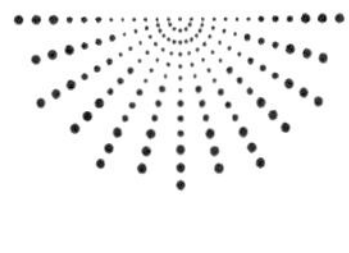

LAILA

I put some sandwiches together and started marinating the chicken for dinner. Milly and I went out to the shed to cut some produce for a salad and sides. When Jeremy and Micah returned, we ate together then spent the remainder of the afternoon on the patio.

As I watched Tink and Micah play together in the yard, I couldn't stop my thoughts from running around one another.

What if this was Lux's plan all along? Let us find Micah, bring him home, settle in, and then boom. Attack. When and where I would least expect it. In the comfort of my home or my happy place on the back patio.

Micah was only about twenty feet away from me, and it still felt too far. It all came back. That awful feeling I never wanted to experience again. The incredible, overwhelming fear of losing my child. Nothing, not a single thing, comes close to describing how terrifying it is to lose a baby. Losing the entire world seemed easier than that.

Around five o'clock, we ate dinner and Jeremy left. Afterward, Micah helped me clean up. The three of us got changed into our pajamas and curled up in my bed. The last time I looked at the clock, it said seven-thirty. I must have passed out by eight.

I remembered.

I sat on a low hanging branch of a large tree that reminded me of an oak but didn't look exactly so. Its green leaves were luminescent, casting a greenish glow on the soil beneath me. It stood about as high as my current home, but its leaves and branches were much lower. Some rested a few mere inches from the mossy ground.

A quiet, almost princess-like hum murmured behind my closed lips. My fingers traced along a patch of moss. As my hand brushed the bark, the moss grew until it engulfed every surface my palm came in contact with. The soft smell of earth mixed with something in the air that felt familiar. Like honeysuckle and flowers almost. Like... like the Fae Realm.

I twisted to reach further up the branch and started to stumble. When I slipped from the branch, I caught myself in the wind. My flowing, green sheer dress billowed around me like Marilyn Monroe in her most famous photoshoot. As my feet touched the ground, my hand coasted to my stomach. My large, basketball-shaped stomach.

"Véa," a voice said behind me. A laugh followed.

My stomach dropped. I knew that voice. Or she did, I guess. He spoke in Enochian but as his words left his lips, it auto translated in my brain.

But I didn't even turn to look at him. Instead, I ran in the opposite direction.

"Véa," he called. His voice was tainted with question, confusion. I heard his footsteps behind me, but I kept running. "Véa, where are you going?"

I kept going. I ran, and I ran, and I ran. And as I did, my stomach kept falling. Aching, sinking. My legs—that had felt so calm against that tree branch—were now gelatin beneath me. My throat and chest were tight. Bringing in air wasn't a mere chore but felt almost impossible. My hands trembled at my sides.

I was terrified.

And I knew why.

Nix had gotten me away from Lux because I was pregnant. I didn't know what our plan was from there, but I knew that him seeing my third-trimester belly couldn't be a good thing.

When I made it to the edge of a rocky cliffside, I lifted the wind beneath me. Just as my feet left the ground, a stronger force ripped me back to the rocks. I stumbled to the ground, landing on all fours.

"I'm sorry, I didn't mean to..." He reached down to help me to my feet but fell quiet when I made it vertical, and he saw my stomach. My heart thudded in my ears. I looked up to meet his gaze. "You... You're..." He looked down at my stomach, head tilting. "But we..."

I looked between his eyes. "It's nice to see you, Lux."

His gaze was locked on my stomach. In the distance behind him, I saw the pretty redhead wearing a soft blue dress. Her eyes were wide. She lifted her hand to cover her small pink lips.

I gave a smile. "Hello, Stella."

Her wide eyes stayed on mine, and she stayed silent.

"What is this?" His brown eyes met mine, flicking back and forth. "Is this why you came here?"

"I don't think now is the time or place for this conversation, Lux." I took a step back, holding my shoulders high, but heart still thudding in my chest. "We should go to my chamber."

His jaw was tight, eyes so firm they could cut diamonds. Fast, erratic breaths left his nose. He took a step closer, and I backpedaled, face still calm and emotionless. "Whose is it?"

"It doesn't matter."

He inched closer. In perfect sync, a gold flash of electricity lit up the orangish sky. "Oh, but it does."

Taking another step back as he drew closer, my foot found nothing. Stella gasped. I stumbled forward to catch myself and dropped into his chest.

He grabbed my biceps so hard that it felt like the bone shattered within the flesh. So strong, he was so *unbelievably* strong. I fought a gasp and yanked my arms away, but he squeezed tighter. "What the fuck did you do, Véa?"

My teeth gritted through the pain of his hands on my arms. "Get your hands off of me before you're a pile of ash, Lux."

He smiled at that. A wicked, crooked half grin. "We both know you can't do that."

My jaw clenched tighter. I let my body warm. Orange flames shot from my arms. Perhaps I couldn't kill him, but second-degree burns weren't murder.

He released my arms, and I didn't waste a second. I dropped backward off the cliffside, summoning the wind to catch me in a cushion.

But before I could make it more than a few feet from where I'd fallen, one arm was around my throat from behind and the other around my chest. The world spun around me, and we were back on that rocky precipice.

This time though, I was face down, gasping for air from his chokehold. His knee was in my back, pushing my stomach into the stone. I flailed, hands aflame, but everything was quickly going black, and I pushed up against him, but he held my hair tighter and pushed his knee deeper into my spine. No matter how hard I was trying, no matter that I was burning him, he wouldn't get off.

Lapse, Véa. I heard my own voice in my mind. It was the first time I heard a thought in one of these. *Damn it, lapse. Lapse!*

He released enough at my throat that I could heave in a gasp. "Whose is it?"

I summoned the wind to pull him off of me, but it only managed to spin his hair into my face. "Get off of me, Lux."

His hot breath was at my ear, voice deep. Thunder cracked above, and his voice was quieter, but it sounded so much louder. "Fucking tell me."

"It doesn't matter!" I screamed, and my already flaming hand shot around toward his head.

And then my face slammed into the rock. My brain pounded, and everything went red. Not in the metaphoric sense; blood leaked from the crack in my head into my eyes. The woman behind me, Stella, gasped again.

I heard a gurgle from his lips, then a cough.

Véa must've tried to gag him on his saliva.

Once more, my head slammed to the stone. Then again, and again.

By then, I'm not sure how I even absorbed what was happening. I could hardly see. The ache in my skull was practically incapacitating, and with his knee in my spine, I could barely bring air into my lungs.

He screamed out something that sounded like a slur, grabbed my head, and tossed me to the side. I'm not sure how I found the strength, but I started to roll back to my knees and stammer to my feet.

But he was on top of me again, kneeling around my chest. His ass planted firm against my stomach, and his hands wrapped around my neck.

My arms flailed again, swatting, fire coursing up them, but he just squeezed harder around my throat.

I'll never forget the way his warm brown eyes looked in that moment.

The fury behind them. The pure, animalistic outrage. The pull in his brows, the flare of his nostrils, the tight grit of his teeth. The hatred. That's about the only image of him I'd ever envision from that point on.

Someway, somehow, I caught his hand at my throat and yanked his fingers backward. He groaned. I raised my fiery fist back to his cheek. The flames were purple now, and I hit him again. He teleported to his feet.

Summoning a strength I don't know how I had, I brought myself onto my knees. But before I could pull my feet beneath me, his foot thrust into my stomach.

I fell back to the ground. And he kicked me again. And again. And again. I don't even know how many times.

All I know is that when I looked down at a mess of blood around the groin of the dress, my heart felt like it was being ripped in half. It was suddenly the only pain I felt. I was breathing, but it felt like the breath had nowhere to go. Like my chest was full of sand.

I heard a thud.

Through the blood and tears in my eyes, I looked up at the pretty redhead holding a thick, heavy tree branch. She dropped it.

"Véa," she whispered with tears in her eyes. I struggled to bring myself onto my knees. She lowered her hands to my armpits. She was tiny and dainty, but somehow with our combined strength, I made it to my feet.

"I would have warned you we were coming if I'd known, Véa," she said as we staggered into the woods. "I—I had no idea."

I tried to make something leave my lips, but I barely heard her over the thumping of my brain in my ears. I just kept staring at the blood pouring down my legs, surely leaving a trail behind me.

I heard his voice.

"Véa!" he called. "Véa!"

"Nix?" Stella looked around. "Is that—"

"Véa." The voice was a few yards in front of me. I looked up. But when he saw me, his jaw dropped. He didn't gasp; he just stared in disbelief for a second.

He teleported in front of me. His hands grasped my shoulders, and Stella released her grip around my waist.

"I fought back," I made out in a mumble.

Tears welled in his eyes as he held me steady. He looked down at the blood over my dress. "Mi lim." *My love.*

A sudden, agonizing cramp began in my abdomen. I gasped and tumbled forward. Nix held me tighter, just as a large gush poured down my legs.

"No," I whispered. Bloody tears puddled down my cheeks. My head shook, teeth starting to chatter. "No. Not yet."

"She needs to lie down," Stella said quickly.

Nix looked at me with slow pants. He held me up but remained silent. In shock, I suppose.

Stella grasped his shoulder and looked quickly between his eyes. "Nix, she *needs* to lie down."

His arm circled my waist, pulling my body into his chest as his other lifted to Stella's shoulder.

I woke with a loud, heaving gasp, clutching my chest.

Micah and Milly flinched but stayed asleep.

I looked around, trying to bring myself back into this moment, trying to breathe, trying to remember that whatever I just witnessed was eons ago. It was okay. My baby was right beside me. I wasn't gushing blood, my head was only throbbing from how fast I sprung up, it was okay.

As I came to grips with reality, it dawned on me.

The sacrifice of the first-born son wasn't only literal, but a poetic, gory retelling of the story that started it all.

My heart raced as I looked at the clock. Nine twelve.

Jeremy wasn't back, but Leah was at the house. I texted her to ask if she could come to sit with the kids. After what I'd just seen, I needed to have some fucking words with the man who'd tortured me for eons.

CHAPTER TWENTY-SIX

JEREMY

"Oui," Papy said into the phone at his desk. "Oui. Merci." He moved the phone from his ear and set it back to the receiver. He took a sip from his scotch and met my gaze. "Thank you for coming back."

"Sure," I said. "Sure, what did you want to talk about?"

"Is it true?"

I knew what he meant. But I hadn't relayed that information to the Chambers for a reason. We all knew how necromancers were viewed. I had no desire to die because of an ability I had that I couldn't change. I'd be damned before anyone tried to wipe out my bloodline for it either.

"Is what true?" I asked.

"Don't play dumb with me, boy." He narrowed his gaze. "Is it true?"

"I'm sorry, but I have no idea what you're—"

"Mon dieu." He raised his thumb and forefinger to rub against his eyes. "Can you resurrect the dead, Jeremy?"

"Of course not."

He pursed his lips. "You're lying."

"No, I'm not."

Papy let out another slow breath. His teeth clenched together. "Your mother could. The only ability the connasse—"

"Alright, don't talk about my mom like that," I said. "I know you didn't get along, but she was my mother and—"

"Fine. I'm sorry. That was the only ability your *mother* had. It'd make sense for at least a few of you to be able to do the same." He looked between my eyes, waiting for a response. "Is it so, Jeremy?"

"No. And how did you know that anyway? We didn't even know until a few years ago."

He chewed his lip. "You're just like your father, do you know that? You both love to lie, even when the person you lie to already knows the truth—"

"I'm nothing like him. I'd appreciate it if you didn't make that reference again."

Comparing the way we looked was one thing. But I was not my father. He abandoned his children. He hanged himself from a ceiling fan and left little eight-year-old me to find him. I was *not* my father.

A huff of a laugh escaped him. "Fine. Fine, Jeremy. Continue to lie. Continue to act as though we don't know what we know. But Thomas was right, wasn't he?" he asked. "The sacrifice was completed. Today's meeting has rerun through my mind a thousand times. That look on your face when he said it, you were terrified, whether you'll admit it or not. But you weren't afraid for yourself, were you?"

"I don't know what you're talking about—"

"The sacrifice didn't bring on the end, did it?" his strict voice questioned. I clenched my jaw. "No, that wouldn't make much sense, would it? A sacrifice to *bring* the end? A sacrifice suggests that God will bestow a reward in exchange. If that were the case, it wouldn't be much of a sacrifice, as only more death would follow. No, no, no. The sacrifice was only a piece of the puzzle, wasn't it, son? You bringing him back. That's what brought on the end."

Damn, he was smart.

I stared between his eyes for a moment. "What do you want me to say, Papy? You already believe what you're saying, and you call me a liar when I tell you it isn't true. So what's the point to this?"

"My point is that you need to be careful who you lie to." His piercing blue eyes darted between mine. "Your people. Your followers. They follow you and your wife because you've been honest with them. Because you've helped them too, but primarily because of your transparency.

"The Elders and the Council are the opposite, and that's why these people like you. But now you're lying to them. If they find out that you kept this from them, the alliances you've built will mean nothing. If you don't want enemies, if you don't want a civil war in addition to the one we'll be fighting soon, you'll have to be blunt with them."

I gritted my teeth together.

"I am a father too, Jeremy. I've also lost a child. I understand your will to protect them. But if you lie to your people, you will have no people. They will rebel against you. They will lose, most likely, given the power you all hold. But how will you fight a war without an army? Will you kill them for going against you even though you were the one that lied to them? Is that the leader you want to be?"

No. That wasn't the leader I wanted to be. I didn't want to lie to the people who planned to put their lives on the line for our common cause. But I didn't want them to try to kill me for what I was, and attempt to murder my child to prevent what was to come either.

Regardless, I couldn't make a call like that without talking to Laila first.

I remained silent.

"Do what you think is best, Jeremy. We all know what they say about necromancy. I understand why you're reluctant to announce it. I'm sure you have to talk to your wife before even confirming it with me. But choose your next moves wisely. If you want to be a leader, then be a good one. Don't be like the others who have conspired against their followers for all of history. Explain it to them. Let them see your perspective. In the end, we're fighting the same enemy so whether they like what you did or not, they'll have to accept it. But at least they won't be able to call you a liar that conspired against them."

"Yeah. Well, thanks for the tips," I said. "My kids are waiting on me. I should get going. Is that everything?"

"Yes. Your grandmére told me to remind you to get that case of wine. It's in the basement at the guest house."

"Will do."

Truly, that was some good advice he'd just bestowed upon me. The way he'd treated us since our trip began was far kinder than I'd expected. I wanted to tell him how grateful I was for that. But talking to him wasn't exactly easy. I wasn't sure how to put it into words.

He returned my nod. When I didn't teleport away, he made a face. "What is it?"

"Thank you." The words tumbled out sounding better than I'd thought they would. "I know you don't approve of my marriage, but I appreciate that you kept your feelings to yourself for the most part."

"Ah," he murmured. "Well, times are changing. No time for... what was it that you called me at your wedding? A racist bucket?"

I gave a half-laugh. "Bigot, actually."

He smiled. "Yes, a bigot. That's it. The world doesn't have time for such ancient views, don't you think?"

"Couldn't agree more."

"It could very well be your wife or child that saves my life. Or my wife's, or a friend's. And I'd hate to be the racist bigot that called the world's savior a whore."

Well, regardless of how he treated her now, he still, in fact, would be the racist bigot that called her a whore. But at least he hadn't been a complete asshole.

"Either way. I appreciate it. Thank you."

He smiled. "We'll see you at the birthday party next month. Be safe, son."

"I'm looking forward to it."

I didn't expect anything notable to happen when I teleported to the basement of the guest house. In fact, I assumed nothing would happen at all. I'd pick up the box of wines, drop them at Leah's, snag a few bottles for Laila, then go home and sleep in my bed. And I did. But I got a little held up.

As I landed on the tile floor, I heard the hum of the hot tub, breathing in the humid scent of chlorine. I looked up. Chris was inside, which wasn't much of a shock.

It was the other shirtless man that sat on top of him that threw me for a loop.

Their faces were pressed together, hands holding each other's necks. It seemed like a pretty intense moment judging by the heavy breaths I heard over the sound of the bubbling water.

I'm not, nor have I ever been, homophobic. My sister's gay, my wife's bisexual, and it never bothered me in the slightest. It still didn't. But I can't say that I wasn't a bit shocked.

To my knowledge, and based on the fact that Chris had been the one that gave me tips in bed when I was getting to that age, I always assumed he was straight. So yes, it was surprising. But not a big deal.

I did feel bad for interrupting though.

My hands flung to my eyes as I said, "Sorry, go on about your business. Just grabbing this box over here and—"

Chris gasped. The sound of water splashed as I reached around with closed eyes for the box Mémé described. "Sorry again, just getting this wine. You two kids have fun."

I felt the box, peeling open one eyelid to make sure it was the right one. I cleared my throat and started blindly to the steps.

"Jeremy," Chris called after me. "Jeremy, wait."

I turned and met his gaze. "Hey, you walked in on me and Laila last night, and I think you saw her ass so we're just about even."

His breaths were uneven, his lips curled downward. He held a white towel around his bare lower half, a certain part protruding more than I would've liked to witness. "You weren't supposed to see that."

I lifted the box slightly so only his upper half was visible. "Dude, can we have this conversation when you aren't pitching a tent?"

He adjusted the towel at his waist, still trying to bring even breaths into his chest. "Can I get dressed and talk to you outside?"

"It's not a big deal. We've all walked in on each other at some point or another. I've got to get home—"

"Yeah, but not... not in a situation like this." Chris's eyes were practically pleading. "Please. Just meet me outside."

Oh.

He wasn't worried because I just walked in on him. He was worried because I just walked in on him with a man. Honestly, I couldn't have given two shits less. But it was clearly important to him.

"Fine, but I'm dropping this box off at Leah's first."

"Alright. Alright, just... just don't say anything to anyone along the way, okay?"

My brows were still slightly wrinkled in confusion, but I nodded. "Oh. Oh, yeah. Yeah, sure."

CHAPTER TWENTY-SEVEN

LAILA

My tennis shoes squeaked against the steps as I descended the basement stairs. I didn't feel an ounce of fear like I had before when I faced Peterson. He felt so insignificant now, no part of me was afraid of him. The man he was tethered to had become my enemy.

But I didn't fear him either.

After what I'd just seen, I had to understand why in the fuck he felt it necessary to torture us for thousands of years. He'd punished me in the worst way imaginable all those eons ago. Why did he have to repeat it over and over again?

I flicked the light on and looked at Peterson. He coughed a bit as he met my gaze. He smiled. "Laila."

"I'm not here to talk to you. I need to talk to him."

His forehead scrunched down. "It doesn't work like that; I can't just make him come out. He channels me when he chooses to."

"Well, let him know that I'm here. And I remember what he did. And I'm pissed."

"I'm sure he knows you're here. But he won't reveal himself unless he wants to."

"Fine. Fine, you can be the microphone then. But he's going to hear what I have to say."

Peterson swallowed hard and gave a slow nod.

"Infidelity is wrong, and I won't say that it isn't." I looked fast between his eyes. "So if I didn't say it then, I'll say it now. I'm sorry that I hurt you, Lux. What I did was wrong. I know what betrayal feels like, thanks to you I'm sure, and I wouldn't wish that pain on anyone."

Peterson continued to look between my eyes.

I'd been rehearsing what I was going to say on my way here, and for the first time in my life, I got it right. All thought didn't suddenly leave my mind like it usually did when I had something important to say.

"But losing a child is not the equivalent to being cheated on." My jaw tightened. "That was the point though, wasn't it? You didn't want to hurt me as bad as I hurt you. You wanted me to hurt worse than you did. You hated me that much." He looked gently between my eyes, almost remorsefully.

"Which is fine. Hate me. Hate me until the end of time if you want. You're only hurting yourself at this point but fine. But how dare you call yourself a god of love and patience after what you've done? After torturing someone you once loved for eons with the worst pain imaginable? After demolishing the rights of so many people for as long as you have? How dare you expect praise and worship after—"

"God loves his children. You aren't my child. Neither is Nix. Neither are your children." His expression shifted. Lux stared back at me through Peterson's eyes. I could see it in his expression. Not literally, not his power, but him. His soul. "I expect my people to be grateful for what I've given them and thank me for it. I *am* a god of love and patience—"

"Don't call yourself a god to me." My gaze hardened. "You are not my god. You are my equal."

His gaze narrowed, chuckle leaving his lips. "Yeah, we'll go with that."

My teeth clamped together. I was about to rebut something about how he could pretend all he wanted that he was the most powerful creature alive, but that he was too much of a pussy to even show his real face. But It came to me.

A smirk came to my lips, half laugh escaping me. "We aren't equals at all, are we? I'm stronger than you. That's what this was about. That's why you and I married in the first place. You wanted me because you wanted power. That's why you lined up my genealogy the way that you did in this life. My soul was always stronger, but you made sure my body could handle it. And I got even more than I had then. That's why you assigned Mary to birth me. So that I had the abilities of your people along with the power of mine. Because you needed us to be a nuclear fucking plant of power to fight what you started."

He smiled. "Always so smart. Have to connect every dot and cross every t."

I guessed I finally figured something out. "Yeah, I guess so."

He looked between my eyes in silence for a few seconds. "Yes, Véa. I made sure you and Nix were more powerful than ever before. Even more powerful than me. But don't get cocky. I know about weaknesses of yours you don't even realize exist."

"Is that how he disabled my abilities?" I asked. "It wasn't Amy and Nastya, it was you."

"The two of them the first time around. I helped later." He smiled. "Used a friend of yours actually."

My brows fell far over my eyes. "What?"

He chuckled. "No one betrayed you if that's your concern. They didn't know what they were doing."

"Chris?" I questioned. "Is that who you're referring to?"

He laughed again. His head shook. "You know what you are? An ant. And I'm a kid with a magnifying glass on a sunny day."

"Don't change the subject. Who did you use against me, Lux?"

"I'm not sure how well you know him yet. Time will tell." His smile widened. He laughed.

I wasn't an ant. The magnifying glass would kill me if I were. I was a spider. He was pulling off each of my legs and watching me struggle to run away before he ripped off another.

"You're a dick, you know that?" I said.

He smiled. "So I've been told."

I tightened my jaw and looked between his eyes. "Time has a lot to do with everything you've caused. That's an ability of yours, isn't it? Jeremy has the key to the afterlife, and you have the key to time. That's how you'll hide from us when this is over and we have the opportunity to deal with your bullshit."

"There you go again. Connecting dots. You're missing a few though. But that's okay. You're close to figuring it all out." He pointed to my head. "Thanks to that bright mind of yours."

My gaze narrowed. "So you know what happens. You know that somehow, we save the world. But we have to figure that part out on our own."

"No. No, I don't know how you do it. I mean, eventually, we'll work together. But you've always loved keeping me out of things, Asherah."

I chewed my cheek, thinking hard for a moment. "Where does that come from? Asherah wasn't my name."

"It's a symbol. Something like a title that turned to a nickname. In our time, it meant 'in the wood.' Tree of life, in the wood, you see the parallel."

He smiled, It turned to a laugh. "It's funny now, isn't it? When you think about your connection to them. You even wore two on your wedding day."

That wasn't entirely true. I'd learn it later as I did more research. Asherah was actually a wooden pole engraved with a serpent. The word in Ugaritic literally translated to 'she who treads the sea dragon.' Although prior to that, yes, it did come from Enochian in relation to a tree. Since Véa was apparently the snake in the garden, those parallels lined up perfectly.

"I was also tending to one when you showed up and beat me into premature labor." His expression grew dismal, eyes softening a tad. I tightened my jaw. "Why would you do that to yourself anyway? Why would you watch me marry him?"

His gaze narrowed. "Do you think it still hurts me? Because it doesn't. I'll always think you're a slut, but it hasn't hurt for a *very* long time."

Judging by the way his hand clamped to a fist, I highly doubted the legitimacy of that statement.

"You wouldn't hate me if you were over it," I said. "Hatred isn't a real emotion. It's a secondary emotion typically caused by pain."

"Funny, I don't remember you studying psychology."

My gaze narrowed. "Well, thanks to you, I've had to spend a lot of money on a good one. That's the advice she gave me."

He rolled his eyes. "Regardless. Quite literally, it's history, Véa."

Clearly, it wasn't. It was still unfolding before us. But I had other questions.

"What happened to Stella?" I asked.

He tightened his jaw. "I'm sure you'll remember soon enough."

"Did she cheat on you too?" I asked. "Is that why you hate women so much?"

"No, she had the decency to leave before she fucked someone else." His jaw grew tight. "Wasn't my brother either."

She didn't actually. She cheated too. He just never found out.

"Why did it even matter? It's not like you actually loved me. I was just a political tool."

He squinted a bit. "I loved you more than anything. I loved you more than I loved her. I loved you more I loved my own family. Before this world came to be, there was nothing in the universe that meant more to me than you. Even after you left." His eyes shifted fast between mine. "For a while, anyway."

"You didn't love me the way that I deserved to be loved. You loved me the way a middle-aged man loves his sports car. I was property to you."

"That's what wives were then," he snapped. "That was my culture. Yours was different, and I understood that but I'm pretty sure sneaking off into the woods to fuck your husband's brother was pretty taboo to you too, Véa."

"I never said that what I did wasn't wrong. But can't you admit that you were wrong too?" I barked. "Can't you admit that you were at fault? You sent your brother to pick me up for our wedding. You didn't fight beside me on battlefields. You didn't give me a say in the decisions you made about wars. You hid every political aspect you took part in from me because I was a woman even though I was a queen on my first home, and I knew what the fuck I was doing. You had me killing innocent people—"

"You could have stayed home. But you wanted to fight." He furrowed his brows, head shaking. "Don't blame me for that."

I clenched my jaw. "It's the premise. I was a queen with a following of her own. Why would you expect me to blindly follow and agree with you? That wasn't me, you knew that before you married me—"

"Fine," he snapped. "Yes. I realize that if I would have treated you differently, things may not have turned out the way that they did." His nostrils flared as he stared into my eyes. "There. Is that what you wanted to hear?"

Not an apology, but an admission of fault was something.

"Yeah. It is." I clenched my jaw. "You know what though? I'm really curious what the fuck you did that made us want to lock you up in the first place. If we terraformed earth together, that means we moved past what happened between me and Nix. And we can't take the souls back to the first heaven, that's what Heylel told us. So what did you do? Why can't we take the souls back there?"

He tightened his teeth together. "There is no first heaven. It's gone. So is the great green."

My heart thumped harder. "What do you mean it's gone?"

"I had to do what I had to do. They were going to hand them over on a silver platter. The souls we cultivated, the ones we called our children. The people here." He gestured around. "There was no diplomatic answer, Véa. We looked. We tried to reason and barter, but they wanted their souls. They wanted us to give up the lives that we created. It was only a matter of time before they came for them, and I refused to let them get close. You took risks, you tried to talk about things and work it out without war and it could have cost us every soul on Earth. I couldn't get the rest of you to listen, so I took matters into my own hands."

I processed that for a moment, chest tightening. "You destroyed our home worlds."

"And I'd do it again if it meant that I got to keep the souls we have here safe. Wouldn't you destroy a world to save your children, Véa?" That condescending half grin played at his lips.

I walked over those words in my mind once more.

The curse. It'd been a comparison. He wiped out our planets because they sided with Wormwood. That's what we were punishing him for, for destroying our homes.

So he wanted to teach us a lesson.

That we too would let a world burn for our children.

My eyes widened, breaths getting close together. "Are you saying that you killed my son to prove a fucking point?"

"Among other reasons. Poetic irony, the currency of his soul. And as I said before, a bit of vengeance. He is the offspring of your blasphemy, you know."

I teleported in front of him and cracked my fist against his cheek.

But I wrongly anticipated his strength. I guess he stayed in the restraints for my comfort, not because he couldn't get out of them.

The cemented metal in the wall broke free like the center of a flip-flop in a puddle of mud. It swung to the ground with a clatter. His palms flung to my throat. I gripped his hand as he stood, but he was stronger than anyone I'd ever encountered. Even Wyatt and Celena weren't as a brute.

He didn't squeeze; he wasn't trying to hurt me. It was a hold meant to signify dominance. I'd used the same tactic on people I fought that were smaller than me, which was rare but did happen from time to time. And it works. Holding someone by their neck has a way of making someone feel inferior and controlled.

He looked furious. But not the way Peterson did the day his hand tightened at my neck. He didn't look like Peterson at all to me at that moment. No, he looked like he did the day I lost Micah for the first time. Full of rage and pain, whether he'd admit it or not.

"You might have married him in this life, Véa, but it doesn't change the way it happened the first time. It doesn't change that your son's soul was the product of something awful."

I teleported out of his grasp to the ground behind him. My arm spun around his neck to stabilize him. I ripped the air from his lungs. A heaving gasp left his lips as he struggled against my hold.

"He was the product of something beautiful. Maybe it's a little too forward-thinking for you to understand but we were in a toxic, emotionally abusive relationship." I lowered his struggling body to the ground and kept my hand around his neck. "And Jeremy was my way out. Our child brought an end to a terrible arrangement that should have never been made in the first place."

"Say it, ol boaluahe. Nix. Not Jeremy." *My love.* Ol boaluahe meant my love. His voice was deep, but near a whisper. He turned slightly, peering at me over his shoulder. "This little love story you've worked up between the two of you in this life isn't who you really are. You were an adulterer. You were a whore. You were the reason your son didn't make it to birth the first time around."

He reached up and swiftly grabbed ahold of my ribs. I tried to move from his grip, but he lifted me through the air quicker than I could teleport. I barely realized I was upside down until I felt the back of my body slam to the cement.

He climbed over me and pinned my arms to the ground. His eyes darted between mine. "Betrayal is betrayal. You betrayed me—"

I slammed my knee into his groin. He gasped, fell sideways, and released his hold at my neck. I teleported over him, rolling his body to meet my gaze as I shoved my knee into his chest.

Just as he'd shoved his into my pregnant belly.

"*I* betrayed you. My son did nothing. He is and always was innocent. You never should have brought him into this."

"Children will pay for the sins of their parents," he made out in a struggle to breathe.

That's when I blacked out. I can't say what was running through my mind or how bad it hurt when he hit back. I didn't even see what I was doing.

A strength inside of me that I didn't know existed pummeled his body more times than I could count judging by how bad my wrists hurt when I was done. He must have gotten a few good hits in because my face was as swollen as a can of soda whose top and bottom had ascended after a fall.

I stood over Peterson's body panting heavily, looking hard over the crimson running down my hands to the cocktail of our mixed blood beneath his body. His pale face had already turned purple. A deep cut, probably from the diamond in my ring, streamed blood down his chin. Both eyes were swollen shut.

The sound of my thudding heart soared against my eardrums. I saw Jeremy land in front of me. I felt him grip my face and turn it up to meet his. I saw his wide, scared eyes. His lips seemed to mouth 'are you okay,' but I didn't hear him. Nothing was processing. I'm not even sure that I was breathing. I felt absolutely nothing.

Honestly, it was kind of peaceful.

CHAPTER TWENTY-EIGHT

JEREMY

I leaned against the railing to the basement stairs with a joint between my lips. The aroma of fertilizer and crisp wind danced into my nose as I took in a slow drag. I looked out over the field and then turned my gaze up to the clear, dark blue sky.

The stars were so bright that night. Or maybe they shined as bright as they always did but I paid more attention to them than I once had.

Chris used to say he wanted to be an astronaut when he grew up, but I never understood it. The thought of leaving Earth's atmosphere always freaked me out. Sure, outer space is pretty and everything. But there's a certain level of comfort that comes with standing on solid ground. It was hard to believe that at one point, I lived in a world that wasn't this one.

But as I stared up at Orion twinkling in the distance, that fear started to dissipate. Maybe that was the place I once called home.

"Hey," Chris said at the bottom of the steps.

I glanced at him and smiled as he ascended the stairs. "See, now that you're wearing more than a towel, we can have an actual conversation."

He cleared his throat. "I'm really sorry you saw that."

"I'm not five." I laughed. "And you're not a priest. I didn't expect you to be celibate for the rest of your life."

He swallowed hard and gave a nod.

I raised a brow. "Wait, do you think I care that you're gay?"

"I'm not gay."

"Making out with another guy naked in a hot tub seems a little gay, bro." I thought for a second. "Or, ya know, whatever it is that you guys were doing. I can't see it being that comfortable with the lack of lubrication but hey, nothing's ever gone up my ass so I'm no—"

"Alright. Alright, just..." he said. "I'm not *gay*. I still like girls."

"Bi's cool too. I really don't give a shit who you fuck."

He shuddered.

I was sure Laila would be very offended at his cringe over the word bi. But I also recognized that she didn't grow up being taught that homosexuality was blasphemous. "Nobody cares about that shit these days, man. Gay marriage is legal in almost every first-world country around the globe. And everyone in our family is really left leaning. Leah's the most open lesbian you'll ever meet."

"Yeah. Yeah, I know. But..." He shook his head. "Can you just keep this to yourself please?"

I took another slow hit off the joint. "I mean, yeah. Yeah, sure. But there's no reason to keep it a secret. You know that nobody's going to care—"

"I care," he said quickly. "And it's my business. I'll tell people when and if I want to. But it'd be nice if you could just respect my—"

"Woah, there." I held up my palm. "Chill. I won't tell anyone, Chris. I get it. That's a personal journey."

Although I didn't know much of what it was like to come out of the closet, I did understand privacy. He was right; that wasn't my place. I didn't tell Laila's story to other people either, because when someone confides in me, that means something. I was good at keeping secrets. I didn't see why he *wanted* to keep it secret, but if he did, I wouldn't out him. It's not like I made a habit of talking about my sibling's sex lives anyway.

A pressure in my hand vibrated up my arm.

Laila. She hit someone. I peeped into her mind and saw her punch Peterson. Which was odd since she said she didn't want anyone else to watch the kids. But if she were down there with him, he couldn't get to them. So I brushed it off. If she needed me, which was rare, she'd ask. She was more than capable of fighting her own battles.

"You can tell everyone, or not tell everyone, whenever you're ready. But we have a lot of telepaths in this family. Laila's in and out of my head all the time. I can't promise that she won't see it. I should be able to keep it from everyone else though." I paused. "Wait, does Leah know?"

"Just you. And the pool boy." He gestured toward the basement.

I laughed. "That's a little cliché, isn't it?"

He smiled. "Well, at least we know Mémé isn't fucking him, right?"

I laughed again. "Well, for the record, no one, and I do mean *no one*, is going to care if you do come out. So if that's part of why you haven't, don't let us be the reason. All any of us want for the others is for the others to be happy. And, ya know, if sucking dick is what does it for you—"

He shoved me and tried not to laugh. I chuckled and took another hit off the joint.

"I'm just saying, man. Do whatever it takes to be happy. You deserve it. Just don't bring your Grindr guys back to the house, alright? I don't trust anyone enough to let them onto our property unless we've known them for a while."

"I've been going to them," he muttered.

"Them?" I asked. "You've only been back for a little over a month, how many people have you hooked up with?"

"I've been imprisoned for ten years. And the last three, I was in a tiny room with your son. My balls were bluer than the sky."

I laughed again.

A sudden ache ascended over my entire back. I grasped the railing to keep me on my feet. My head pounded behind my eyes as if I'd just been punched in the back of the head. I gasped and leaned forward as the pain faded.

"What's wrong?"

"Laila. I've got to go."

I focused on her mind for a second.

But I didn't feel her.

Her pain, I felt. The blood pumping through her skull, the ache in her lower back, but her thoughts weren't touchable.

Just like they'd been three years ago when he held her captive.

The basement. I saw her punch him in the face a few seconds ago, that's where they were.

I tried to teleport there. But I shot back to where I stood like a rubber band.

"What is i—" Chris began.

I teleported to the basement door. I heard talking, followed by groaning as pains soared over her body. Her cheek, her hands, her ribs. Her knees, as if she fell to the ground.

I tried to spin the heavy-duty metal handle, but it was locked firm and wouldn't budge. Good move to put a thick, solid steel door on the steps that led to our torture chamber.

Or so we'd thought until one of us was stuck down there with an enemy.

I screamed her name, pounding on the door until my arms ached. But her pain was a lot worse. Everything hurt. Her arms, her face, her neck.

"What's going on?" Wyatt called from the maid stairs.

"I can't get down there," I yelled.

I heard her groan. A thud pounded against her ribs. A gasp left my lips. I felt her head slam into something. Not a fist, something harder. Like her head was forcefully clunked to the ground.

"Open the damn door!" I slammed my fists into it again.

"Here, move." Wyatt brushed past me to the handle.

But then pain soared from her knuckles up her arms. Then again. And again, and again.

Silence followed. My heart raced. I attempted to teleport again.

But it worked that time.

My jaw dropped. She looked like she'd just finished an MMA fight. I could barely make out her eyes behind all the blood and swelling.

She stood over her opponent with bloody hands tightened to fists. Fast, erratic breaths left her lips. I glanced at Peterson and then back up to her. "Laila, what happened?"

She stared down at her shaking, dripping hands. She struggled to bring an even breath into her lungs.

"Baby, are you okay?"

She stayed silent, staring at her palms. I grasped her face and turned it up to me. "Are you okay?"

She blinked hard for a few seconds.

I glanced back at Peterson lying in a puddle of blood and then to her. "Okay. Okay, you need to sit down."

She didn't move. I'm not sure she even heard me.

I grabbed a chair from the foot of the steps and set it beside her. My hand went to her shoulder, carefully tugging her toward the chair. She took in slow pants and dropped onto it.

I turned to Peterson. As I lowered myself beside him, part of me prayed that she'd lost control and finished him off. But his fast, dull heart thudded against my fingers.

"Is he..." Laila whispered.

"No. No, he's alive." My gaze caught the chains at his wrists. His hands were covered in blood too, but where they hung in the wall was now a hole leading to the earth behind it. I turned to her. "How did he do this?"

"It wasn't Peterson," she murmured.

My jaw tightened. "Lux did this to you?"

Her head shook before it turned to a nod. "It was mutual."

Clearly.

I supposed two bloody, nearly unrecognizable figures was what I'd imagined the end of a brawl between two gods would look like.

"Well. Looks like you got the last hit in," I muttered.

She grew quiet again. I took in a slow breath as I looked over him. I grabbed the other chair and tugged it to the center of the room. After struggling a bit, I managed to get his body up into a sitting position. His head rolled back to face the ceiling. I walked to the armoire, found some rope, and started tying him up.

When I finished, I walked to Laila and kneeled in front of her. I'd never seen her so fucked up. I'd seen her stabbed at least a handful of times by then, even shot a time or two. But never beaten. Actually, I'm not sure I'd ever seen *anyone* beaten so badly. Except for Peterson in the chair behind me.

I physically couldn't find her features through the blood and swelling. Blood poured from the back of her crown to her spine. More from her forehead to her cheeks. They were so big and puffy, I couldn't see her eyes. A sliver of red poked through one, blood vessels burst in the whites. That must've been the only bit of vision she had, so I looked into that one.

The adrenaline was wearing off as I touched her chin and turned her face to mine. She winced and raised her hand to wipe blood from her eye. But when they made contact, we both grimaced at the pain.

I lifted my palm from her chin to heal her face, but she pushed it away. "Just... Just give me a minute."

My head lifted in a nod.

After a few minutes, she let me take her back to the house. I told Leah what happened, and she said she'd keep an eye on the kids until I healed Laila and she got cleaned up. When I came back into the bathroom, she was sitting on the floor beside the bathtub with her hands clamped to fists in her hair.

I lowered myself beside her and gently took her hands from her scalp. I raised my hand and healed her busted lip and swollen eyes. She didn't even wince as I drifted the energy from her head down either arm, her ribs, and finished up with her legs.

I lifted her chin and searched her gaze. "Baby, what happened?"

Her lip quivered. Tears puddled in her bloodshot eyes. "I remembered something."

I waited for her to go on.

"When I was—I mean, when Véa was pregnant, you-you helped me get away from him, remember?" I gave another sympathetic nod. "I-I, I mean Véa. She was sitting outside. In a tree, like... She was just sitting there and helping the moss grow up the branches." She swallowed hard again. "And she heard his voice. But she didn't even turn to look at him. She just took off. And I-I could feel how scared she was. Not for herself but for the baby. She had to be at least six and a half months in."

I raised my thumb to brush a tear from her cheek. She cleared her throat and lifted her palm to rub her mouth. "And she kept running, and he was following her until she got to this cliffside. She tried to fly but he... He like, telekinetically pulled her back down. and then when he tried to help her up, he saw her stomach and..."

She took in a slow breath. "He was reasonably upset, I guess. He kept saying to tell him whose it was, and she wouldn't, and... I don't know, it..." Her eyes filled with tears. "He just, he just started beating the shit out of her. And she fought back, but he's really strong. And he-he slammed her face into the rocks and put his knee on her back and pushed her belly into the..." Her head shook as her eyes closed. "She was bleeding. Like, like a lot of blood. Not from where he hit her but the baby."

I wrapped my arm around her shoulders. She rested her head against my chest as she struggled to stifle her sobs. I held her close to me as she tried to regain a normal breathing rhythm.

"That girl, his other wife—she was there. She hit him over the head with a branch and helped Véa up. They started walking through the woods, and then you were there. And you held me. And I woke up. And I just—I was so angry. He took my baby. He took my baby so many times."

I held her tighter as her cries got closer and closer together. She pushed her hand far into her mouth to hush the sound. Her head shook again and again. "I didn't deserve this. I cheated on him, but I didn't deserve this. Micah didn't deserve this. And I told him that, and he said that 'the children will pay for the sins of their parents.' And I punched him, and he just ripped himself out of the wall. I... I don't remember what happened after that. I blacked out."

I lifted my head in a gentle nod and touched my lips to her forehead.

I didn't know what to think.

It was obviously a big part of her history. That's why her mind showed it to her. But it didn't come as a shock.

That was the man he was. A god of war, a jealous god. He referred to himself that way in his holy book. That's who he'd always been and would forever be.

It hurt. But mainly because it hurt her. Yeah, it was unfortunate, but it didn't matter to me now. It mattered in the sense that she needed me, but I couldn't let my heart shatter because of something that happened hundreds of thousands of years ago that I couldn't change.

We had our babies back. And no one would ever take them from us again. That's all that mattered now.

We stayed like that for a while; me just holding her. Maybe an hour, maybe two. I don't know. But then we took a shower together. I helped her wash off the blood. We got dressed and ready for bed. I told Leah the coast was clear, and she was good to go back to the house.

The kids were asleep by then. So we sat on the couch and smoked a joint. I didn't need it, but her still shaking hands told me that she did. She curled her head against mine and fell asleep. I teleported us to the bedroom and tried to squeeze in where I could between her, the kids, and Tink.

I lay there staring at the ceiling for what felt like forever. The knowledge she'd gotten from that memory didn't affect me the way that it affected her. I'd almost assumed it. But it made me hold my son and daughter a little tighter that night.

CHAPTER TWENTY-NINE

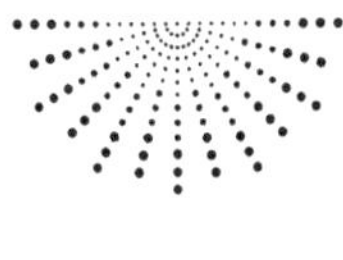

LAILA

"Scrambled or dippy?" Jeremy asked at the stove. I heard him but it didn't process. It was one of those moments where life didn't feel real. I just continued to stare vacantly out the window watching a hummingbird sipping from the feeder on the patio.

"Lai," Jeremy said again.

"Huh?" I turned to meet his gaze.

He sent me a gentle smile. "Do you want your eggs scrambled or dippy?"

"Oh. I don't care, whatever you're having."

"Dippy it is."

"Mommy." Micah laughed behind me. "Mommy, look."

I turned. He stood beside Tink. He'd pulled a gray cardigan through her shoulders and buttoned it at her chest. I laughed as she panted up at me. "I think that's a little small for her, don't you?"

He grinned. "She likes it."

"Damn it. The yolk broke. Sorry, guys, looks like we're all getting scrambled," Jeremy said.

"That's okay." Micah climbed up the chair beside me and turned to Jeremy. "I like both."

"Ya know, I was thinking." He turned over the island to pass me a cup of coffee. "Since we left Paris early, I have a couple of days before I have to go back to work. How about we check some places off our list? We don't have to go global, but there're some cool places in the states we could check out. Yellowstone's pretty this time of year."

I smiled. "Yeah, let's do it. No overnight's though, we'll just visit and teleport home. It's too hard with the baby."

"Yeah, it's a waste of money anyway." He turned to Micah and grinned. "Do you want to go to Yellowstone?"

He made a face. "I don't want to see a wock."

"It's a park, kiddo. It's not an actual stone," I said.

"It might be a little cold in Montana still anyway," he said. "Where do you want to go then, buddy?"

Micah thought for a moment. He grinned with wide eyes. "The beach."

"The beach." Jeremy smiled. He turned his gaze to me. "What do you say, Mommy? Wanna go to the beach?"

I gave a smile. "Sounds like a plan to me. Florida's probably the way to go, huh? Warmer water?"

"Yeah, Florida's our best bet. I'll check the weather after we eat. But Micah, get that sweater off of Tink before she gets stuck on something."

"She likes it."

"You like it. The dog doesn't." He pointed between them with the spatula. "It's warm out, and she already has a coat."

Micah frowned. He slowly pouted his way off the stool and mumbled, "She *does* like it."

I laughed.

Jeremy sighed. "He got your attitude."

"Yes, he did." I grinned.

I took a sip of my warm coffee, relaxing in the warmth that filled my stomach. I closed my eyes and breathed in the smell. My hands gently embraced the heat around the mug.

That was something my therapist had recommended to do when I was at my worst with the anxiety attacks. To envelope myself in one object as a grounding tool. It'd been a cigarette before, but I hadn't smoked since before I was pregnant with Milly. Coffee was better anyway.

The smell brought me peace. The taste brought me warmth. It was a good way to focus on the moment in front of me. I needed to focus on this, not a life I lived thousands and thousands of years ago.

Jeremy glanced at Micah over my shoulder then looked over me carefully. *Are you alright?*

I tilted my head to the side. *Yeah, I'm fine. Why?*

Just seem a little off. He tilted his head slightly. *Yesterday was a pretty rough day.*

Well, just from lunch on. We had breakfast in Paris, we saw the Luxembourg Gardens, it wasn't all bad. I smiled. *The night before was pretty good too. We should do that more often.*

Yeah, we really should. He flashed a quick grin. Then his lips curved down at the ends. *You're okay though?*

I held my smile. *I'm fine, baby.*

Well, let me know if you aren't, and I'll try to help.

I know. But I'm okay. Really.

He gave a gentle nod. *We need to talk about something then.*

And what's that?

Some things Papy said last night. He made some pretty valid points.

"No," I said. "We talked about this two days ago, I thought that we were on the same page."

"We were. We are, I just..." He closed his eyes, chest broadening with a deep inhale. "Look, I know how it sounds—"

"It sounds like you want to publicly announce that our son isn't only the reason the world is ending, but also a way to prevent it from happening—"

"That's just a theory. We don't need to tell anyone that."

"But they'll figure it out on their own. If they knew his soul was the bartering tool for the planet, they'd hand it over in a—"

"They won't come near him," he said quickly. "No one will, Laila.

You didn't see the way that they looked at me when I got back there with Thomas. They like us, they like us a *lot*. They're pretty scared of us, too. We're blunt, and we fight for what we want, and we follow through. But we're not being blunt about this. And I'm not even worried about the other Chambers; I'm worried about the masses. Rumors trickle and when they do, they get diluted. After that meeting yesterday, they've probably already started. We should address them head-on—"

"You don't know that. You don't know that they won't come after him." My jaw tightened. I looked at Micah at the rose bush in the corner of the yard with Tink. My head shook again, face screwing up in anger. "How can you even consider this after yesterday? He almost died, so did she." I gestured to Milly in his lap.

"They didn't almost die," he muttered.

"You weren't there. He couldn't stop crying for hours. It wasn't even crying; it was a panic attack." I tightened my hand to a fist on my lap. "I'm glad you're getting the hang of diplomacy and everything, but keep my children out of it, Jeremy."

"This revolves around them. The end of the world is centered around *our* child, Laila." He clenched his jaw. After a moment of me glaring at him, he took in a calming breath. "Do you think that I want to do this? Because I don't. All that I've ever wanted is to be normal, but we aren't. We never will be. Neither will Micah or Milly. But if I've learned anything in the past few years, it's that lying to people who trust you hurts everyone."

Oh yeah, real smooth. Bring up our separation as if that even remotely compares to this.

"Yeah, your wife," I snapped.

"And the people you expect to risk their lives for your cause."

"It's *their* cause. This is their world—"

"This was *our* world," he said. "We brought them here. It's our job to protect them. And if we lie to them, we're no better than him."

I felt my eyes glow. "Don't ever make that comparison again."

"It's true—"

My voice was at a whisper so Micah didn't hear, but dumped out like the snarl of a beast. "It's entirely different. I'm lying to protect my child; he lied to protect himself."

"We can keep Micah safe. You know that we can. And if we're honest with them, if we tell them everything, they won't fuck with us, Laila. No one will." He looked quickly from my left eye to my right. "I know it's crazy, and I know it seems risky, but not telling them is riskier."

"You want to tell them everything? You want to tell them I was married to God in a past life and cheated on him with you? That he beat the shit out of me when I was pregnant and then, what, exactly? A few hundred thousand years later, give or take another few hundred thousand years, we decided to come here and cultivate a planet? You think they'll believe that?"

"I don't care if they believe it. But as long as we tell them, they can't say that we hid it from them. If they want to believe it, they can. If they don't, then they don't."

I clenched my jaw and stared him down for a moment.

"Either they'll be too scared to fuck with us because they know that we're gods and can wipe them from existence. Or they'll think we're cult leaders and leave us alone because they think we're quacks that will *still* wipe them from existence. Either way, it's a win-win."

I may not have liked it, but he did make a good point. Telling the survivors what we'd learned at the banquet last fall had formed me an alliance with the masses because I was honest. I walked them through what I lived step by step, and they appreciated that truth-fulness.

Plus, the Chambers knew better than to fuck with my kids after yesterday. No one could get to us in the perimeter; the kids were safe. Except for the bastard that was already here.

I ran my hand over my mouth. "I'll think about it, Jeremy."

"That's all that I'm asking." He placed his hand on my thigh and gave a gentle squeeze. But I wasn't in the mood for his cuteness. I pushed it away.

I watched Micah chase after Tink for the toy car she had clamped between her teeth. "We need to set a date for the execution. I need to feel safe in my home again. If Lux wanted to let Peterson out, he could do it without batting an eyelash."

"Yeah, we should get it over with. We'll go over the list of questions and make sure he answers the most important ones before we do."

"And we've got to cut his dick off first," I muttered. "And Chris gets to cut his eyes out."

"Seems fair."

CHAPTER THIRTY

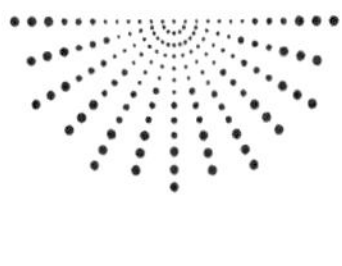

JEREMY

We spent the day on some Florida beach I can't remember the name of. Micah marveled at the feel of warm sand between his toes, then gasped in terror when a large wave trawled him to the ground. He recovered quick though.

Milly giggled at the cool salty water when it brushed her legs at Laila's hip. She even paddled around a bit when I held her in the water.

We walked along the boardwalk, ate some shitty street tacos for lunch, and returned home for dinner. Overall, it was a pretty good day. At least, in terms of spending time together and acquiring an experience that we'd hold onto for years to come.

But Laila was bitchy most of the time. Not with the kids, but she was pissed at me. Granted, I understood her concerns. I had the same ones. But it didn't change the facts.

Papy and I didn't agree on much, but he couldn't have been more right about this. The men and women who vowed themselves to fight our cause deserved to know the truth. Last year when we had the banquet for the survivors, Laila felt the same way. We didn't have all of the information then that we had now though, so I understood her newfound hesitation.

Hell, I wasn't one hundred percent certain it'd be a good idea either.

But we only had a few options on the table and lying is rarely the best one.

The truth was, I had no idea what the reaction would be. I knew there'd be some hostility. I knew there'd be some faithful followers regardless of Micah's role in the end of the world.

One way or another, though, they'd find out. Either from the rumor mill that Thomas started, or they'd come to their own conclusion just as Thomas had.

But it would happen, and we'd be in the same situation. From first-hand knowledge, I'd learned that the best way to address a conspiracy is to get on top of it before the theories go too far off the wall.

However, telling the masses we were once gods that ruled the planet seemed as far off the wall as we could get.

It was a lot. Explaining what we knew to dozens of people wouldn't be easy. It'd be long, difficult, and most likely wouldn't end well. Some people were going to go ape shit. A few would probably try to go after Micah. When they did, we'd have to fight our own to keep him safe. I hoped we wouldn't have to kill anyone but if it came to that, then so be it. No one would lay a finger on my children.

But that brought us back to the political issues. *"You'd choose your children over the world?"*

Yeah. I would. A thousand times over.

Any parent who truly loves their child would. Maybe turning my baby over for a greater cause was the ultimate sacrifice after all. But not one I was willing to make, even if it was a permanent solution rather than a temporary one. I didn't believe one could call themselves a good leader if they willfully sacrificed innocent lives that had no choice or understanding in what they were doing. A child could not make that decision. They never should have had to. But I damn sure wouldn't make it for them.

Hopefully, the fact that it *was* temporary would be the saving grace that made the people see our perspective.

Laila plopped down to the chair diagonal from the couch. She didn't attempt to meet my gaze as she picked her copy of *The History of the Peloponnesian War* by *Thucydides* off the end table. She peeled it open and stared down at the words on the pages.

"Still mad at me?" I asked, still lightly strumming the guitar on my lap.

She didn't even look up. "I'm not mad at you."

"Uh-huh," I murmured.

She turned with a glare. "I'm not mad at *you*. I'm mad that I have to make this decision. I'm mad that we didn't get the opportunity to enjoy our son before we had to face the fact that he's the match that lights the powder barrel to the apocalypse." She clapped the book shut. "I'm mad that every moment of our lives was predetermined before we lived it. I'm mad that I lost my baby for the millionth time, I'm mad that I got into that fucking van, I'm mad that they're never going to be remotely close to normal. I'm mad at our life. But I'm not mad at you."

Well, yeah. That was fair. "Yeah, me too."

"And I'm mad that you're right." She turned her eyes to the floor, rubbing her temples. "There's going to be some anarchy after we tell them. But as long as he stays here, he's safe. I'm not working anyway; I just won't take him out in public for a while. Maybe quick trips by teleportation but nothing more. It's not ideal. But I guess there's a pretty good chance that no kid alive is going to have a normal life in a few years. Bitter pill but one we all have to swallow."

Ah. So we were on the same page then.

"When do you want to make the announcement?" I asked.

"There's a Chamber's meeting at the La Fay mansion the week after Milly's birthday. We'll go. We'll tell them everything that we know. We'll make sure Kai and Celena are here to watch the kids. They're almost as powerful as us."

"No, we'll make sure the whole family's here. I don't think there's anyone powerful enough to get through the barrier spells, but we're going to take every precaution." I put my guitar on the ground. "The Chambers probably won't touch us. They're smart; they know we'll kill them. But their people. They might try to get a swing or two in."

"Did you get my text?" Brody said anxiously, suddenly appearing behind the couch.

"Jesus Christ, Brody." Laila's hand flew her chest.

"Get your phone out right now," Brody said with wide eyes.

I reached into my pocket for it. "What's going on?"

"Oh, just open any social networking site there is. You'll see," he said quickly. "But I sent you the link. Just watch it."

I opened my texts as Laila moved beside me. I clicked the blue URL to YouTube.

The video was titled:

Don't Say We Didn't Warn You

I looked at Brody as the loading symbol spun in circles. "This wasn't one of us, right?"

"Not that I know of. Papy said the Chambers are freaking the fuck out. Just watch it."

I turned back to the video. A robotic, female voice started over the speaker. It gave off an *Anonymous* kind of vibe but a lot less creepy. Rather than a V for Vendetta mask, the speaker was merely a black silhouette on a white backdrop. Female, judging by the narrow shoulders and accompanying voice, but entirely indistinguishable.

"Hello, ladies and gentlemen. People of planet Earth," she began. "We have a message for you. Whether you choose to believe it is up to you. But I'm begging that you hear me and that you listen.

"I hoped that I wouldn't have to do this, but it's inevitable now. I want you to know that we did try to stop it. Unfortunately though, destiny can't be avoided. The end of life as we know it has already begun.

"But let me make something clear. The end of the world we know does not equate to the end of all things. It means that reality is shifting. We already phased out a portion of the first wave of what's coming. In 2020 when the global pandemic hit, we were able to beat it. How did we do that? We listened to what our governments told us to do and together, we saved our loved ones and ourselves. As many as we could, anyway. Once everyone listened. And if everyone listens now, we can do that again.

"As for the authorities, we argued for a while over whether or not this announcement should be made. I'm sure you can see where they stood by the quality of this video. And since we don't have any government seal on the cover of this, I'm sure many of the people watching will immediately see it as a hoax. And I don't blame you. If I were in your shoes, I would do the same. But I promise you, this is real. This is happening. And I'm begging you to heed my advice. You can't fight what's coming but you can listen. Because we're going to help you. But we can't if you don't listen.

"Now isn't the time to hoard survival gear. You won't need it. Now isn't the time to stock up on medical supplies and toilet paper because you won't face the threat. Anyone who has a decent head on their shoulders will do as they're told when the time comes. When they do, they'll be moved somewhere safe from all of this. That, I can promise you.

"When that time comes, we'll be standing beside your president and prime ministers and kings and queens who will then tell you what I'm telling you now. If you do as we say when that day comes, you will live. I promise you that.

"But of course, your governments don't want you to panic. They know we have a bit of time. They don't want the stock market to crash and have to deal with unneeded resource scarcity in the meantime. And they're right, you don't have to panic because if you listen when the time comes, you *will* be safe.

"But I'm giving you this message as a preview. If you hear the words I'm saying to you now, they won't come as too much of a shock when they're confirmed. This may seem like a lot to take in, but what's coming will be even harder to understand. Your instinct will tell you not to take it seriously because we fear what we don't understand. You won't be able to process what is actually happening because coming to grips with the fact that your entire existence has been a façade isn't easy. Learning that an apocalyptic war between good and evil is more than just a story in an old book will be terrifying. Realizing so many things that you know as make-believe are real won't be easy either. But you don't need to be afraid because we're going to do everything within our power to keep you safe.

"In the meantime though, know that your time left here is limited. Enjoy it now. The comforts of air conditioning and central heating. The convenience of running water and public sewage systems. Enjoy your cushy office jobs. Eat at your favorite restaurants and save the recipes that mean the most to you.

"If you hate your job, quit it and cash out your assets. If you've been holding onto some expensive items to cash out on a rainy day, that day is today. Sell them and live the life you've dreamed of living.

"Go skydiving. Ride in a hot air balloon. Swim in all four oceans, ride a zip line, kiss someone you love at the top of a Ferris wheel. Take that trip to Disney. Visit the Himalayas. Do whatever it is that you've always wanted to do. Live your life. Then get a single backpack together of things that you'd hate to lose most and keep it somewhere convenient—maybe in your car, maybe by your front door.

"Make sure you invest in a pair of heavy-duty boots. Anything else that means a lot to you, put it somewhere safe and don't forget where it is. Think time capsule, not a storage facility. I'm not talking about antique furniture; I'm talking about wedding dresses. Photo albums. Things you want to pass down to the next generation that won't fit in your backpack. But be certain you pack that bag. And if you have pets, put whatever supplies they'd need to survive in it too.

"This isn't a threat. It's a message of preparedness. And I hope that you listen."

The voice grew quiet for a few seconds.

"We'll see you again in a couple of years. Enjoy your lives, people of Earth. Your whole existence is going to shift soon."

It ended.

Whoever the hell that was, they had a plan. To take the people somewhere. But where? And they said they could bring their pets? Kind, but an odd thing to say when referencing the end of all things.

A thought dawned on me. Those mystery CIA people.

We're handling it, they'd told Adam.

"This had to be someone in our community," Laila said. "The shift, Peterson's said that before."

"The CIA told Adam to give us the same advice," Brody said. "To live our lives and enjoy the time we have left. How much do you want to bet whoever came that day to interrogate him is the same person that made this video?"

I tightened my jaw and took in slow deep breaths. "They said they're going to keep the people safe. If they belong to our community, why wouldn't they come to the Chambers with information like that?"

"Clearly, they want to remain name and faceless." Laila gestured to my phone. "They probably have beef with the Council too."

"No one's going to listen to this anyway."

"Hey, maybe they won't take it completely serious, but look at how many views it has. This shit is viral," Brody said.

"Wait, why would they tell us to stock up on essential items but not the general public?" I asked.

Laila lifted her hand to her mouth and chewed her thumb nail. "They're moving the people somewhere safe when shit hits the fan. But they'll need us on the front lines."

Kind of. Sort of.

CHAPTER THIRTY-ONE

LAILA

Jeremy yelled into the phone at his ear in French, spitting some pretty harsh words like vomit. I bounced Milly at my hip while I poured myself a cup of coffee. He huffed. He snapped something else before he pulled the phone from his ear and tossed it to the counter.

For obvious reasons, we hadn't gotten any sleep.

"'I told you to be transparent with your people, Jeremy. Not the entire world.'" He spoke in his grandfather's thick accent, then clenched his jaw.

"The Chambers think that was us?" I asked.

"Papy does. I don't know about everyone else." He rubbed his thumb and forefinger against his eyelids. "Why do they care anyway? Whoever they were, they didn't do anything wrong. They told people to enjoy their lives while they still have them. They didn't publicize any secrets; they didn't condemn our kinds. They sent out a simple warning. I don't see why that would be an issue for anyone."

"I don't know why they'd care either. But they aren't the only ones that think it was us." I slid my phone across the counter. "Helena texted. So did Moriah, Brendon, and the Wilsons. Everyone thinks we're the ones who put that video out. I told them we didn't, but I don't know. I kind of wish we had. The supernatural community knows; the general public deserves that knowledge too."

He chewed his lip. "Yeah. Yeah, I agree. But you know what, fuck it. I don't give a damn what the Chambers think. This had nothing to do with us."

Sure was ironic timing. Just as I'd concluded that Jeremy was right and we needed to be transparent with the supernatural world, a video of someone telling the entire world that it'd end soon—posted only an hour prior—goes viral. Coincidence or more, the fact remained.

"Yeah, fuck 'em," I muttered. "But I'm taking that video as a sign."

"A sign of what?"

"That we're doing the right thing. Telling everyone what we've learned, I mean."

"Oh," he said. "Yeah. Yeah, I think so too. Do you still want to wait until the next Chamber's meeting? Because apparently, they're calling an emergency one this afternoon. They want us there. I told Papy to piss off, but I can call him back."

Rubbing my temples, I said, "Yeah, we might as well. Like you said. Let's stop the rumors before they start."

He released a slow, calming breath. "I'll check with Celena and Kai to see if they can watch the kids. If they can't, one of us can stay here."

"Works for me."

Jeremy's phone rang beside the flowers in the center of the island. *Heylel.*

That reminded me. We'd wanted to talk to him as soon as we got Micah back, but shit had been hectic. I'd been pushing all of this out of my mind and simply enjoyed being a mother before the Chamber's Meeting. It was about time we addressed him too.

"Haven't heard from him in a while," I said. "Put it on speaker."

He slid the green bar and clicked the speaker button. "Hey, man, what's up?"

"Oh, good. I'm glad you're awake," Heylel said on the other end. "I'm sure you've seen the video by now then."

"Oh yeah. We saw it." I huffed. "Wasn't us though, if that's why you're calling."

"No, I know," he muttered. "No, I was calling because I'd like to meet with you. Both of you. In fact, I'd like to meet with all of the world leaders. Rumor has it you've made some friends in that area."

Wouldn't call them friends. Allies, but not exactly friends. Having him with us would be good though. No one was gonna fuck with the king of hell.

"Rumor made it downstairs that quick?" Jeremy asked.

Heylel chuckled. "You know how that goes."

"That I do," Jeremy muttered. "So what are you thinking? You want to come with us to the Chamber's meeting?"

"If you don't mind."

"Might give us a bad rep, my man." I smiled.

Heylel chuckled again. "I never thought that mattered much to you, Laila."

"Yeah, it doesn't," I said. "What time's the meeting, baby?"

"Two their time." He glanced at the clock. "So two hours?"

"I can make it there within the hour if you'd like to meet me at the end of the path. We should probably do a bit of catching up anyway."

"Yeah, we've got a lot to talk about," Jeremy said. "Call me when you're here and I'll bring a necklace down."

"Will do. See you soon."

<hr>

"It sounds like you two have remembered a great deal then." Heylel took a sip from his coffee and looked out over the garden. "Those begonias are doing wonderful. What do you use for fertilizer?"

"We compost," Jeremy said. "But did you know about any of this?"

"About you being married to my father?" He looked at me.

I nodded.

"No, I can't say that I did. I knew there was bad blood between the three of you. I always thought it was out of jealousy. The fact that you were bound, and he never had that connection with someone else. You have to bear in mind, I wasn't born until a few years after you moved to this world. You were all much older than me."

"How old were the kids then?" Jeremy asked. "When... When he did what he did."

"Fairly young. We measured years a little differently then, but no more than ten," he said. "You used to say that he should have been older. I never knew what you meant by that until now."

"What do you mean?" I asked.

"Well, remember that I told you his soul couldn't reside in just any body? It had to be held? That is what makes him so innocent?" Heylel met my gaze.

I nodded, and he looked at Jeremy.

"I can't be certain. But the two of you, you didn't just create life, you created souls. His was always incredibly powerful. The first merging of light and dark on both sides, a cosmic collision. And given your power over the afterlife, I think it was you who held his soul first. My guess would be that you placed the same soul that left his body that day into the new life you conceived together later after his death in your womb."

I thought for a moment. So I didn't lose my baby that day. I lost his first body, but Nix moved that same soul into the next child we conceived. At least, that what it sounded like he was saying.

I gave a careful nod.

"Did you know that I could do that?" Jeremy asked. "That I was a necromancer?"

"I knew that Nix was," Heylel said. "But Nix and you are not the same, Jeremy. You are him, yes, but you don't share all things. Nix was Elvan, after all. You have many different attributes than your past self. Véa certainly had none of my blood in your first lives. Many things have changed. I didn't know what abilities passed along."

Jeremy rubbed a hand against his mouth.

"You spoke with him, you said." Heylel looked at me. I nodded. He ran his tongue over his lips. His gaze shifted to his coffee. He cleared his throat. "Does he still hate me?"

"Seemed like he kind of hates everything except for the humans," Jeremy muttered.

"Even you?" Heylel tilted his head to the side a bit.

Turning his gaze down, Jeremy said, "No. No, it kind of seemed like he respected me."

"Always did," he murmured. "I suppose that's a brother thing. Mine aren't quite as loyal." He chuckled. "And I never screwed their wives."

I narrowed my gaze. "Ha-ha."

"Yeah, well. Seems like mine did me pretty dirty too," Jeremy muttered.

"We'll have to swap horror stories some time."

"Once I have a clearer memory of what happened."

Heylel was quiet for a moment. He said, "He didn't want to hurt the humans, you said."

"No, they're his top priority," I said. "He won't hand them over to Wormwood. That's why he made sure I was so powerful in this life, so that I'm strong enough to fight them."

"I did think that it was odd for him want to kill them. Temporarily, sure. Killing them off and starting anew isn't something he's a stranger to. But souls are power, and he doesn't like losing power. This, this makes more sense. He's always had a particular affiliation for the humans. His precious little advanced monkeys."

Precious little advanced monkeys. I had to chuckle.

"Mommy," Micah said at the patio door. His hand rubbed against his mopey, tired eyes. "What'we you doing?"

I smiled as I stood. "Me and Daddy are just talking to our friend. I'm sorry, baby, did we wake you up?"

He shook his head, gazing over Heylel and clutching his stuffed lamb close to his chest. A half smile tugged at his sleepy lips. "Hi."

Heylel smiled and brought himself to his feet. "Hello there."

I brushed past Heylel and lifted Micah to my hip. "This is an old friend of ours. His name's—"

Micah's smile lifted. "Lucy."

My forehead crinkled. Heylel's brows rose. He laughed and gave a fast nod. "You remember."

"Maybe a little bit. I don't know whewe I wemembew you though."

"Lucy," Jeremy said. "As in, Lucifer."

"As I said before." Heylel smiled. "I've gone by many names. But they all ring the same bell."

CHAPTER THIRTY-TWO

JEREMY

Watching Micah and Heylel together was incredibly strange. They'd never met, not in this life, but they knew one another. Old friends reunited after centuries and centuries apart.

I'd thought that Micah attached to us so quickly because of the dreams where we communicated for the months before we found him. But as I looked at the two of them laughing like old pals, I realized that was hardly the case. He knew us because he remembered us from eons before. He remembered us before we remembered him.

That thought led to another chain-reacted realization. I'd always thought I was just a sensitive guy. I thought that was the reason I was so obsessed with Laila's pregnancy and keeping her safe. But now I saw that wasn't it either.

My subconscious mind knew what my conscious couldn't understand. Some part of me deep down knew that we'd lose him again. Maybe some part of me knew that the brother I'd betrayed in my first life was the one behind it all too. Maybe that's why I blamed myself for her disappearance even though I knew she was the one who willingly climbed into that van.

Regardless, it was a pleasant breakfast. But we didn't have any more time to discuss what we'd learned. I didn't get to ask the million questions I'd compiled for him. Although, I wasn't sure he could answer them anyway. Like he'd said, he wasn't born until centuries after our origin.

Laila and I got the kids ready and packed their diaper bags. We teleported them to Celena, Wyatt, and Leah. Adam and Jenna arrived with Hannah and Kai just as we were leaving. I felt a little better knowing they were all there to watch over them in our absence.

When we landed in the hallway to Mémé and Papy's dining hall, I took in a long, steady breath. I opened the door and held it for Laila and Heylel. As we entered the room, the hushed chatter grew to a sudden halt.

All eyes turned to Heylel. He sent the crowd a gentle smile and lowered his head in a soft nod, but it didn't seem to matter. His reputation sent a chill through anyone with our world's knowledge who crossed his path.

Papy's eyes widened as our gazes met. He stood, grasped ahold of my bicep, and pulled me away. "What are you doing, Jeremy? Are you out of your mind?"

"I'm doing what you told me to do." I yanked my arm away. "And he's the only person who can corroborate what we're about to tell everyone."

"You shouldn't have—"

"Well, I did," I said. "And it's too late now, isn't it?"

He tightened his jaw and exhaled a careful, shaking breath. His head, and he walked to his seat. As I lowered myself to the chair between Laila and Heylel, he muttered, "Doesn't like me much?"

I chuckled and looked at Papy at the end of the table. Laila tightened her hand to a fist, nearly holding her breath. I ignored the gazes of the other shocked Chambers and placed my hand just above her knee. She glanced at me and put her fingers over mine. Papy cleared his throat.

"Thank you all for coming again today. We all know why we're here. So let's just get to it then, shall we?" he said. "Who would like to begin?"

"Um, yeah. Hi, over here." Blair Martin stood. I didn't know her well, but we'd met at affairs like this a few times before. She, like me, came from a powerful family. Full-blood Guardian with a lot of reign over Northern Australia. Her parents died a few years back, and she took over in their place. Her values weren't much different from theirs from what I'd heard. She was just as much a stickler for the rules as my grandparents. "What the fuck is Lucifer doing here?"

"Ouch." He frowned. "Pleasure to meet you too, Miss Martin."

"This is obscene." She scoffed. "I agreed to work with you and your family, Jeremy. I did not agree to work with Satan himself."

"Love, I don't think you know what a satan is." He pronounced the word differently. Blair had said it as say-tin. Heylel said it as sah-I. "And not even if we're fighting for the same cause?"

"You and I will never be on the same side, mate," she said.

"Believe it or not, he is," Laila said. "He doesn't want the world to stop spinning any more than the rest of us."

"Oh, no? Then what is it that you want?" Blair crossed her arms. "To assert yourselves? To show us just how powerful your other allies are?"

"No." I stood. "No, we have a lot to share with you all today. We got a little side-tracked last time we were here. My wife and I didn't have the chance to properly explain what we've learned in the past few months. And Lucifer is here to serve as a witness. Because he has a lot of information that the rest of us can't imagine."

"Like what?" Dayo knitted her brows. "How to defy good nature?"

"Were any of you present when this world became our home?" Heylel stood beside me and looked around. "Did any of you witness the War of the Gods? Do you even know what that is? No. Of course you don't. Because your souls were infants then. But I remember it. I remember everything. I have sat at the hand of the god you pray to, and you think I have nothing worth sharing? Why? Because of the way I have been personified in your popular culture and folklore fan fiction?"

"Maybe because of the lives your children have ripped from our arms." Janis Wilson stood with a furious gaze.

"That isn't fair. You've had many children that have not done you justice as a parent, Janis," Heylel said.

Her fangs shot out of her gums. Elijah gripped her arm.

I noticed how he addressed them each by name. I wasn't sure if he did that for the sake of formalities or simply to make it clear that he knew them better than they knew him. Either way, I liked his style.

"Whether we like it or not, we all have to stand together." Laila stood and shook her head. "This is insane. We're talking about a biblical war of the worlds here, and you guys are worried about Lucifer? The man who's been around for eons and hasn't caused any problems? You're more worried about him than the unknown threat soaring through the galaxy kill everyone on this world? Then take our home too? Lucifer's got big guns, and we're going to need the biggest arsenal anyone has ever seen. And he's not asking for a damn thing. Not your soul, not even your respect. He's willing to help us for nothing. So how about you all keep the judgment to yourselves."

"This is about principle." Thomas La Fay smacked his palms against the table as he stood. "This is about decency."

"Don't go throwing stones when you live in a glass house, Thomas," Papy said.

Laila snapped her head toward him, eyes lighting up. "You'll keep your mouth shut if you want to walk out of this room."

"Don't you threaten me, little gi—"

Laila teleported behind him and gripped him by the back of his hair. He reached for the dagger at his hip before she grasped ahold of it and flung it to his throat. "You can call me Laila. You can call me Missus Callidy, or miss, or ma'am. But do not call me a little girl." The room grew eerily quiet as she spoke into his ear. "I can deal with a lot of shit. But do you know how I deal with someone who goes after my babies?" She pushed the blade slightly into his neck. "You're on thin ice, Thomas. Keep your fucking mouth shut."

Damn. Why'd that turn me on?

She dropped his blade to the table and turned back to the anxious faces. As she walked to her place beside me at the table, she said, "While I have your attention, I'd like to clear the air. My family didn't put out that video. No, we don't have a plan to save the world. We don't have shit. If we did, we'd have briefed you on the subject by now. So you can all stop blowing up our phones."

"Well, who does then?" Roland asked. "I doubt whoever that was decided to talk out of their ass to the entire planet."

"We don't know," I said. "But honestly, I don't give a shit. If they have a plan, then awesome. The burden isn't ours to bare. If they're going to save the world, we don't have to. But—"

"That's not what they said," Moriah uttered.

"What?" Laila asked.

"We all saw that message. But who was it targeted toward?" Moriah said. "The humans. Whoever that was, they plan to help the humans stay safe. They said something about how 'it will be hard for you to accept that all the things you believe as imaginary are real. But *we're* going to help you.' They'll need our help for whatever they're planning. That's why I believed it was you two in the first place. Saving the world isn't a one-man job."

Huh. I supposed they had.

That brought me back to the same conclusion we'd drawn last night. They told us to have a stockpile for a reason. Peterson built us an army of supernaturals.

People with abilities—hopefully—capable of fighting an alien race.

But then another thought came to me.

Why had they told us to cash out our accounts?

"Well, if it wasn't you, we need to learn who it was. They said that the world politics won't come forward with this information. That must mean they've been in contact," Roland said. "Raphael, you have some government connections, don't you?"

"I could do some digging," Papy said.

"I can help. My telepathy, I mean," Laila said. "Give me some names, I'll do some research and a little stalking. Might be able to get to the bottom of it."

"Excellent," Papy murmured. "I'll make some calls when the meeting ends. I'll contact Jeremy once I have something for you."

I cleared my throat. "Well, that checks one thing off the list."

Onto the dreaded topic.

"What is it that you needed to share with us today, Jeremy?" Papy asked.

I looked at Laila. She took in a slow breath and twined her fingers between mine. "Until the start of this year, we didn't know any of this either. And in all honesty, I don't really want to share it with you or anyone else."

"Not necessarily because we want to keep it from you," Laila said. "But because it's some far-fetched shit. And I'm not sure you're going to believe it. But we don't want to lie to the people who are going to risk their lives fighting behind us."

"So here it goes."

CHAPTER THIRTY-THREE

LAILA

We spent the next three hours recalling the information we'd started to gather on December 26th, 2021. Jeremy and I opened things up, and Heylel took the reins for a while. After the word 'god' was mentioned, profanities began to toss back and forth.

On more than one occasion, Jeremy held his pointer finger up in a hushing motion and retorted something like, 'You can talk when I'm finished.' Which I'd never seen him do, and it was actually incredibly sexy. His voice fell to this deep, masculine octave, and, I won't lie, I got a little wet.

The stages they experienced were relatively similar to the ones of grief. It started with denial. "This can't be true. You're lying, you must be lying." It moved to anger, although that one remained for most of the meeting. Someone even threw a glass of water at me. I caught it, of course—even kept the liquid from spilling. Nonetheless, we pissed off a lot of people.

Bargaining came next. "But what if this is just some trick? Powerful demons are known to play mind games. I'm not saying that you're lying but maybe you were lied *to*."

I went on to explain the dreams. The deep connection I had to them, how I recognized the way Micah felt inside my womb in either lifetime. The way that Nix felt as real to Véa as Jeremy did to me. I reminded them that they didn't have to believe it. But I knew it to be true.

Sadness followed. They may not have believed it with every fiber of their being, but the seed of question was planted, and their redwood of blind obedience was struck by lightning.

As that person on the video had said, learning everything you've been taught is pretend is a terrifying realization.

And all of that was before we even made it to the part where I was married to their god. The air in the room got thicker then.

By the time I made it to my recollection of losing my child, the room was boiling. The words 'whore' and 'slut' were tossed around quite a bit.

Jeremy jumped to my defense before I proudly proclaimed that maybe I was. And so the fuck what.

Infidelity is never just cause for murder and torture. The only reasonable response to cheating when one party wants to leave the marriage is divorce. Not violence. Not death. Once I phrased it like that, those rich, shameful bastards grew pretty quiet. Undoubtedly, plenty of them had been involved in similar scandals.

Then we carefully treaded onto the topic of Micah. That proved the hardest of all.

"So you did then." Thomas scoffed. "You brought your son back and let my daughter die."

"Yes, Thomas. I did. And I won't apologize for it," Jeremy said. "Your daughter tortured my toddler. She helped Peterson kidnap him and disguise his location for three years. Not to mention the thousands of others her actions affected. And had it been a Demon instead of your daughter, you'd have done the same thing."

"Honestly, I agree," Roland muttered. "Somebody should have taken care of that cunt years ago. No offense, of course."

Thomas's jaw clenched.

"What does that mean then?" Dayo murmured. "Does that mean..."

I looked between her eyes, knowing good and damn well what she was getting to. She was the last person I'd expect to say it, but that's probably why she trailed off.

"What does what mean?" I asked.

"Killing him could be a pause button," Eric said at the end of the table near Papy. "If we sacrifice the child, we will buy ourselves some—"

"Over my dead body," I said.

His gaze narrowed. "That can be arranged."

I laughed.

That little Witch? Really? First of all, he was a man. Male Witches weren't shit. And secondly, I'd love to take out the resentment I held for his daughter on his wrinkly little face.

"Oh, can it?" Jeremy raised a brow.

"I would love to see you try." I smiled. "It's been a while; I could use a good fight."

"I'd watch who I spoke to that way, young lad—"

I wagged a finger. "The next person to call me 'young lady' is getting a knee to their nuts, pal."

"That is out of the question," Heylel stated with a piercing gaze. "The three of us created an entire world. You're a piece of dog shit on the bottom of my shoe, Eric. Don't voice an opinion like that again until you hold at least a quarter of the power just one of us has. This conversation is a courtesy. To touch a hair on that child's head, you'll have to get through all three of us. And everyone in this room knows that isn't possible."

"You wouldn't do it willingly?" Blair asked. "You wouldn't give up one child to save the world?"

My face screwed up in disgust tied together with fury. "Would you?"

"With a heavy heart," she said. "But of course I would. One child to save a million? That seems like a simple question."

"Are you a parent?" Jeremy asked with an expression similar to mine.

"I am."

He scoffed. "Well, you shouldn't be."

"Excuse m—"

"I will never sacrifice my child. Never. Because the world means absolutely nothing without him. And aside from that, what kind of person would I be if I condoned something like that, let alone worked to help it happen? No, I'm sorry, but nothing is worth my two-year-old's life. Nothing. And no one should be put into the situation where they're expected to even think something that awful." Jeremy's eyes darted between hers.

She narrowed her gaze, lip curling in disgust.

Honestly, I couldn't give a shit less. She could glower at us for as long as she wanted. That didn't make her right.

They all were acting as though it was us defying good nature. As if sacrificing a healthy, beautiful child was the logical thing to do, or the right thing to do. As if *we* were the villains here.

"Don't look at me like that, Blair. I'm not the one who set this up. You know who did?" Jeremy asked. "The man you fall to your knees and beg forgiveness to. The man who tells you to keep your mouth shut and ask your husband's permission for every single thing that you do. The man who smote villages and said rape is okay so long as you pay the woman's father afterward. No, I'm not the villain. The one who assembled this game is. Don't you get it?

"We're pinned to look like the bad guys. But who's the one who bartered their brother's child as a payment? Who's the one who killed his kid and told some great big story about how it was to save you from your sins? He set up that philosophy, sacrificing the only begotten son, in anticipation of this day. He knew this would come to a head. He wants you to view something your instincts tell you is disgusting as some beautiful, poetic, sacrificial sign of love. But that isn't love. That is mass manipulation at its finest."

The room fell quiet.

"Is that who you are?" I looked between the sea of uncertainty. "Do you believe it's okay to make child sacrifices?"

"If it's to save the world," Eric said.

"Okay, you know what." I rubbed my temple. "Alright everybody, think about this for a second. Let's say you're human. For the sake of this metaphor, imagine you're a middle-class person working on your own to care for your two children. Both of your children are sick with the same disease, but they were diagnosed at different times so their scripts run out at different times.

"From time to time when money's short, you give one of your kids the other one's medication and pay it back when you can afford to fill the second script. You get paid today; you're going to grab the second script when you pick the kids up from school.

"But something cataclysmic takes place. Say the apocalypse starts. Everything shuts down and you can't pick up that script. Both of your children will die without those meds, but you can't loot for that medicine right now.

"You know you have enough to last a week and a half for both of them. But if you only give it to one kid, that kid will live for three weeks, and the other will die tomorrow. So what do you do? The same outcome's going to happen either way. You're going to run out of pills eventually, whether it be in a week and a half or three weeks. So do you let one kid live for three weeks? Or both kids live for a week and a half?"

"Well, obviously, you'd give the medicine to both children. But—" Blair said.

"But the outcome is the same either way. One day, it's going to happen, and you're going to have to fight to make sure your children survive." I locked my gaze with hers. "And as it stands right now, we're as prepared as we can be for an unknown threat. We have people ready to fight. In a hundred or two hundred years, everyone will have forgotten. And by then, the two of us might not be around. Or we will, and we won't remember who we are. Or we will, and we won't be as powerful as we are in this life."

"The reality is, the two us were designed to fight this," Jeremy said. "The dominoes were put into place long before we were born by your god himself. Having our son was just the thing that tapped them over. You can add more to prolong the end. But ultimately, it still ends. And there's nothing any of us can do to stop it."

"Do you expect us to believe that the lord himself called upon a man to torture nearly a thousand of our people?" a woman at the end questioned. "The holy people, the ones he tasked with caring for the human race?"

"God's 'holy people' were imprisoned many times, love." Roland sipped his wine. "I don't know why any of you are shocked by this. You act as though you've never read the man's work. He loves a good sob story."

"So what is this then, hmm?" Blair asked. "Do you expect us to worship you then? You expect us to bow to you instead of him?"

I laughed. "Did I say that?"

"Well, gods typically expect praise."

"*Your* god expects praise," I snapped. "But no, bitch, I don't want shit from you. Ya know what I want? To go back to work at my diner. I want to take orders and pour coffee and talk to old people about how to use Facebook to talk to their grandkids. I want to be able to send my son to the same shitty, American public school I went to without fearing for his life. I want my biggest problem to be a car that keeps breaking down.

"I want to be pathetically simple. I don't want to be who I am any more than you want this to be true. I want to tell destiny to fuck off. But I can't. This is coming whether any of us are ready for it or not."

The room grew quiet once more.

Moriah ran her fingers through her long copper hair and rubbed her scalp. "What do you want us to do with this information, Laila?"

"Whatever you see fit," I answered. "Tell your people. Disregard it as rambles of a couple of psychos. I don't really care. But we aren't hiding. We've said our peace. We've told you what we know. We're keeping nothing from no one."

"Will you then?" Papy asked at the foot of the table. "Tell all the people?"

"We'll tell anyone who asks," I said.

"But if you do spread the word," Jeremy began, "make sure you spread it loud and clear. Make sure your people know we have no known enemies. But the moment you threaten our children, there's an immediate price on your head."

"We won't tolerate so much as a threat against these children," Heylel stated. "Be certain to make that part abundantly clear."

"In the meantime, we should prepare," Roland said with a nod. "We don't know when this is coming. But while the humans are enjoying their remaining time, let's train ours. Sparring, training exercises."

"We should work on strengthening our barriers around the underground hospital systems," Papy murmured. "Many of them have attached spaces for refugees."

"Not to mention the libraries," Moriah said. "We can transform those spaces. Prepare to use them as war medic stations and store excess supplies for resources. We can border them off with powerful spells to have a safe space for our soldiers to reside when and if we need them. Many of them are already running on renewable resources, but we should think a bit broader. Perhaps start some gardens? Widen areas for meals to feed the masses?"

"We should try to recruit some Fae," Janis Wilson murmured. She looked at me. "People like you will be commodities for something like this. The ability to heal and manufacture food and fresh drinking water? We'll need that."

"I can try," I said. "But the way we've been treated by this community isn't going to do us any favors. Honestly, I'm sure a lot of my people will return to the Fae Realm when that time comes. There aren't many on this plane anyway, and no one's going to want to leave their homeland to come fight a war that isn't theirs."

"You and your siblings plan to stay, don't you?" Roland asked.

"Honestly, we didn't always," Jeremy said. "We planned on leaving if we couldn't stop it. But that was before we remembered who we were."

"We're staying," I said. "And we'll do everything that we can. But I agree with Roland, we should work on training. Perfecting abilities, hand-to-hand combat, even shooting. Guns, arrows, maybe give spears a try too. We don't know what type of war this is going to be. We don't know how we'll have to fight. So let's work on perfecting everything."

"And that boy of yours," Papy said, "as powerful as his soul is, his power will be needed. You'll be training him as well, I'm sure."

Jeremy's jaw tightened. "Yes, we're helping him learn to use his abilities. But he's not even three. He won't be at the front of any army until he's old enough to make that decision for himself."

"Well, intergalactic travel takes some time." Eric sipped his wine. "Maybe ten or twenty years until this war lands. At least if he's trained from such a young age, he'll be prepared to fight in what's coming."

That sent a shiver down my spine, but he wasn't wrong.

"Both of our children will be taught to properly use their powers. But as with any child, none of them will be expected to fight until they're of age," I said. "We won't send babies to fight a war. Not our babies, not anyone else's."

"And what is that age?" Elijah asked. "I'm not one for proposing children fight our battles either, but we can't expect them to be twenty-five before they fight in this. We may not make it that long without them."

"I think that should be judged on a case-to-case basis," Papy said. "Some children may be ready to fight at fifteen. Others, perhaps not until their later teens."

"That decision should be left to the parents and the child," Roland said.

"I can get behind that," Jeremy said.

"Well, I am glad that we are all on the same page," Heylel murmured. "We'll spend whatever time we have left preparing for what's to come."

"And enjoying the world we love," I said.

CHAPTER THIRTY-FOUR

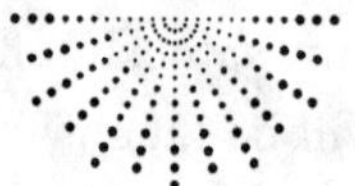

MAY 29, 2022 - JEREMY

The last few weeks moved like lightning. Between organizing the kid's birthday party, me returning to work, and every member of the family working somewhere in the supernatural community day in and day out to prepare for the apocalypse, it's fair to say that we were stretched a little thin.

When I wasn't at work, Laila and I were working on mastering each other's abilities. She got a handle on my energy manipulation faster than I knew was possible. Neither of us had so much as dipped our toes into the afterlife though. I had to give Hannah credit because mastering that ability was the hardest thing I ever did.

But I was having a hell of a time getting a grip on Laila's powers. Fire came easily. It was as easy as thinking of something that pissed me off. Air wasn't so bad either. But I hadn't so much as wiggled a raindrop or brought a single flower to bloom.

I started to understand a bit of Peterson's point during that time. Still hated the fucker. But I got it. Tapping into those other powers was extremely difficult. Laila only mastered them all so quickly because she had to in order to protect herself. But it felt like it'd take me years before I could come close to doing what she could.

The kids were coming along though. Micah was a boss with his abilities. He and Laila were close to equal in their elemental powers. Even Milly was learning quicker than me. She'd started to toddle around the week before, just around the time that she learned to catch me on fire when I changed her diaper. I found myself pretty grateful for my recent immunity to flames right about then.

Neither of us had gone to the basement since that day. Honestly, we'd asked all the questions we could get an answer to. He wasn't going to tell us what was coming, and we'd essentially figured him out. We understood his motives, we understood the ins and outs of what he believed. All that was left was his execution.

We scheduled it for June 29th, 2022. The three-year anniversary of the first escape. Closing the door on the same day it was opened, at least for me, Laila, and Micah.

Since it was a public execution, we'd have to take the barrier spell down around the house. We couldn't afford to have it put back up, so it made sense to do it somewhere else. Wyatt had the land and privacy at his old home in West Virginia and was more than willing to let us borrow it for the night.

The day of his execution, every survivor would get their opportunity to torture Peterson as they saw fit. Brutal, I guess. But only fair. We'd had him captive for months, and the family had all gotten their chance to hurt the guy. The other survivors deserved that closure too.

Chris and Laila planned to go through with their last revenge the week after the party. Then they'd let him rot in agonizing isolation until his final day. But the guy was already dead in my eyes.

The world seemed to be moving like an old VHS on fast forward. Just flicking right past me. Every day was a task. Go to work, do the paperwork, fix that leaky sink, make sure to call the bands and have the bar stocked for the weekend shows, and so on. Then come home, relax for ten minutes over dinner, play with the kids, get them ready for bed and spend the following two hours struggling to get them to actually stay in their beds. Afterward, I'd spend two to three hours practicing entering and exiting the abyss, then working on Laila's abilities. I'd get five hours of sleep and rinse repeat Monday through Saturday. I took Sundays off to have fun with Laila and the kids. We'd checked off a few places on our lists already, but we still had plenty to get to.

Overall, it was a challenge. I hadn't had time to pick up my guitar since it started. I'd barely gotten the chance to kiss my wife for more than two seconds. Life wasn't easy.

But it was so much easier than the previous three years had been. Yeah, I was a little overwhelmed. But I didn't have the time to even think about getting high or fucking things up, which is a good thing for an addict. All that I could think about was a preparedness to keep my life as close to what it was in that time as possible. Busy, yes, but being busy for the people I loved and a cause that matters was a beautiful thing.

CHAPTER THIRTY-FIVE

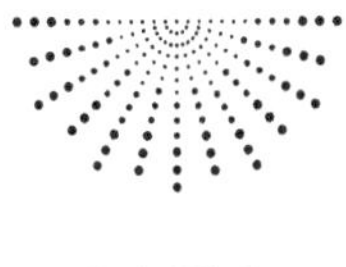

LAILA

The past month was weird. It was filled with this odd sense of peace bound with urgency. We could see the clouds rolling in, but the sun was still shining. And we were dancing in its rays while hastily weatherizing the windows.

Things were a mess. The beautiful mess I'd dreamed of living for years, but a disaster. I never gave mothers enough credit, and if not for my own, I would have lost my mind during that time.

Jeremy was handling the diner. But I had a full-time job training with people in our community in addition to my children and myself. We'd started something of a training course. Five days a week, I worked with people who were preparing to fight in the coming war. While I sparred with swords and superpowers, my Mom helped a lot.

She decided to finally retire the week after that Chamber's meeting. She said she wanted to be a full-time grandma from there on out. I think that video that came out played a part in that. Jenna needed a sitter for Luka now that she was back to work too. Four hands are better than two so Mom brought Luka over almost every day. She was there on the porch with the kids while I trained in the yard.

At first, I was hesitant for my son to see the violence. The first day or so, I told Micah I had to go work with Jeremy. But the kid had powers. He teleported to me while I was in the middle of a faceoff with Helena in the backyard of the main house.

Being the little hero that he was, he got Helena on the ground with the wind in the blink of an eye. I explained what we were doing. She wasn't trying to hurt me; we were practicing. At which point, he released his hold and proclaimed that he wanted to practice too. Suddenly, my son and I were throwing balls of fire and water at one another like a game of dodgeball.

And honestly? It brought the fun back to a scary time.

It wasn't just Helena, though. I'd battled with almost every important person in our world at that point. Roland was a damn good fighter. For a Werewolf, he moved like a swan. I'd never even witnessed Moriah cast a spell, but she was a badass bitch in action too.

When I wasn't training people in the day, I was traveling throughout the underground hospital system with my children. Micah, Milly, and I were setting up indoor gardens to prepare if our people had to go into hiding. While we were there, he got a little practice in on healing on command.

Milly amazed me every day that ticked by too. She could grow a sprout to a vegetable in a second. She could barely say more than five words, but she had her own garden. We'd even put some flowers on the windowsill in her bedroom. Every morning that I walked into her room, the flowers had grown more vibrant and resilient than they'd been the night before.

She'd started walking the week before, just after her first birthday. And I was there. I was so grateful that I got to witness that moment. She toddled her way from me to Jeremy on the hardwood floor in the kitchen after dinner. Micah cheered her on, and Tink licked her face when she stumbled to Jeremy's lap. We even got it on video. That moment was one of the best in my life.

On her actual birthday, we went out to eat at this restaurant I went to every birthday growing up. They sang to her and brought her an ice cream with candles and sparklers. I worried that Micah would be jealous, but he got to eat most of it, so he didn't mind. He asked if we could come back for his birthday.

I promised we'd come back for every one of his birthdays. But the moment I said it, I wished I hadn't because I didn't know how many birthdays he'd see before the end came.

I pushed that thought from my mind as quickly as it came.

That's the only option when the world's going to shit, and there's no way to stop it. I did what I could and kept moving, finding a way to be happy even though I knew I wouldn't be for long.

It's true what they say. Ignorance really is bliss.

Originally, I planned two separate parties for the kids. Jeremy and I ultimately decided it made more sense to have one big party rather than two. It's not like there'd be that many kids, and I didn't want to have to rent a bounce castle twice. In a way, it *was* both of their first birthdays.

Again, I worried that he'd be jealous, but Micah didn't mind sharing his day with his sister, and Milly was too little to give a shit. It also helped with expenses. We weren't broke by any means, but we were told to get as much money together as we could. It'd take a while before we figured out why, but we would need that stash soon enough.

And if I'm being completely honest, I didn't have the time to plan two parties. Between all of the things I was doing in the supernatural world while still trying to be a mother and find time to take a shit without conversing with a child, planning one party was hard enough. A joyous kind of hard that I was incredibly grateful for, but still not easy.

No one had threatened Micah again after that day, another thing I was incredibly grateful for. Rumor spread around fast after the Chamber's meeting. I was pretty shocked at the response. I suppose I expected an uproar. But the only hostility we faced came from their leaders. I guess a lot of people already idolized me enough that learning I was a goddess didn't come as much of a shock. I still didn't let my guard down. But the people seemed to hold the same respect for me that they always had, if not more than before. People love to have a hero they can see with their own eyes.

Since the dream when I remembered losing my baby, the memories had lightened. Rather than brutal fights and odd threesomes, I saw

Jeremy. Or Nix, I guess. It was mostly just flashes. The sound of his voice as he sang or a quick image of him smiling accompanied by a laugh.

I preferred them to the whole story. I didn't want to remember who I was then. I wanted to live *my* life.

Still though, we'd found something of a balance throughout the chaos. Although more hectic than my life had ever been, they were also some of the best times I'd ever live.

CHAPTER THIRTY-SIX

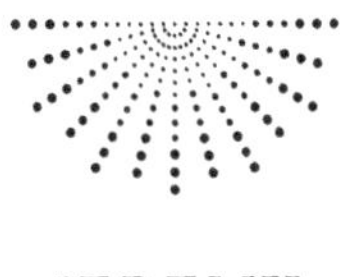

JEREMY

"Where do you want the cake, babe?" I called, walking in the front door. "Out there with the food?"

"Uh," Laila muttered from the patio. "Just leave it on the counter. I don't want the icing to melt."

"Alright." I set it on the island. Just then, Milly erupted in violent sobs. When I turned, she was lying face down beside the coffee table. "Damn it."

"Is she okay?" Laila yelled.

I walked across the room and picked her up. Noticing a red mark on her forehead, I sighed. "Yeah, she's fine. Might have a goose egg later though."

"Of course." She walked into the living room. "Where's Micah? Did you get him dressed?"

"Wight hewe!" He trotted down the steps with Tink at his tail. "I got dwessed all by myself."

I chuckled as I met his gaze. Despite the uncanny resemblance, I sometimes wondered how the hell he was my kid. He wore a pair of brown khakis and a blue button-up with a sweater vest over top.

"Well, don't you look handsome." Laila smiled while I bounced and hushed Milly. "Didn't even miss a button."

He grinned as he approached, then frowned when he looked to his sister. "What's wong, Milly?"

"She bumped her head. She'll be alright," I said.

"Hewe," he murmured. He raised his hand. White light radiated from it. I reflexively pulled her back.

"No, it's okay," Laila said. "It barely tickles when he heals."

"Really?" I asked.

"Weally." Micah smiled and placed his hand against Milly's forehead. Her cries softened, but she pushed him away. "See? You's all bettew now."

Huh. When he'd healed Chris's eyes, I'd assumed Chris bit through the pain like we did. But I supposed not. I wondered why that was. Did it have something to do with the fact that he was a hybrid? Or was it the purity of his soul?

Micah turned to me. "Can we eat the cake now?"

I laughed. "No, we have to wait for everyone to get here."

He frowned. "But I's hungwy."

"There's a whole buffet out there. Go eat some fruit, kid." Laila ran her fingers through his hair. "Everyone's getting here soon. Once everyone eats some real food, then you can have cake."

He frowned. "Well, when's evewyone coming then?"

"I'm sure they'll be here soon." She smiled. "Go get a cookie, I'm right behind you."

"Cookie?" His eyes widened. He scampered out the back door.

Laila laughed and shook her head. She reached for Milly. "He doesn't look like it, but he's definitely my kid."

I chuckled, moving throughout the room to pick up the miscellaneous toys scattered around. "So it doesn't hurt when Micah heals?"

"It does if it's bad. The real nasty injuries seem to feel about the same as when I heal. But he healed this lady at the hospital—she just had a cut on her hand—and she described it as a pins and needles type of sensation."

"No shit," I muttered.

"Yeah. Pretty cool, huh?" She sat on the couch and began changing Milly's diaper. "I'm sure it'll come in handy."

"Hey, guys," Chris called, jogging his way down the steps. "I'm going to pick up the ice, do you need anything else?"

"No, I think we're good," Laila said.

"Oh, if you could grab some extra napkins." I folded the throw blanket and laid it on the back of the couch. "Might be a little low on those."

"Sounds good." He started to the back door.

"Hey, before you go," Laila began, buttoning Milly's pink dress, "we should probably touch base on something."

"What's that?"

"Heylel's coming today." I turned to meet his gaze. His brows dropped, but I continued before he could go on. "Look, I know you have opinions about him. But meet him and judge for yourself. Micah loves him; he's the one that asked if he could come today. And it's his day. I couldn't tell him no."

Chris clenched his jaw. "Like you said. He's your kid. It's not my place."

"I'm glad you see it that way," Laila said. "But we don't want you to feel uncomfortable. He wouldn't dream of hurting—"

"Again. Not my place." Chris grabbed the doorknob. "Let me know if you need anything else while I'm out."

"Will do. But hey, don't take the Subie. Take the charger, it's been a while since I started her up." I gestured toward the keys on the wall. "Could probably use a drive."

"Shit, that's cool." He smiled. "Does it need gas?"

"No, you should be good."

"Alright, awesome. I'll be back."

That'd been something on my mind lately.

I loved that car. It was my baby. But it was his first. I only got it because we thought he was dead, and Adam didn't want it. He could've bought his own, but that was our dad's. It had sentimental value. And I never drove it anymore; it was too much of a pain in the ass to move the car seats around.

As he started out the door, I turned to Laila. "I think I should give it to him."

"What—the Charger?" I nodded as she stood. "But that car's your child."

I chuckled. "Yeah. Yeah, it was. Now I have *actual* children though. And it was supposed to go to him anyway. It did actually, it went into his name when he turned eighteen. When he disappeared, it went to me. But we don't need it. It's just sitting there. Might as well go to someone who will use it."

She smiled and lifted her head in a nod. "Yeah, I think that's a good idea."

"Daddy!" Micah yelled in the doorway with wide eyes. "You got to come see this."

"What's that?" I asked.

His eyes twinkled with joy and amazement. "You just got to see it."

I laughed. "Alright, I'm coming."

He took my hand and hastily carted me out the back door, down the steps, and into the tent where the buffet was set up. He pointed to the cupcakes Laila was up until three a.m. working on. Although she wasn't known for her artistic abilities, I could *almost* tell that they were supposed to be shaped like a saxophone.

Probably wouldn't have known if she hadn't told me, but there was a bit of a resemblance.

"It's a sasophone!"

I laughed. "It kind of looks like a saxophone."

"And I can eat it?" He looked up with wide eyes and an even wider grin.

"Yeah, go ahead. But just one, alright?"

"This is the best day evew." He lifted a cupcake to his mouth.

CHAPTER THIRTY-SEVEN

LAILA

Everyone arrived at the party by two-thirty. I tried explaining to Micah that he was supposed to play first, then open presents and eat cake, but the concept flew right over his head. He wanted that damn cake. He didn't care much about the massive pile of toys. Just wanted the cake. So we hurried onto singing happy birthday and did the cake before the gifts.

It felt hectic as it was happening, but I remember it in slow motion now. His little laugh when Adam showed him how to use the remote-controlled drone, his giant smile when he opened the beginner guitar that Jeremy picked out, and the joy that flooded over him as he jumped in the bounce castle. Milly tried to jump too, but it was a little out of her age range. Instead, Micah jumped around her and forced her to topple. He'd help her up and do it again.

She looked so perfect that day too. Mom and I had picked out the cutest pastel pink dress a few months prior, and I was ecstatic that it fit. I pushed her little black waves from her eyes and pinned them back with a cute pink barrette. Of course, I had to fix it a thousand times, but it looked adorable for a moment or two.

Watching them eat cake and run through the grass felt like something from a dream. I nearly pinched myself a few times, practically unable to believe we made it here.

A year before to the day, we were in the Fae Realm. We hadn't met Micah yet. We didn't know that I was once Véa and Jeremy was once Nix. We didn't know we were gods. We didn't know there were other par animarum aside from ourselves and Celena and Wyatt.

All that we had was each other and that little girl.

In that moment, I began to realize what Peterson meant that day on the cliffside. I needed her. That little girl gave me a reason to keep living. She gave me a reason to keep fighting. Magically speaking, we wouldn't need her for decades. But Milly was the medicine keeping me alive as I fought to bring my other baby home. I gave birth three years prior, but Milly was the one that made me a mother.

Jeremy's hand went to my hips from behind as I poured myself a glass of water. "I think we pulled it off," he murmured at my ear.

A quiet laugh left my lips. I turned my head up to meet his gaze. "What, the party?"

He smiled. His hands went around my waist, looking at Micah and Milly playing in the grass with Luka and my mom. He rested his chin on top of my head. "No, just... just everything. We're here, you know? They're here, they're safe, they're happy and they're healthy." I rested my head against his chest. His arms tightened around me. "We pulled it off."

"Barely." I twisted my arms around his and squeezed. "But we did. We pulled it off."

"Too bad we started the apocalypse along the way," he muttered.

"Yeah, let's not talk about that today. Let's just be happy."

"That's a reasonable request." He kissed my hair. "Where are we going to put all these toys?"

"All over the house, I'm guessing." I laughed. "He liked the guitar though."

"Milly liked the keyboard too. Maybe I should start Micah on a keyboard too; piano's one of the best ways to learn to identify pitches as notes."

I craned my head up with a smile. "What are you going to do if they end up hating music?"

"Give them up for adoption." He grinned. I laughed, and he chuckled. "I don't know, make them play sports. Or dance or some shit, I don't know. But they've got to be passionate about something."

I put my hands to my hips. "You say dance of some shit before you even mention writing."

"Writing's cool too." He held his playful grin. "If, ya know. They actually do it."

He just had to call me out like that.

I narrowed my gaze. "Wow, okay. I see how it is."

He laughed. Then his phone rang in his pocket. He lifted it out and checked the text. "Heylel's here. I'm gonna go grab him."

"Alright. We'll be here." I pressed my lips to his and walked to the kids.

"Mommy, look." Micah raised his hand to show me three lightning bugs crawling on his palm. "I caught them all by myself."

Mom laughed. "He sure did."

"Look at that. Three just like you." I smiled. "Almost, anyway."

"Do they light diffewent colows? Or just gween?" he asked.

"Just green, I think," I said.

"I wish they was blue. I like blue. Ooh, or yellow."

"I wish they were pink." Mom smiled. "Pink's my favorite color."

"I like pink too," Micah said. "But I like yellow the best."

"Where'd Jeremy go?" Mom asked.

Milly climbed into my lap. I situated her dress against my legs. "Just to grab our friend at the end of the driveway."

"Lai!" Celena called a few yards away. "Can I pack up a plate to take home?"

"Knock yourself out, girl. Take it all," I yelled.

"Awesome." She grinned and turned back to the food.

I smiled.

This was what it meant to be happy.

I was surrounded by family, doing menial things. Watching light-ning bugs pulse in my son's palm, listening to the birds chip in the tree-tops, breathing in warm spring air. Life was good. This was all anyone wanted and deserved.

Damn. I wished I could take this day and stretch it out. I wished I could live in it for the rest of my life. This was a dream come true.

"Max?" Mom asked.

"Huh?" I asked.

"Is that who Jeremy's grabbing?" Mom asked.

"Oh. No, Max is around here somewhere. Probably around the front smoking a joint with the guys. Where's Jenna?"

She chuckled. "I told her to spend some time with Adam. They've both been working a lot lately; she needed a minute kid-free."

"Ah." I laughed.

"Who's this friend then? Someone I know?"

Ugh. Now to tell my mom that the devil would be at my kid's birthday party. Not that she was ever the judgmental type, but that word packs a punch.

"Uh, no. No, you haven't met him. His name's Heylel; maybe you've heard me mention him a couple times."

"Oh, I see," she murmured.

I cleared my throat. "He kind of has a bad reputation. I don't want to go into the details but... Yeah, just don't be surprised if some of Jere-my's siblings are a little intimidated by him. But he's harmless, don't worry."

Micah's glanced over my shoulder, and his eyes widened. He grinned and started to his feet. He brushed past me and ran in a full sprint to Heylel. Micah wrapped his arms around his legs and looked up at him with a smile. Jeremy laughed. Heylel kneeled beside him and exchanged some gentle words.

"Damn, he's a good-looking boy," Mom murmured. "Does he have a dad?"

What a pleasant thought. My mom with my ex-husband. Who was also my grandfather.

I grimaced. "Not one you'd be interested in. But he's older than everyone here combined. So ya know. Go for it, Mom."

She laughed and shook her head. "I'm just kidding."

I started to my feet and hoisted Milly to my hip. "Come on over, I'll introduce you."

She stood from the grass and started toward them with me. "You should pull your hair back more often, that looks nice," she said to Jeremy.

"I like to switch it up from time to time," he said.

In fairness, I liked his hair better down. Yeah, on special occasions, I liked it up. But I loved his wild waves. They reminded me of the messy man I fell in love with. It did look cute pulled back though.

Heylel smiled as he stood. I gestured between them. "Well, Heylel, I'd like to introduce you to my mom, Rachel. And Mom, this is Heylel."

"Pleasure to meet you." He sent a warm smile and extended his hand to hers. "Missus Callidy then, I presume."

"That's me." She smiled back and shook his hand. "Nice to meet you too, hon."

He held his polite smile, turning to me. "I'm sorry I'm so late. Things have been... Well, hell."

I laughed. "Don't worry about it. We're just glad you made it. Micah really wanted you here."

"I did." Micah nodded quickly. "I've got to show you my pwesents."

"While we're on the subject." Heylel reached into his suit pocket and retrieved a small trinket wrapped in blue paper. "I've got something for you. Oh, and one for V—" He paused. "Milly. And for Milly, too."

"What is it?" Micah asked with a big smile.

"Open it and find out." He smiled. Micah ripped the paper and tossed it to the ground. I looked at the small, wooden figurine in his hand. I couldn't make out what it was actually supposed to be, but as I stared at it, that deja-vu moment flashed behind my eyelids. Only for a split second.

I saw it in a child's hand and heard a little boy's quiet giggle. I heard Heylel's voice, laughing as he spoke in a language I couldn't clearly make out.

Micah gasped, staring down at it. He laughed. "I lost this long times ago, whewe'd you find it?"

Heylel forced a smile. "It doesn't matter where I found it so long as it's back with its owner, right?"

Micah laughed and gave a quick nod. "Wight."

Heylel smiled and retrieved a smaller box from his pocket. "I suppose it isn't much of a gift if they were theirs to begin with. But it's about time they're returned."

I took the box and flipped it open. A small necklace laid over top a layer of purple tissue paper. The pendant was a blackish purple, Elvan ore sphere on a silver chain. A similar deja-vu moment passed over me, but it wasn't the sound of my son's laughter that I heard. Just silence and an image.

That pendant laying on the ground in a puddle of blood. And a small child's hand lifeless beside it.

And a horrible, sinking sensation in my stomach. Then pain. The sensation of my throat sealing shut. The taste of salty water running down my throat.

I shuddered and flipped it shut. Heylel met my gaze, eyes gentle. "I take it you didn't remember the day you made it?"

I swallowed and shook my head.

"Ah, well, I brought a gift for you as well. For the both of you, I suppose, but not something you're likely to use, Jeremy."

"That's alright," Jeremy said.

He extended a small flask. Obsidian colored when I looked at it head on, but purple when the light reflected against it. I remembered it clear as day. The one Nix and Véa drank from together the night that they met.

My mouth fell open and my eyes glimmered with tears. I looked up and smiled. "Thank you."

He smiled. "Try it. I've got a bit more I could bring by, but my crop is limited so I don't have much."

I passed Milly to Jeremy. "What is it?"

"You'll remember. Just go easy on it; it's much stronger than drinks you're used to."

Behind me, I heard someone clear their throat. I spun around. Chris held a broad stance. His jaw was tight, and his hands were balled to fists on either side.

I pulled the cork from the flask.

"Heylel, this is my brother Chris," Jeremy said. "And Chris, this is our friend Heylel."

Heylel smiled and extended his hand. "Thank you. Thank you so much."

Chris reached out to shake his palm. "I'm sorry, what for?"

He tilted his head to the side a bit. "You are the brother who was with Micah all of that time, aren't you? The one who kept him company and helped him learn to be the boy he is?"

Chris puzzled at him for a moment. "Yeah. That was me."

"Well then." Heylel smiled. "Thank you."

CHAPTER THIRTY-EIGHT

JEREMY

The smell of burning wood coasted into my nose. Shadows of the dancing flames bounced on Laila's cheek to my left. Laughter filled my ears, echoing from my own lips too. I sipped my water, shaking my head.

"No, no." Leah laughed. "That is not what happened."

"That is definitely what happened," I said.

"I did not fall asleep in my vomit." She shook her head. "I fell asleep. Then vomited and fell back to sleep *beside* said vomit."

"She's right," Laila agreed. "That was the order."

"Fine, I got the order wrong, but you still get sloppy," I said. "So no, you cannot have any more magic liquor at my children's birthday party."

Heylel laughed. "I could bring you a bit. It takes a few years to prepare, but I could probably spare a flask worth."

"I like this guy." Leah grinned. "If I weren't gay, my man."

He gave an awkward chuckle again. Something of a grimace crossed his face—and it'd take years before I realized why. He took a sip from his glass. "It isn't magic either, by the way."

"What is it then?" Laila lifted the flask to her nose and sniffed. "It's way sweeter than wine."

It did smell really good. Sure, like something one would use to sterilize a surface, but also incredibly sweet. But I was content sober. I'd gotten a taste off of Laila's lips, and that'd do.

"We called it yeshlbawa," Heylel said. "It comes from a fruit similar to that of grapes although still quite different. Much sweeter, like you said. Blue, clearly. The texture was similar to that of a... A—What are those called? Those little pink balls with the white fruit and black seeds inside?"

"Dragonfruit?" I asked.

"Ah, that's it," he said. "Yes, a bit like dragon fruit."

Celena wiggled her fingers at Laila. "Let me have a sip."

"Can I twy it?" Micah asked from my lap.

"In eighteen years," I said.

"Eh, maybe fifteen," Laila said.

Probably. We weren't exactly sticklers.

I'd make sure my kids knew the dangers of drugs, but I wouldn't make a big deal if I caught them with some liquor in their teens. 'Just say no' doesn't work. Curiosity and experimenting with drugs is normal. Should it become more than an occasional occurrence, that'd be a whole other thing.

"I'll bring you some of the fruit next time I visit," Heylel said. "But no, you're too young for a drink like this."

"That was delicious," Celena murmured.

Heylel smiled. He looked between her and Wyatt. He turned his head to the side. "I can't quite place the two of you. You're familiar to me, but I can't quite put my finger on it."

"Not the top bitches." Celena glanced at Laila and I with a grin.

"No, it isn't that. All of you were equals, really. But the three of us were family." He looked from me to Laila. "Just a different dynamic."

"Yeah, so about that," Brody said from his seat on the other side of the fire. "Can you give us a little more history there? We know how it ended, but I'm really confused about a couple of things."

"And what's that..." Heylel raised a brow, unsure of his name.

"Brody," I said.

"Right. Brody. I apologize, there's a lot of names to remember here," Heylel said.

"It's fine," he muttered. "No, but what I'm wondering is the time-line. You were there on the last planet, right? The one they all came from?"

"No. I was born here."

"But what did you all call it?" Hannah asked. "Not just heaven, right?"

"No." Heylel smiled. "No, they all called it Matriaza."

"Enochian, right?" I asked.

"Similar, anyway. Angels now refer to heaven as Matriax. But yes, Matriaza is what the Angelic homeland was called."

"So how did you know it was them?" Chris asked. He raised his beer and gestured between me and Laila with the end. "That they were who they are, I mean."

"Well, after the second compound was taken, that's when I started to see the parallels. I'd heard the rumors about two possible paired souls, and then two more, but I didn't know for certain until we met. Abbadon played a part in that as well. He was certain it was so."

"And he came along after us, right?" Laila asked.

Heylel nodded. "He was also born here. We have different mothers though."

"It's so weird." Adam laughed and wiggled his arm around Jenna's shoulder. "Like, just to think about, you know? I've known both of you for so long. And then finding out that you're both go—"

"So gosh darn in love." Laila widened her eyes and glanced at Micah.

We weren't sure about a lot of things as parents. But we were sure that we didn't want our kids growing up calling themselves gods. They didn't need that prideful chip on their shoulder.

Even we didn't like calling ourselves that. We only did because it sounded better than aliens that cultivated human existence on earth.

"Oh. Right," Hannah said.

"It is weird though," I muttered.

"Yeah. Really fucking weird." Chris stood. "I could use another drink. Anybody want one?"

"Yeah, can you grab me a water?" I asked.

"More wine, please." Leah handed him her glass.

"Can you get me another beer?" Adam said.

"Mine's getting a little low too," Brody muttered.

"Jesus, I only have two hands, people."

"I'll help." Heylel stood. "My legs are getting a bit tense anyway."

Chris glanced at me with an unsure gaze. He forced a civil smile and started to the house with Heylel close behind.

"I always knew me and the devil would get along." Leah glanced at him walking into the house.

Rachel's eyes widened. "I'm sorry, the what?"

"We don't like that wowd," Micah said.

She looked at him with confusion and turned to Laila. "Okay, you're going to have to fill me in here, baby."

Laila shook her head. "Things aren't black and white. Stories get twisted and turned and misconstrued."

Her head tilted to the side a bit. "But that's him. That's the king of hell."

"He's not a king," I said. "Just a leader. Think of him kind of like the president. But ya know, without the elections."

"And you knew each other?" She made a face. "In a past life?"

"Yeah, to make a long story short," Laila said.

"Wait a minute now. Hang on. If you knew him in a past life, does that mean that you knew his dad?"

Laila awkwardly shifted in her seat, as if even the mention sent a chill down her spine. "Yeah. Yeah, we did."

She thought for another moment. "As in... *The* dad."

"If you want to call him that," I muttered,

"Have you met him?" she asked. "In this life, I mean."

"Unfortunately," Laila muttered. She glanced at Micah listening on my lap. "But we'll talk about the details after the party."

Rachel looked at Micah then back to Laila. She gave a slow nod.

"I like him," Jenna said. "But I didn't think he'd be so pretty."

"He is really pretty, isn't he?" Hannah chimed in. "Like a gentle kind of sexy."

"I didn't expect him to be so respectful," Wyatt muttered. "He's more polite than me, and I'm from the south. That's saying something."

"Neither did I," Adam said. "But I like him too. He fits right in around here."

"I think I see what you mean now," Celena said. "He feels like a part of the family. I remember him too. Vaguely, just his face really, but I do. I remember him."

"Yeah, me too," Wyatt agreed.

"Is it possible that I could too?" Kai asked, eyes shifting between Laila and me. "It's hard to explain. But I feel like we've met before too."

We had dillydallied around with the idea of Kai and Hannah being par animarum like us. The only reason we didn't know yet was because they were both holding onto their virginities. But that wedding was coming soon. Then we'd know for sure.

"I think it's possible." I squinted at him. "I could see you being Venark. You look a lot like him."

"He was Véa's brother, I could see the parallel," Laila said. "I don't know. Seal the deal and we'll find out."

"Yeah, Kai. Seal the deal." Hannah grinned.

He smiled and touched his lips to her cheek. "Another month, love."

She leaned back in the camping chair. "Yeah, yeah."

"Everything's ready, right?" I asked.

"Yup," Hannah said. "I'm going for my dress fitting on Wednesday when I get off school. You're coming, right, Lai?"

"Wouldn't miss it." She smiled. "We have to pick up Milly's dress anyway."

"And your tux." I poked Micah. He giggled, and I smiled.

"You're going to be the cutest ring bearer in the world," Hannah said. "You won't lose the rings, will you?"

He smiled and shook his head. "I'll hold them weal tight."

"Where is my drink?" Leah craned toward the house. "It doesn't take this long to pour a glass of wine."

"Yeah, well. Those two should probably talk," I said. "Chris needs to see him the way that we do. He's so brainwashed, ya know? None of us ever fell for that Council bullshit. You'd think everything that's happened would make him see things from a different perspective, but he just blindly respects them."

"We all picked shit up from Mom," Leah said. "Chris remembers you guy's dad clearer than the rest of us."

"Yeah, but Dad didn't fall for their shit either. Just about the only thing I can give the guy credit for," I said.

"No, but he was a stickler for the rules too," Adam said.

"And a 'man of faith,'" Brody muttered with air quotes.

"Yeah, well," I said, "either way. Chris needs to chill. This isn't the world he disappeared from ten years ago. Everything's changed."

"You've got to cut him some slack, baby," Laila said. "Our life is a lot for anyone to take in. But he's dealing with his own shit too."

"Yeah, I know. You're right. I just trust Heylel. About as much as I trust everyone here. And he doesn't have to feel the same way, but it'd be nice if he didn't look at me the way that he did for believing in him."

"Give him time," Leah said. "He'll come around."

"Who wants to hold this baby so I can take a piss?" Laila asked.

"I'll take the birthday girl." Hannah smiled, reaching for her.

CHAPTER THIRTY-NINE

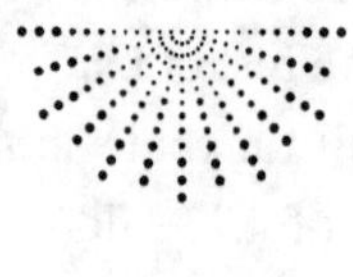

LAILA

I'd only drunk maybe two shots worth of that blue juice, but my legs felt like gelatin beneath me. I could walk a straight line, I wasn't shit-faced, but I certainly had a buzz going. Definitely wouldn't have felt comfortable behind the wheel, but still functional enough that I didn't mind being around the kids. Although I was a little tipsy, I certainly wasn't hallucinating. But I felt like I was for a moment.

I meandered past the kitchen to the powder room. My hand grasped the doorknob, but as I tried to turn it, the function clacked against the frame. Heylel called, "Just a second."

I leaned against the entry table, mindlessly glancing down at my very neglected fingernails. I remember thinking that I really needed to clean up my cuticles.

Then the door opened. Out walked Heylel wiping sweat from his brow.

"Tough go in there?" I gave a joking grin.

He laughed. "Sorry about that. It's all yours."

As I turned to let him pass, I glanced in the kitchen and saw Chris. He looked a bit out of breath too. And he hadn't been there a moment before when I walked past.

And the bathroom smelled like the air freshener in the corner. Not like something messy had just gone down the toilet.

I looked between them for a moment, both seeming like they'd just run a marathon. And Chris's shirt was mis-buttoned.

"Okay, hold up," I said. "Wait, did you two just fuck in my powder room?"

"What?" Chris asked.

I put my hands at my hips. "You heard me."

"You're crazy." Chris laughed, cheeks going red.

I arched a brow at Heylel. "You totally just fucked my brother in-law."

He laughed. "Laila—"

My head tilted. "That's kinda weird, isn't it? Since Jeremy was your uncle?"

He raised a finger, as if proving a point. "Nix was my uncle. Jeremy is not."

"They still look a lot alike." I glanced at Chris. "Guess more like Jeremy than Nix though, huh?"

"I'd say." He took a long gaze over him.

"Ah-ha, so you admit it." I smiled. I turned to Chris and cocked my head to the side. "I didn't know you were gay."

"I'm not gay," he claimed.

My shoulders lifted, head tilting from one side to the other. "I think fucking a guy in my bathroom's a little gay, man."

"We didn't fuck," Chris said firmly.

"Well, where were you when I walked in then? And why's your shirt not buttoned right when it was ten minutes ago? And why are you all sweaty?"

"Can you just drop it?" he asked. "Does it really matter?"

Of course it didn't. Adam and Jenna had gotten away earlier. They probably fucked in my powder room too. But to my understanding, Chris hated Heylel. So it was a bit of a surprise.

But judging by Chris's adamant proclamation that he was straight and insistence on not admitting otherwise, I took it that he wanted to keep it quiet. Which was fine. I didn't really get why, but it wasn't my place to judge either.

"Well, no. No, I don't care. Good for you guys. But ya know, you could have met up afterward instead of hooking up in the bathroom at your niece and nephew's birthday party." I looked at Heylel, giving a teasing half-smile. "Just bad manners."

"Laila—"

"Just use the other bathroom and clean your dicks off before you go out there. Celena and Wyatt'll smell it. Since I'm assuming you don't want people to know, and we're all aware of how this family likes to poke and prod. Oh, and do it quick because Leah's waiting on her wine."

Chris swallowed. "Thanks."

"Yeah, yeah. But lying about being gay is stupid, no one gives a fuck."

"I'm not gay," Chris said again.

"Guess it makes sense that the devil swings both ways, huh?" I poked Heylel with my elbow. He laughed. He cleared his throat. "Alright, sorry. Sensitive material. I'm just not used to the whole hiding your sexuality thing. But hey, it's your life." I turned to Chris. "Does anyone know?"

He pressed his lips together. "Jeremy does. Nobody else though, so I'd appreciate it if you kept it to yourself."

"Will do. And keep your dick to yourself at the next kid's birthday party, alright?"

He curled his lip. "Please never say that sentence again."

"Keep your penis in your pants. That better?"

"Oh, yeah. Perfect, thanks."

Jeremy lifted a cookie from the buffet table to his mouth. I put my arms around his waist from behind and laid my head against his back. He laughed, turning to meet my gaze. "Hey, you."

"Hey." I leaned onto my tiptoes and pressed my lips to his.

He curved back. Wiping his mouth, he nearly gagged at the taste of my lips. "It wasn't bad earlier but damn, babe."

"Oh, sorry." I covered my mouth. "That stuff is pretty strong."

"You aren't kidding," he muttered.

"So keep this quiet." I glanced at Heylel walking out the back door. "But I just walked in on your brother and him."

He wrinkled his brows before he raised one. "Doing what?"

"Well, they were in the bathroom. I don't know the details," I said. "But they were doing something, I know that."

He took another bite of his cookie. "When I told him to judge for himself, I didn't mean like that."

I grinned. "Well, hey, at least they're getting along."

"Fucking and getting along are two very different things. Haley and Leah were 'getting along' too until they weren't," he muttered. "But yeah, must trust him to some extent."

Nah, I wasn't picking up on those vibes. They were just fucking around. It'd hurt Chris's pride too much to actually date the devil.

I did enjoy the irony though considering how condescending he'd been about Heylel.

"How'd you find out he was into guys?" I asked in a hushed tone.

"Walked in on him with the pool boy at Mémé and Papy's."

"Damn. He's a hoe. I love it."

Jeremy leaned against the table. "Ten years without sex, I would be too." He looked over Chris walking out of the back door with hands full of drinks. "Must have had a pretty intense conversation before you walked in there."

"I'll say," I said.

Jeremy's phone buzzed in his pocket. As he pulled it out, I said, "Who is it?"

"Papy. They're probably here. I'll be right back."

CHAPTER FORTY

JEREMY

"My goodness." Mémé's gaze slid over the front of the house. "And you built this?"

"With a lot of help." I smiled, giving a happy nod. "But yeah. Yeah, this place is my pride and joy."

"Well, you should be proud." Her head shook as her eyes danced across my home. "This was just a little cabin when Jeán bought the land, wasn't it?"

"It was. Laila and I were living in the apartment above our diner when she got pregnant with Milly. We were looking for Micah, and it was only a one-bedroom. We didn't have the space for two kids. So we decided to build. And we had a lot of memories here. It made sense."

"It's very nice," Papy said. "Quaint. Very American, but nice."

I laughed. "Yeah, well, we're American."

"I suppose," Papy muttered.

That may not have sounded like a compliment, but coming from my grandfather, that was the closest to an accolade as I was going to get. And hey, I'd take it. In his own way, that was him jumping with excitement.

"So do you guys want a tour? Or do you just want to get to the party?"

"You can show us around after. I want to see those great-grandchildren of mine." Mémé smiled. "Sorry we are so late, by the way."

"It's still early your time," I said. "Don't worry about it. We did do the cake already though, so you won't get to sing to them. But there's still plenty of food if you're hungry."

"That's alright, we just ate," Papy said. "Just wanted to make an appearance."

Of course. Our American birthday cakes weren't exactly to their level of taste. They were more souffle and créme brûlée kind of people. It was okay though. I was just happy they came, and that Mémé would get to spend some time with the kids.

I gestured around the house. "Alright, this way then."

As we rounded the corner, Mémé took in a quiet gasp and gestured to the flower beds. "Wow," she murmured. "Quite the green thumb your wife has. These blooms should have passed by now."

"A Fae gift, I guess." I unclipped the gate to the backyard. Tink came barreling out. She jumped at Papy's legs with bared teeth. He shouted curses and pushed her away. I grasped her collar and tugged her back down. I wanted to say something about how glad he should be that Laila didn't see him call her fur baby a name but decided against it. "Sorry, she's weird around new people."

"My." Mémé held her hand over her heart. Her mouth hung open beneath her wide eyes, watching Tink fighting against my hold with snarling teeth. "Does it act this way around the children?"

"No, she likes them." I shot Papy a snarky smirk. He narrowed his gaze and pushed down his unwilling smile, brushing dog hair from his slacks. "Go ahead in, guys."

"I'm sure you remember Rachel, Laila's mom." I gestured between them. "And this is our friend Max. He's head manager at our diner."

"Of course." Mémé smiled and shook Rachel's palm.

Rachel smiled. "Nice to see you again."

Papy forced a smile and looked over Max. He glanced at me with a raised brow. "Il est humain?" *He's human?*

"Oui," I said.

He forced a smile as he shook his hand.

Obviously not his preference. But he was a great friend, and I was happy to introduce them. Max was a good guy, and he'd been busting his ass at our diner for years. He was practically a part of the family.

"And Max, Rachel, this is my grandma and grandpa, but you can call them Raphael and Adele," I said.

"Wow, I can definitely see the resemblance." Max laughed, eyeing the three of us. "Those eyes are a powerful gene."

I laughed. "Skipped right over Mills."

"Guess so, huh?"

Laila smiled, stood, and started toward us. Papy's eyes flicked over Heylel at the fire. "He's around quite a bit."

"He's a good friend." I smiled.

"Mm."

"I'm so glad you guys made it." Laila placed a hand on my back. "Are you hungry? It's not as fancy as you're used to but still tastes pretty damn good."

"Thank you, but we're fine." Mémé smiled. "But the decorations are beautiful. Truly. Absolutely stunning."

"Well, thank you. I tried but all the streamers are a little crooked. Kids don't really care though, you know?" Laila said. "But I insist that you try the cake. We use this little bakery in town, and everything that leaves their doors is amazing. Take a slice home if you want."

Mémé fought the frown that tugged at her lips. "Sure. Sure."

"But what about a drink?" She looked between them. "We've got it all. Water, soda, wine, brandy. You name it."

"Any scotch?" Papy asked.

Laila smiled and lifted her head in a nod. "I'll see what I can find. And a glass of red, Mémé?"

"Yes, please. Thank you."

"Alright, I'll be right back. You make yourselves at home." She touched her lips to mine and started into the house.

"I've got a few seats saved this way." Rachel gestured toward the camping chairs by the fire pit.

"Great, thank you," Mémé said.

"Can I speak with you for a moment, Jeremy?" Papy asked.

"Sure." I took a step back.

Rachel started to the fire with Max and Mémé.

I expected it to be something pertaining to the Chambers. Perhaps another meeting they wanted us to attend; maybe something they wanted us to know. But his gaze was soft. His shoulders were relaxed, his normally tense forehead was eased.

Unusual.

"What's going on?" I asked.

He smiled—which almost made me think I should talk to Mémé about having him seen for dementia. "Well, these sorts of things aren't usually handled on a first and third birthday. But we don't know where the world will be when they turn eighteen so now seems a good a time as ever."

Eighteen. That's when I got my hundred grand from them. Was that what he was getting at?

My forehead wrinkled. "You set up trust funds for my kids?"

He reached into his coat pocket. "No. No, because we don't know if the banks will be around much longer. I presumed you could hold onto it for them."

Which did seem reasonable. It was a good idea. We had been told to secure our assets, after all.

He handed me a check. I saw the numbers, and my eyes widened, counting six zeros behind the one.

"A million dollars?" I looked up at him. "You're giving them each five hundred grand?"

"We're giving them each three-hundred thousand dollars," he corrected. "To be used for college, or a home, or to start a business when they're old enough. Some worthwhile investment. I ask that you keep control over it. This kind of money can be wasted very quickly in the wrong hands."

I laughed. "Don't I know."

He smiled. "The other four-hundred thousand is for you and your wife."

My face screwed up. "Why?"

He looked down. His head shook. "Your father came to me in a dream. I know that it was not him, perhaps a manifestation of my own guilty conscious. But he said you'd need money. That you'd use it for the others. Your brothers and sisters, your children. And truth be told, this is a drop in what we have. But I believe you need it more than us."

Kind as that may have been, Laila and I were doing fine financially. We weren't billionaires, but prior to the house, she was nearly a millionaire. We didn't need his four hundred grand. Laila would be incredibly embarrassed if I accepted that kind of money based on the notion that we *needed* it. And truthfully, it hurt my pride a bit too.

"We don't need it," I muttered. "We aren't as wealthy as you but we—"

"Jeremy, this is not to slap your cheek," he said with a firm twitch between my eyes. "When your grandmother and I go, the five of you will get much more than this. This is practically your money already. Is there nowhere you can think to spend four-hundred-thousand dollars to prepare for what's to come?"

There were a thousand. We could set up a big ass greenhouse on the property. We could build that makeshift hospital Laila mentioned. Small homes, more composting toilets, other off grid living items we might need in an apocalypse.

I chewed my lip.

"I know that you are comfortable." He gestured to the house. "Like I said before, you made a nice little life for yourself. And I'm proud of that. But this may help you one day. Stash it away, or invest it in equipment, or housing, or medical supplies. If you don't need it, then split it amongst the children when they're old enough. But if you do, you will have it."

Well, he did make a good point. And it made my stomach feel fuzzier than it should have to hear that grumpy old bat tell me he was proud of me. But my kids weren't his only grandchildren.

I glanced at Luka in Adam's arms. "Do you have anything set up for him?"

"Three-hundred-thousand," he said. "But today isn't his day. I'll give Adam his check on his son's first birthday."

"Sounds fair," I murmured. "Alright. Alright, thank you."

He smiled. "So where's that drink?"

CHAPTER FORTY-ONE

LAILA

As the night drew on, we made some of the best memories we'd ever have as a family. In fact, that's what the remainder of 2022 and all of 2023 was all about. Spending time together. Loving one another. Enjoying our lives as one big, happy family.

It's bittersweet when I look back on it now. But for the remaining year and a half, we'd mostly just taste the sweetness.

Micah fell asleep in my lap and Milly in Jeremy's. The guests all left around eleven, so Jeremy and I got the kids to bed, cleaned up from the party, took a quick shower, and collapsed to the bed. As I lay back onto the pillow and blew out a long, heavy sigh, Jeremy inched up the bed and pressed his lips to mine with a wide grin.

I raised a brow, lips lifting in a smile. "What are you grinning about?"

"You know how Papy pulled me aside when they first got here?" He pushed hair behind my ear. I nodded. Jeremy reached into his pocket and handed me a slip of paper. As I unfolded it and realized it was a check, I read the numbers.

$1,000,000

One Million Dollars and 0/100 Cents

My mouth dropped open.

"Holy shit." I sprung forward and squinted over it a moment longer. "What... Why did he give you a million-dollar check?"

"Three-hundred-k for each kid. Then four-hundred for us."

I still didn't understand. "Why?"

"He said my dad came to him in a dream and told him we'd need it more than him," he said. "I figure it was probably the telepaths working with the CIA that came here that day. Maybe they made a mirage type of hallucination in his mind to get us more money? I don't know."

"Did you tell him we didn't need this?" I questioned.

"I did. But he insisted. Said it'd be all of us kid's money when they die anyway, and they aren't going to use it by then. They're loaded, babe, this isn't even a dent to them."

I scoffed. "How is a million dollars not a dent to anyone?"

"I don't know how much they have, but I know this isn't much. Maybe a dime of their worth? Less even? Who knows, they're a part of that one percent. Inherited wealth bullshit. And he's right. Those people told us to get as much money as we could. This does more than replenish our savings. This is more than you initially had when you got Moe's estate if you add it to what we already have."

I thought for a moment. "Last I checked, we had about a hundred-thousand left in the account."

"And a little over four hundred in the safe," he said. "So not including the kid's money, that takes us to about nine-hundred-thousand."

"Holy shit," I murmured. "That makes us millionaires."

It suddenly felt very hypocritical to talk about eating the rich. However, once I saw how our socialist mindsets would spend that money, I'd be back on my 'eat the rich' mentality.

He chewed his lip. "But we won't be for long. If we need this money, that means we'll need to spend it."

I ran my hand over my mouth. "Why would we need a million dollars? How is that going to help us save the world?"

Jeremy chewed his lip. "I have no clue."

"Well. Let's cash it out."

"Might need a bigger safe."

"Or maybe just bigger bills," Jeremy murmured.

Funny, that'd been what the CIA said. To cash it out in big bills. The oldest big bills we could get our hands on.

CHAPTER FORTY-TWO

JEREMY

Such a great fucking day. Only to fall to sleep and recall the worst—yet most formative—memory of my soul's existence.

As it flashed behind my eyelids, I was just as afraid as Nix. But I felt a little bit calmer than him because I knew how it ended. Although, I think he knew how it'd end too.

I remember holding her swaying shoulders and yelling for Venark as Stella and I helped Véa onto something like a couch composed of Elvan ore lined with fabric. I can still see the thick red blood dripping from her gown onto the green, velvet-like fabric. I can still feel her hot, tear drenched face in my hands as I insisted that she open her eyes.

The worst of it all was the deep connection I had to the afterlife. Because as she fought for her life, I struggled with every fiber of my being to hold onto our child's. I could feel the energy fighting to leave their bodies. Whatever Lux had done damaged our son's beyond repair. When Venark made it into that room and began healing her and the baby, I felt blood of my own stream from my nose.

Nix tried so fucking hard to keep that baby alive. But it was useless. His body wasn't developed enough to survive out of her womb.

Venark managed to heal Véa. The swelling around her face had receded, the abrasions over her knuckles, even the blood pouring from her legs lightened. She was better. But the baby wasn't.

The water had broken. She had no choice. Once labor begins, there's no stopping it. Especially not in a world without medical care like we have today.

Véa cried. I cried. But I kept telling her it was going to be fine. I didn't believe it, neither did she, but we pretended to because we had no alternative.

Most of the labor went on in flashes. She cried as I cradled her from behind and fought to keep her from seeing my tears. Part of Nix broke in those moments. His heart imploded inside of his rib cage with a pain more unbearable than anything I'd ever felt.

It was the same level of powerlessness I felt in my current life when she lost Micah in that cold, tiny cell.

The blame and self-hatred he felt then never entirely faded. I still feel it now, thousands of years later.

When our son came into the world, there was no eruption of tears. There was no flash of white light. The only cries came from Véa's lips. They wanted to fall from mine too, but I fought them with everything I had.

Stella tried to get him breathing. Véa tried pushing air into his lungs. I was still holding his soul inside of his body, but his heart wouldn't beat.

His whole body was blue. Dark, breathless blue.

I tried shocking him.

Véa tried healing him.

Venark attempted to suction the liquid from his esophagus.

But nothing worked. He was gone. He hadn't even lived, and he was gone.

Véa's steady sobs turned to heaving gasps as she coddled his blood and mucus-covered body to her chest. Tears drizzled from my eyes too, but I couldn't sob. I had to comfort her. I had to keep lying and telling her it would be okay as she cradled our dead child in her arms.

Stella said something softly before Véa screamed something I think translated to, "Get the fuck away from me!"

Giving a sad, gentle nod, Stella headed out the door I'd struggled her in through. Venark tried to finish healing her, but she shoved him back with the wind and continued to rock the corpse back and forth. The only person she didn't scream at was me. She let me hold her shoulders, resting her head against the lifeless child in her arms.

I watched her become the Laila I know. I watched fury boil out of her in the form of tears. Our son died that night, but the massive calamity I'd always known her to be was born. This messy, gorgeous combination of pain wrapped up with rage and love all tied into one. The beauty and peace within her collided with hatred and agony to create this awful, yet magnificent intricate balance.

I didn't attempt to tell her to put him down. I didn't say a word once Venark and Stella left. I just held her. She seemed grateful for that.

Somehow, I still held his soul inside of that dead body. I don't know what I planned to do with it when I had to let go, but I held onto it with everything I had. I couldn't let him leave us. He was dead. There was no resurrecting that body. But I held it there, I supposed, because I couldn't let it just disappear into the abyss.

We must have stayed like that for hours. I watched the blue sun rising in the window as she continued to cry in my arms. At that point, my brain thudded like a jackhammer behind my eyes, blood pouring from my nostril. I wiped it with my sleeve.

I kissed her forehead and whispered, "I don't know how long I can keep him here, mi lim," in Elvan.

Her cries intensified then, head rolling from her chest to my shoulder.

I kissed her forehead. I whispered, "But I... I think I can hold him somewhere else."

Lips still shaking, eyes still watering, she turned to meet my gaze. "What do you mean?"

"I-I'm not sure. I've never done it. But I—I think I can keep him from being born into anyone else. We can put his soul into a new body once we create one." I looked between her eyes and swallowed hard, blinking at the salty liquid over my irises. "I've never done it, but I-I can try."

"You can do that?" she whispered.

I licked my lips. "I can try. I-I'll try, mi lim."

Her trembling lips curved down. Her spilling eyes shut. She lifted the bluish baby back to her chest and touched her lips to his forehead. After a long minute, she bobbed her head in a slow nod.

———

Of course, my mind wouldn't show me how I managed to trap a soul in the afterlife and move it to a new body. No, that'd be too easy. Skipped straight past that part.

Instead, I then saw Nix helping Véa into a bath she clearly didn't want to take in a large hunk of stone that didn't come close to resembling a tub. She rolled away, sunken green eyes gazing off at something I couldn't see. I spoke to her, but she wouldn't say a word. She'd stopped crying and moved to absolute silence. Heartbreak.

It felt eerily familiar. The same level of helplessness I felt when she made it back from the capture in 2019. I bathed her that night too.

There was no comforting her when she was in a state like that. She didn't want comfort. She wanted the wrongs done to her made right. She wanted to shift the course of time that led her to that place. Not that I blamed her. I felt the same way.

I helped her to the modest, yet large bed in a massive bedroom covered in doors that led to the outside world. I suppose they were more of windows than doors since one would fall to their death if they took a step out of them. But it almost made me wonder what the point of having walls at all was. It felt more like a rooftop than a bedroom.

But I helped her falling body into the blankets and tucked them around her. I tried to get her to talk to me a time or two, but she was silent. She just stared vacantly at the bundled corpse in the bassinet beside the bed.

I lay beside her, running my fingers through her hair and whispering a quiet melody. She held our twined fingers close to her chest. I felt the weight of both our heavy hearts as I touched my lips to her cheek.

After a few hours that felt like years, I eventually managed to sing her to sleep. A few moments after her eyes closed, I slowly stood from the bed and walked to the bassinet.

I just stared at him.

He hardly looked like a baby. He looked... He looked like the personification of pain.

His lips were bluer than his eyes should have been. He had a head of dark hair and a tiny little nose. His skin was so pale, tainted with the same bluish, bruised color of his lips.

Fighting sobs as warmth spilled from my eyes, I lifted him to my arms.

But holding him almost hurt worse. Because he was so cold. He was supposed to be a ball of warmth in my arms, but his little cheeks were cooler than the wind that blew in from the window. I bunched the blanket tighter around him, as if that would somehow make it better. As if warming him up would bring him back.

I took in that soft smell of his newborn body coated with the early stages of decay, and my tears got heavier. Still, I fought the sobs. But one did escape. Véa stirred, and I held my breath to keep the next one inside.

His little blue hand was smaller than that of the water baby Milly carried around day in and day out. His thumb couldn't have been bigger than the bloom of a baby's breath.

I stood there for longer than I could keep track of.

Then Lux flashed behind my eyelids.

And when he did, my chest grew tight, heart banging at my ribs. My jaw clenched. Iron filled my mouth from a snag of my cheek between my teeth.

I carefully laid the body back to the cot. I touched my lips to Véa's forehead and tiptoed from the room. Venark called for me as I descended a winding Elvan ore staircase, but I ignored him. He caught my arm at the landing.

I flung it away. "What?! What do you want?"

"What are we going to do, Nix?" His glowing emeralds flicked between mine. He spoke behind gritted teeth. "Something has to be done. This cannot go unpunished—"

"*We* are not going to do anything." I turned and started away.

"So that's who you are. You stand beside the man who—"

I teleported to him and thrust his body to the wall. His eyes glowed brighter. "I stand beside her. *Her.* Only her. Not him, not you, no one but her and my child. Don't tell me who I am or what I have to do."

He clenched his jaw and shoved me off of him. "Take care of your brother or I will, Nix. Our *people* will."

"Oh, I plan to."

I felt his power the moment I left the palace doors. My mind followed it like a sailor to the North Star.

I pushed open a creaky wooden door. The aroma of stew and bread wafted into my nostrils. Stringed instruments and drunken words poured into my ears accompanied by billowing laughter. The people reminded me of the Open Lands in the Fae Realm—ranging in skin colors from white to blue to black, some with pointed ears and others with tusks and protruding jaws and some that looked as close to human as Véa and Lux.

And there he was. Hunched over the bar with a glass of dark brown liquid in his swollen hand. The sight of him sent an explosive fury through my extremities. Once I was a foot or two away, I said, "Lux."

As he turned, his face screwed up in confusion. I slammed my fist into his jaw.

The room fell silent as he stumbled off the chair. He staggered to his feet. I grabbed ahold of his shirt and banged my fist into his cheek again.

"I told you." Fast breaths panted in and out of my chest, squeezing the shirt of his tunic so tight I was surprised the fabric didn't rip. "I fucking told you to never put your hands on her again."

He telekinetically threw me off of him. His nostrils flared as he wiped blood from his lips and looked between my eyes. "Why don't you mind your damn business?"

Others within the bar stood, watching carefully with furrowed brows and tight jaws.

"How would you know anyway?" His gaze narrowed. Then his eyes flung wide open. His breaths grew short. He straightened his shoulders and balled his hands into fists. "You knew. You knew what the whore did, and you brought her—"

I teleported to him and grabbed him by his throat. He tried to pry my hand away, but I squeezed tighter, watching his eyes bulge as he struggled to bring in an even breath. "Nothing is just cause for the way you reacted. *Nothing.*"

As his face turned blue, he raised his knee and thrusted it into my groin. I gasped, releasing my hand at his throat.

"That's why you brought her here? To protect her little secret?!" He grabbed my hair and forced my gaze to his. "Whose is it, Nix? Who?"

I reached up, wrapped my fingers around his fist, and pushed them further into my scalp until I felt his knuckles crack beneath my own. He cried out in pain. I took hold of his shoulders and slammed him to the ground.

He fought against my weight as I pushed my knee into his chest.

"You're that stupid? You really haven't figured it out?" My brows pulled together, teeth gritted, driving my knee further into him. "Mine. He was my son, your nephew, and you fucking killed him."

His eyes popped. He'd stopped writhing when I'd spoken, but now, his strong grip shifted, slamming my body to the dirt floor. He flung his hands around my neck, jaw clamping shut as he squeezed the breath from my body.

He didn't say a word, but his face said it all. He hated me. He knew what I'd done, and he wanted to kill me for it.

But I teleported over him and slammed my fist into his face. He tried to grab ahold of me again, but I didn't give him the chance.

"Enough of this!" a woman's voice yelled in Elvan from behind the bar. "Outta my shop with all that. Now!"

I didn't even glance at her, just grasped his shirt and teleported outside of the door I'd just entered. As we landed, he threw me off of him and struggled to his feet.

"I hope you had your fun with the whore because she won't breathe for much l—"

I teleported to him and slammed his body to the wall of the pub. The building shook, sending a soft blizzard of dust to the street around us. My gaze darted between his. "You will *never* touch her again."

"Oh, I will. I'll make it hurt too," he said. "She'll be executed—"

I grasped his throat and slammed his head to the brick behind it. His eyes widened, and a gasp left his lips. "You. Will. Not. Touch. Her."

He huffed, half-grin coming to his lips. "She might be your slut, Nix, but she's my wife—"

"She's not. Not anymore." I raised my hand to his throat and let my skin kindle. He screamed, eyes wide. I squeezed too tightly for him to draw in enough air to do it again. "She never wanted to be. She never wanted you because you are nothing. You're a name and an ego. But you. Are. Nothing. And we both know they won't kill her. They can't."

He raised his fist and slammed it to my lower ribs. I lessened my hold on his throat for a fraction of a second. He looked between my eyes with fast pants. "What she did—"

"Could get her killed?" I looked between his eyes with a wide piercing gaze. "Is that what you're going to say? And what do you plan to do with me then? Hmm? Going to have me hanged too?"

"Maybe I should," he spat.

I laughed. I squeezed his throat tighter beneath my palm. "Try. Try, but you will fail. You think Pa'd allow that? Because we both know that'd cause too much chaos. But wait, you think you can if they won't?" I couldn't help the ironic huff of a laugh I let out. "I have you by your throat, esiasch. Your life is inside of my hand."

"It is my right—"

"Yeah, if she fucked a nobody." My gaze darted between his. "If she wasn't a 'chraobh." *The great tree.* "But she fucked a prince. I have as much influence with the Conclave as you." I smiled. "I'm a prince here too. My death would cause wars. But most of all, I love her. And she loves me. And what you just did?" I let out an angry scoff that almost resembled a laugh. "Your marriage is gone. You are a walking target on this world now—you should've seen the look in Venark's eyes. You're nothing to the Fae folk. You never have been. But our people, we need that treaty, don't we?" My eyes rapidly shifted between his. "What do you think the Conclave will suggest to keep it intact? Hmm?"

His jaw tightened as his nostrils flared.

"You just created your own downfall, don't you see that? My son is royalty of two lands, and this world is awaiting his birth." A wave of anguish soared through me, probably at the realization that I'd used the present tense. I squeezed his throat tighter, feeling my teeth clamp together. They trembled in fury as he struggled for air. "Now he's dead. My child is dead because of you."

He reached forward and grasped my neck. I tossed it off and locked my fingers tighter around his skin, watching his eyes slowly close as the memory faded to blackness.

CHAPTER FORTY-THREE

LAILA

A yawn left my lips as my phone sounded on the bed beside my pillow. I rubbed my hand against my eye and dismissed the alarm. I rolled to the side to touch Jeremy's chest, only to find a cold bed.

I craned to glance into the dark bathroom, but he wasn't there either. I stifled another yawn, stood from the bed, and started from the room.

The kitchen was quiet, still clean from the night before. "Jeremy," I quietly called.

When he didn't yell back, I walked to the steps and tiptoed my way up. I glanced into Micah's room. Micah lay on the bed sleeping soundly with Tink tucked up in the arch of his knees.

Jeremy was in the desk chair catty-cornered from the head of the bed. The side of his mop of black hair rested against his open palm. His cheeks were reddened, glistening where the sun shined in from the windows.

"Hey," I whispered.

He looked up and smiled. His hand brushed against his cheek. "Hey."

"What's going on?" I asked. His smile struggled to lift further at the ends. His head shook. I took a few steps into the room and pushed the hair from his face, wiping the wetness beneath his eyes with my thumb. "What's wrong, baby?"

He touched my hips and tugged me onto his lap. His arms tightened around my waist as we both looked at Micah dreaming in his bed. "I remembered the night that we lost him for the first time."

"Oh," I murmured.

He kissed my shoulder. He rested his head against my back and blew out a deep breath. "I just... I had to come look at him. Pinch myself and make sure *this* wasn't the dream, ya know?"

I put my arms around his neck and kissed the top of his head. "I think we got past the bad dream part."

We stayed that way for a while. Just holding one another and watching our baby sleep.

Then Milly cried in her bedroom which in turn woke Micah. But it was okay. I got her dressed, he got him dressed, and we went downstairs for breakfast. At almost every word that left Micah's lips, Jeremy smiled or roughed up his hair with a chuckle.

It's funny how those memories hit us differently. They filled me with rage. But they made him grateful for what we had now and how far we'd come.

He didn't start on some tirade about how he needed to go beat the shit out of Lux inside of Peterson's body. He didn't scream at the sky and stomp his feet. That was my thing.

Jeremy was the one who lived in the moment. He let the past fall away. He didn't let the things incapable of change affect him. That's what I loved about him. His remarkable ability to get back up and move right past the bad things that led him to where he was.

I envied that for a time. But now, I'm grateful for the fire within me. He finds strength in a gentle approach to the world around him. I find strength in pain and anger. But ultimately, both come from a place of love. His gentleness, my pain, they both originate from a point of care. It simply manifests differently.

He called Max that morning and asked if he could handle the diner by himself for the day. He asked if I could cancel my training session with a group of teens I'd helped escape the first compound. I rescheduled for the following day. Then we set out.

Jeremy told me to wear something I could get dirty but wouldn't say why. I squeezed into a sports bra I hadn't worn since before the breastfeeding boobs and grabbed the sling for Milly. He fastened Tink's harness around her shoulders. Micah hoisted on a pair of tennis shoes. Then we loaded into the car and started off.

Micah and I pleaded to find out where he was taking us, but I didn't really want to know. I always said I hated surprises, which wasn't entirely a lie. But as the years went on, I'd grown to love them. That look of glee across his face as we drove down back roads with the mystery of what awaited us made me happy because it made him happy.

After an hour and half in the car and two stops to pee and get a snack, we pulled into a state park Jeremy and I had gone to when we first started dating. We went there a lot in the beginning. He said you could see the stars better there than you could anywhere else on this side of the world. Before I knew what he was, I believed that to be a hyperbole. That was hardly the case though. You could see it all from those mountaintops.

Of course, we didn't stay until dark. But we had the time of our lives climbing small rocks and dipping our toes into creek beds that coasted through the mountains. Jeremy and I sat on the edge of the water with Micah and Milly as Tink chased after dragonflies flying overhead.

We hiked our way to the highest peak in that small forest. Then we ate a picnic of sandwiches and granola bars, gazing out over the miles of thick spring foliage around us. The five of us sat on the same rock Jeremy and I had spent hours getting to know each other on years before. We took in the near silence of the woods, hearing only one another's voices and the distant songs from birds perched high in the trees. I remember Micah commenting on how the air smelled cleaner, and I knew exactly what he meant. The coast of that gentle wind brought with it a wave of tranquility and peace we couldn't get in a town, even one as little as ours.

That day felt perfect.

So many did during that time.

We had it all for a while. A happy marriage. Two beautiful children. The cutest husky-mutt in the world. Financial stability, a wonderful home, and a reliable car.

I can't say that we took them for granted. But we'd certainly miss that repose.

CHAPTER FORTY-FOUR

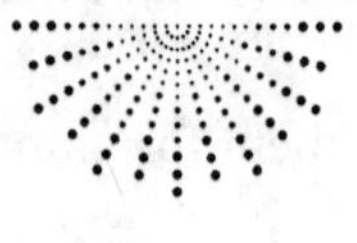

JEREMY

After we hiked for a few hours, we stopped for dinner at some little pub. The food was okay. Our diner was better, but it wasn't bad. We didn't stop there for the food though. We stopped for the live entertainment. Laila and I used to eat there every time we made a trip that way for the music alone. There was something incredibly refreshing about listening to jazz after hearing the stillness of the wilderness.

They had a little stage in the corner where a musician played a saxophone next to the grand piano. I didn't know him personally, but I'd always admired his skills. I knew Micah would too.

Milly seemed indifferent, but Micah stared at the older gentleman in awe. He barely even touched his French fries and apple sauce. He just rested his chin in his hands, eyes gazing over him like he was a work of art.

After he stepped off stage, Micah turned to me and said I should learn to play the saxophone like that. I laughed and told him I'd try. But he could be that good one day too.

And he would be.

On the way home, we stopped at Dairy Queen. It was a bit of a family tradition at that point. Micah and Milly shared a banana split. I ate a chocolate sundae, and Laila got her blizzard.

It was a great day. The kind I'd remember forever. It almost washed away the pain from the memory I'd recalled earlier that morning.

Both kids fell asleep in the car. They stayed asleep as we carried them to their bedrooms and tucked them beneath their blankets.

Laila and I sat on the balcony afterward and smoked a joint. She sipped a glass of wine. I played my guitar. The world felt right. As it should have felt for the last five-thousand or two-hundred-thousand years.

When Laila went to take a shower, I walked to the kitchen to get a glass of water. Chris was at the counter eating leftover cake in his boxers. That was the first time I saw his scars.

They were so much worse than Laila's. Even worse than Daniel's, which I didn't realize was possible.

The ones on his back protruded inches from his skin. They covered every inch. With Daniel's and Laila's, they looked like scars. But on Chris, they looked like a science experiment gone wrong. He didn't seem to care though.

I walked around the counter to the fridge. "Hey."

"Oh, hey." He wiped some icing from his lip. "You weren't saving this, right?"

"Nah, eat it all. We have enough leftovers to feed an army."

"Alright, cool. I ate a couple of burgers too. Those were really good, by the way. What's on them?"

"If I knew, I'd tell you. It was Moe's recipe." I smiled. "Max and Laila are the only living people who know it."

His head tilted, swallowing a bite of cake. "Doesn't Adam work there too?"

"Yeah, but the two of them premix the seasoning. I've tried to master it, but it never comes out quite right. There's definitely garlic and salt and pepper. I thought the red part was chili powder but nope.

Come's out way too spicy. Even tried cinnamon once, but it didn't do the trick either."

"I've never understood the whole secret recipe thing," he said. "If you die, that beautiful taste dies with you. That's just a crime against the people of the world."

I laughed. "Laila actually willed me the recipe. If she dies, I have access to it. But only if she dies."

He chuckled. "Give you something to look forward to in the event of her death, I guess."

"Yeah, I guess." I laughed and leaned against the counter. "So I take it your opinion on Heylel's changed?"

His tongue ran against his teeth. He cleared his throat. "Look, I'm sorry. I know that was kind of rude. It was your kid's birthday party, I shouldn't have—"

"What? No, I don't care. Do you know how many family functions I've fucked Laila at? Get laid, man. I don't care. But I'm curious. You're cool with him now?"

He was quiet for a long moment, studying the plate before him. As if it had the words he was looking for written on them.

"I mean, I don't completely trust him. But after meeting God, I really don't trust anyone. Besides the family, I mean. But... I don't know. He's not how I expected him to be. I always thought he'd be beast-like, you know? Like the other Demons we've killed?"

"Those are later generation Demons. They get deformed because of the species differential. If two first-generation Demons have a kid, they come out fine. If they mate with a Guardian, or Fae, or Angel, or Werweolves, they come out fine. Like me or you. But if they mix with humans, deformities take place, or the mother miscarries."

His forehead wrinkled in confusion. "But Luka's half-human."

"Angels and Demons are different. The rest of us can have healthy offspring with any race. For some reason though, they can only breed with us or each other. Ya know, the whole Nephilim thing? That's Demons."

"No shit," he murmured. "How'd you learn all this?"

"It's kind of a long story, really. But what made you decide you were going to sleep with him?"

"We didn't sleep together," he muttered. "Just a little hand stuff. But I don't know, man. He said something about us. How we both devoted ourselves to a cause that slapped us in the face. How we both busted our asses for that fucker just to be tortured for it. Our culture had us convinced we were doing the right thing, following the right rules. He got kicked out of heaven for having an issue with that fucker killing the rest of you par animarum or whatever, I was tortured for a decade when I did nothing but follow the rules. We both... I don't know, we just... We were both blindly obedient to a piece of shit. We were both sheep led to our own slaughter." He shrugged. "And he's really hot." I laughed, and he smiled. "That's not weird for you? Hearing me call a guy hot?"

"Not really. I mean, can't relate. But yeah, I really don't care, man."

But I could relate to everything else he said.

I'd been like him when I was young. I believed in 'God.' I followed that hoopla. Because I was brainwashed into doing so. For me, the final straw had come as a teenager when I actually read the damn book. But for Chris, it was being tortured by that man.

We came to the same conclusions in different ways. And for vastly different reasons. Clearly, he was battling some internalized homophobia from the indoctrinations we'd been taught as kids. But I wanted him to see the same things that we had.

No one should be punished for love.

I supposed that was a biased statement coming from a man who'd fucked his brother's wife. But it was true. Yeah, we hurt him. But that didn't justify his retaliation. There was no justice in beating a pregnant woman into losing her child. There was no justice in tying our baby into the end of earth.

It was malicious. It was evil.

What we'd done came from a place of love.

If he wanted to hurt us, he should've sued us or some shit.

Chris gave a gentle nod. "Well, that's good to know."

I sent him a slight smile, trying to make sure he realized our generation was a lot different than the ones that came before us. I cleared my throat and said, "So I was thinking about something."

"What's that?" he asked.

I slid the junk drawer open and tossed him the keys to the Charger. "I think you should have it."

His brows knitted, staring down at them. He looked back up at me. "What?"

"I've got kids. I never drive it anymore anyway. And it was yours. Dad gave it to you. It's bad enough Leah stole the house, and we chipped off a piece of the land for ourselves."

He smiled, staring down at the keys in his hand. "Are you sure?"

I smiled back. "Take good care of her."

He looked back up at me with a grin. "Thank you. And I don't care who's name the house is in, by the way. Probably better that it's in Leah's anyway. I can be petty."

I laughed. "Well, I guess it all worked out then."

CHAPTER FORTY-FIVE

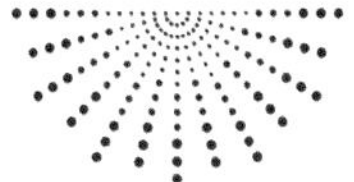

JUNE 26, 2022 - LAILA

Our routines hadn't changed since the party. Jeremy was still holding down the fort at the diner while I trained with survivors day in and day out. Everything was calm.

Two days ago was Micah's birthday. We had dinner at that little restaurant in town. He got an ice-cream sundae with sparklers and ate it cheerfully as we all sang him happy birthday. He looked so happy that day. I expected to feel the same way. But it brought back a feeling of worthlessness.

It was my fault that I didn't get to spend his first or second birthday with him. It just was. The sadness lessened each June 22nd that passed by, but the guilt never would. Neither would the memory of his birth.

Above all else, that was probably the most traumatic event of my life. The rape was a close second. But the date alone carried me back to that night. That helplessness. Knowing that fucker was going to take my baby and having no ability to stop it.

Micah was happy though. And he wouldn't remember that I missed his first two birthdays. He was just glad that I was there for the rest.

In two days, we'd publicly execute Doctor Robert Peterson.

I never thought I'd say that. That I arranged a public execution. That I'd watch people cheer for a man's death.

My hatred for him hadn't changed. But after realizing he'd done the things he had on the word of a god, I can't say that I didn't feel a little guilt. Not that I'd go back on my word. Peterson had to die. The survivors deserved to know that their captor could never hurt them again.

But it didn't feel quite as justified anymore. He didn't want to do the things he had, not really. He'd done them because he was told that it was the right thing. To train the mother goddess of earth. To help create her. To gift her with an army. And to graciously accept that he will forever be his favorite person's enemy.

What Peterson did was selfless in many ways. Still awful. Still just cause for an execution. But he'd done it for the good of humanity and for the future of the world. Not that I agreed. I still passionately believe that training can be done without pain.

But it still made me feel bad for him.

Another thing I'd never thought I would say.

The birds sang in the treetops overhead. Bright summer sun shined on the deep green grass. I couldn't find one puff of white in the blue sky overhead. The humid smell of the air filled my nose, accompanied by fresh-cut grass.

I watched Micah and Milly play in the yard from my seat on the porch. Milly's little black locks were almost as long as her brother's now. His were wavy, like Jeremy's. Milly's was fine but curly. It slipped right out of the cute blue clips.

Tink was always right behind Micah. He spoke to her regularly, and truth be told, I think she talked to him too. Even I didn't know that was possible. But in our world, having a real-life Dr. Doolittle didn't seem too farfetched.

"Hey." Chris bumped my shoulder as he sat beside me on the wicker bench. "Whatcha doing?"

I flipped my notebook shut. "Procrastinating. I'm supposed to be writing, but nothing wants to come out."

"Yeah, I feel you. I've picked up a paintbrush a good hundred times since I've been back. I thought painting would be awesome, ya know? Never thought I'd be able to do it again. But it just won't happen."

I sighed. "The struggles of an artist."

He gave an awkward half-smirk. "Eh, I think writing's a little different than painting."

I made a face. "Are you saying that writing isn't an art form?"

"I mean, it's a form, I guess. But... Eh."

I smacked him with my notebook, and he laughed. "I paint pictures with words, shit head. They don't call it language arts for nothing."

"If you say so." He took a gulp from the beer in his hand. He gestured to Milly lying in the grass with her arms outstretched. "Should I maybe... Go grab her?"

I huffed. "Sure. If you want to hear her scream bloody murder just to teleport over there and do it again."

Chris arched a brow. "What?"

"She's got a connection to the earth, my friend." I sipped my warm coffee. "Just plops down and lays in the grass all the time. I think it's the Fae in her."

A half-smile played at his lips. His head tilted to the side. "Do you ever have the urge to just lay in the grass?"

"Not so much these days. But as a teenager, that's about all I did. Me and my one friend, Adrian, we sat in the field at the park for hours back then. Getting high, mostly, but sometimes we just sat there. Felt a lot like Milly does right now. Almost like taking a nap."

He laughed. "So she's recharging her batteries?"

A chuckle left my lips, and I lifted my head in a nod. "Yeah, something like that."

Chris smiled as his gaze slid over them. "It's so cool to see this. Watching them grow into these massively powerful creatures, you know? I got to see it with Brody. But all he could do was teleport, and he was a little shit. He'd just disappear. Find some quarters around the house and flash down to the candy store. We'd look for him for hours. He'd just show up in his bedroom with a Halloween's worth stockpile of candy."

I laughed. "I'm so glad they don't do that. They can, they could go anywhere they want. But they like it here." My lips curved up, watching Micah collapse to the ground beside his sister. "It means a lot when someone can be anywhere, and they choose to be with you."

He smiled back and gave a soft nod. "Yeah. Yeah, it really does. Especially after everything. It makes me wonder if Peterson kept me for that reason alone. So I could teach him about us. Family and everything, I mean. Because if I hadn't been with him, he might have been an entirely different kid."

I'd thought about that a lot over the years. And yeah, I'd come to the same conclusion. He always wanted Micah to end up where he was now; home with us. But having Chris there made him *want* to end up home with us.

"Yeah, I think that's why he put my cell beside yours," I murmured. "So that you'd know he was your family. You were there when he was born, you felt that energy. You knew it was your nephew when you held him."

"So I'd be more apt to take care of him," he said. "It pisses me off now. When I think about all those little things. Now that I see his plan. All the things that made no sense before that make perfect sense now."

"Makes you wonder if there was a reason for everything." I held my wrist over my lap, grazing the slit where my implant had been. "Like why did he put those things in every one of us? My Guardian abilities still haven't presented so that's not why he put them in me. Haley's a wolf; they didn't do shit to her either. So why did he do it? And Micah. Why didn't he feed him? Why didn't he give him vitamin D and some type of light therapy? There had to be a reason. Had to be."

"We ought to ask him tomorrow," Chris said. "That's still the plan, right? One last questioning before I pluck his eyes out and you cut his dick off?"

"That's the plan," I murmured.

He squinted at me. "You still want to do that, don't you?"

Of course I did. However, it was also an incredibly cringe-worthy thought. Yeah, I wanted the bastard to suffer. I wanted him to know how it felt. But I also wasn't sure I could actually go through with cutting off a penis. Burning him alive, that'd be one thing. But that... I don't know.

I cleared my throat. "Yeah. Yeah, I mean... I want it done. I just... I don't know, something about coming into contact with that part of his body. It freaks me out, you know?"

"Oh," he murmured. "You don't have to, you know. We're killing him anyway—"

"No, it's going to happen. My vagina hurt for weeks after what he did. He deserves to feel violated like that too." I cleared my throat. "Just not really my area of expertise. Never cut off a dick before."

He gave an awkward chuckle. "I don't think that's a particular area that most people educate themselves."

I'd done some reading on the subject. And apparently, that was not true.

My head shook. "It was actually common back in the day. Castration used to be a major type of torture. There's almost an art form to the procedure. But we're not going to care about the technicalities. I don't care what happens to his urethra and shit. He'll be dead the next day. I'll probably burn whatever's left to cauterize the bleeding but that's the extent."

"Ugh, this is making my dick hurt just thinking about it," he muttered. "Fucked up how I can still have sympathy for the guy, isn't it?"

"Hate to admit it, but I feel the same way." I looked at Micah helping Milly to her feet. "I guess empathy is what separates people like us from people like him. He enjoys other's pain. We just want justice."

"Eh. More like vengeance."

I sipped my coffee. "That too."

CHAPTER FORTY-SIX

JEREMY

I got home from work around seven that night. Me and Lai went about our usual routine. I kissed her hello, helped her cook dinner, we cleaned up the house afterward, played with the kids, got them bathed, and ready for bed. Laila hadn't said anything concerning, but she seemed a bit off. I asked if she was okay, and she smiled and said she was fine. I knew she wasn't, but the kids were still up, so I didn't want to prod.

Once they were asleep, I got my shower. When I came back into the bedroom, my chest grew a little tight.

Laila sat on the armchair in front of the patio doors with her knees tucked against her chest. She stared vacantly out the glass with a joint between her lips. She took a long sip of the whiskey in her crystal glass. I knew that face, she was hurting. Not scared, but hurt.

I stood and walked to the door, pulling the other chair so it was beside hers. "Lai."

She kept her gaze out the window. "Hmm?"

"Are you okay?" I asked.

She nodded and took a gulp from the glass.

"Liar."

Her gaze turned to mine, sad smiling tilting up her lips. "No, I am. I'm okay. I just have a lot in my mind."

I leaned forward and put my hand on her knee. "Like what?"

She shook her head a bit. She chewed her lower lip. "I don't know. Everything, I guess. My head's spinning a little bit."

I brushed hair behind her ear. "Is this about the execution?"

"Among other things. Just... Just everything, you know?"

I watched her carefully, waiting for her to go on. When she didn't, I reached for the joint and took a hit. "Anything in particular?"

"I just never thought I'd do this." She sipped her drink again. "Not capturing him. Not ending his life, I knew I'd do that one day. But organizing an execution. I used to be against the death penalty, you know? Killing someone in the heat of the moment to protect myself or someone else is different than this.

"And not that I think we shouldn't do it. I do. But I just... God, the reality to it just makes me feel like a monster. The whole situation. This guy, this fucking asshole, he destroyed me. He took the soft person that I was and turned her into a murdering machine. But he did it because he thought he was doing the right thing. And he really does love me, in his own sick way, and I just... This just feels so twisted. It's right but it's wrong."

There she was. That beautiful, profound, living personification of an oxymoron. She killed as though murder was an artform. One would have thought it was her greatest pleasure watching her in the act. But she felt so guilty for it. Even for him.

"You aren't a monster." I looked gently between her eyes. "He deserves this, Lai. He deserves everything we've done to him."

She chewed her lip. "He was brainwashed. He's sick. He's seriously mentally ill."

"So is Mark David Chapman," I murmured. "He loved John Lennon, too. He shot him in the head. He robbed the world of an amazing person. And frankly, if I could go back in time and kill that bastard to keep John alive, I would. This is the same thing. If we don't end him, he could go on to—"

"No, I know. I know. I'm not saying we shouldn't go through with it." She ran her hand over her mouth. "I just... It feels wrong. The one who's actually responsible for this can't die. Peterson's taking the heat for it. And yeah, he deserves what he's getting. But he's not the one who actually caused it."

I wasn't sure if I should say this next line, but maybe it'd help her feel a little less guilt.

"He's the one that raped you," I murmured.

She looked down and swirled the liquor in her glass. Her head dipped in a nod. She cleared her throat. "Yeah. I know." We both got quiet for a moment. "I don't know how I'm going to handle that."

"Handle what?" I asked.

"Castrating him," she murmured. "That's another thing I'm torn about. I want to do it but I... I don't think that I can. I-I'm not good at calculated torture. I punch, and I stab, and I beat, but I don't... I don't know how to do that. Even going near that part of him..."

Not that I had a particular fascination with cutting of dude's dicks, but I wouldn't mind doing it to him. That wasn't to say I'd enjoy it. But if she weren't going to do it, I would. No ifs, ands, or buts about it. That fucker tore her apart from the inside, and I wanted him to know how that felt.

"It's harder when you're not angry. Even harder when they're begging you to stop," I said. She shuddered. I paused again, watching her shaking hand raise the glass to her lips. "Do you want me to do it?"

She frowned. "I can't ask someone else to do that for me."

"You aren't asking me, I'm offering." I looked between her eyes for a moment. "If you don't want anyone to do it, we don't have to. He's going to be dead in forty-eight hours anyway. But if you want him to suffer like you did, I'll do it."

Her head shook slightly. "That's a lot for me to expect from you."

"It's not," I muttered. "It wasn't my body, Lai, but I felt it too. And that's all that I wanted to do when I felt that happening to you. Well, after slitting his throat." Her solemn expression stayed firm across her lips. "When he did that to you, I think it hurt me more than when Ally did it to me. I... I still don't even remember that. But that night, when I felt that happen to you... I know it hurt you worse, but it fucked me up too. And I'm more comfortable with calculated pain like that. I can handle it. It probably won't bother me at all."

We'd never actually talked about this. It'd been such a sensitive subject for so long, it was too hard for her to verbalize. And I'd never pushed the conversation; it wasn't like I wanted to talk about it either. But it was true. That day fucked me up.

I couldn't help her. I felt him hurting her. I heard her screaming for someone, anyone, to help her, and I couldn't. And I hated myself for it. I hated that I couldn't save her.

And I wanted that fucker to suffer for hurting her like that.

Revenge. I wanted revenge.

Laila's eyes softened. "What were you doing? That night, I mean. When it happened."

I huffed. "Remember when I told you about that fundraiser Hannah and Max set up when you were missing? In your honor or whatever?" She nodded. "Well, they insisted that I perform a song for you. I thought it was stupid, but they thought it'd look good, you know? Get my face out there a little since I wouldn't talk to the journalists and stuff."

Her brows raised, mouth dropping open. "You were on stage?"

"When I felt him grab your neck," I said. "I rushed through the rest of the song and ran up to the apartment. I knew that it was different. It was a Saturday night; it wasn't your back... And I felt him bite your lip. Then your neck. And I puked. I puked a lot. Had a lot of liquor in me already so that might have played a part, I guess. But, yeah. Yeah, it was... It was one of the worst moments of my life."

Tears welled in her eyes. "I'm sorry."

I took her hand. I lifted her knuckles to my lips. "Never apologize for something that wasn't your fault."

"It was though." Her lip quivered, and her teeth followed. "It was. I willingly got in—"

"Stop saying that because it isn't true." I took her face in my hands and looked quickly between her eyes. "They were holding two people that you loved at knife point. No, Laila. It wasn't your fault."

She pressed her trembling lips together. I thumbed the tear that escaped her eye. But her teeth chattered harder together.

I knew she didn't believe me. I knew she'd always blame herself for what happened over those three months and consequentially the following three years. But I wanted her to know that I didn't blame her. And especially that I'd never, *ever* blame her for what he did that day.

"Come here," I whispered. She leaned forward and wrapped her arms around my shoulders, tightly clamping her fists around my back and burrowing her head into my chest.

CHAPTER FORTY-SEVEN

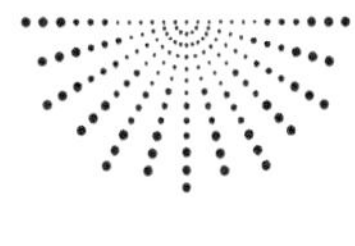

LAILA

"**I** thought you said you didn't have to wowk today," Micah said.

I slipped on my shoes and forced a smile. "Well, me and your dad have a lot of responsibilities. And they aren't all running the diner."

"Like what?" he asked.

Ugh. How was I supposed to tell my three-year-old I was about to go torture a man and publicly execute him? I supposed there wasn't a way to say it. Obviously, I couldn't tell him the truth. I also didn't want to tell him a blunt lie. We weren't going to work; we weren't going to the grocery store. At the end of the day though, we were doing a good thing for the world.

"Well." I cleared my throat and sat beside him on the couch. "We have a duty to other people like us. People that are special. They... They need us for some things."

His big, innocent eyes flittered between mine. "Like those people you help use they powews?"

"Yeah. Yeah, exactly."

"Almost like pwofessow zaview." He smiled.

I laughed. "Who?"

"You know, the guy whose legs don't wowk because of Magnito."

"Oh." I laughed again. "Professor Xavier."

I wished. In no world was I the equivalent to Professor Xavier. He was undoubtedly a good guy. There was no anti before hero when he was involved.

Micah nodded quick with a grin. "Yeah, like him. Like a supew hewo."

"Kind of," I muttered. "A little different though. It's kind of hard to explain. But one day, I'll tell you every detail."

It was a lot different. We weren't comic book characters. We weren't the good guys, not really. There was no infinite good and infinite bad. This story may have revolved around a little boy, but it was no tale for children.

He pursed his lips. "You and daddy always say that."

"Some things are just a little too complicated for kids to understand." I kissed his forehead and brushed his chin with my thumb. "But one day, I'll explain everything. I'm glad you ask a lot of questions though. That's a good thing. You should question everything. But sometimes, you have to accept that some questions have answers you can't understand yet."

He sighed. "But Aunt Hannah's coming, wight?"

"She'll be here any minute." I smiled.

"Uncle Kai too?"

"Uncle Kai too."

"Good." He smiled. "He talks funny, but I like him."

I tried not to hold my breath as we walked down the squeaky basement stairs. I tried to stay levelheaded. Somehow, I managed to maintain my composure. But I couldn't explain how if it was to save my life.

Jeremy's hand brushed mine when we touched the landing. I didn't look up to meet his gaze. I just grabbed the chair and carted it to the center of the room. Brody and Chris silently trotted down the steps behind me. As the basement door closed, Peterson rubbed his hand against his eye and looked around. His gaze stopped on me.

That expression would stay with me the rest of my life. It was almost like the look Micah gave me when he ate my last chocolate bar. That *I'm sorry, I won't do it again,* kind of look.

"Hello, Laila."

"Hi, Peterson," I murmured.

"My final farewell, I suppose." His dark eyes glistened with water, lips pulling into a smile. "Do I get to choose my last meal?"

I chewed my jaw. "You do."

He smiled and nodded back, wiping his shackled hand against his eye again. "Something from your diner. I've always wanted to try it."

"Any preference?"

His head shook. "Surprise me." I pressed my lips together, nodding. His watery eyes were still on mine. "I didn't do a good job after all, did I?" I puckered my brows, and he said, "You feel bad for me."

"I feel bad that you're a puppet. I feel bad that you were used by a man far more powerful than you. I feel bad that you're sick, Peterson." I frowned. "But no. I don't feel bad for *you.* Because you knew what you were doing. You chose to ruin innocent lives."

He swallowed and gave a nod. He smiled. "So I did do a good job then."

True or not, that phrase still sent a shiver down my spine. It made my jaw clench.

"Before it's over, we have a few more questions for you," Jeremy said. He yanked the chains at the wall to sit Peterson up. As he dragged him across the cement floor to a seated position, I got my first good look at him in quite some time.

His dark, salt and pepper hair was nearly to his shoulders, and his beard touched his collar bone. He looked almost as pale as the white wall behind him. He'd lost a lot of weight. His narrow shoulders looked even frailer than they always had.

So little. So minuscule. So weak.

Peterson met my gaze. "What do you want to know?"

"I need you to explain things," I said. "I want to know why you didn't feed my son. I want to know why you attacked us the day my daughter was born. I want to understand your reasoning because I know you. Everything happened for a reason; you *did* everything for a reason. And I want to know what that is."

He turned his gaze to the ground. "We attacked that day to help you. To force you to put up the barrier around your home as soon as possible, for one. But mainly so that you would all cast that spell on yourselves."

"To keep Nastya out?" I asked.

"Yes. Had she been able to enter your head when you came for Micah and Chris, we could have kept you much longer. But since you cast that spell, you were the one in control. You entered her mind, but she couldn't enter yours."

Huh. Shitty or not, he'd done it to help us. To teach us a lesson. Always to teach us a fucking lesson.

"And Micah?" Jeremy's voice was low. "Why didn't you feed him?"

"I did feed him," Peterson said.

"That slop wasn't food," Chris said.

"If I didn't treat Micah as I treated the others, would your people believe you and I weren't working together?" Peterson looked between me and Jeremy. "Would they have trusted you? Would they trust him? I wouldn't torture him, but I couldn't treat him like he was any better than the others. And he had to understand suffering to be grateful for the life you'll give him. Even once the detailed memories fade, the two of you will always be heroes in his eyes. And aside from that, resources were scarce. They weren't in the beginning, but we were moving so frequently. We had to be cautious. We couldn't go to grocery stores, we couldn't order takeout, we had to work with what we had."

"Am I supposed to thank you for that?" I clenched my jaw. "For making us heroes in his eyes?"

"No. But that is why."

"And the bomb?" Brody said. "What the fuck was that for?"

Peterson glanced at Brody then turned to me. "I wish I wouldn't have had to do that to you."

My nostrils flared. "Then why did you?"

He remained silent, gaze steady against the floor. "You had to learn that you cannot save everyone, Laila. You think that you can but not everything you put your mind to will turn out as you want. It's unfortunate but a fact you needed to learn so that you can accept the realities of war. Even gods aren't all powerful, Laila."

My jaw clenched.

I hated that he was right. And looking back on it, I hate that that was another lesson he taught me. But he *was* right. I needed that experience. Because if I hadn't lived through that, and everything else he'd done, I wouldn't be ready for what came next.

"Why did you cut my eyes out?" Chris said. "Twice. Why did you cut my eyes out twice?"

"Isn't it obvious?" He looked at us like we were stupid. "So you couldn't show her the memories of Micah as an infant."

That was why? He blinded Chris to hurt me?

I teleported before him and reached for his throat. He covered his face, head hanging low. "It was him, he told me I had to. Please, I wouldn't have done that to you, Laila. Please."

My hand caught.

Fuck. Why did I feel bad for him? Why could I sympathize with this disgusting excuse of a man?

That was obvious though.

Because it wasn't him that I wanted to suffer. It was Lux.

He'd taken a sick, twisted man and manipulated him into atrocities. He played on an ill person's delusion. Peterson wanted to matter to me. He wanted me to know he existed so badly that he'd do anything he was told to make the largest impact on my life.

And he did just that.

By becoming my villain, he mattered to me.

It was so unbelievably fucked that I felt bad for this man. But I did. Because he was a no one who'd been take advantage of by a man far stronger than he.

We all grew silent for a moment. Then Jeremy spoke. "Why'd you put the implants in everyone? Laila's powers are barely connected to her Guardian abilities."

His gaze turned to Jeremy's. "Do her scars bother you? You don't find her as beautiful as she once was?"

Jeremy's eyes narrowed. "My wife is the most gorgeous woman alive. Don't turn it around and try to make her feel shitty. Just answer the damn question."

"I was told to," Peterson said. "I don't know why he deemed it necessary. Only that he did, and I obeyed." He looked back to me. "I am sorry, Laila. I am sorry you had to suffer."

My jaw hardened. "Are you sorry that you raped me too?"

Tears bubbled in his eyes. "I am. More sorry than I am for anything else that I've done."

"Well, at least there's that," I muttered.

The room got quiet for a moment or two. Jeremy turned to Chris and Brody. "Alright, we ready to do this?"

"I've been ready," Chris said.

"Wait," Peterson said. "Wait, I... Laila?"

"What?"

"When I die... you'll be the one to do it, yes?" I nodded, and he said, "Can you give me something beautiful? When you kill me, can you do it in some intricate, extraordinary way? Not just incineration or a bullet to the brain. Something... something pretty. Like you."

My lips curled slightly.

Such an odd request. But he was a seriously deranged individual. I should've expected nothing less. I was dreading his execution. But if he wanted a pretty death, I'd give it to him.

"That can be arranged."

"Are you staying, Lai?" Jeremy asked.

I shook my head. "I'll be upstairs."

He gave a gentle nod. I stood and pressed my lips to his. I thought it'd be a quick kiss, but it was long and firm. His hand traveled to my waist, pulling me closer into him, squeezing a little. The other held my face. His lips opened against mine, tongue parting through.

I thought about pulling back. But I got it. He wanted to hurt him. He wanted Peterson to see what it was like to kiss me when I wanted it.

Cruel, I guess. But no crueler than cutting off his dick.

After a moment, I took a step back and met his gaze.

"I'll be up soon. You can go back to the house if you want."

"I might." I released his hand and turned to the steps.

When I made it to the kitchen, I heard Peterson's loud, ear piercing scream.

I teleported outside.

CHAPTER FORTY-EIGHT

JEREMY

The grossest thing I've ever done.

I won't go into the details because no one in their right mind wants to hear about that. And because I don't think I could put it into words if I tried.

I told Laila I'd be fine, and for the most part, I was. But I'll put it this way. I'd never be able to look at sausage the same again.

When I finished with that part, Chris took the knife, and I took Peterson's arm. Brody held the other. He screamed a lot when we castrated him, but he was nearly silent when Chris cut his eyes out.

He'd known for a long time that things would end this way. Aside from the heavy breaths, Brody, Peterson, and I were on the same page. This was a necessary evil. But Chris looked almost animalistic. His eyes were wider than oceans, tears drizzling from them. He held that knife as if it were a life jacket, and he was lost at sea. His teeth were gritted to a hard line. He looked the way Laila had after she stabbed Peterson over and over the morning we'd gotten Micah back.

He thought he'd feel relieved. But he was left with the same emptiness we all were when it was over. We'd suffered, he'd suffered. It was over. Hurting him didn't take away what he'd done.

"Alright, I need a shower." I wiped my bloodied hands on my jeans.

"Yeah, me too," Brody grumbled. "I think he pissed on me."

"Gross," I muttered.

"Nix." Peterson's voice crackled behind me.

Ah, fuck.

I turned. "Damn it. How long were you there? Did he even feel that?"

"Popped in after he fainted." His empty eye sockets met mine. I realized in that moment how he did that. It was astral projection, that's how he saw without eyes. He was here in this room, channeling Peterson like a microphone. "Before you go, do me a favor."

I huffed. "How about no?"

"Fine. But it's not actually for me, you know. It's for Véa."

"What do you mean?"

His lips curled up in a devious half-smirk. "Let her know I was the driver."

My brows dropped, and my stomach was close behind. "What?"

"I was the one driving that van." His smile widened. "She was getting inside whether they held a knife to your sister's throat or not."

If he were the person that took her off the road that day, that meant she never had a chance. She wasn't strong enough to take on a god yet. That meant that she'd hated herself needlessly for the last three years.

Heart picking up in my chest, my bloodied hands clenched to fists. It pounded in my ears. It was like I was suddenly seeing through a tunnel, only him ahead.

My jaw clenched, and I took a few steps closer. "All of this time, you let her hate herself for that."

"Well, she's still to blame. She could have gotten away that night if she knew how to use her abilities. But yeah. Yeah, I wanted her to hate herself. She deserved to live with a guilty conscious for a time," he said. "Oh, and by the way, I also helped Amy a bit. That day? When she woke up after Micah's birth? I'm why she believed he was dead. So she can quit blaming herself for that too."

The image of her shaking body the day she found out he was alive flashed behind my eyes. Her lip shook so hard. Her eyes wouldn't stop watering. Had I not put my arms around her, she'd have hit the floor.

She thought I'd hate her because she didn't know he was alive. Because that's how she felt about herself. She hated that she didn't know. It made her think that she was a horrible mother. But it was because of him. It was his fault. It was *all* his fucking fault.

My nostrils flared. I slammed my foot into his chest. He took in heaving gasps, hand flying to his sternum. "I hate you. I fucking hate you. You." I kicked him again. "Worthless." Kick. "Piece." Kick. "Of." Kick. "Shit."

Once he regained his breaths, he released something of a laugh. "Well, at least now she can let go of that self-hatred."

"This is him?" Brody asked. "This is God?"

Peterson's head rolled to follow his voice. "Which one are you?"

"Yeah, this is him." I grumbled, wiping blood from my cheek.

"Oh." He laughed. "You're the brother that loved Véa, too."

"Once upon a time," Brody said. "Never handled it like a little bitch like you though."

"Yeah, guess you wouldn't." He smiled. "You always were a bit softer than us. Even if you do like to pretend that you aren't."

My brows wrinkled. "What?"

He smiled. "See you boys in a couple years."

His head clunked to his chest.

"What the fuck did that mean?" Brody looked up with confusion.

"I don't have a clue," I said.

But if I had to guess? That Brody's soul was probably pretty old too.

After the three of us took turns showering, Chris dropped to the couch beside Leah with a bottle of vodka. Brody and I smoked a joint on the back porch. He clearly had a lot on his mind, barely speaking a word as we passed it back and forth.

Truthfully, so did I. Did that mean he was one of us too? Did he have a soulmate out there somewhere? Maybe so. But if he did, it wasn't Gwen.

Not only that, but Lux knew him. He didn't seem to like him either.

Which was probably why he fell in love with Laila, as some poetic punishment for whatever grudge he held against him.

After a few minutes, I gave him a pat on the back and started back to the house. I could have teleported, but I decided to walk. I needed to figure out how to tell Laila she'd hated herself for the past three years for nothing.

I had it all planned out. I got to the house and saw her sitting on the porch with the kids. Suddenly, I forgot every detail of my little speech.

"Daddy!" Micah yelled. He ran from the steps and wrapped his arms around my legs.

I laughed and lowered myself to the ground. "Hey, bud."

"We'we still getting ice cweam, wight?"

Another laugh. "Yeah, we'll go get some ice cream. But let me talk to Mommy for a minute, alright?"

He ran back up the steps and into the front door, hollering over his shoulder, "I go get my shoes!"

Laila struggled a smile. "Hey."

I sat on the porch swing beside her. "Hey." Milly climbed from her lap to mine, bringing a smile to my lips. I pushed hair from her face, and she plopped her head to my chest. "She's sleepy, huh?"

"Yeah, she'll probably pass out in the car," Laila said. She closed the journal on her lap and met my gaze. "So it... You guys did it?"

I ran my hand over my short beard "Yeah. Yeah, it's done." A slow, shaking breath left her nostrils. "But, uh... when we were done, Lux popped in."

She ran her tongue along her teeth. "And what'd he have to say?"

My throat constricted and I desperately tried to open it back up. "He, uh... He had a message for you."

"For me?" Her brow raised. "What—another 'it had to happen' bullshit line?"

My expression softened. "No. No, he... he wanted me to tell you he was in your head that day. The day you woke up after having Micah. He's the reason you believed Micah was dead."

Her eyes softened, and her mouth parted slightly. "Really?"

"Him and Amy combined. But yeah." I placed my hand over hers. "Yeah, that's what he said."

She looked out over the yard.

Silence set it. I wasn't sure what was going on behind those green eyes. I didn't know if she was angry, or sad, or what. But I waited anyway, just sliding my thumb along the back of hers as she watched the wind rustle the grass and wildflowers.

"That makes sense," she said after a moment. "Once I knew he was alive, I didn't know how I believed he was dead. I knew Amy was in there, but she wasn't powerful enough to override my thoughts. So that... that makes sense."

Relief. That was the closest I could pin her reaction as. Relief to know it wasn't her fault that she believed our son was dead when he wasn't.

I hoped the next tidbit of information would bring her that too. She needed to let go of the blame.

"There was something else too," I muttered. She turned back to me. I cleared my throat and licked my lips. "He was driver in the van. Even if you fought them, even if you would have killed the other guards... He was taking you that day."

Her forehead scrunched down. "What?"

"That's what he said," I murmured. "He was there. You willingly got in that van, but even if you hadn't, they were going to take you one way or another. He let you believe that this was your fault, but it never was. You weren't powerful enough to take him on then. Even if you killed those guards, he was going to take you." I watched her confused expression turn to fury, eyes starting to pulsate in their sockets. "It was never your fault, baby."

Her jaw clenched. She drew in slow, deep breaths. I put my hand on her shoulder as her head shook. "That fucking prick."

"Okay, I's ready!" Micah exclaimed in the doorway. "Can we go get ice cweam now?"

CHAPTER FORTY-NINE

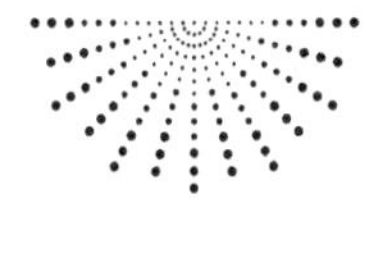

LAILA

Any sympathy I'd mustered up for Peterson dissipated like clouds after a storm once Jeremy told me that. That fucking dick. That piece of shit.

I couldn't believe I hadn't thought it myself. Of course someone had fucked with my head to convince me my son was dead when he wasn't. Even I questioned it at first. But I kept pushing it from my conscious mind because just thinking about losing him hurt too much. Although, as time went on, I did ponder if it was Amy that convinced me he was gone.

But the van. I couldn't have guessed it. I didn't even believe gods existed then. I certainly didn't think the top one had a personal vendetta against me. I'd made comments pertaining to that idea, but they were intended to be ironic. Certainly not in a literal sense.

The fact of the matter was simple. I'd gotten lost in a sea of pity for Peterson. *It wasn't really his fault,* I'd told myself. *He was acting on the words of God.*

But fuck that. No, he knew exactly what he was doing. And he still stood behind his cause. Bin Laden was an extremist too, and I didn't feel guilty when he was killed. Hitler? Same thing. Fuck them all. Fuck any person who stands blindly behind an evil cause sugar-coated in a righteous title.

Everyone knows what is right and what is wrong. Everyone knows that bombing innocent people isn't justifiable for oil or religion. Everyone knows that killing someone for the color of their hair, or eyes, or the god they worship is fucked up. And every fucking person alive knows that kidnapping a child and sacrificing him on a god's word is heinous.

Peterson knew all of that too. And he did it anyway.

He wanted a pretty death? Oh, he'd get it. It'd be beautiful.

And it'd hurt like a son of a bitch.

We took the kids out for ice cream and a quick dinner. We stopped at the playground and let them romp on the swings and the slides. We acted like everything was normal. We shielded them from the reality of what our day had actually been and what tomorrow would bring. We'd get even better at that over the years.

Jeremy was worried about me. I could see it all over him. He kept looking at me like I was on the verge of a break down, but I wasn't. Actually, I was relieved. I didn't feel any guilt for what we'd do tomorrow. I didn't feel remorse. I was ready.

It wasn't about anger anymore. I didn't want to kill him because I hated him. I wanted to kill him in the name of justice and freedom.

Holding Peterson for so long humanized him to me. But once I remembered what he put us through, what he *enjoyed* putting us through, my composure returned.

We got ready for bed, and I slept like a baby. The kids dreamed peacefully through the night. And I woke up ready to shut the gods damned door. Once and for all.

"We probably won't be back until late tonight." I lifted my jacket over my shoulders. "And I'll probably be pretty drunk when we do, so if you want to get the kids a bath and ready for bed, that'd be awesome."

"Will do. Hey, maybe we'll take them down to the creek. Micah loves the water, right?" Hannah said, grabbing a pop from the fridge and lifting herself to the edge of the kitchen counter.

"Yeah, so does Mills. Just be careful with her though. She's clumsy. If she does get hurt, you can let Micah heal her." I looked up the steps at Jeremy trotting his way down. "They still asleep?"

"Yeah, they're out. We should probably get out of here though. Long day ahead of us."

"Alright. Let's do it. Thanks, Han. There's all kinds of food in the fridge, but I left some cash in the junk drawer if you want to order in. Just stay in the perimeter, please."

"You got it." She grabbed an apple from the counter and took a bite. "Good luck, guys."

"No luck needed." I smiled. "The hard part's over."

Jeremy's fingertips touched mine. He sent me a soft, sympathetic smile. I exhaled a long, relieved sigh, allowing a joyous smile to come to my lips. "Time to finish this."

As we landed at the top of the basement steps, Jeremy pulled me in to meet his gaze. His forehead crunched down. "Are you—"

"I'm fine. I'm great, actually." I smiled. He tilted his head to the side a bit, and I sighed. "Alright, I know that sounds crazy—that I'm fine with killing someone—but I'm ready. I'm over this. After what Lux told you, that Peterson knew I never stood a chance... That he let me hate myself for all this time... No, fuck him. That fucker goes on and on about how much he loves me, right? Tells me a million times how happy he is to be a part of this? Well, he'd better be happy to die for it too. He... he chose the wrong god. He *fucked over* the wrong god. And it's about time he gets to see her wrath."

He looked over me for a moment. "That's what we're calling ourselves now?"

"No. I mean, not really. But that's what we were. That's what this boils down to. I'm not going out and expecting praise and—"

"I get it," he said. "You don't have to defend it. It's the truth. And I agree. He should have known better than to get on your bad side. Not a place I'd want to be, that's for sure."

I exhaled a slow breath. "Let's do it then. Let's shut the damn door."

CHAPTER FIFTY

JEREMY

When we got down to the basement, Peterson didn't say a word. He humbly stood and waited for us to remove his shackles and cuffs. Laila didn't so much as wince at the sight of him without eyes. She just waited for me to unlatch him, then grabbed him by his throat and teleported to Wyatt's property in West Virginia.

I teleported close behind. We landed in the high green grass in his back yard. She and I carelessly hoisted him belly down to the makeshift crucifix. He groaned a bit but stayed mostly quiet. I fastened his arms and legs in place, ripped open the back of his filthy shirt, and cut the quartz from his back. He screamed a bit but then Laila kicked him, and he shut up.

Then we sat on the porch and waited.

We didn't talk much either. There wasn't anything to say. It was the moment of solace we'd been waiting three years for.

As the survivors started flocking in, we told them to do whatever they wanted to him. Cut him, whip him, punch him; whatever they deemed fit. But we gave them one rule. Don't kill him.

When Liam arrived with Emma and Benny, just as Emma's brown

curls started bouncing toward the man lain out for torture, Laila pulled Liam to the side.

"I think they might be a little young for this," she said. "Are you sure—"

"Uh-uh," Emma said. "You don't get to make that call, Laila. I've waited for this moment way longer than you have."

"Emma—"

"No, Laila," she growled. "Me and Benny both had our first change in a tiny cell. Do you know what it feels like to be a wolf in cage? All you want to do is run and—"

"Alright." She extended her arms in surrender. "Alright. If you're okay with it, Liam."

Honestly, I agreed. A kid or not, she still deserved justice for what was done to her. If Micah were in his teens and wanted in on this, I'd have let him. It'd bring closure.

And it'd teach a lesson too.

Hurting people the way they've hurt you doesn't make the pain go away. Nothing makes that pain go away. All that helps, even a little, is being sure they'll never hurt anyone again.

Liam huffed, rubbed the bridge of his nose, and pushed up his glasses. "I don't think I have much say. But, yeah, I mean, Emma's right. They were too young to live through what they lived through, and they did. So I guess life experience makes them old enough to see his death."

Laila was quiet for a moment. "Okay. Have at it then. Just don't kill him."

"Me too, right?" Liam asked.

"You too," she said. "Just get in line."

He chewed his lip. "Alright then. But can I talk to you guys for a minute?"

"What about?" I asked. He gestured toward the house.

"I'll stay here and keep an eye out," Laila said. "You go ahead."

I slid my hand over her shoulder and started to the porch with Liam. As I sat on the porch step, I said, "What's up?"

"Uh." He paused, running his fingers over his chin. He cleared his throat. "There's a lot of rumors going around about the two of you."

Ah. He wanted to know if it was true. If Laila and I were truly gods. If he'd fucked one, I supposed. But we'd made it clear to spread the word around the community. Tell everyone the truth. So that's what I did.

"They aren't rumors," I said.

"So it's true then? You guys are..."

"Gods?" I asked. He swallowed hard. "Yeah. Yeah, we are. Or were, I guess, in a past life."

He gestured to the step beside me. "Mind if I..."

I laughed. "I'm not going to smite you, dude."

Liam smiled as he sat. "Sorry, it's just... I've never been face to face with a god before."

"You've been face to face with a few actually," I muttered. "Copped an attitude with a pretty important one, might I add."

An awkward laugh escaped him. "I didn't know you were a god then."

"Well, neither did I."

"Wouldn't have slept with your wife if I knew you were," he murmured. His hand ran along his clean shaved, warm brown jaw. "You aren't going to, like, damn me to hell for that, are you?"

I laughed. "Hell isn't real. I mean, it is. But that's not where we go when we die. But no. No, I don't care. It's not like I didn't fuck other people when we were broken up either. But bring it up again, and I'm punching you in the face."

"Message received." Peterson released a loud, nails on a chalkboard scream a few hundred yards away. "Bet you're glad to finally kill that asshole, huh?"

"Yeah, can't wait." I huffed. "Ready for all this shit to just be over, you know?"

"Yeah, me too. It'll be nice to be able to tell them he can never hurt them again. It's hard when they wake up in cold sweats, ya know? Not knowing where they are, terrified. Benny ran two miles into the woods completely unconscious last month. When I finally caught up to him, he was on the verge of shifting while in the worst panic attack I've ever seen. He was convinced guards were chasing him." He watched the next survivor step up to whip his back. "I hope it'll be easier once he's dead."

I looked at Laila standing beside the young girl. "Yeah, I hope."

"But you got your kid back, right? Micah?" Liam asked. "That's got to be a good feeling."

I smiled. "Yeah. He's perfect. Nothing's going to give us those years with him back, but at least the bastard responsible is going to be gone forever."

"Ain't that the truth," Liam murmured. "How is he? Your boy, I mean."

"He's great. Really great. You wouldn't even know he's been through so much if it weren't for the scars." I grabbed my phone from my pocket and angled it toward him. Micah and Milly were my background, smiling wide in the backyard with Tink at their feet.

"The resemblance with the two of them and two of you is crazy." He laughed. I chuckled, giving a nod. "I'm glad you guys got your big happy family."

"Me too." I smiled down at the image. I looked at Emma and Benny. "I'm glad you got yours too."

He smiled. "Thanks to you guys."

By nightfall, all of the present survivors and their loved ones had gotten their chance. Everyone who wanted to beat the guy had done so. Peterson was in and out of consciousness, sprawled out above a pond of his blood.

It was time.

I asked Laila if she needed me, but she shook her head. She stood from her perch on the steps and started toward him. The crowd of over a thousand people became utterly silent.

I stood to get a better view over their bobbing heads. I watched as she cut the ropes at his wrists and feet, letting his body fall to the ground with a quiet clunk. He was barely alive by that point anyway.

"The moment we've all been waiting for," Laila began, rubbing her hand over her mouth and shaking her head. "I've only waited three years for this. But some of you have waited ten or fifteen." She kicked him. She huffed. "I don't need to give some speech, do I? We all want this to fucking end. We all want to see this piece of shit take his last breath."

Claps erupted from the audience. Some cheered, others waited solemnly for her to continue. Chris was with the latter, taking a long gulp from his flask beside me. He offered it to me, and I made a face. "Right. Sorry."

"It's okay," I muttered. He took a long gulp and looked back to Laila in the field.

"Stand up," Laila said. Peterson struggled to his knees, falling back to his face. She grabbed his shoulders and teleported him back to the wood, this time, facing the crowd.

I heard her murmur something in Elvan. Vines started from his feet, climbing around his body, and buckling each limb to the structure. He didn't struggle. He didn't say a word. He just leaned his head back and closed his eyelids over their empty sockets.

Then, the vines climbing his body started sprouting tiny red flowers.

A huff of a laugh escaped me. Japanese bamboo torture on instant replay.

Laila had started growing those flowers in the garden a few weeks prior. They were called euphorbia milii. Also known as the crown of thorns.

Poetic in so many ways. The color of the plant itself; red, like the blood he'd spilled. The formal name of the flower, which closely resembled our daughter's. That's why I thought she'd liked them, in fact. And of course, the layman's word for it. The crown of thorns would kill him as he lay out bound to a cross.

Had I not known those flowers, I'd have had no idea how much pain he was about to be in. But I'd accidentally grabbed one of them when I was pulling weeds. The stem beneath the bud was coated in jagged thorns in every direction, almost like a thin cactus. Laila had needed to heal the cuts for me because I couldn't even hold a pen in my hand.

He screamed. He screamed louder than anything I'd ever heard. Everyone in the crowd grew quiet once again, leaving only the sound of his cries in the echoing valley.

Slowly but surely, deep green stems coated in crimson started to burst up through his entire body. Blood spilled from each hole. His screams got louder, then turned to gurgles when budding blooms shot through his chest. He was heaving at that point, but still not fighting.

"Goodbye, Peterson," Laila said.

Suddenly, two bright red blooms shot through his eye sockets.

The gurgled screams stopped.

The crowd cheered.

After a long moment of joyous claps and yells, Laila turned to face the crowd. "It's over. It's finally fucking over. We can stop looking over our shoulders. The weight on our chests has finally lifted. It's over, guys. My only regret is that it took us so long to get here. So I'm sorry for that. But we did. We made it. We can enjoy some peace again."

She turned back to his corpse. A bright purple fire started in her palm. She shot it at his feet. His legs went up in flames. As they travelled up his body, she walked through the crowd, smiling and giving cordial nods.

When she made it to the porch, Chris passed her the flask and tucked his arm around her shoulders, pulling her in for a hug. She took it and tilted her head back. She guzzled until it was empty.

"And now, we drink!" she yelled.

They did. They drank. They drank a shit ton. But we had a babysitter, and she always planned to get shit faced that night. So I just sat beside her and watched as she took shot after shot after shot.

I think every time she drank in the past three years, she'd done so to drown out the pain. But that was the first time since before Moe that she drank to relax.

Chris looked happier than he had since he'd been back. The alcohol probably played a part, but the execution was the cuffs falling from his wrists. I knew I'd be carrying them both home, but it was okay. They deserved to let loose.

We stayed there for hours after the death. Survivors approached us, thanking us for everything we'd done. Some even kneeled before us. That was awkward.

When they did though, Laila extended her hand and helped them to stand. She said something about how 'the only time someone should kneel is if they're scrubbing a floor or sucking a dick, but never to another person.'

I laughed. And so did everyone else.

But Laila hugged them with tears in her drunken gaze, telling them how glad she was that they were okay. She showed them the kid's baby pictures and looked at photos the survivors showed her of theirs. She took a few numbers to set up play dates, which was actually a really good thing for Micah. He needed friends. Especially friends that had scars like he did.

When the sun started to rise, Wyatt and I told everyone it was time to start clearing out. I teleported him and Chris back home and came back for Laila.

She fell to the bed with a loud clunk. Hannah asked if everything went well, and I told her it went exactly as planned. She smiled and said she was glad to hear it.

The kids had been good all day, but they went to bed early so they'd be up soon. I thanked her and got a quick shower before I heard Milly on the monitor. Laila began to drunkenly stumble from the bed, but I told her to lie down. She did.

I got Milly dressed and started breakfast. Micah got up soon after. As I poured some syrup over his pancakes, his always entertaining rhetoric began.

"Daddy," he said.

"Micah."

"Whewe's Mommy?" He looked past the counter to the bedroom. "Shouldn't she be up by now?"

"Usually." I smiled. "But Mommy had a long day yesterday. And don't tell her I told you this, but she drank a lot of grown-up drinks last night. So she's probably going to be asleep for a while."

"Oh." He took a bite of his bacon. "Well, what awe we going to do until she wakes up then?"

"I was thinking you could help me set up that new swing set we bought last week." I took a gulp of my coffee. "What do you think?"

He gave an excited nod. "It's gonna be so cool. We'we going to have our own pawk in the back yawd!"

I laughed and nodded back. "We kind of will, huh?"

As I laid the skillet into the sink, Micah spoke again. "Daddy."

"Micah," I repeated.

"Is he gone now?"

I turned with confusion in my eyes. "What do you mean?"

"The doctow. Is he gone now?"

All this time, he knew? He knew we had him here? Did he know we were torturing him too? Did he know the awful things we'd done to him?

But maybe he didn't. Maybe he just knew he was alive. Maybe he just felt the absence of his soul now that he was gone.

"Yeah, he's gone."

He looked down at his plate. "Is it okay fow me to be a little sad?"

I paused, searching for the words. "Yeah, buddy. It's okay for you to feel however you feel."

"I's a little sad," he murmured. "But now he can't huwt no one no more, wight?"

"Right," I murmured.

He was quiet for a moment. "That's good, I guess."

I never told Laila about that conversation. I wish I'd never had it. I wish he'd forgotten about him. But Peterson was right that day on the cliffside.

Some part of Micah would always have some level of love and compassion for that monster.

That kid had compassion for everyone.

CHAPTER FIFTY-ONE

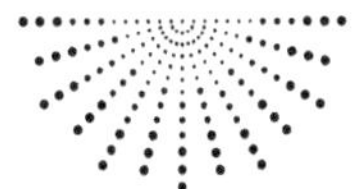

ABOUT A MONTH LATER - LAILA

"I can't do this." Hannah paced back and forth through the kitchen. "I'm not even twenty-two yet. I'm supposed to be going to clubs, and hooking up with random guys, and-and I'm a fucking virgin. God, how does that even work?"

"Instinct kind of kicks in," Celena said. "If it feels good, you keep doing it. If it doesn't, then you stop. It's kind of self-explanatory, really."

"Han." I laughed. "You want to be with Kai, don't you?"

"Well, yeah. Yeah. But, wasn't I supposed to live first? Wasn't I supposed to see the world? Wasn't I supposed to enjoy my youth?"

She sounded like I did when I found out that Jeremy and I were soulmates. As if this realization somehow changed anything between them. The only thing that *might* change their dynamic would be if I were right and they were in fact par animarum.

And I was pretty hype to find out.

I'd never been so excited for other people to fuck in my life. But I had a feeling, and I wanted to know, damn it.

"Divorce is an option," Leah said. "Just do it. If it doesn't work out, then get out."

"Oh, yeah. That makes me feel so much better," Hannah snapped.

I laughed. I fastened the buttons on the back of Milly's cream-colored dress. "You just have cold feet. Once you see each other up there, that'll go away."

"Did you feel like this too?" She plopped down to the breakfast nook, struggling with the bottom of her poofy ball gown.

"Not really. But my wedding was a coping mechanism to help me get through a really rough bout of depression. And I got around a lot before I met Jeremy. I didn't feel like I was missing out on much." I knew what her response would be, but I said it anyway because verbalizing things often helps the mind stop spinning. "It's different for everyone though. If now isn't the time for you, then now isn't the time for you. Do you want to call it off?"

"No," she murmured. "No. I love him. I love him more than I love anything."

I smiled. "Then marry him."

She slowly exhaled a deep breath. "Does my hair look okay?"

"Your hair looks amazing," Celena said.

"And your makeup's perfect." I smiled, eyes moving over her and fighting the water that tried to form across my irises. The little fourteen-year-old girl I met almost seven years before was long gone.

It hadn't really dawned on me that Hannah was grown until I saw her in her wedding gown with her makeup done and hair spun into an elegant updo. She wore a soft brown eye shadow beneath a thin black wing. Her pouty lips were painted a dark, gorgeous shade of maroon. In that big floofy ballgown, she really did look like a princess.

"You look beautiful, Han." Leah grinned. "I wish Mom was here to see this."

A sweet smile came to Hannah's lips. "She'd love Kai."

"She would," Leah said. "We all do."

"Who wouldn't?" Celena smiled. "You guys are perfect."

"We are, huh?"

"You are." I smiled. "So have a glass of wine. Take a deep breath. And enjoy your wedding day."

"My wedding day," she murmured. Her smile widened. "I'm really getting married."

"You really are." I laughed. Milly reached for her sippy cup on the table, and I handed it to her. "And you've got the cutest little flower girl in the world."

"She does look freaking adorable." Hannah reached for her hand and touched her fingertips. "Micah looked so cute in his tux too."

"He was so hype to put it on." I laughed. "He's been itching to wear it."

"Luka's tux looked so cute too," Leah said. "Before he spit up on it, anyway."

Hannah took in another slow breath. She looked up at me. "Can you get me that wine? It's hard to move in this thing."

"Sure." I set Milly on the ground and started to the wet bar.

"I told you not to go with the corset, but no one ever listens to me," Leah muttered.

"I like the corset. It makes my tits look huge," Hannah said.

"Your tits always look huge because they're huge," Celena said.

"Yeah, but they look all perky."

"They always look perky," I said.

And that was true. Lucky bitch. Hannah had the cutest, curvy without being voluptuous figure. A small waist, a large bust and hips, all wrapped up at barely over five foot tall. I hoped Milly would get her figure.

"Kai likes corsets too," Hannah said.

"All men like corsets," Celena muttered.

"Yeah, they're sexy," Leah agreed. "Won't catch me dead in one. But they're fucking cute."

"Exactly," Hannah muttered. "I wonder what the guys are doing right now."

"Probably pouring Kai shots." I poured some white wine into a glass. "Or maybe telling him how to find the G-spot."

"He knows how to do that," Hannah muttered.

I set the glass in front of her, arching a brow. "I thought you were a virgin."

Her cheeks grew red. "I am. But... We've done some stuff."

"Oh, then you'll be fine tonight," Celena said. "It might hurt a little bit at first. But once you relax, it's a good time."

Hannah laughed. "I'm kind of excited for that part though. I mean, I'm nervous. But I'm excited."

"I'm excited to see if you two are paired souls." I grinned. "I think you are. I really do. I remember when you first told me that the two of you kissed, do you remember that?" A grin stretched up her cheeks. "You said something like 'I know it's not the same as you and Jeremy, but I feel connected to him.' And that's how I felt about Jeremy when we first met too."

"Yeah, maybe. It'd be pretty cool if we are. Maybe I'd get some more powers," she said. "And Kai's been hanging out with Heylel, did you know that? They're on the phone all the time. He's convinced they know each other."

"Yeah, Heylel told me that when we had lunch last week," I said. "I wouldn't doubt it. Venark looks a lot like Kai. I think he was my twin in that life too."

"What's up with that?" Celena asked. "Have you guys seen anything lately?"

"Nothing in depth. But we've seen glimpses. I saw Jeremy holding Micah, the original Micah, last week. It was only for a second or two, but it was the best memory I've seen. He looked so happy. Like he does now, you know?"

"He has been really happy lately." Leah smiled. "I think we all have."

"It feels good to feel good, doesn't it?" Celena said. "We're all in a good place at the same time for once."

"Yeah." I smiled, looking over Milly with her doll on the floor. "Let's hope it lasts."

"I think it will." Hannah smiled. "For a while, anyway."

"Hey, guys." Chris appeared in the doorway. "We're all set. The altar's ready, the music's playing, the guys are up there. Just waiting on the bride."

"The bride." Hannah laughed as she stood. "That's me, right?"

"That's you." Chris grinned, glancing over her. His eyes softened, and his lips raised in a grin. "My baby sister's a bride. A beautiful bride, by the way."

"I do look pretty hot, huh?" She smirked, fingers grazing her bodice. "Sucks I only get to wear it once. But hey, maybe my kids will wear it one day."

"Maybe." Chris smiled. "You ready though?"

She smiled. "Let's do this thing."

CHAPTER FIFTY-TWO

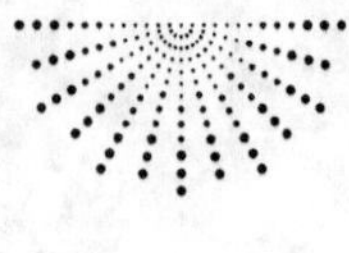

JEREMY

The smell of men's cologne mixed with potpourri filled my nose. Bright sun shined in from the high window to my left, reflecting like glass against the hardwood floors. I glanced at myself in the mirror the maids had brought into the meeting room, adjusting the scratchy dress shirt around my shoulders.

This room felt a lot more homey without the many Chambers sitting around the massive table. Then again, maybe it was just all of my brothers that made it feel that way. Their laughter, shoving one another's shoulders, bitching about how uncomfortable our shoes were.

It was nice. Normal. Practically human.

"You look fancy." Micah looked up at Kai as he fastened his suspenders over his shoulders. "I like it. You should get fancy all the time."

Kai laughed. "I'll keep that in mind, lad."

"That's a cool word," Micah muttered. "Why don't you call me that, Daddy?"

"Because I'm not Scottish," I said as I buttoned my shirt.

"I ain't Scottish neither," Kai said.

"Yeah, but close enough."

"You've got the rings though, lad?" Kai asked.

Micah patted his pants. Then his eyes widened, and he looked up at me. I laughed and reached in my pocket. I set them in his hand.

Micah breathed a sigh of relief, closing his palm tight around them.

He'd been so concerned about the rings. Hannah had made a comment about how if he lost them, he'd be scrubbing toilets for a year to pay Uncle Kai back. Obviously she was joking, but he'd taken it to heart. He was terrified of losing those rings.

"Well, look at you," Adam said in the doorway. "Clean up pretty good there, pal."

Kai chuckled. "That's what everyone keeps tellin' me."

He did look pretty nice. Aside from today, I'd only seen him out of harem pants three or four times. When he helped us take the compounds, he'd worn jeans. At mine and Laila's wedding, he'd worn slacks.

Today though, he wore an expensive black tux. Finely tailored to his size on Hannah's command, of course. He refused to do the vest though. He said he'd wear the rest, but the vest would not happen. She reluctantly agreed. He didn't seem to enjoy the bowtie at his neck either, but there was no way she'd marry a man without a tie.

Adam smiled. "It always shocks people when guys like us wear something decent."

"It wouldn't kill you all to wear something with buttons once in a while, ya know," Brody said, adjusting his cuffs in the mirror in the corner. "Might get laid a little more often if you did."

"I get laid plenty, thanks," I said.

It probably would kill me though. That shit wasn't for me. Slacks suck. Ties are annoying. I liked shoes that didn't make me feel like Big Foot shoved into leather.

"What's that mean?" Micah asked.

"Ask me that in ten—"

"Ugh, I hate when you say that," he said. "I's thwee now. I not a baby anymowe."

I laughed. "Don't I know."

"My, my," Mémé said in the doorway. She wore a long, flowing blue gown. As usual, only a bit of mascara rested above her pale eyes, but her white hair was adorned in a gorgeous updo with little crystal pins. "You boys have grown into fine young men, haven't you?"

"Not so young anymore, Mémé." Brody smiled.

"Younger than me." She chuckled. She looked at Kai as he shook his jacket over his shoulders. "A fine young man you are, too."

He smiled. "Thank you, mistress."

She smiled back. She looked down at Micah. "And look at you! What a handsome chap. Look just like your grandfather all dressed up like that."

"Weally?" he asked. "I never seen him 'cause he died a long time ago."

Her smile curved down. She cleared her throat. "Would you like to see some photos?"

Micah nodded excitedly. He looked up at me. "Can I, Daddy?"

We only had one photo of Dad at the house. It was a family picture with us four boys, Mom, and Dad. Hannah wasn't born yet. It really sucked how we didn't have any with all five of us and both of them. But it was kinda hard to look at pictures of him. Any time I saw him, I pictured him the last way I'd seen him, hanging from the ceiling fan.

But it'd be nice for Micah to know what his grandpa looked like.

"Go ahead, bud." I roughed up his hair. "Just hold those rings real tight. We'll all be in big trouble if you lose them."

"I won't," he said. He ran toward the doorway and took Mémé's hand.

"We have a bit before the service, no?" she asked.

"Ten minutes or so," Brody said. "Chris is helping them set up the speakers now, so it won't be long."

"Then neither will we." She smiled. "We'll just be in the sitting room."

I smiled back and gave a nod.

As the door shut behind her, Kai cleared his throat and looked between us. "The day's finally come, hadn't it?"

"Looks like it." Adam took a gulp from his flask and passed it to him. "You're finally going to become a man."

"I been a man for a long while now." Kai took a sip and sat at a chair near the end of the table.

I laughed. "That's not what he meant, dude."

"What'd ya mean then?" Kai asked.

"You're going to have sex," Brody said. "Kind of a part of manhood where we're from."

I wasn't really sure why the two equated either. I'd started having sex at sixteen, and it wasn't until I had kids that I really started to feel like a man. Fucking isn't what makes one a man.

Kai may have been light and airy for as long as I'd known him, but honestly? I think he'd been a man far longer than I had. Kind of ditsy at times, but also mature. An all-around good guy, really. He was kind, and caring, and always happy.

He was gonna be a good husband. I was happy to say he was my brother when I married his sister, but I was even happier to see him marry mine. I knew he'd be the kind of man she needed.

"Oh," Kai mumbled. He took another gulp from the flask. "Is it that important to the lot of ye?"

"It's a pretty big thing," Adam said.

"It's fun." I shrugged and sat down. "And if you guys are anything like me and Lai, it'll be a hell of a lot more than that."

"But..." He paused. "I, uh... How do you know you're doing it right?"

"If she sounds like she just ran a marathon, you're probably doing it right," Adam said. "Hannah's pretty expressive. I'm sure she'll tell you if you're doing it wrong."

"Right, but... I mean, how do ye..." He paused. "Ye ken. Do it?"

"Aww. Poor guy." Adam laughed. He pulled his phone from his pocket. "Here. Watch this."

Awkward. So very, very awkward.

Not that I'd ever been one for 'locker room talk' anyway, but in reference to my baby sister, it was a lot weirder. It wasn't that I didn't want them to have sex or a good sex life, I just didn't want to think about it. And I didn't want to give him tips based on how I fucked his sister.

Just a lot of awkward going on here.

I bit down my grin as he passed Kai the phone. The moans and dirty talk of some pretty hardcore porn began, and Kai's eyes widened. Then they crinkled. His jaw dropped, and his eyes widened again. "The hell is this?"

"It's porn," Adam said.

His nose scrunched up. "No one will be watching Hannah and I, will they?"

"Don't watch that," I said. "Sex isn't really like that."

"Maybe *your* sex isn't like this," Adam muttered over Kai's shoulder.

"No, no one's going to be watching you guys." Brody laughed. "But Jeremy's right. Porn isn't going to give you a good idea of what sex is really like. Everyone's a lot different, man. You'll get your groove once you've done it a couple times."

"But I want her to enjoy it too," he said. "I don't... I don't want to do it like that, but she looks like she's having a jolly time there."

"Because she's paid to look like she's having a jolly time." I took the phone and shuttered it. "Just do what feels right. And ask her what feels right. Trust me, you'll learn as you go."

"Here." Adam took his phone from my hand and clicked out the S-pen.

Brody shook his head. "Don't show him more porn, man."

"I'm not; I'm drawing him a diagram," Adam muttered, doodling for a moment. He turned the phone to him. "Alright, so the hole down here, that's where your dick goes. Sometimes it can go in the other hole too, but you've got to ask first, or they get mad."

"Jesus," I muttered.

"And this thing here, that's the clit. And that's where the magic happens. Move your fingers around it enough, and she'll be feeling pretty damn good."

"You do realize you're talking about our little sister, right?" I asked.

"Yeah, and I'm trying to help her out. She'll thank me later. Oh, and if you put your tongue on there—"

Kai's face said he was confused as he pointed at the image. "But how the hell can my face be down there while my pecker is?"

"No, not at the same time," Adam said. "You usually start with your mouth and then work into the pecker part."

"Alright, I'm gonna go see if Chris needs any help out there," I muttered.

CHAPTER FIFTY-THREE

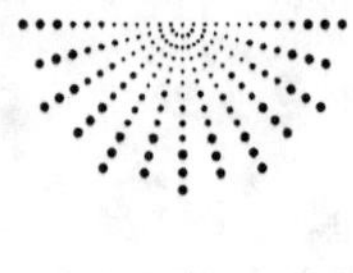

LAILA

Jeremy smiled at me as I put Milly on the ground and adjusted her dress. "Here." He handed me Milly's basket of flowers.

I put it in her hand and smiled. "You've got to throw them, okay? Don't eat them."

She giggled and started toddling down the stone path. Kai lowered himself to the ground at the altar, arms wide for her. She tossed a petal or two before rushing toward him.

"I'm next, wight?" Micah asked.

"You are." Jeremy smiled, fixed his ponytail, and gestured toward Milly. "Just follow your sister. Try and walk a little slower though."

"Got it," he murmured. He slowly took a step forward, pausing at the sound of each thump in the music.

I laughed. "A little, tiny bit faster."

"Oh." He picked up the pace.

"The maid of honor and the best man are next, right?" Jeremy smiled, locking his elbow with mine.

I grinned back. "I think that's how it goes."

He touched his lips to my cheek. "You look beautiful."

"You look pretty damn good too." I bent back to look at him. Hannah was right all those years ago, blue was his color. He looked amazing in dress clothes, on the rare occasion that he wore them. "Look better without it though."

He grinned. "Oh, yeah?" I smirked, and he squeezed my hip. "Maybe we'll sneak off during the reception."

If we wanted to squeeze any in, we'd have to get it done here. Everyone was crashing at our place to clear out the main house for Hannah and Kai. Jeremy and I weren't known for being quiet either, and I wasn't all that into the idea of getting down and dirty as our million siblings slept on the couch.

"Enough empty rooms around here, we can probably pop out for a few minutes." I glanced up with a smile.

"We should definitely fuck in my grandpa's office," he muttered. "Something about that desk, just looks like the perfect place for a quickie."

I laughed, watching Micah make it to the altar. "Seems a little disrespectful though, doesn't it?"

"Eh." We started down the path. "Never bothered you before."

He wasn't wrong. The two of us were always down for a quick fuck on a desk. Wasn't sure why, but it was a great position. He always hit just the right spot at that angle.

I gestured toward the rolling hills of green, fragrant of grapes and berries. "I don't know, something about those vineyards seems romantic."

"You always want to fuck in the dirt," he muttered.

"I love the earth, what can I say?" I murmured, sending smiles to the audience members I knew.

Hannah and Kai didn't know most of them, but we did. Chamber heads, wolf Monarchs, vamp leaders, high priestesses. A far bigger wedding than my taste, but Hannah always said she wanted a big one. At least she'd get some bomb gifts.

"I wonder what Micah and Milly's weddings will be like," Jeremy said. "Micah'll probably want something like this. He's all about the finer things."

"Milly'll probably be barefoot." I smiled, watching Micah try to usher her to a chair before she swatted him away. "She's pretty big about the Earth too."

"I bet she'll wear your dress." Jeremy smiled.

"If she wants to," I muttered. "She's going to be curvier than me though. My dress probably won't fit her."

"We can always have it tailored," he said. "I thought Hannah would wanna wear Mom's dress though. Maybe Milly will want something different too."

"The mermaid style might be outdated by her big day."

How wrong I was about that. She didn't want my dress though. Said it was 'pretentiously pretty and way too tight.'

Jeremy pressed his lips to my forehead, and we parted ways at the altar. I lifted Milly to my hip and watched Wyatt usher Celena down the aisle. Adam and Jenna followed, joining beside the rest of the wedding party. Brody and Chris walked alone with big smiles. Then the dun-duh-du-dun began.

My smile stretched across my lips when I saw the top of Hannah's veiled head bobbing down the terrace. As her body came into view, tears welled in my eyes.

She wore a large, princess ball gown that made her look like as tiny as a Barbie doll. Sheer linen tightly wrapped her arms, sparkling with a glitter like sheen. Her tiny waist looked even smaller beneath the tight, glistening bodice. The large skirt nearly tripped Leah beside her, train extending a good ten feet behind them.

I looked at Kai. His messy brown locks were combed cleanly around his ears, reminding me so much of how Dad looked on the few occasions when he dressed up. He looked at her with the sweetest, happiest smile and wiped a tear from the corner of his eye.

They were perfect together. The two of them shared this remark-able sense of innocence and joy for life. It's funny because Kai's older than me. But he was so much greener to the world then. Hannah was too. But that soft, sweetness they shared never faded.

The audience stood, gazing with smiles as Hannah and Leah walked to the altar. Leah gave her a quick hug and struggled not to cry. I sent her the same, teary eyed gaze. I passed Milly to Mary in the front row. Hannah handed me the bouquet as Micah passed Jeremy the rings and stood at his feet.

Hannah and Kai looked at each other for a moment. Tears welled in their eyes as they smiled. Kai murmured something before Hannah laughed and waved her hand in front of her eyes.

"Now if you'll all be seated," the pastor began. When the audience sat, he said, "Dearly beloved, we are gathered here today to witness these two beautiful souls join in holy matrimony. Two very different souls who've led two very different lives, from two different worlds, in fact."

A few chuckles sounded from the audience. He went on.

The ceremony was amazing. I could feel the two cultures merging as the pastor spoke, considerate to Kai's heritage and to Hannah's. He went through the basic old ceremony everyone had heard a thousand times. He went through a Fae ceremony, reciting Elvan verses that brought a joyous chill to my skin. They repeated the vows, Kai stumbling on a few complex English words he wasn't familiar with. Hannah mumbled some of the Elvan words in the same unsure tongue, giggling when she mixed up a few.

Then they slid the rings over each other's fingers. But before the kiss, Kai lowered himself to the ground and fastened a silver chain around her ankle. Hannah then brought herself to her knee, tightening one around his. Then, on their knees at equal sight, they shared their first kiss as husband and wife.

I cried. I bawled like a baby.

Kai stood and helped Hannah to her feet, kissing again with his hand cupping her cheek. She twisted her arms around his neck and lifted their joined hands for the crowd to see.

Aside from my children's and my own, it was the most beautiful wedding I ever witnessed. Maybe because it reminded me so much of Nix and Véa's.

Hannah and Kai sweetly swayed around the patio. Her head rested against his chest. Then a voice sounded over the speakers. "Alright, ladies and gentlemen. Now that the bride and groom have shared their first dance as husband and wife, it's time for the bride to share a dance with her grandfather. All the fathers out there, get your daughter's hand and join them on the dance floor.

"Still want to sneak off?" Jeremy whispered at my ear.

"Maybe after you dance with your daughter." I laughed and passed her to him. "I want pictures."

"Alright, little lady." He hoisted her in the air. She giggled and pumped her feet toward the sky. He grinned. "Let's get some pictures so I can go have some fun with your mommy."

I laughed and shook my head.

"Can I dance with you, Mommy?" Micah asked, reaching his hand out for mine.

"On the next song." I tugged him into my lap as *Forever Young* covered by Bob Dylan played. "This one's for daddies and their little girls."

"Thewe isn't one for mommies and they little boys?" He laid his head against my chest and looked up to meet my gaze.

"Not usually. But maybe you can have one like that at your wedding."

His eyes widened. "I'm going to have a wedding?"

"Maybe one day." I smiled and kissed his forehead.

"That'd be fun," he muttered. "This is so pwetty."

I smiled, watching Jeremy spin around with Milly on the patio.

It really was. It felt like a fairytale. The twinkling fairly lights over the dancefloor, brightened by a sunset with a hundred vibrant hues. The smell of fancy French food, the taste of sweet wine on my tongue, the sound of the music, the warm summer breeze.

My sister-in-law looked so pretty in that big ball gown. My husband looked so happy with our daughter on his hip, singing that old song and watching her grin. All of my brothers and sisters laughed and sipped champagne. My mom sat at a table with Jenna and Luka a few seats down, even Mary was around here somewhere.

We were all so happy. Life was good.

"You's pwetty too." He looked up with a smile. "I like youw dwess."

I grinned and squeezed him tighter. "Thank you, baby. You look very handsome."

He smiled and turned back to the dance floor.

"Hey, lad," Kai said to Micah. "Mind if I share this dance with yer mum?"

Micah furrowed his brows. "You'we not Mommy's daddy."

He laughed. "Well, can we pretend for a bit?"

"I'll dance with you, bud." Celena took his hand with a grin. "C'mon."

"Hah!" Micah jumped from my lap. "I still get to dance with a pwetty giwl."

We laughed, and I took Kai's hand. The two of us made it to the dance floor. I put my hands on his shoulders, and his rested at my hips.

"This was a great wedding," I said. "Best I've attended, if I do say so myself."

"It was wonderful, wadn't it?" He grinned, looking over my shoulder at Hannah dancing with Papy.

"It was indeed."

He smiled. "Thank you, Laila."

I cocked my head to the side. "What for?"

"You knew her. You showed me her." He gazed at Hannah lovingly over my shoulder. "If you hadn't met him, I'd have never met her."

"Oh." I chuckled. "Well. You're welcome. But thank you, too. Hannah's like my little sister. And there's no one in the world I'd rather see her with. You treat her like she's gold."

"She is." He smiled. "She's the best person I've ever met."

I smiled back.

CHAPTER FIFTY-FOUR

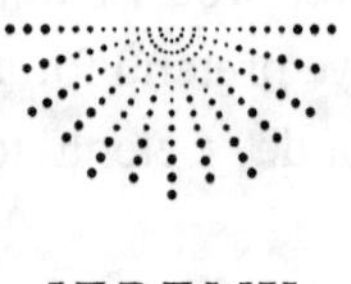

JEREMY

I wasn't surprised that I didn't get the chance to sneak off with Laila. That was usually how things worked now that we were an old married couple with kids. But it was still a great day. Hannah and Kai were the happiest couple I'd ever seen aside from me and Laila.

When it was over, Laila helped clean up while I took the kids home and started their bedtime routine. It was midnight our time, they were exhausted, so we skipped the baths. I just changed them into their PJ's, brushed their teeth, and tucked them into their beds.

I fed Tink as the siblings began flocking in. Celena and Wyatt crashed in Laila's office on a blow-up bed, Leah claimed the couch, and Brody and Gwen took the other blow-up mattress in the last guest room.

Then Laila got home and collapsed to the bed. I hoped I'd get lucky, but she was out the moment her head hit the pillow. So I sighed and lay down beside her.

But I just stayed like that for a while. Lying there, watching the slow rise and fall of each breath she took. I twirled a piece of her long dark hair between my fingers, grazing my thumb against her soft, blushed cheek.

Life was finally as we wanted it to be.

We were normal.

We had our kids. They were both happy and healthy.

Micah was starting to get some skills on the guitar, and he knew all of his ABCs in three different languages. Any of the physical problems he'd manifested in captivity were beginning to dissipate. At his last doctor's appointment, the pediatrician said his legs were looking better —that he wouldn't need braces or surgery after all.

She wasn't happy that he insisted on eating a vegetarian diet, but in fairness, neither were we. She did help us work out a meal plan and supplements to help him gain back whatever he would've gotten from protein. But I was just happy to know that he was healthy, or at least getting close to it.

Milly was growing into quite the little stinker. I loved her with every fiber of my being, wouldn't trade her for the world, but she was a mischievous thing.

She'd made a habit of teleporting into Laila's makeup bag and painting the bathroom sink with foundation and eyeshadow. She *loved* to steal all of her brother's snacks when we loafed around on movie nights. But she had so much personality. She was fun. Kind of rowdy and a little mean, but Daddy's little girl for sure.

And Laila? She'd been so at ease since Peterson's execution. It hadn't been long yet, but she hadn't woken from a nightmare once since that day. Her smile looked more genuine. Everyone was just... Good.

Life was good.

We were probably the happiest we'd ever been. It finally happened.

We'd busted our ass to make it here. To have children, and a simple, human life, but we'd done it. And nothing would take our family away again.

But our lives? Well, those were another story.

CHAPTER FIFTY-FIVE

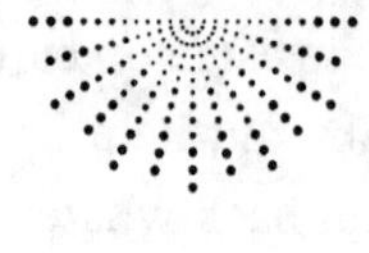

LAILA

It was about three A.M. when I awoke with a sudden jolt. The alarm didn't wake me, neither did the kids, or Tink barking at the crack of twigs outside. It was a feeling. Like a wave of vibrating, soft, yet shocking, energy.

I peeped into Micah and Milly's mind. Micah was dreaming of playing outside with Tink. Milly's thoughts were centered around my azaleas in the garden.

It didn't come from them.

Jeremy sat forward, cocked his head to the side a bit, and turned to meet my gaze. "Did you feel that?"

"I sure the hell did." I stood.

Our bedroom door swung open. Leah looked at me with wide eyes. "You felt that, right?"

"We did," Jeremy said. "What was it?"

She huffed. "Only felt something like that one other time."

My lips curled up in a smile. "When we completed our bond."

Leah let out something of a huff. "Guess you guys were right."

"Should we go congratulate them?" I asked.

"I mean, if we just felt that, then they're probably still doing it," Jeremy said. "Maybe we should, ya know, give them a minute or two."

"Holy fuck," a voice exclaimed from the kitchen. "I can teleport!"

"Or not," he muttered. "Must be a minute man."

"I'm sure you nutted quick your first time too," Leah mumbled.

I rushed through the doorway with Leah and Jeremy at my tail. Hannah stood beside the island, gripping it for support in a camisole negligee covered by a white satin robe. Her long black curls hung in a mess around her creamy cheeks, lipstick smeared down her neck a bit.

Never in my life had I been so pumped to see someone's after sex aesthetic.

"I knew it!" I bounced with excitement.

She looked at me and grinned. She teleported in front of me. Her eyes widened at the landing, grasping my shoulders for support. "Ooh, head rush."

"It happens sometimes in the beginning." I smiled.

I fucking knew it.

And it explained so much.

When I met Hannah, I loved her instantly. She was younger than me by a fair bit, but we instantly hit it off. I'd even told Jeremy, 'I swear she was my sister in a past life or something.' For the record though, I had no biological sisters in my first life.

When I met Kai, I asked if we knew one another. Then when I realized he was my brother, that's what I cracked up the familiarity to. And maybe it had played a part. But I felt the same way when I met Celena and Wyatt.

Once, a long, long time ago, we all called one another family. And now, we were all together again. One big, happy family.

"You'll get used to it." Jeremy leaned against the counter with a smile.

"All these years, I've been the powerless one and now, I've got more abilities than everyone else. Besides you, I mean," Hannah said.

"Well, I think that'd make us equals now, right? Because eventually, you'll be able to use Kai's abilities too," Jeremy said.

She wagged a finger, eyes wide. "Ooh, that's true."

"Well, no, because you can't do the electricity thing," Leah said.

"Oh, yeah. Duh," Hannah said. Her eyes widened. "I should probably get back to him, huh? Just kind of poofed out."

"Might not be a bad idea." I laughed. "Go have fun with your husband. We'll talk in the morning."

She smiled and disappeared.

"Ya know, this is some bullshit," Leah muttered. "You guys get all these cool powers and eternal romance. And what do I get? Suicidal girlfriends, cheating girlfriends, two powers, *and* I have to deal with all of your drama and bullshit."

"Sorry," I mumbled.

"Connor and Naomi aren't related to either of us. But they've got the bond," Jeremy said. "Maybe you have a soulmate out there somewhere too."

"I fucking better," she grumbled. She walked to the couch and dropped down. "Some damn bullshit. I'm going to sleep."

"Sweet dreams." I gave a quiet laugh.

CHAPTER FIFTY-SIX

JEREMY

The smell of warm java filled my nose. Its sweet yet bitter flavor slid down my throat. Bright summer sun shined in from the French door windows. The sound of laughter filled my ears, mostly my own, really.

"No, I agree with Leah," Chris muttered. "This is bullshit."

"Well, I'm sorry," Hannah said. "It's not like we chose it."

Laila laughed and shook her head. "They'll get over it."

"Mhm," Leah grumbled. She poured some jack into her coffee and took a sip. "We've always followed the rules. We've always kept this world's secrets. Just doesn't seem fair. At least you get a reward."

"Yeah, we just get the shit end of the stick," Chris said.

"I think you mean short end of the stick," I said.

"No, Jeremy." His gaze narrowed. "I meant shit."

I laughed again.

Don't get me wrong, I loved my wife. She was my other half. She meant everything to me. But everyone in this room was young. They had time to find the loves of their lives too. Although, I suppose I did see Chris's point to some extent. He'd spent a third of his life in a cell. He wanted to enjoy every minute he had left with the love of his life.

But he'd find him.

Well, actually. *I'd* find him for him. But I'll get to that eventually.

"Would you Debbie downers either say something nice or go somewhere?" Laila looked between them. "It's not fair to make them feel guilty for something out of their control."

"Yeah, yeah," Chris muttered.

"Alright, I'll shut up," Leah said.

I turned to Kai with a smile. "It wasn't so bad, huh?"

He chuckled and kissed Hannah's hair. "Not so bad at all."

"So did you guys see the swirling lights?" Laila asked. "Or was it just the feeling?"

"No swirling lights," Kai said.

"But his eyes glowed," Hannah said. "Like when he's angry. Do yours do that too, Lai?"

"They do."

"So weird," she muttered.

I said, "I don't know, I think it's pretty."

"Aww." Laila smiled.

"No, they are cool. It just kind of threw me off," Hannah said. "I don't know, it was... It was amazing though."

"Felt a bit like flying," Kai said.

"Really?" I asked. "The first time for us made me feel more grounded than I ever have. Like I found a purpose."

"Oh, I don't know, mate. I've felt that way for as long as I've been on this plane." Kai looked at Hannah and smiled. "As long as I've known ye."

She smiled and rested her head against his shoulder. "Me too, baby."

"Ugh. Changed my mind. Too sappy," Leah grumbled. "I'm going outside with the kids."

"Yeah, me too," Chris muttered.

"It wasn't like that for me either," Celena said as she trotted toward the fridge. "Just thought it was some bomb sex."

Wyatt grinned. "I am pretty impressive in that area."

"What about you?" I gestured toward him. "How'd it feel for you?"

"Like goin' for a run on a cool night. Not chasing anything, not on the hunt. Just the wind whirring past me and watching the trees blur together. Like, full of adrenaline. And happy, too. Really happy."

"I guess I can see that," Celena said.

That fascinated me.

The first time with our soulmates was slightly different for all of us, but one thing was common between us all. It was a feeling unlike anything else—one we desperately craved. And it almost seemed to be a sensation that brought us more joy than anything else.

For me, that was stability. For Laila, it was peace and comfort. For Celena and Wyatt, it was freedom. Considering the nomads they'd grown to be, that didn't shock me. And for Hannah and Kai, it was flying. Made sense, those two were always up in the clouds.

"Ya know what I'm wondering?" Hannah asked.

"What's that?" I said.

"We're all connected, right?" she said. "We've all known each other for centuries. Eons, really, I guess."

"Right," I said.

"But then why haven't you seen us in those lives?" Hannah asked. "Why don't you know anything about us?"

"Well, we've met Venark. And I'm pretty sure that was you, Kai." I looked between them and then over to Celena and Wyatt. "Don't know why we haven't seen you guys yet."

"We were the firsts," Laila said. "And the memories we've seen are associated with our origin. You guys must have come along later."

In my opinion? It had nothing to do with that. It had everything to do with what mattered most to us. Me seeing Véa, that's because she was the center of my world. Being there for her was my purpose then just as it is now. Laila seeing Lux, that was so she'd remember how capable he was of hurting her. Because once she remembered, she'd never let him do it again.

"Maybe," Hannah muttered. "I guess that'd make sense."

"So how many of us are there now?" I asked.

"Let's see." Laila counted on her fingers. "Me and you. Celena and Wyatt. Naomi and Connor. Now Hannah and Kai. That makes eight."

"Ten if you count Avery and Asher," I said. "I mean, I'm not sure, they didn't confirm it. But the way we felt about Connor and Naomi is how we felt about them, so it stands to reason."

Ten down, fourteen to go.

"Yeah, that's true. But why wouldn't they just tell us?"

"Connor and Naomi were reluctant, too," I said. "Maybe whoever told them what we are told them not to."

"Yeah, maybe," Laila muttered. "Hey, maybe we should take a trip there soon. Micah would love it."

"If I can get some time off work and you can take a break from your training sessions," I said. "Ya know, we literally had nothing going on two years ago. Now we're booked every day."

"Getting old sucks," Wyatt said.

"Speaking of which." I kissed Laila's cheek. "I've got to sign off on the shipments coming into the diner today. I'm gonna go say bye to the kids."

"Alright, have a good day. Love you," she said.

"Love you too."

CHAPTER FIFTY-SEVEN

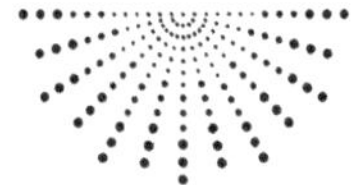

DECEMBER 24, 2022 - LAILA

The smell of apple cider filled my nose. Crackling wood sounded in the fireplace. Multicolored lights twinkled around the windowsills lined with faux snow. *Rudolph the Red nosed Reindeer* sang from the Google Home on the kitchen counter.

"Ya know what, I can't wait until this whole Christmas thing is over," I grumbled, sweeping pine needles into the dustpan. "I'm tired of these little shits pricking my toes. I'm sick of all this glitter. I'm sick of it, damn it."

"Wear your slippers." Jeremy laughed.

"I get it now. I get why my mom always bitched about the holidays. Between shopping, and cooking, and cleaning, I officially hate Christmas."

Although I said it, I didn't really mean it. I was bitching because that's what I did. I loved this though. Every bit of it. Preparing pies, baking cookies with the kids, stringing popcorn, making cut out snowflakes and dangling them all over the house.

It was a lot of work. But it was the best kind of work in the world.

My first Christmas with my babies. And all of my brothers and sisters. My mom would be there for dinner, Mary said she'd make an appearance, even Nikki was coming. All that was missing was Dad, but I supposed he couldn't make it. Being dead and all.

This was great either way.

"We could switch to Hanukkah." Jeremy fixed the star atop the tree. "Not like we believe any of this shit anyway."

"Hey, I never said I had any issues with Jesus. Seemed like a pretty cool guy. He's the one who said it's no longer an eye for an eye and a tooth for a tooth." I lifted the toys from the floor into the bin in the corner. "Never said anything shitty about the gays, or the whores, or the drunks. I like his philosophies; I don't mind celebrating his birth."

"Still seems a little sacrilegious, don't ya think?" He placed his hands at my hips. "Celebrating the birth of our arch nemesis's child."

"Yeah, well, he was up there on the cross saying 'my lord, why have you forsaken me?'" I placed my arms around his neck. "And frankly, I can relate. Our son definitely can."

He laughed and touched his lips to my forehead. I rested my head against his chest and looked around the living room. Bitching or not, it really was a dream come true. The snow was falling outside, the smell of warm apple pies filled the air, the kids were in the backyard making snow angels with their aunts and uncles.

Thick green, fake snow coated, pine garland wrapped the banister. Little Santas perched on every surface. The Elf on the Shelf sat on the mantel over the fireplace.

"It is nice though, huh?" I murmured with a look around.

"It's perfect." He squeezed me harder into his torso. "Our first Christmas all together with the kids, and Chris, and your mom, and your siblings, and my siblings. It's like a Hallmark movie."

Well, kind of. We were a little too metal for a Hallmark Christmas movie. But it was still sweet.

"And you're off for a whole week." I turned up with a grin. "What are you gonna do with all your time?"

"Maybe we can go visit somewhere." He thought for a moment. "We saw the Taj Mahal last month and Great Barrier Reef over Thanksgiving, maybe we could check out the Grand Canyon the day after tomorrow. I showed Micah pictures last week, and he said it looked cool."

"Or." I reached onto my tiptoes and touched my lips to his. "We could spend some time here. Be tourists in our town for a few days. They're still having that Christmas light show at the fairgrounds. The kids'll love it. We had one of our first dates there, remember?"

"I do remember." He grinned. "But I don't think we can fool around in the back seat anymore. The car seats kind of get in the way."

"Could always fool around when we get home." I smiled. "They'll probably pass out on the way back."

"Valid point." He grinned. He touched his lips to mine once more and pulled away. "I'm gonna get some more wood for the fire. Can you call everybody in?"

"Yeah, I'll get the s'mores stuff out too."

2022 had been our year. The first half had some pits, but the peaks soared much higher. We got our son back, we killed the bastard responsible for losing him, and we were in good standing with everyone in our community. We had no enemies, we had thousands of allies, and our family was together again.

It was a great time to be alive.

I'd spent most of the last six months working with others to perfect their abilities and strengthening my own. The power I held over the earth was unbelievably intense. A few months prior, I'd actually prevented a small tsunami in Japan. With Jeremy's help, in fact.

He'd gotten pretty good with my powers too. Not quite as good as me, but he was getting there. He learned to do everything that I was capable of a year before. He was still having a hard time with telekinesis, but he'd get the hang of it eventually.

My kids amazed me. Micah was like a magical prodigy. He could do everything that I could do and more. In October, he shape-shifted in his sleep. I nearly pissed myself when I went into his room to find two

Tinkerbells sleeping in his bed. I screamed for Jeremy, and he woke up and shifted back to his regular form.

Milly had a better handle on all of her Fae abilities than her dad, that's for sure. She could create and manipulate water as easily as she breathed. She kept my garden alive all winter long. And when she was angry, storms as powerful as tornadoes and hurricanes manifested outside. When she was happy, we got blue skies and sunny days.

In August we'd learned that both kids shared Jeremy's ability to manipulate energy. Micah had a habit of flipping the breakers when he had a bad dream. Milly liked to shock me when I picked her up against her will.

Our stockpile was growing. We were well prepared for the end of the world if it came. The guys had finished building the structure we referred to as a toboggan. Really, it was just a weatherized barn. But if need be, it'd house about fifty people. Still not much in terms of an apocalypse but one day, we'd be glad we had it.

It didn't feel like the world was ending any time soon. The world seemed peaceful. We were happy, the family was happy, we didn't have any major life-threatening events going on or people tied up in our basement.

But it never feels like something bad will happen until it does.

CHAPTER FIFTY-EIGHT

JEREMY

Really, I felt like I was living in a movie. My kids were both in bed. Quiet Christmas carols hummed in the background. Only the glow of the tree illuminated the living room. A mound of presents nearly as tall as my son was perched beneath it.

Which, granted, they didn't need. But it was our first Christmas together. Laila and I had the finances to spoil our kids a little, so that's what we did.

"Do you think Micah's going to like the train set?" I situated the box beneath the tree. "He wanted the one that sings but they were sold out."

"I'm sure he'll love it either way, baby." Laila plopped to the couch. "You know how he is about toys. He'll like it if you like it."

"Maybe I should unwrap it and set it up," I murmured. "That'd be cool, right? It'd add to the whole holly, jolly Christmas ambiance we've got going on here."

"It's fine the way it is." She laughed. "Just sit down with me and relax."

I turned to meet her gaze. "I just want his first Christmas to be perfect."

"It will be." She stood and took my hands. "It already is. Just look around. There's a million gifts under the tree, a blizzard outside, and there's enough food to feed an army back at the main house."

I glanced out the window and smiled. Every naked tree in the yard was coated in a soft blanket of white. The moon tinted the world a near blue color.

"Are you responsible for that?"

"I am not." She shook her head and gazed out the window. "Just good old Mother Nature."

I pushed hair behind her ear. "Isn't that technically you though?"

She laughed. "I don't know. Maybe. I guess in a way. But I think the par animarum just set the cycles of earth in place, ya know? It's been on autopilot for a few thousand years. I'm just blessed enough to put it into manual when I feel like it."

I chuckled and rested my head against hers. "Fuck, we're weird."

"In the wise words of Marilyn Monroe, it's better to be absolutely ridiculous than absolutely boring."

"The wise words of Marilyn Monroe." I laughed. "I wonder how it'd make her feel to know that the supreme earth goddess quotes her."

"Probably like the boss bitch she was." Laila took my hand in hers and hauled us to the couch. "Ya know, we've had some shitty times in the past few years. But at least we got answers this year. We figured a lot of shit out."

Not everything though. There were still so many variables left open. We knew about everything we needed to pertaining to Peterson and the survivors, but there was a lot we'd yet to learn about everything else. And I don't even mean the apocalypse.

Our first lives, that was one of many. I hadn't had a detailed dream in a while. I really missed them, actually. In a way, I supposed I missed Véa. I knew she was right there beside me. But I did miss seeing her in that life. I missed feeling what it was like to be Nix. He seemed like a good man. I'd have liked to get to know him a little better.

Aside from even that though, there were plenty of things I still wondered. That day at the second compound. That was one of them.

I bit my lip. "Actually, I was thinking about something the other day."

"What's that?" She cocked her head to the side.

"We still don't know who it was that saved us that day on the cliff-side." I squinted slightly, recalling the memory. "You know, when you were pregnant with Mills?"

"Huh," she muttered. "Almost forgot about that."

"Yeah. Yeah, I know someone saved you." The image of those people in hoodies and Chuck Taylors flashed behind my eyes. "Two someones. But I don't know who. And I still don't know how I got out of the tides that day."

"You said that you had a dream that day, right?" she asked. "You said it was you. That you were talking to yourself."

"Well, yeah, in the dream. But I woke up. It was like my subconscious telling me what I already knew. I had to keep you and Milly safe. Not that you needed me. You never really *need* me."

"Well, that's not true." She frowned. "I always need you. I don't know where I'd be without you."

I smiled and tucked my arm around her shoulders. Our fingers twined together. I lifted her knuckles to my lips. "You say that, but you'd be just fine without me."

"No." She shook her head and turned up to me. Her smiling lips fell as she looked from my left eye to my right. "No, I'd be lost without you."

She could say that to stroke my ego all she wanted. But Laila Callidy could do anything with or without me by her side. I'd like to be there. If I weren't though, she could still get the job done.

I smiled. I lowered my lips to hers. She kissed me back for a moment. She reached for the button on my jeans. I laughed and pulled back. "Chris could come down at any minute."

"He drank a lot of yeshlbawa tonight. He'll be out for a while." She grinned as she tugged the zipper down. Her hand snuck into my boxers. "We're too young to only have bedroom sex."

I laughed and slipped my hand into waistband of her pajamas. "We're actually old as shit, but I'm in no position to argue."

She laughed. "Just kiss me."

The past five months were the life I'd always dreamed of living. They may have been the best times of my life. I was clean, I had my wife, I had my kids, I had all of my siblings, I had a good job with a steady income.

I had it all.

I can't say that I took it for granted. I cherished every moment. But every great moment has to end.

Still, we had some time before that inevitable doom dawned on us.

I'd gotten further glimpses into our first life in the past few months. Just that though—glimpses. Neither Laila nor I had any detailed memories since that devastating one where I held our stillborn son.

But what I had seen was stunning. I think I'd gotten a flash into our first wedding. I'm not sure though, it wasn't like any wedding I'd seen. There wasn't an altar nor rings we slid over each other's fingers. But I did fasten an anklet around her calf, and I saw her do the same for me. All that I saw was that moment though. Clicking the bracket over her foot, then a gaze over her perfect face before our lips molded into each other's.

It reminded me of the day that I proposed. When I got down on one knee, and she lowered herself to my eye level. I guess some things from that life stuck. Like the way we held hands and kissed each other's knuckles.

Véa and Nix weren't us anymore. But they still were in a lot of ways. That's how it goes with everyone though. It's just how life works. Who we are now isn't who we were a year ago, or a decade ago. We change. We evolve. Everyone does.

Little did we realize; our evolution was still commencing. In fact, it'd never really stop.

CHAPTER FIFTY-NINE

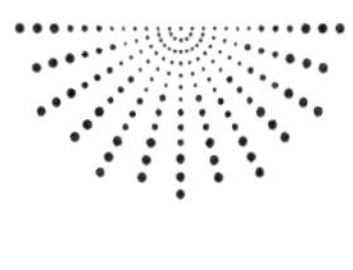

LAILA

"**M**ommy!" Micah jumped on the bed. "Daddy! You was wight! Santa *did* come!"

Milly climbed on my chest and held my eyelid open with her thumb and forefinger. "Wake up, Mama."

"I'm up." I groggily pushed her hand away. "How'd she get out of her crib, Micah?"

He grinned. "It don't matter. C'mon. We have to open the pwesents."

I sat forward with a yawn. Jeremy lifted the blanket over his head. "C'mon, Daddy. Let's go open presents."

"Five more minutes," he grumbled.

"Daddy!" Milly reached over and smacked him in the face.

I struggled not to laugh as I said, "No hitting."

We were working on that. I wasn't even sure where she learned to hit. Then again, I playfully smacked Jeremy's chest on a regular basis. Maybe it was my fault.

He tugged the blanket down with furrowed brows. "Did you just hit me, little girl?" She giggled and leaned into my chest. He craned over and tickled her side. Her bubbly, baby laugh billowed through the high ceiling. He scooped her up and tossed her to the bed.

"How about you go wake up Uncle Chris?" I told Micah. "I'll go pee and change her diaper. *Then* we'll open presents."

"Good idea." He disappeared.

"'Have kids' they said," Jeremy muttered as he climbed from the bed. "'It'll be fun' they said."

"Oh hush. Once you have your coffee, it *will* be fun."

"Wow, Santa got evewything on my list!" Micah yelled. I picked up wrapping paper scraps and shoved them into a plastic bag. "Even the twain!"

Jeremy smiled. "Even the train."

"Did Santa bwing you anything, Mommy?" Micah asked.

"I don't know, did Santa bring me anything, Jeremy?" I grinned at him.

He looked up from the Lego box he was struggling to rip open. He smiled. "I don't know, Laila, did Santa bring *me* anything?"

I put a hand at my hip. "No, but I did."

"Santa didn't bring you anything either, but I did too." Grinning, he stood, and a bag appeared in his hand. "Merry Christmas, baby."

"Aww, aren't you sweet." I lowered myself to the couch and gestured toward the tree. "Yours is in the back."

"Right under my nose, huh?" He reached into the branches and threw Chris a small box. "It isn't much, but I think you'll like it."

"Oh, cool. Thanks." Chris smiled as he ripped the wrapping paper off.

I started digging in the bag, pulling out the green paper. I lifted a plush throw blanket to my lap. Tears formed in my eyes as I held it out in front of me. It was one of those throws with a photo collage printed on it. In the center was a picture of me with Milly and Micah on my lap from Thanksgiving, smiling wide with whipped cream on our noses. Dozens of others framed the edges, some from the trips we'd taken around the world, others with my siblings, a few with my mom.

"Baby," I murmured with teary eyes.

He smiled and gestured to the bag. "There's some other stuff in there."

I reached inside and retrieved a small box. "Jewelry?"

"We go through this every time." He rolled his eyes and pulled the paper off of the box in his hands. "I had some help picking it out, chill."

I lifted it open and smiled. It was two interlocking circles on a silver chain with two stones on each one. Two amethyst on one—mine and Jeremy's birthstones—and an emerald and moonstone on the other—Milly and Micah's.

"This is beautiful, baby. Thank you." I reached inside for the last one. My lips lifted even higher. A custom plaque of the dates most significant to us. The day we met, the day we completed our bond, the day he proposed, our wedding day, and the day we moved into our home. "Aww, this is adorable. I saw this online; I've been wanting it for months."

He grinned. "I'm a great gift giver, what can I say?"

"Open yours." I bounced with excitement, putting everything back in the bag.

He tossed the paper to the ground and smiled. It was a wallet imprinted with a picture of him, Micah, and Milly. "I've been needing a new one of these."

"Couple other things down there," I said. "Way in the back, you might have to dig a little."

As he lowered himself to the ground, Chris gasped. "Dude. Dude, this is awesome."

"What'd he get you?" I asked.

He turned the Fitbit box to face me. "One of those cool fitness watches."

"Yeah, it's waterproof too," Jeremy said, pulling the large box from beneath the tree. As he ripped the paper, he said, "Why's it so big?"

"Two gifts in there." I smiled.

"What is it, Daddy?" Micah asked.

Jeremy grinned as he lifted the first box out. "A new record player, and..." He trailed off, gazing at the other box. He tore off the tape and lifted the bubble wrapped telescope to his hand. Custom made with a wooden base and neck. "'I love you as much as the sky is wide,'" it read.

I'd seen it online, and it grabbed my attention. Our love story started out there in space. Maybe if he looked through that thing enough, he'd find out where.

He looked up at me and smiled. "This is awesome, baby. Thank you."

"But what is it, Dad?" Micah asked.

"It's a telescope." Jeremy smiled. "So that I can see the stars and moon and stuff better."

"Oh," Micah murmured. "Like Aunt Leah's glasses fow the sky?"

I laughed. "Exactly like glasses for the sky."

CHAPTER SIXTY

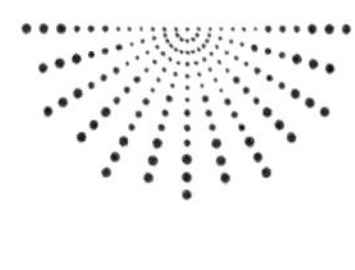

JEREMY

"Hewe, look, Luka," Micah murmured. He pulled the race car back on the hardwood floor and let it go, giggling as it rushed through the kitchen and slammed into the counter. Milly toddled toward it and brought it back to her brother like a golden retriever to a tennis ball. Luka reached for it, but Micah pulled it away. Then Luka busted out in tears.

"Alright, give it back," Laila said.

Micah said, "But we was shawing."

"Yeah, but he doesn't want to share any more. It's his turn; give it back."

"But—"

"No buts. Listen to your mother," I said. He huffed and handed it back to his crying cousin.

Fuck, I loved saying that. It made me feel mature—like a parent. It was one of those timeless phrases that dads spoke in every family show in the history of modern television. It made me feel normal. Human.

"Damn, we're old." Adam plopped to the breakfast nook next to me. "Telling our kids to listen to their mothers and shit."

I laughed and took a sip from my coffee. "We're not even thirty yet. We're not old."

"Old enough," he muttered.

"And just getting older." I smiled as I looked over the crowded kitchen.

We were getting old. Not really *old*, but finally grown. We weren't the kids we'd been a few Christmases before. But I wouldn't change it for the world.

Aside from the powers and pending apocalypse, we were living the American dream. One big, happy family sitting around a loud, busy kitchen on Christmas eating until our belt buckles burst and reminiscing about the good old days. One day, this would be a good old day too.

Kind of, anyway.

"Where's Chris at?" Hannah said from the island with a look around. "I haven't seen him yet."

"He said he was going to pick someone up," I said.

"Like a girlfriend?" She raised a brow. "I didn't know he was seeing anyone."

"He sees a lot of someones," Laila muttered, sipping her wine.

"I saw him talking to a lass at the wedding," Kai said. "Maybe that's who he's bringing."

"Maybe."

I doubted it. Not once had I seen my brother check out a girl's ass since he came back. Well, okay, once when we were at a swim park over the summer. He made a comment to Laila under his breath about how her ass was way too small for those bottoms. I hadn't actually seen said ass, so I couldn't be a judge, but either way. I had a feeling that whoever he was bringing wasn't gonna be a lass.

"Oh, great," Leah grumbled. "So it's back to me being the only single person in the family again."

"Maybe if you'd leave the house once in a while," Brody said at the wet bar. He looked over his shoulder at Gwen by the steps. "Do you want a drink, babe?"

"Wine, please," she said.

"I do leave the house. We just live in bumfuck Egypt and there's no fellow gays around here." Leah plopped to the island with a plate of pumpkin pie.

"Let's go up to the city after the holidays then," Laila said. "I'll be your wingman."

"Hey, I'll come too," Jenna said. "I love when women hit on me. They're so much pickier than men, it's a lot more flattering."

"Well, gee. Thanks." Adam took a bite from his pie.

"Might take you up on that." Leah sipped her drink. "Hey, is Heylel coming? I'd kill for some of that magic liquor."

"Nah," Laila said.

"He said celebrating Christmas is against his religion," I said. "Can't say I blame him. But it's more cultural than religious for us."

"Still stand by what I said." Laila wagged a finger. "Jesus was a cool guy. No shame in celebrating his birth."

"It would make more sense for us to celebrate the solstice though, wouldn't it?" Leah asked.

"No one's stopping you."

Truthfully, it was all a little arbitrary. I liked the holidays because I liked spending time with my family. I liked the music in the background, and the food, the marshmallows around the fire. I supposed it was more about the tradition than the actual holiday.

A gust of wind blew in from the front door. Tink erupted in barks. I heard Chris laugh accompanied by some hushed talking.

"Is there any ham left over there?" I gestured toward the island.

"Yeah, and another one in the oven. Go crazy," Leah said.

"Alright, cool." I stood and started to the counter. As I grabbed the tongs and ripped a piece of ham from the bone, Chris spoke in the doorway.

"Hey, guys." I looked up and smiled. Called it. He stood beside a well-dressed guy with a scar across his neck like Laila's. He had long blond hair and pale blue eyes beneath a pair of thick black glasses. "This is Noah."

"Nice to meet you, Noah," Leah said. "Do you eat? Please eat. I don't want to be stuck with all this food tomorrow."

He laughed. "I'm a wolf, watch out or I'll eat it all."

"Hey, I wemembew you." Micah smiled and stood from the floor.

"Oh, yeah?" Noah raised a brow.

He gave a fast nod. "You sat beside us on the aiwplane."

Noah squinted at him. "You were a newborn. How do you remember that?"

"I don't know, you was nice."

I knew Micah remembered bits and pieces of our past life, but I didn't realize he remembered infancy. How could he? Well, come to think of it, maybe he didn't. Maybe Chris thought about Noah from time to time in captivity, and he remembered him through his uncle's memories.

"I vaguely remember you too." Laila smiled. "You were the tenth or so door I opened at the second compound."

"I was. I'm surprised you remember that. I looked a lot different then."

"Yeah, well." Laila laughed. "We all did. I'm glad you're here though. Make yourself a plate."

"Thanks." He smiled.

"So how'd you two get in contact?" Laila asked.

Chris laughed, lowering himself to the island. "I'm a creep."

"No, you aren't." Noah laughed. "I told you to find me if we ever got out and you did."

"I went to the hospital you took everyone to." Chris smiled. "There were only three Noahs so it wasn't so hard. Little bit of cyber stalking, and the rest is history."

"Wait." Brody's head tilted as he looked between them. "Are you like... like a thing?"

The room got kind of quiet. Not eerily quiet, but awkwardly quiet.

Chris cleared his throat and smiled. "Yeah. Yeah, we're a thing."

"Oh," Brody muttered. "Oh, cool."

Not some grand coming out story. But when your family is all relatively forward thinking, there typically isn't any heartfelt interaction over it. When Leah came out, Annie said, 'Alright, you still have to wash the dishes.'

I don't know. Maybe he wanted a bigger moment. Maybe someone should've said more than cool. But around here, it just really didn't matter.

"Wait, you're gay?" Leah asked. "And you didn't tell me?"

"Who wants whiskey?" Laila hopped from her perch at the island. "Noah, do you like whiskey?"

He smiled awkwardly. "I love whiskey."

"Alright, two whiskeys then."

"Make it three," Chris said.

CHAPTER SIXTY-ONE

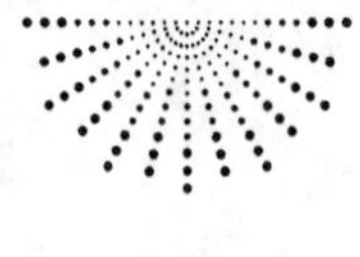

LAILA

I looked out over the snowy field and tightened my sweater around my waist. Leah bitched as I looked up at the dark blue sky twinkling with a million stars. The cold winter air wafted into my lungs, and I took a sip from my whiskey.

"You knew?" Leah asked. "Why did he tell you and not me?"

"He didn't tell me. I walked in on him with someone," I said. "But c'mon, Leah. It's not a big deal."

"That he's gay? No, of course it's not a big deal. But it's a big deal that he kept it from me," Leah said. "Do you know how many times I cried to him about how I wished that I liked guys? Do you know how many times he told me it was nothing to be ashamed of, and that I had to accept myself for who I am?"

"It's hard to take your own advice. We both know that." I swirled my glass. "We all have to figure out who we are in our own time. Maybe he didn't realize in high school, maybe he realized it when he was in solitary confinement for ten years. And he's been adjusting to normal life out here. He probably thought that you all have an image of him in your heads and didn't want to disturb it until he knew for sure. And he's probably been experimenting, trying to figure out who he is and what he really wants. I doubt he wanted to announce it until he knew for sure."

She leaned against the snow-covered banister and grabbed my whiskey from my palm. She tilted her head back and chugged. "Wait, who did you walk in on him with?"

Not my place.

"Great question. Ask him." I frowned at my empty glass. "That was rude."

"Your face is rude," she muttered. "I just don't get it. I tell him everything. Keeping something this big from me is not what we do."

"Well, talk to him about it."

"No, he'll make me rationalize. And I don't want to rationalize, I want to be mad."

"Then be mad. Go stomp your feet and throw yourself on the floor." I looked inside at Milly as she pushed Luka to the ground. "Like my daughter is about to."

"Did she just push him?" Leah asked.

"Looks like it," I muttered, starting toward the patio door.

"Such a feisty little shit."

"Hey, everyone," Mary's voice said in the cased opening to the living room. I looked over her with a smile. A pretty red shirt hung over her neat slacks. She carried a large gift bag in each hand and wore a sweet smile across her lips.

"I didn't know you were coming. We didn't get you anything," I said from my seat on Jeremy's lap.

"That's okay, these are just for the kids," she said.

"Well, go get something to eat," Leah said. "I just put everything away though."

"That's alright, I already ate," Mary said. She walked to the tree and set the bags down. She sat beside Chris on the other couch.

"What, had to have Christmas dinner with your other family first?" Chris joked.

She laughed and shook her head a bit. "Something like that."

Something like that indeed.

"Mawy!" Micah released Mom's hand in the doorway and barreled toward her. She laughed and extended her arms out to his, wrapping them around his shoulders.

"Hello, sweetheart." She pushed hair from his face. "Are you enjoying your first Christmas?"

"I love it." He grinned. "I got so many pwesents."

She laughed. "I bet you did. Mommy and Daddy are probably spoiling you rotten, huh?"

"We just got what he put on the list," Jeremy said. "And ya know. Santa got him some stuff too."

"Nah, they're all a little spoiled," Jenna said.

The night drew on with laughs and smiles. We sipped eggnog and hot chocolate and apple cider. The guys played some Christmas carols, the kids ran rampant through the house, we sat around talking about our year and making memories that'd last a lifetime.

I often wish I could go back to that night. Relive those moments when we were all together. When we were all so happy. When it was a beautiful time to be alive.

When Mom was around every day. When Mary and I had a relationship. When I was at home with my kids just enjoying being a mom. When our family made sense. When *the world* made sense. When we were still ignorant to reality.

A year prior, I was dying inside. My little boy was being held captive by a madman. I had my baby girl, but I needed my son too. I needed him like I needed air in my lungs and blood beneath my skin.

And for the first time in years, I could breathe again. I wasn't a depressed sack of bones with nothing but fire running through my veins. The hot embers inside of me finally cooled.

2022 taught us so many things. It showed us who we once were. It was the reward we'd waited eons to achieve. We'd stumbled many times along the way, but for once, for *fucking once,* it felt like we'd won.

And we had.

But no matter how beautiful things look, there are always ugly cranks shifting behind the curtain.

CHAPTER SIXTY-TWO

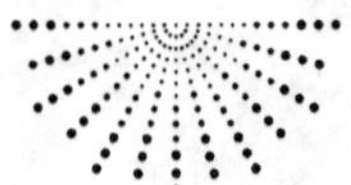

FEBRUARY 12, 2023 - JEREMY

The smell of pancakes wafted up my nose. Sweet syrup dance on my tongue. Morning light brightened by the blanket of snow outside shined in through the wall of windows ahead. Quiet wind whistled through the branches. I carefully set the glass plate on the TV tray on the countertop.

"We've got to be really quiet," I whispered with a finger over my lips. I knew that was a damn near impossible request from my chatty son, but I at least had to try.

"Or what?" Micah murmured with wide eyes.

I passed him the fork and spoon. "Or Mommy'll wake up."

"But isn't this fow Mommy?" he asked. "Awen't we waking hew up anyway?"

"Yeah, but if we wake her up, it won't be breakfast in bed."

"You know, Mommy says we awen't allowed food in ouw beds."

I laughed, turned back to the stove, and flipped a pancake. "No, *you* aren't allowed food in your bed because you leave half eaten candy everywhere and we get ants."

He neatly placed the silverware beside the plate. "Well, the ants was hungry."

"Well, feed them outside."

He plopped to the couch beside Tink. "They like it inside."

"They don't pay rent."

"But—"

"Can you go let Tink in for me?" I gestured toward the back door.

"Yeah." He started to his feet and darted to the patio.

My kid was the light of my life. But sometimes, I just had to cut off the silly rhetoric. He talked so much that he made my throat hoarse. I didn't even think half as many words as that child spoke.

I breathed out a sigh, enjoying the quiet for a moment. Chris laughed as he came down the steps. "Kid loves to talk."

"Yeah, you aren't kidding." I smiled. "At least he's entertaining."

"That he is." He reached for a piece of bacon on the plate. I smacked his hand with the spatula. "Ow."

"There's more by the stove. That's for Lai," I said.

"Oh. What is it? Your anniversary or something?"

"Her birthday," I said.

Kind of a big one, actually. It was the first life we'd lived in a few thousand years where we both made it past twenty-four. So I made plans. When I was a teen, I'd visited Angels Falls in Venezuela once. And I'd sworn I was gonna take the girl I planned to marry there. I'd yet to do that. Why not take her to the most romantic place I'd ever been on perhaps the most important birthday of her life?

"Any big plans?" he asked.

"Yeah, Hannah and Celena are gonna watch the kids. I thought about taking them too, but we took them to Niagara Falls a few months back, and Micah said the water was too loud. Milly didn't care for it either," I said. "Probably a good idea to have a date night without the kids once in a while, ya know?"

"Yeah, if you ever want to make any more." He laughed.

"You're telling me," I muttered.

"Is that in the cards for you?" He leaned against the counter and chomped on a piece of bacon. "More kids, I mean."

"I don't know, probably. Haven't really thought about it."

"Might want to start thinking about it soon." He gestured toward

Micah on the patio with Tink. "He's going on four. You don't want them to be too far apart."

I shrugged and poured Laila's coffee.

That was a big fat lie. I had definitely thought about it. In that exact context, in fact. I assumed we would have more, but it wasn't something Laila and I had talked about. But I did want more kids. I grew up in a big family. I was close with all of my siblings, and I wanted them to have that too.

Like Chris said, I didn't want them to be far apart in age. Plus, I was already a few years older than Laila. I'd aged six years since we got together, and she hadn't. She wouldn't. She was an Angel. She had at least a hundred years before she'd age to thirty. Maybe even longer.

Neither Micah nor Milly were planned. It felt like time to do it the right way.

CHAPTER SIXTY-THREE

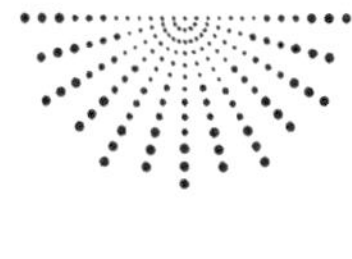

LAILA

"**H**appy birthday!" Micah yelled, jumping on my stomach.

I grumbled and rubbed my eyes. "Can Mommy sleep for five more minutes for her birthday?"

"If you really want," Jeremy said. "But your breakfast will get cold."

I opened my eyes and looked up at him standing beside the bed. He held a serving tray with a grin so wide it reached his eyes. Micah turned to sit beside me as Milly struggled to climb the ottoman at the end of the bed.

Well, there was no going back to bed when they were looking at me that adorably. And not when the coffee and pancakes smelled so good.

I smiled and sat up. "You made me breakfast in bed?"

"I helped!" Micah said.

"Me too," Milly chimed in.

Jeremy smiled, sitting down beside my legs. He put the tray on my lap. "Eat up, you're going to need your energy."

"Oh yeah?" I grinned, lifted the coffee, and took a sip. "We working out today?"

"No." He took a piece of bacon from my plate and chewed on it. "But trust me, you're going to want a full stomach."

"Where ya taking me?" I asked. "Disney World?"

"It's a surprise."

"Okay, well should I wear pants or shorts?"

"Jeans and a hoodie should do," he said.

Well, that one threw me off. He usually took me to tropical places. Like the Bahamas and Fiji. It was a well-known fact that I liked being warm. So why the hell was he taking me somewhere that I'd need a hoodie?

"Ew." My nose curled. "You're taking me somewhere cold for my birthday?"

He nibbled away on the bacon. "I didn't say it was cold. I said you'd be comfortable in jeans and a hoodie."

"Daddy doesn't know me one bit, Mills," I murmured as I handed her a blueberry.

"She ate plenty, don't let her con you into thinking she's hungry. She's just chunky." Jeremy poked her belly, and she giggled.

"It's okay, I'll share." I grabbed the fork and cut the corner of the egg. "But you know, I'd be very happy if I knew where we were going."

"Eat your damn eggs." He smiled.

"I said no peeking," Jeremy said with his hands over my eyes.

"You always say that like your hands aren't literally holding my eyelids shut," I muttered.

He laughed and grazed my hips. "Alright, but keep them closed."

"They're shut," I said.

"You ready?"

"Yes, I'm ready. But if you keep making me wait—"

"Hold on tight."

The world spun around me. As we landed, I stumbled forward a bit. A loud roar vibrated to my ears. Jeremy gripped my hips tighter. Elevation change didn't usually bother me, but I was suddenly a tad dizzy.

My eyes peeled open, and my stomach danced with butterflies. I wasn't sure what I was looking at, but it brought me a warm fuzzy feeling.

Water fell from a cliff above us like a curtain. Warm, wet air drifted into my nostrils. The loud roar of running water bounced off the mountainside, and I smiled.

I turned to meet his gaze. "Where are we?"

"Venezuela." He smiled, pushing hair behind my ear. "The highest waterfall in the world."

I rolled onto my tiptoes and touched my lips to his. "Angel Falls, right?"

"Figured it'd be poetic." He smiled, pulling away. "And peaceful. Things are pretty hectic back home."

"A fun hectic," I said.

"But hectic," he said. "I love our kids, but we haven't been away together since we... Well, ya know. And we should spend some one-on-one time together once in a while. Doing something besides executions and hunting rogue Demons."

My smile edged higher, arms twisting around his neck. "Yeah, but I like fighting rogues with you."

And I did. That was the closest to a date we'd gotten since we had both kids, but it was fun. It brought me back to the good old days when hunting rogues was our biggest problem. Granted, we hadn't had too many of those lately, but it was still a good time.

"Well, so do I. But this is a big day." He grinned, hands coasting over my waist. "You're twenty-five. We're both past twenty-four."

I laughed. "It's about damn time."

"It really is." He smiled, turned away, and gestured to the ground. A blanket laid out on the damp rock of the small cavern. On top of it were a few pillows and a wicker basket. "Come on. Sit down."

I couldn't pull my smile down as I brought myself to my knees on the blanket. Jeremy sat beside me and opened the basket, pulling out the essentials. A bottle of wine, a few pre-rolled joints, a couple plates, and an array of junk food.

"Guess I was wrong. You know me better than I thought," I said.

He smiled and raised the joint to his lips. A flame came to the tip of his finger, using it to spark the joint. He took in a long drag and passed it to me. I breathed in a hit and laid my head against his shoulder.

And don't get me wrong, it was nice. Pretty, and peaceful. But I wasn't used to this sort of thing. I liked my hectic life. Mom life kept me busy. It'd only been a few minutes, and I already missed the noise of my children.

"It's so quiet," I murmured. "Almost forgot what that sounded like."

He chuckled and kissed my forehead. "Refreshing, isn't it?"

I smiled and gave a nod.

I couldn't make out much beyond the wall of running water, but it was oddly beautiful to watch those waves cascade before me. However, I needed something to fill up the silence. I turned up and pressed my lips to his. He held the side of my neck, pulling it closer to his.

After a moment, our lips opened against one another's. I took the joint from his hand and set it on the rock beside us. My knees opened over his lap, his hands travelling to my hips. I reached for the button of his jeans.

He didn't waste a second teleporting my pants to the ground beside us. It was a little too chilly, splashes from the waterfall smacking against my ass. But I couldn't remember the last time I got laid, and I was ready to go, damn it. I laughed against his lips. He teleported his body over mine, lying me against the damp blanket.

I yanked his pants and boxers down his legs, sneaking my hand to his groin. His fingertips slipped between my legs. As they pulsed inside of me, I breathed out a long, quiet sigh.

Holy fuck, I forgot how good it felt to be touched. Married Mom life was great, but so was sex. With his fingers inside me, that was the first time in so long that I didn't think about all the things I needed to get done.

Thoughts drifted away, and sensation overtook me. Pleasure, comfort, love. My stomach flipped with anticipation, and chills rose over my skin.

His lips turned to my neck, ear close to my face as I moaned in ecstasy.

A moment or so later, he moved his dick to my opening. But then thought returned.

I pulled back slightly, forehead touching his. "Do you have a condom?"

He leaned on his palms above me. "Maybe in my wallet. But do we really need one?"

I laughed. "Well, we don't need another baby."

He smiled and touched my cheek. "Why not?"

Well, that escalated quickly.

I cocked my head to the side. "What?"

A quiet laugh left his lips. "I don't know, what's wrong with having another baby?"

"You mean, aside from the fact that we have to go to another continent to get a little bit of peace and quiet?" I sat forward. "I don't know, babe. We haven't even had Micah for a year yet."

It wasn't that I wasn't open to the idea, he just kind of sprung it on me. I'd love more kids. But I also wanted to give Micah the attention he'd missed out on when he was gone. I wanted Milly out of diapers. I wanted a little while longer with the family we already had.

Jeremy smiled. "Yeah, but he loves being a big brother. He won't mind."

I huffed. "Maybe, but I will."

He looked between my eyes for a moment. "You don't want more kids?"

"No, I do." I laughed. "But I just... I don't know, we're still young. We have time."

A sad smile lifted his lips. "*You're* still young."

As if he were approaching a senior citizen discount.

I laughed. "You aren't even thirty yet, Jeremy."

"Yeah, but you have a lot more time left than I do." He looked between my eyes. "Your body is still in its early twenties, Lai. When I'm sixty, you're going to look like you're twenty-five. And when you're a hundred, I'll probably be dead."

My chest tightened, hands sweating a tad. I didn't want to think about that. In fact, I never really had. And for a good reason.

Rationally, I knew my life expectancy was far longer than his. It was the unavoidable reality I'd learned when I found out what I was. But I never thought about it because I didn't want to.

Losing him would kill me. He was my best friend. He was my baby. Just the thought of never seeing him again made my stomach hurt.

"Don't talk like that." I frowned. "We don't know that. I might figure out that tree of life thing and—"

"Might," he murmured. "But I... I want a big family. I've always wanted a big family. And I don't want my kids to be ten years apart. I want them to be close, like I was with my siblings, like you are with yours."

"Baby," I whispered.

He licked his lips, growing quiet for a few seconds. "Can we just... can we set a time frame when you think you will be ready to have more?"

That was a reasonable request. I may not have been ready in the moment, but I would be one day. I just needed a little more time with things as they were.

And for him to not bring up dying again.

I chewed my lip. "2024. We can start trying in 2024. That'll give me enough time to enjoy Micah and Milly at this age. He'll be getting ready to go to school, and I'll miss having a baby around." I gave a gentle nod. "Next year."

He smiled. "2024 then."

I willed a smile. "Now put that condom on and fuck me."

CHAPTER SIXTY-FOUR

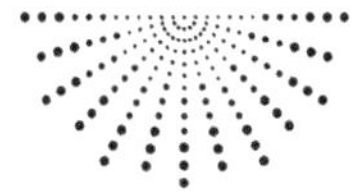

JULY 4, 2023 - JEREMY

I struggled the last camping chair into the back of the Forester, jamming it against the cooler. My hand wafted beneath my sweaty armpit as the humid summer air drifted into my nostrils. I clicked the back door shut and leaned against the car.

"But I don't get it," Micah said. "Who's birthday is it again?"

"'Merica's." Adam grinned.

"What's that?" he asked.

"The country we live in," I said.

Micah shook his head, eyes moving between mine. "I don't get it."

"Alright, let me give you a little history lesson here." I squatted down to meet his gaze. "So a few hundred years ago, the only people living in America were Native Americans. Then this guy, a real butt head actually, came here on a boat because he was trying to get to India."

"That's where the Taj Mahal is, right?"

I gave a smile. "Yep, that's the one. Well, this guy landed here and thought he made it to India. That's why some people call Native Americans Indians, because Christopher Columbus was an idiot and didn't realize he made it to an entirely different continent."

His face screwed up. "America was found by an idiot?"

"Technically, he didn't find shit." Adam leaned against the Jeep beside us. "There were already tons of people living here. Christopher Columbus came here and just pillaged Native American culture. But yeah, dude was an idiot, and a horrible human being."

"Also true," I said. "But that's kind of off topic. Basically, people from England just kinda started taking over. They were actually really bad people, and I'm not exactly proud of our heritage here. They…"

How could I tell my four-year-old the truth about our country's origins without whitewashing the story? Yeah, the whole religious freedom thing was a nice thing to tell kids, but that's not actually true.

The pilgrims had religious freedom. They came to America because there was a market of goods here that they wanted to tap into. And they did so by mass genocide on an entire continent of people.

But we did have a few Native Americans in the family. Maybe they could relay that part of the history in a better fashion to a kid. He was asking about Independence Day anyway.

"Well, basically, the people that came and stole this land from the Native Americans wanted to be their own nation. So they fought a big war with England. And they won, and when the king of England finally said they could be their own country, they put off fireworks and celebrated. It was called Independence Day because we got Independence from England. So now, we go out and watch fireworks and have big barbecues to celebrate it every year," I said. "Does that make sense?"

"I don't know, kind of."

"What are you talking about out here?" Laila said, trotting down the porch steps.

I smiled and straightened back up. "Just a brief history lesson."

She set Milly down and adjusted her shorts at her hips. "What are they telling you, kid?"

"Dad said Christohpew Columbus was an idiot," Micah said.

"Teaching him right early." Laila raised her hand to mine for a high five. "Did you tell him how to knock down the statues of him yet?"

I laughed. "The trick's to tie the chain really tight on both sides around the top and have people tug evenly back and forth on both sides at the same time. Then run before it falls."

Micah furrowed his brows at me. Adam laughed. Laila smiled.

Not like I knew any of that from personal experience or anything.

"Daddy." Milly tugged the bottom of my shirt. "Daddy, look." She jumped and spun in a circle.

She looked... Like my daughter.

I glanced at Laila. *What am I looking at?*

"Her dress." Laila laughed. "She's all kinds of excited about that dress."

"Oh." I laughed and looked over it. It was white, covered in blue and red flowers. "You look very pretty."

She grinned and spun again.

"We should get going. The traffic's going to be crazy getting into the city," Laila said.

"Alright. You get him, I'll get her?" I glanced between the kids.

"Works for me," she said.

2023 had been a fun year. There hadn't been any major life-threatening situations. We helped out a few allies with small cases but nothing major—just a few rogue Vampires and Demons we put a quick stop to.

We'd been attending Chambers meetings monthly but nothing big had happened. It was mostly formalities, discussing worldwide issues. Laila had gotten the ball rolling on helping with issues we couldn't prior to being involved with the Chambers. She'd started planting— and growing—vegetation in areas hit by wildfires and places damaged from deforestation. She made it her mission to regrow the rainforests. A big task, I suppose, but not so difficult for us. We still had to tread lightly because if humans realized desolate areas miraculously started to flourish, we'd risk exposure.

It was nice though. We were using our powers for good. We were genuinely making a difference in our world.

The kids were great. Micah had finally been able to stop the supplements and vitamins he was put on when we got him back. He looked healthy now, like he always should have. And he was smart as hell. Way smarter than I was at four. His grammar was near perfect, and he could finally annunciate the letter R—for the most part.

Milly was amazing. She wasn't as sociable as her brother, not as sweet, but a doll either way. She reminded me so much of Laila, but a little meaner, to be honest. Far more emotional too. But I guess two-year-olds tend to be more emotional than the rest of us.

She wasn't quite as advanced as Micah was at two, but she certainly wasn't behind for her age. In fact, she'd hit most of her milestones a few months early.

Laila and I were the best we'd ever been. We were happy and in love. A different kind of love than we'd once had, not chaotic and passionate anymore, but maybe deeper than it'd ever been. Married love. Grown, mature love.

She'd decided to go back to work a few days a week in March. Since then, the housework and the diner were split fifty-fifty. And I had to give her credit. Managing the diner was a lot easier than managing a busy household with two kids, three adults, and a dog.

But it was fun. Life was fun. Old, boring fun, but the kind of fun I'd fantasized about for years. We were giving our kids the life I wished I'd had growing up.

Life was good.

But that time everyone kept telling us that we had? Well, the sand in the hourglass was getting low.

CHAPTER SIXTY-FIVE

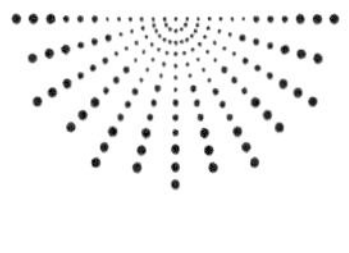

LAILA

Jeremy, the kids, and I sat on a yard blanket in a crowded field at The Point Park in Pittsburgh where the three rivers met, waiting for the fireworks to start. Jenna and Adam sat on a blanket beside ours while Luka toddled between us. We hadn't made a trip to the city in a while, but the festival they threw every July was too much fun to miss. We hadn't gone last year because we were too busy helping Kai and Hannah plan the wedding. And because we'd just killed Peterson and I was still a little too emotional to enjoy an outing like that.

But the weight on our shoulders had lifted in 2023. We weren't thinking about psychopaths and the apocalypse. We hadn't even experienced retrocognitive memories from our past lives in a while. I'd get a glimmer here or there, a passing thought at times. But the detailed retellings had stopped.

Truthfully, I was grateful for it. We'd learned enough. I got the picture now; I didn't need all the details. I didn't want them. Véa may have been me at one point but she wasn't anymore. I was Laila Callidy. Wife to Jeremy Skoulda, mother of Micah and Malina Skoulda. I was a diner owner, a mother, and a matriarch in the supernatural community. I didn't want to be a god. I didn't ask to be a savior. And during that time, I just wanted to enjoy my life. So I did.

For a while.

"You want a beer, Lai?" Adam asked, tilting one toward me.

"Ew, beer." I curled my lip. "I'll pass. But thanks."

"Suit yourself." He popped off the top and dropped it into the garbage bag.

"Are you allowed to drink here?" Jeremy asked.

He shrugged and took a gulp. "Probably not."

"I'm so glad we came early enough to get good seats," Jenna said. "Remember when we came with Mom and Dad, like, ten years ago and we had to watch from the car?"

"Yeah, that was when we got that bad summer storm, wasn't it?" I asked.

"Yeah, we were soaked."

"And Mom was pissed because she just got the Corolla, and we were covered in mud." I laughed.

No summer storm today though. A cloudless sky, though impossible to see through the lights of the city. The moon was pretty though, almost full in fact. Bright and white, like a disco ball above the incline on the other side of the water. Only warm humid air, the peace of the river ahead, and the zillion smells. Gyros, and hotdogs, and cotton candy, and deep-fried Oreos. Micah loved those.

"Good times." Jenna smiled, leaned back on her palms, and looked up at the sky.

I laid my head against Jeremy's shoulder. "These are better."

"They are, huh?" Jenna smiled too. Adam put his arm around her shoulders.

"It's crazy, isn't it?" Adam asked. "Just thinking back on the last few years. Never thought we'd make it here. We're all parents and shit now. Never thought I'd see the day, ya know?"

"I did." Jeremy touched the top of Milly's hair and smiled. She leaned her head against my chest, craning her gaze up to him. He tickled her belly, and she giggled.

"Mommy, what's that?" Micah asked, pointing to the trolley moving up to the peak of Mount Washington.

"That's the incline," I said. "You can ride in it and get to the top of the mountain."

His eyes widened. "Can we do that next?"

"I think they're getting ready to close for the night," Jeremy said. "Maybe one day next week."

That sounded like a good idea actually. I hadn't been to the incline in ages. When I was a kid, I'd loved it. It reminded me of Mister Roger's Neighborhood. Micah would equate it to Daniel Tiger's Neighborhood.

Still though, the overlook was amazing. He'd love it.

"Okay," he muttered. "It's pretty though."

"It is. The view up there is beautiful. You can see all the rivers and every building in the city. We have some pictures from up there somewhere, don't we?"

"Yeah, somewhere," Jeremy said.

"We could just fly up there," Micah said.

I laughed. "Not here, buddy. There's too many people."

He looked around at the shuffling crowd. "Why can't we show other people again?"

Jeremy said, "People aren't always nice about things they don't understand, kiddo."

"But we can make them understand." He smiled. "We're nice, they'll like us."

I roughed up his hair. "Maybe one day."

The first boom sounded. Milly jumped. I laughed. My arms tightened around her, and Micah rushed to Jeremy's lap. He groaned when Micah plopped to his groin. I laughed and looked up at the burst of blue and white.

A red one shaped like a flower followed. I smiled at the pretty colors. But Milly's hands flung to her ears. Her head shook, turning to meet my gaze. "I don't like it."

"You don't?" I asked.

"It's loud," she said with wide eyes. "I don't like it, Mama."

"It's okay, I've got you." I smiled and kissed her forehead. "It'll be over soon. Then we'll go home."

She pushed her head closer to my chest.

"If you want to take her back to the car, I can bring him when it's over," Jeremy said.

I slid my fingers over her curls. "No, she's tough. Huh, Mills?"

She nodded.

"It's not scary," Micah said, looking up at the colors booming in awe. "It's pretty, Milly."

"It's scawy to me," she muttered.

My little girl. That was one thing I'd always admire about Milly. Micah was always quick to proclaim his fearlessness. But Milly openly stated when she was intimidated. Yet, she didn't run away.

When she was young, she'd curl against my lap and count on me to protect her. But as she aged, she stood on her own two feet to anything that came her way. Even when she was petrified, she didn't hide it. She just fought whatever came at her. I guess she got that from Jeremy. Micah got his ability of denial from me.

CHAPTER SIXTY-SIX

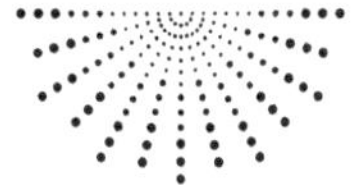

DECEMBER 31, 2023 - JEREMY

The second half of 2022 and all of 2023 flew past us like mile markers on a highway. I suppose it's true. Time flies when you're having fun. And we really were.

Life was perfect then. Every single one of us was happy. Some more than others, but still. We were at the best we'd ever been.

After Chris came home, Leah's depression I'd grown so accustomed to faded away. She was no Leslie Knope, but she was the most content I can ever remember seeing her.

Chris was in a great place too. The guy he'd brought to Christmas dinner last year was long gone and a few others had passed by.

No girls, although he still readily proclaimed that he wasn't gay. But he was single then, which was good considering what was about to go down. He was joyously living off of his trust fund, but he helped me with stuff at the diner from time to time.

Adam's situation hadn't changed either. He and Jenna were discussing marriage, although loosely. He told her that marriage "seemed like the next logical step." She probably would have agreed to it if he'd, ya know, asked.

But Laila said she was pissed he considered it *logical* rather than romantic. Still, they were pretty happy. Luka was doing good too, he'd just teleported for the first time in November. Jenna wasn't thrilled about that, but he needed to teleport to keep up with his cousins.

We didn't see much of Brody those days. But he was doing great. He and Gwen spent almost all of their time together. When he wasn't working, that is. He'd landed a great job at a local bank in the city. The kind where he wore ties and pressed slacks every day. Not really my taste, but he seemed to be in his glory.

Hannah and Kai were doing good too. They still acted like newly-weds, kissing at every available opportunity, and sneaking off at every family function as if we didn't know what they were doing. They were happy though. That's what mattered. I guess they always were. Happiness was their strong suit.

Celena and Wyatt were in a good place too. They were still living at the main house with Leah and Brody, but we teleported them around a lot. Sometimes to West Virginia so Celena could see her mom and Wyatt could see his brother, others to New York to see Celena's dad.

And as for my sector of the family?

We were perfect.

Laila and I had started trying to get pregnant again in the beginning of December. And let me just say, sex is not nearly as much fun when doing it on a schedule. But I counted my blessings. At least we were having frequent sex again.

She'd been writing a lot. Usually, she wrote when she was stressed. But not then. When I asked what the matter was, she said nothing at all.

That she was happier than she'd ever been, and she wanted to write about it. Because when things got bad again, as we both knew they inevitably would, she wanted to read the words she'd written when she was in a better state of mind.

She said they'd remind her that things get better. *'Even when it feels like your life has been ripped out from beneath you, things get better. Sometimes, you just need to remember that things always get better.'* There was some poetic irony there that I'd see later.

Micah was an absolute angel. He'd come so far in the past year and a half. I almost had a hard time believing there was ever a time when I didn't see him every day; he was my little shadow now.

He was preparing for kindergarten. We weren't sure how we were going to go about that yet. He really wanted to go to regular school, but Laila and I were hesitant to send him anywhere without one of us.

Although we held good standings with everyone in the supernatural community, that could very well just be to our faces. There was no way to know what they all thought when we turned our backs. Or what someone like Thomas La Fay would do if we put our guards down.

Milly was an antagonistic little turd. I loved her with every fiber of my being; she was—and always would be—Daddy's little girl. But damn, she was a bitch sometimes.

Her temper tantrums in those terrible twos were intense—especially as she was teething. And by intense, I mean blaring hailstorms, winds that tore off sections of the roof, and snowfalls that forced us to teleport outside because our door was barricaded. For being so predominantly in touch with the Fae, she was ferocious. As she got older, she reminded me more of Leah than her mother. Although, when she smiled up at me with those twinkling emerald eyes, she was as sweet as honey. All she had to do was give me that look, and I caved.

The kids were pretty spoiled. If they wanted it, they got it. We had the money, and we overcompensated to deal with the guilt of losing Micah. They both had iPads, toy boxes full of games and trinkets they rarely touched, and enough clothes to start our own secondhand shop. But I can't say that I feel guilty for that. I just wish we would have been able to spoil them the years that followed.

CHAPTER SIXTY-SEVEN

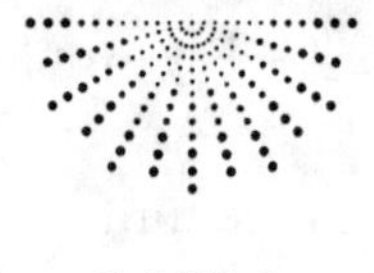

LAILA

"She already had her cold medicine, and she's out cold," I said to Brody. "It has melatonin in it so she should sleep through the night, or at least until we get back. But if she wakes up and starts bawling, just give me a call. I can come home whenever."

"I'm sure she'll be fine, love." Gwen smiled.

"Yeah. Yeah, I know. I just hate leaving them when they don't feel good, you know?"

In fairness, it was just teeth coming in. She was fine. But I knew she was hurting. She'd been running a low-grade temp on and off for a few days. I just wanted to make her feel better, but I couldn't make her teeth grow in faster.

"Well, we'll let you know if we need you. You kids have fun." Brody plopped to the couch and brought his feet to the coffee table.

"You guys are sure you don't mind staying home?" I asked. "I mean, I don't mind. Jeremy can take Micah."

As much as I did want to go, I was kind of hoping he'd say he didn't want to deal with my whiney baby. I loved the idea of getting to kiss my husband when the clock struck midnight, but I just didn't want to leave my baby girl.

"Nah, we're good," Brody said. "It's refreshing to stay in once in a while."

"I'm not one for concerts anyway." Gwen sat beside him and took a sip from her wine on the table. "Go on, have a good time."

"See ya next year." Brody grinned.

"Ha-ha." I rolled my eyes. Such a washed-up joke.

"You ready, babe?" Jeremy said from the stairs.

"Yup, I'm all set." I buttoned my jacket. "Where's the kiddo?"

"He's coming." Jeremy smiled, turning his gaze up the steps. "Ladies and gentlemen, I present to you the one, the only, Micah Skoulda."

I laughed as he appeared on the staircase. He wore a giant smile across his lips. A blue V-neck laid over his shoulders covered by a black jacket, a pair of dark washed blue jeans, and a set of black Chuck Taylor's. His long black hair hung to his shoulders in loose waves.

Definitely not my son's taste. But absolutely fucking adorable.

"Well, don't you look handsome." I smiled.

"I look like Daddy." He grinned.

I laughed. "Yeah, just like him."

"He's pretty excited for his debut show." Jeremy smiled.

"Yeah, I want to look like a musical."

"Musician, buddy." Jeremy laughed.

"Oh. Right. Musician."

Micah had been preparing to play a song with his dad on stage for the past two months. We figured the New Year's Eve show would be the best time to do it. It always brought in a big crowd. Jeremy said he needed to conquer the fear of public performance early so he didn't wind up like him, terrified to go on stage at twenty despite having great musical talent.

I guessed getting to see that was worth being away from my grumpy, teething baby for the night.

"Let's head on out then." I smiled. "The car's running."

The smell of bar food and beer filled my nose. It was hot and sweaty—typical concert vibes. The taste of wine rested on my tongue, smile against my lips. Bright lights shined on the small stage in the corner. Micah looked so cute up there with his dad. Awkward and a little scared, but so freaking cute.

"Alright, how's everybody doing tonight? We all ready for 2024?" Jeremy said at the microphone, looking over the crowded basement with a friendly smile. I clapped along with the cheering crowd, and he laughed. Micah swallowed hard, looking out at all the people. "Awesome, so are we. Well, for those of you who don't know us, I'm Jeremy, and this is my son Micah. My wife and I own the place, and luckily, I'm a half decent musician so when we have some empty slots, I fill them. But tonight is a really big night because my son here" —he roughed up Micah's hair— "is a budding musician too. And I finally convinced him to come up here and sing a song with me. He's never been on stage before, but I'm sure you all are gonna be pretty impressed."

"Wooo!" Leah yelled beside me, cupping her hands around either side of her mouth.

Micah smiled when the crowd clapped. Admittedly, I think they only roared so loud because of how cute he was, but it was still sweet.

"He wanted to sing the Paw Patrol theme song, but I figured that might be a little too forward-thinking for some of our audience here." The crowd laughed, and Jeremy smiled. "So we decided to go with a classic. This is *All You Need is Love* by The Beatles."

I clicked record on my phone, grinning as Jeremy started strumming his guitar. He smiled at Micah, nodding toward the microphone.

"He's so freaking cute up there," Leah said. "I love that he's not dressed like a prep school kid."

"He likes his khakis, and you like your hair purple. We all have our preferences," I said.

"I'm not hating." Leah laughed. "Whatever floats his boat."

"And I think he looks cute in his khakis," I said.

"He does." She smiled and took a sip from her brandy.

As his little voice started with Jeremy's at the mic, tears welled in my eyes.

My little boy wasn't so little anymore; his head almost reached Jeremy's chest. He was four and a half going on forty. He always had something to say, and his opinions were usually pretty valid.

Earlier that year, he'd advocated that we needed a larger vegetarian menu at the diner. We eventually gave in. Although he was only one of four customers to ever order it, we officially served tofu.

He'd mastered counting to one hundred, he could say his ABCs in four different languages, and he could easily play a guitar. The kid had a knack for the ukulele too. He hadn't made it to the sax yet, but Jeremy was teaching him chords to play once he had the lung capacity. Sometimes I pondered if Jeremy had cloned himself, because the kid barely had an ounce of me in him.

Milly, on the other hand, could be my carbon copy. Although, Mom said she wasn't nearly as sweet as I was. Not to toot my own horn, but I believed it. Milly was a force to be reckoned with.

That was actually my favorite part of her. She was unruly and exciting. Of course, she drove me crazy at times because she practically never sat still. Except for when she was in the grass or climbing a tree. And yes, I let my two-year-old climb trees. Honestly, I didn't have much say in the matter.

If she wasn't climbing them, she was teleporting into them. Also yes, she'd fallen a number of times. But falling from those trees is how she perfected her control over the air. She figured out how to use it as a cushion of sorts. But she hadn't quite gotten the hang of flying yet, which I was incredibly grateful for.

2023 had been a great year. The worst thing to happen was that damn toilet in the diner basement that kept overflowing. But everything else had been normal. Fun, and simple, and happy. Our lives were centered around our family and our friends. But mainly, they were centered around our kids. Our perfect, happy, wonderful children.

As the song wrapped up, I cheered. Leah yelled, clapping along with the crowd. Jeremy asked Micah if he wanted to do an encore. The crowd yelled some more, in a sweet, happy to see a kid so happy sort of way. He nodded fast and they started singing the song *Home* by Blue October—Jeremy's favorite band.

I continued recording, but a call from Moriah appeared on my screen. Enjoying the show, I slid the reject button. A second or two later, Roland's name lit across my screen.

My heart picked up speed in my chest a bit, but I ignored it. It was the first night my son was on a stage; I wanted him to know that his mom was in the crowd cheering him on. And honestly, if something was going down, I didn't want to know until the night was over.

After rejecting that call as well, another name flashed against the screen. Tina.

Fuck.

"Can you record this?" I said to Leah. "I've got to take this."

"Who is it?" she asked.

I turned the screen toward her. "Federal Bureau of Investigation."

CHAPTER SIXTY-EIGHT

JEREMY

"Did you see that?" Micah exclaimed, jumping up and down and reaching for my hands. I took them with a laugh, helping him jump higher with each stamp of his feet. "Did you see, Daddy? I got it all right; I didn't miss a note at all."

"I know, you were awesome." I laughed, and he jumped again. "You've got a great stage presence there, kid."

"I wanna do it again. Can we do it again?" he said with wide eyes.

"It's someone else's turn now, maybe we can do another show next week." I roughed up his hair and looked around. "Do you see your mom anywhere?"

He raised himself onto his tiptoes. "I'm short. I can't see nothing."

"Here." I lifted him up and placed him on my shoulders. He giggled and squeezed ahold of my head for stability. "What about now? See her anywhere?"

"Nope. But I see Aunt Hannah in the back." He lifted one hand and waved. "No Mommy though."

"Maybe she'd upstairs with Uncle Max. Watch your head." I started down the steps from the small stage.

"Jeremy." Adam's voice called somewhere in the distance. I

scanned the room before his waving hand shot up a few yards away. "Jeremy, over here!"

"I'm coming," I yelled, holding Micah's calves tightly as I pushed through the shuffling crowd.

When his head became visible, I saw the look on his face, and my stomach dropped. His eyes were wide, unblinking. Sweat beaded his forehead.

The last time he looked like that was when Laila died seven years ago.

He looked up at Micah and forced a smile. His gaze turned back to me. "Where's Laila?"

"I'm not sure, why?" I asked.

He gestured toward the steps. "Come on. We need to talk."

"What's wrong?" I said.

He looked up at Micah and then back to me. "Let's go upstairs."

"Should I get Laila—"

"Just told Leah to find her. Come on, hurry up."

My heart started to slam against my rib cage. I felt my throat begin to tighten. But I gave a nod and lowered Micah to my hip.

As I followed him up the steps, I hopped into Laila's mind. She was outside by the back door talking to someone on the phone. I just popped in; I didn't see much. But I sent her a quick message.

Something's happening. Meet me upstairs.

"You sit in here with Aunt Jenna for a minute, alright?" I said to Micah.

He sent me a concerned gaze. "Is something wrong, Daddy?"

I smiled and shook my head. "I'm sure everything's going to be fine."

Jenna shot me a nearly petrified expression, just like Adam's. She cleared her throat and pasted an unwilling smile to her lips. "Come here, buddy. Let's watch the ball drop."

"What's that?" he asked, climbing up her bed.

I turned and started from the room. Adam stood in the doorway with his phone in his hand. Just as I was about to ask what was wrong, he clicked the door shut and handed me his phone.

As I looked at the video, my brows fell. Just a black backdrop. But when I pressed play, white words appeared across the screen.

The Gods Live Among Us

My heart picked up speed in my chest. 60K views. And posted forty-five minutes ago.

The screen flashed to an image I'd seen before. A montage of them, actually.

My wife. Naked. Tied to a metal table with dozens of bright red lashes against her bare back.

Peterson's voice sounded over the speaker, instructing two men to whip her again.

Fuck.

Fuck, fuck.

"Who the fuck posted this?" I met Adam's gaze.

"If I didn't know better, I'd say Peterson. There are hundreds of them, dude. Maybe thousands, actually. Like, all of his documentation. Not just Laila. There's some of Chris, and the others too. There's... There's even one of when he..."

My stomach clenched, and my chest got heavy. "Laila's rape is on YouTube."

He chewed his lip and drooped his head in a nod. "It's only been up for an hour. I flagged it, but it hasn't been taken down. And it has some fifty-thousand views."

I felt my breaths get closer together. "I've got to go find her."

"Yeah, but we have bigger fish to fry here, dude," he said. "This is mass exposure. Like *mass* expos—"

"Obviously I fucking know that, Adam." I snapped. "All the more reason I have to find her." I handed him the phone and started past him, but he caught my elbow.

"Wait, Jeremy," Adam said.

"What?" I snapped.

"You're in these too. When you got Micah back, when you two

were in that cell. He recorded himself stabbing her. And then you shocking her, and then you bringing her back and healing her—"

"Great. Fan-fucking-tastic." I ripped my elbow back and darted to the door. "Do me a favor and get Micah out to the car. We've got to get home."

He nodded quickly.

As I slammed the door shut behind me, I felt a sharp ache at the back of Laila's head.

Shit.

CHAPTER SIXTY-NINE

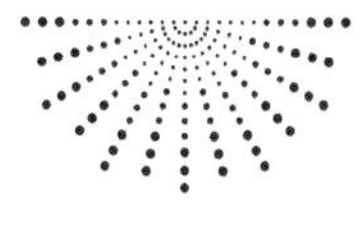

LAILA

"Hey, lady," I said into the phone, trudging up the steps to the back of the diner. "Long time no talk."

"Too long," Tina said quickly. "Are you alright?"

I gave Max a quick smile at the grill. He smiled back, and I started to the back door. "Yeah. Yeah, we're all good here. Just ringing in the new year."

"Is that—Do I hear music?" she said.

"Yeah, we're at the diner. Micah just did this cute little father son show at the venue downstairs. It was adorable. I'll have to send you the video."

"Shit. Shit, okay. Alright, you've got to get home. Like now."

"What?" I made a face and shut the back door. "Why? What's going on?"

"It's starting, Laila."

My brows furrowed. "What do you mean? The apocalypse?"

"Among other things. Where are they? Is Jeremy with you? And the siblings, all of you. Are they there?"

"Around here somewhere." My stomach swirled, and a knot formed in my throat. "What's going on, Tina? How do you know it's starting?"

"We'll talk about everything. But you need to listen to me right now, Laila. You need to get your baby and *get home.*" Tina spoke fast with a ferocity I'd never heard in her voice. "And your siblings. Adam and Jenna too, and their little boy. Everybody in that place who has powers needs to get out of there right now. They need to watch their backs. But you especially. You need to get out of there."

I looked around at the quiet night. There was no one around, I didn't think I was in immediate danger. But I rarely did until disaster struck.

"Okay. Okay, sure. Jeremy and Micah are just finishing up their song—"

"Fuck their song," a woman's voice said. My face screwed up, knowing that voice from somewhere but somehow unable to place it.

"Who the hell is that?" I snapped. "Who did you tell about us, Tina?"

The voice let out something between a snort and a laugh. Tina said, "Just get your family home, Laila. And don't check your notifications."

"Who the fuck is that?" I barked.

"If you don't get the fuck out of there, you're about to find out, dumb ass," she said. Not Tina, the other woman. "Just get home. Now. You're safe there."

"Who the hell are you?" I said again.

"Fucking Christ, would you just stop being so fucking stubborn for a damn minute?" the woman said. "We just told you you're in danger, just listen. For once in your life, just listen."

Well, fair enough. I did have a habit of being stubborn. If my family were at risk, I'd listen and get home to safety. But I was still gonna chew Tina's ass out for evidently telling someone about us.

I gritted my teeth together. "You have a lot of explaining to do, Tina."

"And I'll be happy to. But for now, you need to listen to me and get the hell home," Tina repeated. "And I mean it. Don't check your notifications."

"Why?"

"Just trust me. You don't want to see it."

My stomach clenched. "Alright. Alright, I'll go get Jeremy, and we'll go home."

"Good. Hurry up," the other woman said.

I brought the phone from my ear and clicked the end call button. I took in a deep calming breath, fighting the urge to click into the Facebook app where I had 36 notifications.

Something's happening. Meet me upstairs, Jeremy's voice said into my mind.

My heart hammered. I turned to the door.

A voice behind me called, "Laila. Laila Callidy?"

I turned, and a smile came to my lips. Camuel. An Angel, one of the few I liked, actually. He helped us the day I broke us out of the first compound.

"Oh, hi," I said. "It's nice to see you, but I'm kind of in a hurry—"

"That's alright, this won't take long." He smiled as he ascended the steps. "You look well, how have you been?"

"Pretty good, but I really have to—"

Before I could finish, he teleported in front of me and thrust my body into the door. My head hit the metal with a clunk. I was about to rebut something, but before I could, he raised a blade to my throat. I teleported behind him and raised my flaming hand around his neck.

He screamed, flinging me backward. I started to fall but used the wind to balance myself. As I staggered to my feet, he grasped ahold of my shoulder and raised the blade to my abdomen. But I grasped ahold of it, ignoring the pain as it sliced through the palm of my hand.

I used water, summoning the bile in his stomach up his esophagus and down into his lungs. Suffocation couldn't kill an Angel, but it'd slow him down. Which was all I needed.

I ripped the knife from his hand and grasped his throat in my bloody palm. "What the fuck do you think you're doing?"

He choked, gargling through the vomit in his lungs. Then his eyes widened, a gasping grumble coming from his throat.

His hands reached out for my shoulders, pale blue eyes flicking between mine.

Only then did I notice the projectile sticking out of his chest. I blinked hard. It yanked out the other end.

He started falling toward me, but I pushed his body sideways to the ground. I looked at the person who'd stabbed him.

I froze solid as a statue.

"I told you to hurry up," she snapped.

Her long brown hair was combed up into a neat ponytail at the top of her head. Those piercing, glowing green eyes darted between mine for a moment. I took in the scars and the tattoos that covered them.

Roses and daisies. Delicate green vines. A butterfly covering a round bite mark on the left side of her neck.

"Who the hell are you?" I said.

"I think that's obvious," she said. "I'll take care of him. You go get—"

"Laila!" Jeremy's voice called from the front of the diner. I turned to the sound of him, then back to the woman. Just as she disappeared with the body.

CHAPTER SEVENTY

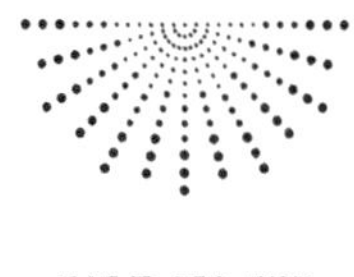

JEREMY

"Laila," I called, looking around the parking lot. "Laila!"

When she didn't respond, I popped into her mind. She stared down at her bloody, shaking palms at the landing of the stoop at the rear of the diner. I took off in a sprint.

As I rounded the corner, my stomach clenched. She stood with short breaths over a puddle of crimson on the ground. I ran toward her and took her hands, healing the deep cuts on her palms.

"We have to go," I said quickly. "Micah's in the car."

She blinked hard for a moment. Her tongue ran along her lips. I raised my hands to her cheeks and looked between her eyes. "We have to move, Laila."

She gave a fast nod.

I took her hand and lugged her to the front of the parking lot. "Who did you just kill?" I whispered.

She shook her head. "I didn't. Or... or I-I guess, maybe I did."

"What do you mean?" I clicked the beeper on the key fob, searching around for our car.

"I-I don't know. I-I was talking to Tina and then—and then Camuel showed up and he... he tried to kill me," she murmured as we rushed to the car. "She showed up and she—she just... Stabbing an Angel doesn't kill them. How did she..."

"Who?" I asked, reaching for her car door.

She looked down at her hands. Her eyes turned back up to me. "I think it was me."

My brows dropped. "What do you mean?"

"I-I don't know. I don't know, she said we had to go."

For a moment, I thought she'd lost her mind. But it was quite the contrary, really. All the puzzle pieces were finally lining up. We were about to see the big picture.

"Let's go then," I said, pulling open her door.

"Good, you're here," Adam said in the back seat. "He's all strapped in, you're good to go."

"You need to get back to the house too," Laila said with a quick look his way. "And Jenna and Luka and-and everyone. Tell everyone they need to get home. Now. Like yesterday, now. And tell Max to kick everyone out."

I felt my brows fall further, but I pushed the door shut and jogged to the driver's side. As I sat down, Adam said, "What? Why?"

"I don't know," Laila snapped. "Just do it. Just get back to the house. *Now.*"

"I'll spread the word and tell Max to close up."

I nodded to him in the rearview mirror as I started the car. He teleported out.

Laila reached for her phone in her pocket. I snatched it from her hand. "What the fuck, Jeremy?"

"You don't want to see that right now," I said, backing out of the parking space and shoving her phone into my jeans.

"I was just going to call Moriah back—"

"You can call her back when we get home. Just-just breathe for a minute."

"I can breathe and talk at the same time—"

"You won't be able to breathe after what she is about to tell you," I said. "Just trust me, okay? When we get home, we'll talk."

"Mommy?" Micah whispered in the back seat. "Daddy?"

"Yeah, bud?" I glanced at him in the rearview as I turned onto the highway.

His scared eyes moved from me to Laila's bloody hands. "What's happening?"

I thought for a moment, unsure of how to respond.

The whole world just found out we're gods. The whole world just saw your mother get raped. The whole world just saw your uncle and your mother being tortured by the man who held you captive for the first three years of your life. The whole world just saw me resurrect your mother from death.

Of course, I couldn't tell a four-year-old that. So I smiled and shook my head. "Everything's alright, bud. But when we get home, I need you to go to your room and lie down, okay?"

"But I didn't even get to see the ball drop," he said.

"I'll show you the video in the morning. Tonight, you need to get some sleep. Okay? Can you do that for me, kiddo?"

He gave a nod and looked at Laila. "Mommy?"

"Yeah, baby?" She turned to face him.

"Are you okay?"

She forced a smile. "I'm fine. You listen to your dad, alright? When we get home, it's time for bed."

He lifted his head in a slow nod. His eyes fell on her hands again. "Is you hurt?"

She looked down at her palms. She rubbed them against her jeans and shook her head. "Just a little accident in the kitchen. Daddy healed it for me, everything's fine."

"You promise?"

"I promise."

LAILA

"Can I have my phone back now?" I said as I dried my hands on a dish towel at the sink.

Jeremy was quiet, rubbing a hand against his scruff. "We need to talk first."

"What the hell is going on?" Brody said at the other end of the island. "Whose blood is that?"

"An Angel's." Gwen sniffed. "How did you kill an Angel?"

"I didn't," I said.

"I thought you said you did," Jeremy said.

"*Someone* did. Someone who... she looked just like me." I leaned against the counter and massaged my temples. "I don't know. I don't know, maybe I did. Maybe I'm losing my shit." I rubbed my tense face. "But-but the body was gone. You-you didn't see a body, did you, Jeremy?"

"Just the blood," he said.

I gripped the counter for support. My vision got blurry around the edges, my heart palpated behind my ribs, my teeth started to chatter. I took in a deep breath through my nostrils and blew slowly out of my mouth in a desperate attempt to come to grips with whatever it was that had just happened.

"What do you not want me to see on my phone?" I looked up at Jeremy.

He chewed his lower lip, eyes softening.

"Tell me what the fuck is going on, Jeremy," I said.

He closed his eyes. His thumb and forefinger them. He met my gaze. "Somebody put the videos on YouTube."

"What videos?"

"Peterson's. His documentation of everything he did to you guys in there."

"What?"

"There's hundreds of them. Maybe thousands," he murmured. "One of me and you, I guess. When we were in there, and I healed you. A bunch of them beating you guys. And... and the one where he... when he..."

My heart hammered. "No."

"We're gonna figure it out," he said fast. "It-it'll be okay, baby. We'll figure it out."

"Are you... Are you saying that the..." I pointed to my neck. "When I got this, that's on the internet?"

He gave a slow nod.

Suddenly, it was like my lungs sealed shut. I was breathing. Rationally, I knew that I was breathing. But I didn't feel like I was.

My legs went numb. My hands clenched so tight that my fingernails drew blood from my palms. My stomach spun.

I gripped the counter, using it to keep me steady as I rushed to the garbage can.

I felt his hand on my back and shoved it away. I heard him speaking, telling me that everyone was going to say that it was fake anyway, but I wasn't even thinking about the exposure.

One of the worst moments of my life was out on the web where anyone who wanted to could see it. The few minutes of my life that made me feel weaker than anything else ever had. The scar on my neck was bad enough, but for the entire world to see it?

Fuck.

I puked again.

My entire body was still quivering as Jeremy led me to the bedroom.

He held my face in his hands and promised that we'd be okay. That we'd take care of it, that somehow, we'd get that video, and all the others, down.

But I wasn't stupid. I knew how the internet worked. I remembered those classes in middle school, the cyber bullying prevention sessions.

"Once something's on the worldwide web, it's there forever. Even if you've deleted it, anyone could have already saved it to their own computer. They could have shared whatever you posted on a million different websites, even in just a few minutes of being posted."

Who the fuck would even watch something like that?

Perverts, that's who. Oh, what a comforting thought. A bunch of sick fucks sitting at their computers watching my bony, pregnant ass being—

Fuck, I puked again.

"Baby, baby," Jeremy whispered, pushing my hair from my face and handing me a tissue. I struggled to retain a normal breathing rhythm. He lifted my face in his hands. "It's going to be okay. It's going—"

"Tina said it's started," I whispered through crying gasps. "She-she said the apocalypse has started."

"What?" he asked. "It starts with this? With mass exposure?"

My teeth trembled. "I-I don't know. I don't know. She said she'd be here in a few hours, and we'd talk about everything."

"Okay. Okay, we'll talk to her soon then. But you need to breathe, alright?" he whispered, gently looking between my eyes. "You need to stay calm. That's over. What happened on those videos is over. Peterson is dead. He can't hurt you again—"

"I'm not worried about that," I snapped. "I know that no one can hurt me again. But that doesn't change the fact that there are videos of me butt naked being beaten and raped going viral and I-I... I murdered people, Jeremy. I murdered more than twenty people in there, and he had it all on tape. What if the kids see that one day? What if—what if my mom opens her news feed in the morning and-and she sees that piece of shit—"

"I'll go get her," he said gently, warm blue eyes moving between mine. "I'll go get her, alright?"

"And Max. Can you—can you go get him too? And tell him not to look at his phone?"

He touched his lips to my forehead. "Yeah, I will. Why don't you lie down? Try and get some rest."

I struggled to clamp together my chattering teeth. "I need a shower."

"Brody and Gwen are here. Leah and Hannah are coming too. They said they'd keep an ear out for the kids. You just try to relax, okay?"

I nodded.

But of course, I didn't relax.

When he left, I got my laptop from the nightstand. I went onto Facebook. I didn't read the comments there, nor did I read the list of more than fifty of my so-called friends that tagged me in the posts they'd shared.

But when I got to the actual videos, the comments were all that I could see. I didn't actually watch them. I knew good and damn well what happened. But the comments made me sick with humanity.

Some weren't too bad.

Fake news.

Clearly this isn't real.

Then they got gross.

Who'd want to fuck her anyway? She's pregnant and shit.

What did dude say? Did he just call her a god?

Ew, I know that girl. We went to school together. She always was a weirdo.

Jeremy was right. I shouldn't have read them.

Because as I did, it felt like someone jumped onto my chest. I could barely breathe. It *hurt* to breathe. I couldn't see straight. My hands were trembling, my stomach ached, and my throat felt swollen shut.

Lie down. I needed to lie down.

I leaned back against the pillows and practiced my breathing exercises. *In for five, hold for three, out for seven. Or wait, is it in for three, hold for five? I know it's out for seven. Or maybe it's in for seven.*

Fuck, held my breath for too long.

I think I stress fainted.

CHAPTER SEVENTY-TWO

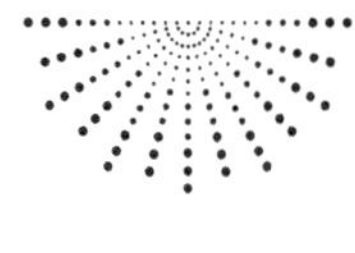

JEREMY

My phone rang. *Papy* slid across the screen. I swiped the red bar, dropped my face to my hand, and shook my head.

"It's chamomile, drink." Hannah set a cup of tea in front of me. "Who was that?"

"Thanks." I took a sip. "Papy. Moriah a few minutes ago, Dayo half an hour ago," I said. "Hasn't stopped ringing all night."

"You should answer them," Chris said from the table. "They just want to know what's going on—"

"I don't know what the fuck's going on, Chris," I barked. "All I know is that someone put those videos up—"

"And now we're all going to have a price on our heads. The entire supernatural community is in danger and—"

"Right now, I really don't give a shit about the politics," I said.

His gaze pierced mine. "Well, as a god of this fucking planet, don't you think that you should?"

"Alright guys, we aren't fighting each other here," Leah said. "This happened *to* us. No one here is at fault."

"I bet it was Lux," Brody muttered. "That fucker hates you guys. What better way to hurt Laila than to put those videos out there?"

"No, there had to be a reason," Celena murmured. "I mean, maybe it was him. But this wasn't done just to hurt Laila. Chris's videos are up there too, so are hundreds of others."

"Yeah. There's even one of Haley," Leah muttered. "She changes in it. I called her. She's a mess. She didn't want to talk. But no one's identified her yet."

"No, looks like the only one they have is Laila," I said. "Guess incinerating someone on contact has a way of sticking out in people's minds."

"What the fuck is happening?" Jenna said with a shake of her head. "This is... it's just unbelievable. Are people actually believing it?"

"Some are," Wyatt muttered. "Some aren't. It's about a fifty-fifty split."

"Did they take that one down yet?" I said with a look at Adam. "The one where he..."

"Yeah. Yeah, it's not on YouTube anymore. But it got uploaded to a bunch of other websites, it's still circulating."

I raised my hand to rub my eyes.

"How is she?" Celena asked. "She was already barricaded in her room when I got here."

"She's out cold," Rachel murmured from her seat at the table. "Probably cried herself to sleep. I've been checking in every few minutes, but I think she'll be out for a while."

"Probably best," I muttered. "It's so fucked up. We killed that bastard; how does he still get to hurt her like this?"

"That's what trauma does, bud," Wyatt said quietly.

"Yeah. Yeah, I guess." I looked down at Laila's phone, watching it vibrate with another Facebook notification. "Think she'd be mad at me if I delete her account?"

"Yeah, she definitely would," Max said.

I sighed and rested my chin back to my palm.

"God, I just want this to be over." Chris shook his head. "I thought it was. Now it's gotten so much worse."

"We're probably going have a flock of journalists at the gate by morning," Leah muttered with a shake of her head. "CNN and Fox News already put out articles about it. People are freaking out."

"Yeah, let's just hope the cops aren't with them." I ran my shaking hand through my hair. "There are what? At least three videos of Laila murdering someone out there right now?"

"At least," Hannah whispered.

"Wait," Brody said. "Wait, did you guys see this one?"

"Which one?" I asked.

He passed me the phone. "Click play."

Everyone herded around me as I did so. The camera shifted back and forth before settling on Peterson's face.

"Hello, world." He smiled at the camera. "My name is Doctor Robert Peterson. And yes, I'm the man conducting these experiments. But no, this isn't government testing. They wouldn't dare. They know they don't stand a chance against these people. These aren't super soldiers either, not like the ones in sci-fi movies.

"These are people. Very special people. People that have already given so much. And now, they will give more. They will be the reason the human race survives what the coming years will bring.

"Some are even gods, gods that love you and plan to help you. Believe it or not. The choice is yours. Soon, you will have no choice. But my point in broadcasting these videos is to show you all who these people are. To give you some future insight.

"This world is about to become a terrifying place. And when it does, these are the people that will save you. Have faith in them. Rely on them. And please, for the love of all that is good in this forsaken world, please, *please* listen to them.

"The time left for the life that you know has run out. I'm sorry to say, but the end is no longer near. It is here.

"So please. People of earth. Listen to the words I'm telling you. Have faith in the gods that live among you. They are powerful. They are gracious. And they love you. And they will save you. But you have to do as you're told."

A long pause drew in as he bit his lip.

"And I'm sorry, Laila. But it had to be this way. Everything had to happen. Even this. Still, though, I will never be able to put into words how truly and deeply sorry I am for what I've done to you. Please forgive me.

"And Jeremy. Please have mercy on my soul. I know that's asking a lot. But please."

The screen cut to black.

That fucking rat bastard.

He put those out so the world would know how powerful we were. What we were capable of. To fear us, to listen to us.

I stood. "I need to smoke a joint."

CHAPTER SEVENTY-THREE

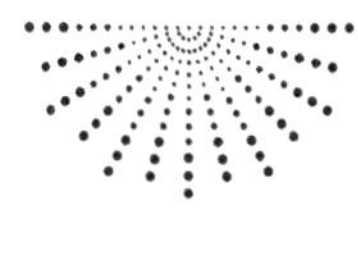

LAILA

I awoke to the sound of birds chirping outside and the bright sun reflecting against the snow. The bed was cold beside me. I rolled over, rubbing my eyes.

Was it a dream? It had to be. That couldn't have happened. It couldn't have.

I lifted my laptop and opened my notifications. With one quick glance, I realized it was far from a dream. I slammed it shut along with my eyelids.

Somehow, I found the will inside of me to scoot up the bed. I tucked my knees to my chest and stared out the window. It looked so peaceful out there. Just a snow-covered backyard in the countryside.

It didn't look like the world was about to end. It didn't look like life as we knew it was soon to change forever.

My last moment of naivety, I like to call it.

Everything was about to shift. I was finally about to understand the complexities of my life. But I didn't know that yet.

I just stared out the window a moment longer.

I heard the bang of dishes clattering in the kitchen and Micah's sweet little voice.

Regardless of what happened last night, my kids were counting on me. I had to get it together—and keep it together. They needed me. I'd be there for them until I took my last breath. I'd uproot their lives and take them to the Fae Realm if I had to, but I wouldn't give up. As their mother, it was my responsibility to keep them safe. Even from my own reputation.

One thing was for sure. I had to take their iPads away. Couldn't have them stumbling upon a video of Mommy growing a tree through a man's chest.

I stood from the bed and slid my arms through my pink robe. I stepped into my slippers and looked at myself in the mirror for a moment.

The girl looking back at me looked tired, but I forced a smile to my lips, and she looked better. I didn't feel much better, but it felt easier than the frown.

I walked to the door and stepped into the hallway. I took a few steps into the kitchen and looked around at my busy, shuffling family. Mom stood at the stove flipping pancakes and sausage. Jenna was a few steps away pouring a cup of coffee. Adam, Brody, Gwen, Max, Hannah, Kai, and Chris sat at the dining table. Celena and Wyatt were chewing on some toast at the couch. Micah was at the island sipping a cup of orange juice with Leah at his side.

He turned to me and smiled. "Look, Mommy. Gammy made me pancakes, and they look like Mickey Mouse."

I smiled back. The room grew quiet. I took a few steps toward him, wrapping my arms around his chest and resting my chin on the top of his head. "Are they any good?"

"They is so good." He took a bite. "You gotta try them."

I looked up at Mom and forced a smile. "Can you make me some Mickey Mouse pancakes too, Gam?"

Her lips lifted in a sad smile. "Chocolate chips?"

"And whipped cream," I said.

"You got it, baby."

Just as I went to sit down, I heard Milly cry upstairs. Leah started to stand, but I said, "I got it."

"Are you sure?" she asked.

"Yeah, I'm good. Just save me some sausage," I said.

I started up the steps.

As I walked up each stair, I had no idea that my entire perspective on the world was about to change. I had no idea. Not until I heard a woman's quiet laugh and hushed singing from my daughter's bedroom.

Everyone was downstairs. No one else was capable of entering my land without a necklace.

Or so I thought.

I teleported to her doorway. As I landed, my jaw hit the floor.

She stood my height, about five-four to five-five. Her long brown hair reached just below her shoulders. She wore a cute white lace blouse and a pair of dark washed blue jeans.

And she was holding my daughter.

"Put my baby down." A ball of fire appeared in my hand. "Put her down right now or I swear to God, you'll be a pile of ash."

She turned with a soft smile. The same smile I'd seen in the reflection two minutes prior. More genuine though. She laughed. "She's my baby too, ya know. Mine's just a lot bigger now."

"I'll do it, bitch—"

"Yeah, and then you'll ruin this adorable outfit." She grinned. "But it won't hurt me."

"Put my daughter down or—"

"Alright, damn. Chill, bitch." She set Milly back to the crib. "But just look at me for a minute, would you?" She turned back to meet my gaze. "Shapeshifters don't carry the scars of the people they copy. Theses tattoos are the exact same one's covering your body, aren't they?"

"Get away from my baby," I said with wide eyes and flaring nostrils. "Get the fuck away from my baby right now."

She smiled and raised her hands in surrender. "I'd never hurt her, Laila."

I rushed across the room and lifted Milly from the crib. Quickly, I glanced over her for marks or bruises. But she looked happy as ever, just as she did every morning.

Clenching Milly against my chest, I spun back to the woman with wide eyes. I brought a ball of fire to my hand. "Who the fuck are you?"

She laughed and lowered herself to the rocking chair. "My name has been Lila Salesky for the past twenty-four years. But for the twenty-five before that, it was Laila Callidy."

That was bullshit. All of it was bullshit. She... she was my age. She was... I didn't know who she was, or what she was, but that was a lie. All of that had to be a lie. Yet the only thing that came out of my mouth was, "You're not forty-nine."

"Almost fifty, actually." She shrugged. "Immortality has a way of keeping ya looking damn good for your age."

What is this?

What the fuck is happening?

My breaths got closer together. My head shook. Words spilled from my lips like vomit. "What are you? Why are you here? *How* are you here?"

She smiled and kicked her feet back on the pedestal of the rocking chair. "Well, I'm you. So ya know, fifty percent Angel, twenty-five percent Fae, and twenty-five percent Guardian. I'm here to help you figure out the latter and keep your kids from having to grow up in an apocalypse. And I'm able to be here because, in the wise words of Tina Turner, twenty-some-odd years ago, my blood was used to put the barrier around this home that keeps my family safe."

"You're lying, you're—"

"She's not," Mary said in the doorway.

My head shot toward her, and my eyes widened.

"Laila, meet Laila."

CHAPTER SEVENTY-FOUR

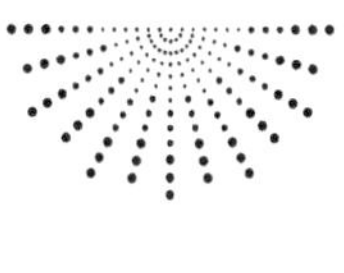

JEREMY

My eyes surveyed the quiet, early morning yard. Birds chirped in the treetops as the sun rose above them. I hadn't gotten a wink of sleep. I couldn't if I tried.

I had no idea what today had in store for us. Was I going to have to kill cops when they tried to arrest my wife for her murder sprees? Was I going to have to pack a bag and hop into another dimension?

Was I going to lose the life we'd worked so hard to build?

I took a deep drag off the joint between my shaking fingertips. Tears bubbled in my eyes, and my throat seemed to swell shut. I tried to blink them away and swallow it down, but it wouldn't budge.

Before I knew it, I was sobbing with my head in my hands beside the air conditioning unit next to the house.

How can things go from so good to total shit in a single night? Why does my life eternally get destroyed just as I'm on the verge of my happily ever after?

I stood and began to pace along the house. The sad sobs morphed into angry yells.

"Why?" I looked up at the morning sky. "Why do you put me through this shit, Lux? Was it really that bad? You hate me this fucking much because I ended up with her and you didn't? Well, ya know what, fucker? I wouldn't do this to you! Even if she chose you, I still wouldn't put you through this shit! I wouldn't rip your life away from you every fucking time you're happy. I'd accept my fucking fate and move on. And I damn sure wouldn't hurt your kids! And that's what makes us different. That's why she chose me, you evil piece of shit!"

"He can't hear you," a man's voice said a few feet away. "The barrier keeps everything in here quiet to the outside."

I shifted quickly.

As our eyes met, my jaw dropped.

Six foot four. Short, salt and pepper colored hair. Brilliant blue eyes and a thick, yet well-maintained black beard. Gray V-neck under a black jacket. Dark blue jeans and a pair of black and white Chuck Taylor's.

"Who the fuck are you?" I snapped with wide eyes.

He smiled and lifted his shoulders in a shrug. "I've gone by a lot of names. My family calls me Jeremy, though."

I shook my head and spun a ball of vibrating electricity to my hand. "*I'm* Jeremy."

"Yeah, and so am I. But c'mon, put that away. You throw it at me, and both of our wives are going to be in a world of pain for literally no reason. We fight the same way, dude, I'm not even sure who'd win."

I threw it.

As it struck his body, he stood steady as a stone. He licked his teeth.

"Alright, you little shit," he said. "Guess we're fighting then."

The story continues in *The Shift*. Turn the page for a sneak peek, or click the link below to download now:

https://www.amazon.com/gp/product/B0973L2BKF/

Sign up for Charlie's newsletter and receive a free copy of the Eluding Destiny prequel, *Blood Bar*:

https://liquidmind.media/eluding-destiny-prequel/

If you enjoyed this story, please consider leaving a rating or review on
Amazon:
https://www.amazon.com/gp/product/B096L15NND/

Join Charlie's private reader group on Facebook and discuss all things
Eluding Destiny and Charlie Nottingham:
https://www.facebook.com/groups/661440911724435/

THE SHIFT CHAPTER ONE
JANUARY 1, 2024 - LAILA

My heart slammed against my ribcage as it rose and fell fast with the heavy breaths panting in and out of my lungs. I held a ball of bright violet fire in one hand and my daughter against my hip in the other.

I couldn't believe it. No one in their right mind could.

It wasn't possible. I was the queen of impossible but this... It couldn't be real. It couldn't be. Doppelgängers aren't a thing, not even in our world. There cannot be two of the same people existing in the same place, or two different places, for that matter, at the same time.

And yet, here I stood before myself.

I blinked a few times, hoping I'd wake up in my bed. Hoping it was all a nightmare. Not my typical post-trauma terrors, I'll admit, but I'd rather it have been a dream than reality.

If the past twelve hours had been a terrible manifestation of my own mind, the world still had a chance. We'd still have time. We wouldn't be standing at the edge of the apocalypse.

"Laila, put the fire down," Mary said. "You need to relax—"

"You need to shut the fuck up," I snapped.

"Ouch," the woman in the rocking chair said.

I looked between the two them. "What the fuck is going on here?"

"I told you what's going on." The woman's gaze was nonchalant, yet serious. "I'm you."

"You aren't me, I'm me." I shook my head quickly. "I'm me, and this... This isn't real. This isn't happening."

"C'mon, quit with the dramatics." She rolled her eyes, sat forward, and exhaled. "You don't have to act all big with me. I know you. I *am* you. Older, smarter. But I am, Laila. I'm you."

My breaths drew closer together, and my head shook.

Not possible. This is not possible.

"Throw it at me." She gestured to the flames in my hand. "Go ahead, Lai. Throw it at me and see that it does nothing. I'll have to borrow some clothes then."

We stood in Milly's bedroom. If I threw it, I'd run the risk of catching that four-hundred-dollar rocker on fire. Had she been a threat, I would have done it without a second thought. But she was sitting there with a calm demeanor, waiting for me to settle down so we could talk. And although I was one to throw punches and stomp my feet, I couldn't bring myself to do it. Some part of me knew she wasn't lying.

She sighed and raised her palm. Bright licks of purple flames ascended through the air. I felt the wind pick up and watched as the fire turned to a ball of swirling water.

"How is this possible?" I asked. "This isn't—it can't be possible."

"The tree of life has a number of attributes." She closed her hand to a fist around the water. "It's not just about immortality, not in this life. It's tied up with time."

"What the fuck does that mean?" I asked. "You—you're a time traveler?"

"Thanks to Lux's careful genome mapping that led Mary and Dad to have us in the first place," she said. "Look, this is going to be a long and complicated conversation. Put your fire out. Tell Celena and Hannah to take Micah up to the main house. I'll put on a pot of coffee, and the five of us will talk."

"The five—wait, why would I let Micah leave?" I asked. "Is something going to—"

"Might confuse him a little bit if he sees two of his mommies sitting down for a cup of joe, don't ya think?" She arched a brow.

I swallowed hard but kept the fire in my palm. "Who's the five of us?"

"Me, you, my Jeremy, your Jeremy, and Mary," she said.

Granted, I was incredibly flustered. I had no clue what was going on. But one thing was made incredibly clear.

Mary had been lying to us about something huge. Evidently for quite some time.

My throat swelled as I looked between the two of them. "You know her?"

Mary turned her gaze toward the ground. "Yes. Yes, I have for a while now."

"And you kept this from me?"

"I told her she had to," Laila said. "But we'll get there. For now—"

"Why the fuck should I believe any of this?" I squeezed Milly tighter, eyes darting between them. "Clearly, you're a fucking liar. And you—you're—I don't even know you."

"Yes, you do. Twenty-four years ago, I was you. I was standing exactly where you are right now. And I remember how that felt. I remember the fear, and the uncertainty, and the shock you're feeling. But you know what else I remember?" Her green eyes cascaded between mine. "I remember thinking about all of the signs. The messages, the mystery CIA that showed up here and tortured my prisoner, the strange woman on that viral video. And I didn't want to believe it either because learning something like this isn't easy to accept. But we both know some part of you believes me. Some part of you even trusts me."

Well, when she put it like that.

Yeah. Some part of me did. I didn't understand it. But she wasn't giving off any vibe that suggested I should be scared. She didn't hurt my daughter a moment before. And, well, if this were real, if it were true, then a lot of things I hadn't been able to understand were starting to line up.

I pulled Milly tighter to my hip. "You keep saying that. Twenty-four years ago. What do you mean?"

She rubbed a hand against her mouth. "In twelve days, once you see what's about to happen to our planet, once I teach you what you need to learn about the tree of life, you're going to go back. To the year 2000."

Even if that were possible, could I do that? How could I leave all of these people behind? I'd built an army. I had thousands of people counting on me. I couldn't leave them all behind. "What?"

"I told you. This is going to be a long, complicated conversation. Your head's going to hurt. And—"

"I can't just run away from this; this is our war—"

"You're not running away. You're collecting extra time," Mary said. "Time that you need. You're not ready to fight this, Laila. She is."

You have time.

That's the message the CIA gave us. That's what Lux had said too. That's what that woman on that video last year said.

My gaze kept bouncing over the two of them. I felt my heart hammering away in my chest, trying to grasp what was happening. But the more that I thought, the angrier I became.

If she'd been around for the last twenty-four years, where the hell had she been? Why hadn't she helped us? If my son was her son, how in the fuck did she let that man take me hostage and steal him from us?

"You've been around all this time, and you just let all of this horrible shit happen to us?" I snapped. "You knew I'd be kidnapped, you knew where Chris was, you knew where my baby—your baby— was and you just—"

A sudden ache slammed across my cheek. The other me, the older me, ran her fingers over her knuckles. "Damn it. Mary, get the others back to the main house. Laila, meet me outside."

She disappeared.

I felt an ache in my hand then too, and another in my gut. Jeremy.

"Laila," Mary began.

"Don't," I said. "Just don't."

I teleported to the back patio.

THE SHIFT CHAPTER TWO

JEREMY

He had to be a shapeshifter. Maybe a Demon. Or, or an Angel. We knew we weren't on good terms with them, especially after the one Laila killed last night. But how could he be here? He wasn't wearing a necklace. The barrier spell kept anyone who wasn't tied to it or wearing a gem encrypted with our DNA out.

But if he was a shapeshifter, or a Demon, or an Angel, how was he here?

And why didn't my energy affect him?

Unless he's telling the truth.

I stood there in disbelief, staring blankly as I watched the blue energy dissolve into his skin.

He appeared in front of me. His fist raised and thrust into my cheek. As the pain soared through my jaw, I teleported behind him and put an arm around his neck. But just as I teleported out of the perimeter to the muddy, snow covered outskirts of our property, he teleported in front of me once again, gripping my shoulders and sending us back to where we'd been a moment before on the edge of the house.

"Listen to me, Jeremy," he said, hands tightly clamped to my shoulder blades. "Listen to me—"

"Who are you?" I exclaimed with wide eyes.

"I just told you who I am." His gaze shifted between mine. "I'm you, Jeremy. An older you, but I'm—"

I teleported a foot back and bludgeoned my fist to the side of his face. The pain swelled up my arm as he spit blood to the sidewalk. He disappeared. I looked around because I knew this trick. I'd done it a thousand times. He'd reappear before I even had enough time to realize he was back and—

Boom, a fist to my gut.

I doubled over; wind knocked out of me. He grasped my shoulders and lifted my gaze back to his. "Stop being a little shit and fucking listen to me. Just listen."

"How are you—"

"Jeremy." I heard Laila's voice rounding the corner from the fence. "Jeremy, stop."

"Get the kids and—" I began.

But I stopped dead in my tracks.

She stood beside the fence in a white blouse, pair of jeans, and a full face of makeup. She'd been a wreck last night. Not that I blamed her, but I expected her to still be in her pajamas with her hair in a messy bun. And I would have just assumed she was doing her typical, 'everything's fine, I'm going to fake it 'til I make it' persona.

But another Laila appeared beside her. My Laila. Wearing one of my T-shirts, a pair of bleach-stained sweatpants, and holding our two-year old against her hip.

She teleported to me and held her hand over my bloody lip, casting white light into the split skin. I barely felt the pain as I looked between her and the... well, the other her.

I grabbed ahold of her hip, pulling her away as the other me appeared beside the other Laila.

My gaze slid between the three of them. "What the fuck is going on?"

"Well, if you hadn't tried to kill me, you'd know," the man said.

I looked at Laila, then at Milly, checking over her for any signs of pain or trauma. But she was fine. Her eyes were wide, her hands were trembling, but she was fine.

"I don't know," Laila whispered with a fast shake of her head. "I don't know."

"Like I said," the woman beside the gate said. "Let's put on a pot of coffee and talk."

Enamored with *The Shift*? Click the link below to download now!
https://www.amazon.com/gp/product/B0973L2BKF/

ALSO BY CHARLIE NOTTINGHAM

The Eluding Destiny Series

Eluding Destiny

The Horrors That Created Us

Aftershocks

The Precipice

Land of Light

The Quiet Army

Sacred Sins

Flash Back

The Shift

Lost to Time

Gods Among Us

The Cover Up

Blank Slate

Eluding Destiny Prequels

The Last Beginning

Blood Bar

Raven's Cry Series

(MMFM Paranormal Romance)

Raven's Cry

Raven's Song

Celena's Story Duology

(Completed—paranormal romance, urban fantasy)

New Normal: Celena's Story Part 1

Reprisal: Celena's Story Part 2

Origins of the Gods

(Completed Trilogy—fantasy romance, more information on the origins of the Fae and Angels, how life began on earth, where Guardians came from, and— most importantly—a badass forbidden romance)

Origins

The Thrones of Ore and Ice

Creation

Stand Alone Novels

Curse of the Gods: The Bridge Between Origins of the Gods and the Eluding Destiny Series

Sign up for Charlie's newsletter and receive a free copy of the Eluding Destiny prequel, Blood Bar:

https://liquidmind.media/eluding-destiny-prequel/

ABOUT THE AUTHOR

Charlie is a... Okay, talking about myself in third person is weird.

Nice to meet you! My name's Charlie Nottingham, and my whole world revolves around fantasy. When I'm not writing a new book, I'm either hanging out with my dogs, talking with my fans online, or reading some amazing urban fantasy, paranormal romance, or fantasy romance series (always a series, never a stand-alone, because I hate to fall for a character and never see them again). Or re-watching some Buffy or Supernatural. (They never get old!)